*He lifted her nearly off her feet
to bring her mouth to his...*

She could smell his skin. He wore no powder or pomades or perfume; it was purely him, and she was driven mad by his scent. She wanted to tear the coat from his shoulders, rip off his shirt and neckcloth, and bury her nose in his naked neck. The desire was animalistic and nearly out of control, and that was what finally made her stop. She pulled her head back and saw that he watched her almost analytically. His eyes were far more calm than she felt.

Damn him! How dare he not be as affected as she?

He studied her face. "You argue with me, enrage me, until I can't stand it anymore and kiss you."

"You say that as if I plan to make you kiss me."

"Don't you?"

"Of course not."

"I think you do," he whispered. "I think you feel you can only accept my touch when it is forced upon you."

"That's not true!"

"Then prove it," he murmured as his head lowered to hers again. "Sheath your claws and kiss me."

Praise For Elizabeth Hoyt's Novels
The Serpent Prince

"4½ Stars! TOP PICK! Fantastic...magically blends fairy tale, reality, and romance in a delicious, sensual feast."
—*Romantic Times BOOKreviews Magazine*

"Exquisite romance...mesmerizing storytelling...incredibly vivid lead characters, earthy writing, and an intense love story."
—*Publishers Weekly*

"Wonderfully satisfying...delightfully witty...with just a touch of suspense. Set in a lush regency background, Elizabeth spins a story of treachery, murder, suspense, and love with her usual aplomb."
—RomanceatHeart.com

"A delight to read...It is fun and flirtatious, serious and sincere, menacing and magical. If you haven't read this series, I enthusiastically recommend it to you."
—Rakehell.com

"With an engrossing plot centered on revenge and a highly passionate romance between Simon and Lucy, *The Serpent Prince* delivers a steamy tale that packs an emotional punch. The three-dimensional characters, high drama, and sensuous love story make it a page-turner. The attention to detail when describing the time period and the traditions of the day, such as dueling, add to the overall satisfaction. I highly recommend *The Serpent Prince*."
—RomRevToday.com

The Leopard Prince

more...

The Raven Prince

"A sexy, steamy treat! A spicy broth of pride, passion, and temptation."
—Connie Brockway, *USA Today* bestselling author

"A very rich, very hot dessert."
—BookPage

"Hoyt expertly spices this stunning debut novel with a sharp sense of wit and then sweetens her lusciously dark, lushly sensual historical romance with a generous sprinkling of fairytale charm."
—*Chicago Tribune*

"Will leave you breathless."
—Julianne MacLean, author of *Portrait of a Lover*

"Hoyt's superb debut historical romance will dazzle readers with its brilliant blend of exquisitely nuanced characters, splendidly sensual love story, and elegant writing expertly laced with a dash of tart wit."
—*Booklist*

"I didn't want it to end!"
—Julia Quinn, *New York Times* bestselling author

"4½ Stars! TOP PICK! You'll adore Hoyt's intelligent characters and their spicy dialogue as much as the heated love scenes."
—*Romantic Times BOOKreviews Magazine*

more...

TO TASTE
TEMPTATION
~

OTHER TITLES BY ELIZABETH HOYT

TO TASTE TEMPTATION

~

Elizabeth Hoyt

FOREVER

NEW YORK   BOSTON

Copyright © 2008 by Nancy M. Finney
All rights reserved. Except as permitted under the U.S. Copyright Act of 1976, no part of this publication may be reproduced, distributed, or transmitted in any form or by any means, or stored in a database or retrieval system, without the prior written permission of the publisher.

Cover illustration by Franco Accornero

Forever
Hachette Book Group USA
237 Park Avenue
New York, NY 10017
Visit our Web site at www.HachetteBookGroupUSA.com

Forever is an imprint of Grand Central Publishing. The Forever name and logo is a trademark of Hachette Book Group USA, Inc.

Printed in the United States of America

First Printing: May 2008

10 9 8 7 6 5 4 3 2 1

Acknowledgments

Thank you to my fabulous editor, MELANIE MURRAY; to my sensational agent, SUSANNAH TAYLOR; to the energetic Grand Central Publicity team, particularly TAN-ISHA CHRISTIE, MELISSA BULLOCK, and RENEE SUPRIANO; to the creative people in the Grand Central Publishing art department, especially DIANE LUGER; and finally—and possibly most importantly—to my wonderfully persnickety copyeditor, CARRIE ANDREWS, who has yet to miss any of my imaginative grammatical errors.

Prologue

Once upon a time long, long ago, there came four soldiers traveling home after many years of war. Trimp tramp! Trimp tramp! Trimp tramp! sounded their boots as they marched abreast, heads held high, looking neither to the left nor right. For so they had been taught to march, and it is not an easy thing to forget the ritual of many years. The wars and battles were over, but I do not know if our soldiers had won or lost them, and maybe it does not matter. Their clothes were tattered, their boots more holes than leather, and not one of the soldiers journeyed home the same man as had left it.

By and by, they came to a crossroads, and here they halted to consider their choices. One road led to the west, the way straight and well paved. One road trailed to the east into a dark and secret forest. And one road pointed north, where the shadows of lonely mountains lay.

"Well, fellows," the tallest soldier said at last, taking off his hat and scratching his head, "shall we toss a coin?"

"Nay," said the soldier to his right. "My way lies there." And he bid his companions adieu and marched off to the east, never looking back as he disappeared into the dark forest.

"I am partial to that way," said the soldier to the left, and he gestured to the mountains looming in the distance.

"And as for me," the tall soldier cried, laughing, "I will take this easy road, for such has always been my choice. But what of you?" he asked the last soldier. "What road will you take?"

"Ah, me," that soldier sighed. "I believe there is a pebble in my boot, and I will sit and take it out, for it has been plaguing me these many miles." He suited action to word and found a nearby boulder to rest against.

The tall soldier clapped his hat back on his head. "Then it is decided."

The remaining soldiers shook hands cordially and went their separate ways. But what adventures befell them and whether their travels led them safely home I cannot tell you, for this is not their story. This is the tale of that first soldier, the one who walked away into the dark forest.

His name was Iron Heart....

—from *Iron Heart*

Chapter One

*Now Iron Heart got his name from a very strange
thing. Although his limbs and face, and indeed all
the rest of his body, were exactly like every other
man created by God, his heart was not. It was
made from iron, and it beat on the surface of his
chest, strong, brave, and steadfast....*
—from *Iron Heart*

LONDON, ENGLAND
SEPTEMBER 1764

"They say he ran away." Mrs. Conrad leaned close to im-
part this bit of gossip.

Lady Emeline Gordon took a sip of tea and glanced
over the rim of the cup at the gentleman in question. He
was as out of place as a jaguar in a room full of tabby cats:
raw, vital, and not quite civilized. Definitely not a man she
would associate with cowardice. Emeline wondered what
his name was as she thanked the Lord for his appearance.

Mrs. Conrad's afternoon salon had been paralyzingly dull until *he* had sauntered in.

"He ran away from the massacre of the 28th Regiment in the colonies," Mrs. Conrad continued breathlessly, "back in fifty-eight. Shameful, isn't it?"

Emeline turned and arched an eyebrow at her hostess. She held Mrs. Conrad's gaze and saw the exact moment when the silly woman remembered. Mrs. Conrad's already pink complexion deepened to a shade of beet that really didn't become her at all.

"That is . . . I . . . I—" her hostess stammered.

This was what one got when one accepted an invitation from a lady who aspired to but didn't quite sail in the highest circles of society. It was Emeline's own fault, really. She sighed and took pity. "He's in the army, then?"

Mrs. Conrad grasped the bait gratefully. "Oh, no. Not anymore. At least I don't *believe* so."

"Ah," Emeline said, and tried to think of another subject.

The room was large and expensively decorated, with a painting on the ceiling overhead depicting Hades pursuing Persephone. The goddess looked particularly vacuous, smiling down sweetly on the assembly below. She hadn't a chance against the god of the underworld, even if he did have bright pink cheeks in this portrayal.

Emeline's current protégé, Jane Greenglove, sat on a settee nearby, conversing with young Lord Simmons, a very nice choice. Emeline nodded approvingly. Lord Simmons had an income of over eight thousand pounds a year and a lovely house near Oxford. That alliance would be very suitable, and since Jane's older sister, Eliza, had already accepted the hand of Mr. Hampton, things were falling into place quite neatly. They always did, of course, when Emeline consented to guide a young lady into society, but it was pleasing to have one's expectations fulfilled nevertheless.

Or it should be. Emeline twisted a lace ribbon at her waist before she caught herself and smoothed it out again. Actually, she was feeling a bit out of sorts, which was ridiculous. Her world was perfect. Absolutely perfect.

Emeline glanced casually at the stranger only to find his dark gaze fixed on her. His eyes crinkled ever so slightly at the corners as if he was amused by something—and that something might be her. Hastily she looked away again. Awful man. He was obviously aware that every lady in the room had noticed him.

Beside her, Mrs. Conrad had started prattling, evidently in an attempt to cover her gaffe. "He owns an importing business in the Colonies. I believe he's in London on business; that's what Mr. Conrad says, anyway. And he's as rich as Croesus, although you'd never guess it from his attire."

It was impossible not to glance at him again after this information. From midthigh up, his clothing was plain indeed—black coat and brown-and-black-patterned waistcoat. All in all, a conservative wardrobe until one came to his legs. The man was wearing some type of native leggings. They were made from an odd tan leather, quite dull, and they were gartered just below the knees with red, white, and black striped sashes. The leggings split in the front over the shoes with brightly embroidered flaps that fell to either side of his feet. And his shoes were the strangest of all, for they had no heels. He seemed to be wearing a type of slipper made of the same soft, dull leather, with beading or embroidery work running from ankle to toe. Yet even heelless, the stranger was quite tall. He had brown hair, and as far as she could tell from halfway across the room, his eyes were dark. Certainly not blue or green. They were heavy-lidded and intelligent. She suppressed a shiver. Intelligent men were so hard to manage.

His arms were crossed, one shoulder propped against the wall, and his gaze was interested. As if they were the exotic ones, not he. His nose was long, with a bump in the middle; his complexion dark, as if he'd lately come from some exotic shore. The bones of his face were raw and prominent: cheeks, nose, and chin jutting in an aggressively masculine way that was nevertheless perversely attractive. His mouth, in contrast, was wide and almost soft, with a sensuous inverted dent in the lower lip. It was the mouth of a man who liked to savor. To linger and taste. A dangerous mouth.

Emeline looked away again. "Who is he?"

Mrs. Conrad stared. "Don't you know?"

"No."

Her hostess was delighted. "Why, my dear, that's Mr. Samuel Hartley! Everyone has been talking about him, though he has only been in London a sennight or so. He's not quite acceptable, because of the..." Mrs. Conrad met Emeline's eyes and hastily cut short what she'd been about to say. "*Anyway.* Even with all his wealth, not everyone is happy to meet him."

Emeline stilled as the back of her neck prickled.

Mrs. Conrad continued, oblivious. "I really shouldn't have invited him, but I couldn't help myself. That form, my dear. Simply delicious! Why, if I hadn't asked him, I would never have—" Her flurry of words ended on a startled squeak, for a man had cleared his throat directly behind them.

Emeline hadn't been watching, so she hadn't seen him move, but she knew instinctively who stood so close to them. Slowly she turned her head.

Mocking coffee-brown eyes met her own. "Mrs. Conrad, I'd be grateful if you'd introduce us." His voice had a flat American accent.

Their hostess sucked in her breath at this blunt order, but curiosity won out over indignation. "Lady Emeline, may I introduce Mr. Samuel Hartley. Mr. Hartley, Lady Emeline Gordon."

Emeline sank into a curtsy, only to be presented with a large, tanned hand on rising. She stared for a moment, nonplussed. Surely the man wasn't that unsophisticated? Mrs. Conrad's breathy giggle decided the matter. Gingerly, Emeline touched just her fingertips to his.

To no avail. He embraced her hand with both of his, enveloping her fingers in hard warmth. His nostrils flared just the tiniest bit as she was forced to step forward into the handshake. Was he *scenting* her?

"How do you do?" he asked.

"Well," Emeline retorted. She tried to free her hand but could not, even though Mr. Hartley didn't seem to be gripping her tightly. "Might I have my appendage returned to me now?"

That mouth twitched again. Did he laugh at everyone or just her? "Of course, my lady."

Emeline opened her mouth to make an excuse—any

excuse—to leave the dreadful man, but he was too quick for her.

"May I escort you into the garden?"

It really wasn't a question, since he'd already held out his arm, obviously expecting her consent. And what was worse, she gave it. Silently, Emeline laid her fingertips on his coat sleeve. He nodded to Mrs. Conrad and drew Emeline outside in only a matter of minutes, working very neatly for such a gauche man. Emeline squinted up at his profile suspiciously.

He turned his head and caught her look. His own eyes wrinkled at the corners, laughing down at her, although his mouth remained perfectly straight. "We're neighbors, you know."

"What do you mean?"

"I've rented the house next to yours."

Emeline found herself blinking up at him, caught off guard once again—a disagreeable sensation as rare as it was unwanted. She knew the occupants of the town house to the right of hers, but the left had been let out recently. For an entire day the week before, men had been tramping in and out of the open doors, sweating, shouting, and cursing. And they'd carried...

Her eyebrows snapped together. "The pea-green settee."

His mouth curved at one corner. "What?"

"You're the owner of that atrocious pea-green settee, aren't you?"

He bowed. "I confess it."

"With no trace of shame, either, I see." Emeline pursed her lips in disapproval. "Are there really gilt owls carved on the legs?"

"I hadn't noticed."

"*I* had."

"Then I'll not argue the point."

"Humph." She faced forward again.

"I have a favor to ask of you, ma'am." His voice rumbled somewhere above her head.

He'd led her down one of the packed gravel paths of the Conrads' town house garden. It was unimaginatively planted with roses and small, clipped hedges. Sadly, most of the roses had already bloomed, so the whole looked rather plain and forlorn.

"I'd like to hire you."

"*Hire* me?" Emeline inhaled sharply and stopped, forcing him to halt as well and face her. Did this odd man think she was a courtesan of some sort? The insult was outrageous, and in her confusion she found her gaze wandering over his frame, crossing wide shoulders, a pleasingly flat waist, and then dropping to an inappropriate portion of Mr. Hartley's anatomy, which, now that she noticed it, was rather nicely outlined by the black wool breeches he wore under his leggings. She inhaled again, nearly choking, and hastily raised her eyes. But the man either hadn't observed her indiscretion or was much more polite than his attire and manner would lead one to believe.

He continued. "I need a mentor for my sister, Rebecca. Someone to show her the parties and balls."

Emeline cocked her head as she realized that he wanted a chaperone. Well, why hadn't the silly man said so in the first place and saved her all this embarrassment? "I'm afraid that won't be possible."

"Why not?" The words were soft, but there was an edge of command behind them.

Emeline stiffened. "I take only young ladies from the highest ranks of society. I don't believe your sister can meet my standards. I'm sorry."

He watched her for a moment and then looked away. Although his gaze was on a bench at the end of the path, Emeline doubted very much that he saw it. "Perhaps, then, I can plead another reason for you to take us on."

She stilled. "What is that?"

His eyes looked back at her, and now there was no trace of amusement in them. "I knew Reynaud."

The beating of Emeline's heart was very loud in her ears. Because, of course, Reynaud was her brother. Her brother who had been killed in the massacre of the 28th.

SHE SMELLED OF lemon balm. Sam inhaled the familiar scent as he waited for Lady Emeline's answer, aware that her perfume was distracting him. Distraction was dangerous when in negotiations with a clever opponent. But it was odd to discover this sophisticated lady wearing such a homey perfume. His mother had grown lemon balm in her garden in the backwoods of Pennsylvania, and the scent pitched him back in time. He remembered sitting at a rough-hewn table as a small boy, watching Mother pour boiling water over the green leaves. The fresh scent had risen with the steam from the thick earthenware cup. Lemon balm. Balm to the soul, Mother had called it.

"Reynaud is dead," Lady Emeline said abruptly. "Why do you think I'd do you this favor simply because you say you knew him?"

He examined her face as she spoke. She was a beautiful woman; there was no doubt about that. Her hair and eyes were dramatically dark, her mouth full and red. But hers was a complicated beauty. Many men would be dissuaded by the intelligence in those dark eyes and by the skeptical purse of those red lips.

"Because you loved him." Sam watched her eyes as he said the words and saw a slight flicker. He'd guessed right, then; she'd been close to her brother. If he was kind, he'd not presume on her grief. But kindness had never gotten him much, either in business or in his personal life. "I think you'll do it for his memory."

"Humph." She didn't look particularly convinced.

But he knew otherwise. It was one of the first things he'd learned to recognize in the import business: the exact moment when his opponent wavered and the scales of the negotiation tipped in Sam's favor. The next step was to strengthen his position. Sam held out his arm again, and she stared at it a moment before placing her fingertips on his sleeve. He felt the thrill of her acquiescence, though he was careful not to let it show.

Instead, he led her farther down the garden path. "My sister and I will only be in London for three months. I don't expect you to work miracles."

"Why bother engaging my help at all, then?"

He tilted his face to the late-afternoon sun, glad that he was outside now, away from the people in the salon. "Rebecca is only nineteen. I am often occupied with my business, and I'd like her to be entertained, perhaps meet some ladies of her own age." All true, if not the whole truth.

"There are no female relatives to do the duty?"

He glanced down at her, amused by her unsubtle question. Lady Emeline was a small woman; her dark head came only to his shoulder. Her lack of height should've made her seem fragile, but he knew Lady Emeline was no delicate piece of china. He'd watched her for some twenty minutes in the damnably small sitting room before approaching her and Mrs. Conrad. In that time, her gaze had never stopped moving. Even as she'd talked to their hostess, she'd kept an eye on her charges as well as on the movements of the other guests. He'd lay good money that she was aware of every conversation in the room, of who had talked to whom, of how the discussions had progressed, and when the participants had parted. In her own rarified world, she was as successful as he.

Which made it even more important that she be the one to help him gain entry into London society.

"No, my sister and I have no surviving female relatives," he answered her question now. "Our mother died at Rebecca's birth and Pa only months later. Fortunately, my father's brother was a businessman in Boston. He and his wife took in Rebecca and raised her. They've both passed on since."

"And you?"

He turned to look at her. "What about me?"

She frowned up at him impatiently. "What happened to you when both your parents died?"

"I was sent to a boys' academy," he said prosaically, the words in no way conveying the shock of leaving a cabin in the woods and entering a world of books and strict discipline.

They had reached a brick garden wall, which marked

the end of the path. She halted and faced him. "I must meet your sister before I can come to any decision."

"Of course," he murmured, knowing he had her.

She shook out her skirts briskly, her black eyes narrowed, her red mouth pursed as she thought. An image of her dead brother suddenly rose up in his mind: Reynaud's black eyes narrowed in exactly the same manner as he dressed down a soldier. For a moment, the masculine face superimposed itself over the smaller, feminine face of the sister. Reynaud's heavy black brows drew together, his midnight eyes staring as if with condemnation. Sam shuddered and pushed the phantom away, concentrating on what the living woman was saying.

"You and your sister may visit me tomorrow. I'll let you know my decision after that. Tea, I think? You do drink tea, don't you?"

"Yes."

"Excellent. Will two o'clock suit you?"

He was tempted to smile at her order. "You're very kind, ma'am."

She looked at him suspiciously a moment, then whirled to march back up the garden path, which left him to follow. He did, slowly, watching that elegant back and those twitching skirts. And as he followed her, he patted his pocket, hearing the familiar crinkle of paper and wondering, how best could he use Lady Emeline?

"I DO NOT comprehend," Tante Cristelle pronounced that night at dinner. "If the gentleman did indeed wish the honor of your patronage, why did he not pursue you through the channels usual? He should compel a friend to make the introduction."

Tante Cristelle was Emeline's mother's younger sister, a tall, white-haired lady with a terribly straight back and sky-blue eyes that should've been benign but weren't. The old lady had never married, and privately Emeline sometimes thought it was because the males of her aunt's age must've been terrified of her. Tante Cristelle had lived with Emeline and her son, Daniel, for the last five years, ever since the death of Daniel's father.

"Perhaps he wasn't aware of how it's properly done," Emeline said as she perused the selection of meats on the tray. "Or perhaps he didn't want to take the time to go through the customary maneuvers. He said they were to be in London only a short while, after all." She indicated a slice of beef and smiled her thanks as the footman forked it onto her plate.

"*Mon Dieu,* if he is such a gauche rustic, then he has no business attempting the labyrinths of *le ton.*" Her aunt took a sip of wine and then pursed her lips as if the red liquid were sour.

Emeline made a noncommittal sound. Tante Cristelle's analysis of Mr. Hartley was accurate on the surface—he had indeed given the appearance of a rustic. The problem was, his eyes had told another story. He'd almost seemed to be laughing at her, as if *she* were the naïf.

"And what will you do, I ask you, if the girl is anything like the brother you describe?" Tante Cristelle arched her eyebrows in exaggerated horror. "What if she wears her hair in braids down her back? What if she laughs too loudly? What if she wears no shoes and her feet, they are so dirty?"

This distasteful thought was apparently too much for the old lady. She beckoned urgently to the footman for more wine while Emeline bit her lip to keep from smiling.

"He is very wealthy. I discreetly inquired about his position from the other ladies at the salon. They all confirmed that Mr. Hartley is indeed one of the richest men in Boston. Presumably, he moves in the best circles there."

"Tcha." Tante dismissed all of Boston society.

Emeline cut into her beef serenely. "And even if they were rustics, Tante, surely we should not hold lack of proper training against the chit?"

"*Non!*" Tante Cristelle exclaimed, making the footman at her elbow start and nearly drop the decanter of wine. "And again I say, *non!* This prejudice, it is the foundation of society. How are we to discern the well-born from the common rabble if not by the manners they keep?"

"Perhaps you're right."

"Yes, of course I am right," her aunt retorted.

"Mmm." Emeline poked at the beef on her plate. For some reason, she no longer wanted it. "Tante, do you remember that little book my nanny used to read to Reynaud and me as children?"

"Book? What book? Whatever are you talking about?"

Emeline plucked at the bit of gathered ribbon on her sleeve. "It was a book of fairy tales, and we were very fond of it. I thought of it today for some reason."

She stared thoughtfully at her plate, remembering. Nanny would often read to them outside after an afternoon picnic. Reynaud and she would sit on the picnic blanket as Nanny turned the pages of the fairy-tale book. But as the story progressed, Reynaud would creep unconsciously forward, drawn by the excitement of the tale, until he was nearly in Nanny's lap, hanging on every word, his black eyes sparkling.

He'd been so alive, so vital, even as a boy. Emeline swallowed, carefully smoothing the raveled ribbon at her waist. "I only wondered where the book could be. Do you think it's packed away in the attics?"

"Who can say?" Her aunt gave an eloquent and very Gallic shrug, dismissing the old book of fairy tales and Emeline's memories of Reynaud. She leaned forward to exclaim, "But again I ask, why? Why do you even think to agree to take on this man and his sister who wears no shoes?"

Emeline forbore to point out that as of yet, they had no intelligence concerning Miss Hartley's shoes or the lack thereof. In fact, the only Hartley she knew about was the brother. For a moment, she remembered the man's tanned face and coffee-brown eyes. She shook her head slowly. "I don't know exactly, except that he obviously needed my help."

"Ah, but if you took all who need your help, we would be buried beneath petitioners."

"He said..." Emeline hesitated, watching the light sparkle on her wineglass. "He said he knew Reynaud."

Tante Cristelle set down her wineglass carefully. "But why do you believe this?"

"I don't know. I just do." She looked helplessly at her aunt. "You must think me a fool."

Tante Cristelle sighed, her lips drooping at the corners, emphasizing the lines of age there. "No, *ma petite.* I simply think you a sister who loved her brother most dearly."

Emeline nodded, watching her fingers twist the wineglass in her hand. She didn't meet her aunt's eyes. She had loved Reynaud. She still did. Love didn't stop simply because the recipient had died. But there was another reason she was contemplating taking on the Hartley girl. She felt somehow that Samuel Hartley hadn't been telling her the whole truth of why he needed her help. He wanted something. Something that involved Reynaud.

And that meant he bore watching.

Chapter Two

Iron Heart walked for many days in the dark forest, and during that time, he met neither human nor animal. On the seventh day, the wall of trees opened up, and he emerged from the forest. Directly ahead of him lay a shining city. He stared. Never in all his travels had he seen such a magnificent city. But soon his belly rumbled, waking him from his awe. He needed to buy food, and in order to buy food, he must find work. So off he tramped into the city.

But though he inquired high and low, there was no decent work to be found for a soldier returning from war. And this is often the case, I think. For though all are happy enough to see a soldier when there is a war to be fought, after the danger is past, they look upon the same man with suspicion and contempt.

Thus it came about that Iron Heart was forced to take the job of a street sweeper. And this he did most gratefully....

—from *Iron Heart*

"I thought I heard you come in late last night," Rebecca said as she placed some coddled eggs on her plate the next morning. "After midnight?"

"Was it?" Samuel replied vaguely. He was sitting at the breakfast table behind her. "I'm sorry I woke you."

"Oh! Oh, no. You didn't disturb me at all. That wasn't what I meant." Rebecca sighed inwardly and took the seat opposite her brother. She wanted rather badly to ask him where he'd been last night—and the night before that—but shyness and a certain hesitation held her tongue. She poured herself some tea and strove to open a topic of conversation, always a bit hard in the morning. "What are your plans for today? Are you conducting business with Mr. Kitcher? I...I thought if not, that we might go for a drive about London. I hear St. Paul's Cathedral—"

"Damn!" Samuel set his knife down with a clatter. "I forgot to tell you."

Rebecca felt a sinking in the pit of her belly. It'd been a long shot—her brother was so often busy—but she'd hoped nevertheless that he'd have time to spend with her that afternoon. "Tell me what?"

"We've been invited to tea by our next-door neighbor, Lady Emeline Gordon."

"What?" Rebecca glanced involuntarily in the direction of the grand town house that adjoined their house to the right. She'd glimpsed her ladyship once or twice and had been awed by their neighbor's sophistication. "But...but when did this happen? I didn't see an invitation in today's post."

"I met her at the salon I attended yesterday."

"Goodness," Rebecca marveled. "She must be a very

pleasant lady to invite us on such little acquaintance."
Whatever would she wear to meet a titled lady?

Samuel fingered his knife, and if she didn't know better, she would've said her older brother was uncomfortable. "Actually, I asked her to chaperone you to some
gatherings."

"Really? I thought you didn't like balls and social gatherings." She was pleased, of course, that he'd
thought of her, but his sudden interest in her schedule
seemed rather odd.

"Yes, but now that we're in London..." Samuel let his
sentence trail as he drank some coffee. "I thought you
might like to go out. See the city, meet some people.
You're only nineteen. You must be bored to death, rattling
around this place with just me to keep you company."

Well, that wasn't quite true, Rebecca reflected as she
tried to think of a reply. Actually, she was surrounded by
many other people—servants. There seemed to be scores
of servants in this London town house Samuel had rented.
Just when she thought she'd met them all, an odd maid
or bootblack boy who she'd never seen before would
suddenly pop up. Indeed, right now there were two footmen standing by the wall ready to wait on them. One she
thought was named Travers, and the other...fiddlesticks!
She'd quite forgotten the other's name, although she knew
for certain that she'd seen him before. He had jetty hair
and amazing green eyes. Not, of course, that she should
be noticing the color of a footman's eyes.

Rebecca poked at her cold eggs. She was only used to
Cook and Elsie at home in Boston where she lived with
Samuel. Growing up, she'd eaten most of her suppers
with Cook and the elderly maid, until she was deemed

a lady and made to sit in the dining room with Uncle Thomas. Her uncle had been a dear, and Rebecca loved him, but dining with him had been rather a trial. His dinner conversation had been so flat when compared to the lively nightly gossip she'd had with Cook and Elsie. The conversation at meals had improved a little when Samuel had come to live with her on the death of Uncle Thomas, but not by much. Samuel could be terribly witty when he wanted to, but so often he seemed distracted by business affairs.

"Do you mind?" Samuel's question broke into her rambling thoughts.

"I'm sorry?"

Her brother was frowning at her now, and Rebecca had the sinking sensation that somehow she'd disappointed him. "Do you mind that I've asked Lady Emeline to help?"

"No, not at all." She smiled brightly. Of course, she'd rather that he'd spent the time with her, but he was in London on business, after all. "I'm flattered that you thought of me."

But this answer made him set down his coffee cup. "You say that as if I consider you a burden."

Rebecca dropped her gaze. Actually, that was exactly how she reckoned he thought of her. A burden. How could he not? She was much younger than he and brought up in the city. Samuel, in contrast, had been raised in the wilds of the frontier until the age of fourteen. Sometimes she thought the gulf that separated them was wider than the ocean. "I know you didn't wish me to come on this trip."

"We've been over this before. I was happy to include you once I knew that you wanted to travel with me."

"Yes, and I'm very grateful." Rebecca carefully straightened the silverware at her place, aware that her answer wasn't quite right. She peeked at him under her brows.

He was frowning again. "Rebecca, I—"

The entrance of the butler interrupted him. "Mr. Kitcher has arrived, sir."

Mr. Kitcher was her brother's man of business.

"Thank you," Samuel muttered. He stood and bent to kiss her on the forehead. "Kitcher and I are to see a man about arranging to visit Wedgwood's showroom. I'll be back after luncheon. We are expected at her ladyship's house at two o'clock."

"Very well," Rebecca replied, but Samuel was already at the door. He exited without another word, and Rebecca was left to contemplate her eggs all alone. Except, of course, for the footmen.

THE COLONIAL GENTLEMAN was even more imposing standing in her little sitting room. That was Emeline's first thought that afternoon when she turned to greet her guests. The contrast was stark between her pretty sitting room—elegant, sophisticated, and very civilized—and the man who stood so motionless at its center. He should've been overwhelmed by the gilt and satin, should've seemed naïve and a little crude in his plain woolen clothes.

Instead he dominated the room.

"Good afternoon, Mr. Hartley." Emeline held out her hand, belatedly remembering their handshake of the day before. She held her breath to see if he'd repeat that unorthodox gesture. But Mr. Hartley merely took her hand and quite properly brushed his lips in the air an inch above her knuckles. For a moment, he seemed to hesitate there, his nostrils flaring, and then he straightened. She caught the amused gleam in his eyes. Her own eyes narrowed. The scoundrel! He'd known all along yesterday that he was supposed to kiss her hand.

"May I present my sister, Rebecca Hartley," he said now, and Emeline was forced to marshal her attention.

The young girl who stepped forward was pleasingly attractive. She had her brother's dark hair, but where his eyes were a warm brown, hers held sparks of green and even yellow. A most unusual color but very pretty nonetheless. She wore a simple dimity frock with a square neckline and a bit of lace at the sleeves and bodice. Emeline noted that the wardrobe could certainly be improved.

"How do you do?" she said as the girl made a passable curtsy.

"Oh, ma'am—I mean, my lady—I'm so pleased to meet you," Miss Hartley gasped. She had a pretty, if unpolished manner.

Emeline nodded. "My aunt, Mademoiselle Molyneux."

Tante Cristelle was sitting at her left, perched at the very edge of her chair so that several inches of air was between her ramrod-straight back and the chair's back. The older woman inclined her head. Her lips were pinched, but her eyes were staring at the hem of Miss Hartley's dress.

Mr. Hartley smiled, his mouth twisting rather raffishly at the corners as he bowed over her aunt's hand. "How do you do, ma'am?"

"Very well, I thank you, monsieur," Tante said crisply.

Mr. Hartley and his sister sat, the girl on the yellow and white damask settee, her brother on the orange wing chair.

Emeline settled in an armchair and nodded at Crabs, the butler, who immediately disappeared to order the tea.

"You said yesterday that you were in London on business, Mr. Hartley. What kind?" she asked her guest.

Mr. Hartley flicked the skirt of his brown coat aside to set one ankle across the knee of the opposite leg. "I deal in the import and export of goods to Boston."

"Indeed?" Emeline murmured faintly. Mr. Hartley seemed not at all self-conscious to admit engaging in trade. But then what else could one expect from a colonial who wore leather leggings? Her gaze dropped to his crossed leg. The soft leather fit closely to his calf, outlining a lovely masculine form. She averted her eyes.

"I hope to meet Mr. Josiah Wedgwood," Mr. Hartley said. "Perhaps you've heard of him? He has a marvelous new crockery factory."

"Crockery." Tante Cristelle employed her lorgnette—an affectation that she used mainly when she wished to cow others. She peered first at Mr. Hartley and then returned to her fascination with Miss Hartley's lower skirts.

Mr. Hartley remained uncowed. He smiled at Emeline's aunt and then at Emeline. "Crockery. Amazing how much crockery we use in the Colonies. My business already imports earthenware and such, but I believe that there is a market for finer stuff. Things that a fashionable lady might have at her table. Mr. Wedgwood has perfected a process to make creamware more delicate than anyone has ever seen. I hope to persuade him that Hartley Importers is the company to best bring his goods to the Colonies."

Emeline raised her eyebrows, intrigued despite herself. "You will market the china for him there?"

"No. It will be the usual exchange. I will buy his goods

and then resell them across the Atlantic. What's different is that I hope to have the exclusive right to trade his goods in the Colonies."

"You are ambitious, Mr. Hartley," Tante Cristelle said. She did not sound approving.

Mr. Hartley inclined his head to her aunt. He didn't seem perturbed by the old woman's disapproval. Emeline found herself reluctantly admiring his self-possession. He was foreign in a way that had nothing to do with being American. The gentlemen of her acquaintance didn't deal in commerce, let alone discuss it so bluntly with a lady. It was rather interesting to have a man regard her as an intellectual equal. At the same time, she was aware that he would never belong in her world.

Miss Hartley cleared her throat. "My brother has informed me that you have kindly agreed to chaperone me, ma'am."

The entrance of three maids bearing laden tea trays prevented Emeline from making a suitable retort—one that would wing the brother and not the girl. He'd taken her assent for granted, had he? She noticed, as the maids bustled about, that Mr. Hartley was watching her quite openly. She raised an eyebrow at him in challenge, but he only quirked his own back at her. Was he flirting with her? Didn't he know that she was far, far out of his reach?

When the tea things had been settled, Emeline began to pour, her back so straight that she put even Tante to shame. "I am considering championing you, Miss Hartley." She smiled to take the sting out of the words. "Perhaps you'll tell me why you have—?"

She was interrupted by a whirlwind. The sitting room door slammed against the wall, bouncing off the woodwork and putting yet another chip in the paint. A tangle of arms and long legs lunged at her.

Emeline jerked the hot teapot away with the ease of long practice.

"M'man! M'man!" panted the demon child. His blond curls were quite deceptively angelic. "Cook says she has made currant buns. May I have one?"

Emeline set down the teapot and drew in a breath to castigate him, only to find Tante talking instead. *"Mais oui, mon chou!* Here, take a plate and Tante Cristelle will pick out the buns most plump for you."

Emeline cleared her throat, and both boy and elderly aunt looked at her guiltily. She smiled meaningfully at her offspring. "Daniel, would you be so kind as to put down that bun clutched in your fist and make your bows to our guests?"

Daniel relinquished his rather squashed prize, and then regrettably wiped his palm on his breeches. Emeline took a breath but refrained from commenting. One skirmish at a time. She turned to the Hartleys. "May I present my son, Daniel Gordon, Baron Eddings."

The imp made a very correct bow—beautiful enough to cause her bosom to swell with maternal pride. Not, of course, that Emeline let her satisfaction show; no need to make the boy vain. Mr. Hartley held out his hand in the exact same gesture that he'd given her yesterday. Her son beamed. Grown men didn't usually offer their hands to eight-year-olds, no matter their rank. Gravely, Daniel took the much larger hand and shook it.

"I'm pleased to meet you, my lord," Mr. Hartley said.

Daniel bowed to the girl, and then Emeline handed

him a bun wrapped in a cloth. "Now run away, dear. I have—"

"Surely your son can stay with us, ma'am," Mr. Hartley interrupted her.

Emeline drew herself up. How dare the man interfere between her and her child? She was on the point of giving him a set-down when he caught her eye. Mr. Hartley's eyes were wrinkled about the edges, but instead of amusement, they appeared to reflect sorrow. He didn't even know her son. Why, then, would he feel pity for the boy?

"Please, M'man?" Daniel asked.

Her consternation should've only grown stronger—the boy knew better than to beg once she'd made a decision—but instead something inside her melted.

"Oh, very well." She knew she sounded like a grumpy old woman, but Daniel grinned and took a seat near Mr. Hartley, wiggling back in the too-big chair. And Mr. Hartley smiled at her with his coffee-brown eyes. That sight seemed to make her breath come short, which was a ridiculous reaction from a mature woman of the world.

"So, then, this is most pleasant," Tante Cristelle said. She winked at Daniel, and he squirmed in his chair until he caught his mother's eye. "But now, I think, we must discuss Mademoiselle Hartley's clothing."

Miss Hartley, who had just taken a sip of tea, seemed to choke. "Ma'am?"

Tante Cristelle nodded once. "It is atrocious."

Mr. Hartley set his teacup down carefully. "Mademoiselle Molyneux, I think—"

The old woman rounded on him. "Do you wish your sister to be laughed at, eh? Do you want the other young ladies to whisper behind their fans? For the young men to refuse to dance with her? Is this what you aspire to?"

"No, of course not," Mr. Hartley said. "What's wrong with Rebecca's dress?"

"Nothing." Emeline set down her own dish of tea. "Nothing at all if Miss Hartley only wants to visit the parks and some of the sights of London. I'm quite sure what she's wearing now is sufficient even for the fashionable of Boston in your colonies. But for the London *haut ton*—"

"She must have the frocks very elegant!" Tante Cristelle exclaimed. "And also the gloves and the shawls and the hats and the shoes." She leaned forward to thump her stick. "The shoes, they are most important."

Miss Hartley glanced at her slippers in alarm, but Mr. Hartley only looked faintly amused. "I see."

Tante Cristelle peered at him shrewdly. "And all of these things, they will cost a pretty penny, *non?*"

She didn't add that he would be providing a wardrobe for Emeline as well. It was understood in London society that this was the way in which Emeline would be recompensed for her time spent chaperoning his sister.

Emeline waited for some type of protest from Mr. Hartley. Evidently he hadn't realized the expense involved in a young chit's season. Most families saved for many years for the event; some even went into debt purchasing a girl's costumes. He might be a very rich man in Boston, but how did that translate to London wealth? Would he be able to afford such an unexpected outlay? She was oddly disappointed at the thought that he might have to abandon the entire endeavor.

But Mr. Hartley merely took a bite from a bun. It was

Miss Hartley who made the protest. "Oh, Samuel, it's too much! I don't need a new wardrobe, truly I don't."

A very pretty speech. The sister had given the brother an honorable out. Emeline turned to Mr. Hartley with raised eyebrows. Out of the corner of her eye, she noticed that Daniel used the opportunity of the adults' distraction to filch another bun.

Mr. Hartley took a long swallow of tea before speaking. "It seems you do need a new wardrobe, Rebecca. Lady Emeline says so and I think we must rely on her advice."

"But the expense!" The girl looked truly distressed.

The brother did not. "Don't worry over it. I can bear it." He turned to Emeline. "When shall we go shopping, then, my lady?"

"There's no need for you to accompany us," Emeline said. "You may simply give us a letter of credit—"

"But I'd enjoy escorting you ladies," the colonial interrupted her smoothly. "Surely you'll not deny me so simple a pleasure?"

Emeline pressed her lips together. She knew he'd be a distraction, but there was no polite way to discourage him. Her smile was tight. "Of course, we would be glad to have your company."

He gave the impression of grinning without actually changing his expression, the lines deepening on either side of his mouth. Extraordinary man! "Then I repeat, when shall we make this expedition?"

"Tomorrow," Emeline replied crisply.

His sensuous lips curved slightly. "Fine."

And she narrowed her eyes. Either Mr. Hartley was a fool or he was richer than King Midas himself.

*   *   *

HE WOKE IN the night, covered in sweat from the nightmare. Sam held himself still, his eyes straining in the darkness as he waited for the thundering in his chest to quiet. The fire had gone out, dammit, and the room was cold. He'd told the maids to bank it well, but they never seemed to do so adequately. By morning, his fire was usually mere embers. Tonight it was entirely dead.

He swung his legs out of the bed, and his bare feet hit the carpet. He stumbled through the blackness to the window and pulled the heavy drapes aside. The moon hung high over the roofs of the city, its light cold and pale. He used the dim glow to dress, shedding his drenched nightshirt and donning breeches, shirt, waistcoat, leggings, and his moccasins.

Sam stole out of his room, the soft moccasins making his steps nearly silent. He padded down the great marble staircase and into the lower hall. Here he heard footsteps advancing toward him, and he merged into the shadows. Candlelight flickered closer, and he saw his butler dressed in a nightshirt and holding a bottle in one hand, the candlestick in the other. The man walked past, only inches from where he hid, and Sam caught a whiff of whiskey. He smiled in the dark. How the servant would start if he knew his master was lurking in the gloom. The butler would think him mad.

Sam waited until the glow of the butler's candle had disappeared and his footsteps faded. Another minute ticked by as he listened, but all was quiet. He drifted from his hiding place and stole through the empty back kitchen to the servant's entrance. The key was kept on the mantelpiece of the great fireplace, but he had a duplicate. He let himself out, the latch clicking closed behind him. It was pleasantly chill outside, and he repressed a shiver. For a moment, he lingered in the shadows by the back door, listening, watching, and scenting. All he caught was the scurrying of a rodent in the bushes and the sudden mewl of a cat. No human nearby. He slid through the narrow walled garden, brushing by mint and parsley and other herbs whose scents he couldn't name. Then he was in the mews, checking for a minute here as well.

He began to run. His footfalls were as quiet as the cat's, but he kept to the edge of the dark shadows near the stables. He hated to be found out when he stole into the night. Perhaps that was why he didn't bother with a valet.

He passed a doorway, and the stink of urine wafted into his nose, making him veer away. He'd never seen a city— a small town, really—until he'd been ten years old. Three and twenty years later, he could still recall the shock of the smell. The terrible stink of hundreds of people living too close together with no place to dispose of their piss and shit. As a boy, he'd nearly heaved when he'd realized that the trickle of brown water in the middle of the fine cobblestone street was an open sewer. One of the first lessons Pa had taught him as a lad was to hide his waste. Animals were canny. If they smelled the odor of people, they'd not venture near. No animals, no food. It had been as simple as that in the great forests of Pennsylvania.

But here, where people lived cheek by jowl and let their waste pile into corners, where the reek of man seemed to hang like a fog that had to be fought through, here in the city it was more complicated. There were still predators and prey, but their forms had warped, and sometimes it was impossible to tell the two apart. This city was far more dangerous than any frontier with wild animals and raiding Indians.

His feet carried him to the end of the mews and to an intersection. He dipped across the lane and continued running down the street. A young man was entering the gate of a town house—a servant returning from an assignation? Sam passed him not a foot away, and the man didn't even turn. But Sam inhaled the smell of ale and pipe smoke as he ran by.

Lady Emeline smelled of lemon balm. He'd caught the scent again as he'd bent over her white hand this afternoon. It wasn't right. Such a sophisticated woman should have worn patchouli or musk. He'd often found himself overwhelmed by the smell—the stink—of society ladies. Their perfumes hung about them like a fog until he'd wanted nothing more than to cover his nose and choke. But Lady Emeline wore lemon balm, the scent of his mother's garden. That dichotomy intrigued him.

He loped across the entrance of an alley and jumped a foul puddle. Someone lurked here, either for shelter or in ambush, but Sam was past before the form had time to react. He glanced over his shoulder and saw the lurker peering after him. Sam grinned to himself and picked up his pace, his moccasins brushing soundlessly on cobblestones. This was the only time he almost liked the city— when the streets were deserted and a man could move without fear of bumping into another person. When there was *space*. He felt his leg muscles begin to warm with his exertion.

He'd deliberately chosen the rented house next to Lady Emeline when they'd come to London. He'd had a need to find out how Reynaud's sister had fared. It was the least he could do for the officer he'd failed. When he'd discovered that the lady enjoyed introducing young girls into society, asking for her help with Rebecca had seemed like the natural thing to do. Of course, he hadn't told her the real reason that he was interested in London society, but that hadn't mattered to him. At least until he'd actually met the lady.

Because Lady Emeline wasn't what he'd expected. Somehow, without realizing it, he must've imagined her to be tall like her brother and with an equally aristocratic air. The aristocratic air was indeed there, but he was hard-put not to smile when she attempted to look down her nose at him. She couldn't be more than a couple of inches over five feet. Her shape was nicely rounded, the type that made a man want to cup her arse in his hands just to feel the feminine warmth. Her hair was black and her eyes just as dark. With her rosy cheeks and snappish voice, she might've been a saucy Irish maid, ripe for a flirtation.

Except she wasn't.

Sam swore softly and halted. He braced his palms on his knees as he panted, trying to catch his breath. Lady Emeline might look like an Irish maid, but in her elegant clothes and with an accent that could cut ice, no one in his right mind would mistake her for one. Not even an unsophisticated backwoodsman from the frontiers of the New World. His money could buy a lot of things, but a woman from the highest tiers of the English aristocracy wasn't one of them.

The moon was beginning to set. Time to go home. Sam looked around. Small shops lined the narrow street, their overhanging upper stories looming above. He'd never been in this part of London before, but that wouldn't stop him from finding his way back. He started at a slow jog. The return journey was always the hardest, his initial freshness and energy blown away. Now his chest labored to draw breath, and his muscles began to ache at the continued exertion. Then, too, the areas where he'd been wounded made themselves known, throbbing as he ran. *Remember,* the scars groaned, *remember where the tomahawk sawed your flesh, where the ball burrowed next to bone. Remember that you are forever marked, the survivor, the living, the one left to bear witness.*

Sam ran on, despite aches and memories. This was the point that separated those who would continue from those who fell by the wayside. The trick was to acknowledge the pain. To embrace it. Pain kept you awake. Pain meant that you still lived.

He didn't know how much longer he ran, but when he again ducked into the mews behind his rented house, the moon had set. He was so weary that he almost didn't see the watcher in time. A man lurked, big and solid, beside the corner of the stables. It was a measure of Sam's tiredness that he nearly ran by him. But he didn't. He stopped and slid into the shadows of his neighbor's stables. He peered at the watcher. The man was barrel-shaped and wore a scarlet coat and a battered tricorne, fraying gray about the edges. Sam had seen him before. Once today, across the street as he and Rebecca had left Lady Emeline's house, and yesterday as Sam had entered his rented carriage. The shape and the way the man stood was the same. The man was following him.

Sam took a few seconds to steady his breath before drawing two lead balls from his waistcoat pocket. They were small things, no bigger than his thumb, but they were useful for a man who enjoyed running the streets of London in the dark. He curled his right fist around the balls.

Silently, Sam rushed at Scarlet Coat, catching the bigger man's hair from behind with his left hand. He punched the man swiftly in the side of his head. "Who sent you?"

Scarlet Coat was fast for a big man. He twisted and tried to elbow Sam in the belly. Sam punched him again, once, twice, his fist connecting each time with the other man's face.

"Sod it!" Scarlet Coat gasped. His London accent was so thick, Sam could hardly make out the words.

The man aimed a fist at his face. Sam leaned to the side, and the blow glanced off his chin. He punched quick and hard at the man's exposed armpit. Scarlet Coat groaned, bending over his hurt side. When he straightened, he had a wicked blade in his hand. Sam circled, his fists held ready, looking for another opening. Scarlet Coat struck with his knife, but Sam knocked the man's arm aside. The knife spun to the ground, moonlight gleaming on what looked like a white bone handle. Sam feinted to the left, and when the other man lunged, he caught his right arm and pulled the man in toward himself.

"Your employer," Sam hissed as he wrenched the man's arm.

The man twisted violently and caught Sam a second blow to his chin. Sam staggered and that was all Scarlet Coat needed. The other man was off, running away down the mews. He ducked and grabbed his knife as he ran past it, and then he disappeared around the end of the mews.

Sam started after him instinctively—the predator always pursues a fleeing prey—but he stopped before the mews spilled onto the cross street. He'd been running for hours now; his wind was no longer fresh. If he did catch Scarlet Coat, he'd be in no condition to make the other man tell him what he knew. Sam sighed, pocketed the lead balls, and headed back to his own house.

The dawn was already breaking.

Chapter Three

One day as Iron Heart was sweeping the street, a procession rode by. There were running footmen dressed in gilt livery, a brace of guards mounted on snow-white chargers, and finally a gold carriage with two footmen clinging behind. Iron Heart could do naught but gape as the carriage came closer. When it was directly beside him, the curtain shifted and he saw the face of the lady within. And what a face it was! She was perfectly formed, her complexion so white and smooth she might've been ivory. Iron Heart stared after her.

Beside him a voice cackled. "Do you think Princess Solace beautiful?"

Iron Heart turned and found a wizened old man standing where before there had been no one. He frowned, but he had to admit that the princess was most lovely.

"Then," said the old man, leaning so close that Iron Heart could smell the stink of his breath, "would you like to marry her?"

—from *Iron Heart*

Emeline stepped into the afternoon sunshine and gave a sigh of pleasure. "That was a most satisfying shop."

"But," Miss Hartley panted beside her, "do I really need all those frocks? Won't one or two ball gowns do?"

"Now, Miss Hartley—"

"Oh, please, won't you call me Rebecca?"

Emeline tempered her stern tone. The girl was terribly sweet. "Yes, of course. Rebecca, then. It is most important that you be properly attired—"

"In gold leaf, if possible," a masculine voice cut into Emeline's homily.

"Oh, Samuel!" Rebecca exclaimed. "Your chin looks even worse than this morning."

Emeline turned, carefully smoothing out her brow. She didn't want Mr. Hartley to see either her vexation at the interruption or the odd flutter of excitement she felt low in her belly. Surely, such tumult wasn't altogether becoming in a woman of her age.

Mr. Hartley's chin was indeed a darker shade of plum than it'd been since Emeline had last seen him. Apparently, he'd run into a doorway sometime in the night. An oddly clumsy accident for such a graceful man. He was now leaning against a lamppost, his booted feet crossed at the ankle, looking like he'd been there for quite some time. And he had if he'd been waiting in this way since the ladies had entered the dressmaker's three hours ago. The awful man couldn't have been standing out here the entire time, could he?

Emeline felt a twinge of guilt. "Mr. Hartley, you do know that it's quite acceptable for you to leave us whilst we finish our shopping?"

He raised his eyebrows, and the sardonic expression in

his eyes said that he knew perfectly well the niceties of a ladies' shopping day. "I wouldn't dream of abandoning you, my lady. I apologize if my presence is irksome."

At her side, Tante Cristelle clicked her tongue. "You talk like a courtier, monsieur. I do not think it becomes you."

Mr. Hartley grinned and bowed to her aunt, not at all put out. "I am suitably reprimanded, ma'am."

"Yes, well," Emeline interjected. "I think the glover's next. Just down here is the most wonderful shop—"

"Perhaps you ladies would like some refreshment?" Mr. Hartley asked. "I'd never forgive myself if you fainted away from the exertion of your labors."

Emeline was forming a suitably regretful reply when Tante Cristelle spoke first. "Some tea would be very welcome."

Now Emeline couldn't decline him without looking churlish, and the dratted man knew it. The corner of his mouth curled as he watched her with warm brown eyes.

She pursed her lips. "Thank you, Mr. Hartley. You're very kind."

He inclined his head, straightened away from the lamppost, and held out his arm to her. "Shall we?"

Why did the man only remember the proprieties when it suited him? Emeline smiled stiffly and placed her fingertips on his sleeve, conscious of the muscle beneath the fabric. He glanced at her hand and up at her, cocking an eyebrow. She tilted her chin and began walking, Tante Cristelle and the girl following behind. Her aunt seemed to be lecturing Rebecca on the importance of shoes.

Around them, the fashionable Mayfair throng ebbed and flowed. Young bucks loitered in doorways, gossiping and eyeing the grandly dressed ladies. A dandy strolled past in a pink-powdered wig, his long walking stick extravagantly employed. Emeline heard a snort from Tante Cristelle. She inclined her head to the Misses Stevens as they passed. The elder girl nodded most properly. The younger, a pretty if vacuous redhead in overwide panniers, giggled into her gloved hand.

Emeline lowered her brows in disapproval at the girl. "How do you find our capital, Mr. Hartley?"

"Crowded." He dipped his head close to hers as he spoke. She caught a pleasing scent on his breath but couldn't place it.

"You are used to a smaller city?" She lifted her skirt as they approached a puddle of something noxious. Mr. Hartley drew her closer to him when they skirted it, and for a moment she felt the warmth of his body through wool and linen.

"Boston is smaller than London," he replied. They separated and she was chagrined to realize that she missed his warmth. "But it is just as crowded. I'm not used to cities at all."

"You were raised in the countryside?"

"More like the wilderness."

She turned in surprise at his answer just as he must've leaned toward her again. Suddenly his face was only inches from hers. Fine lines surrounded his coffee-colored eyes, deepening as he smiled at her. She noticed that a thin, pale scar lay under his left eye.

Then she looked away. "Were you raised by wolves, then, Mr. Hartley?"

"Not quite." His voice was amused, despite the sharpness of her words. "My father was a trapper on the Pennsylvania frontier. We lived in a cabin he'd built from logs that still had the bark on them."

This sounded very primitive. Actually, she had trouble imagining his home, it was so foreign to what she knew. "How were you educated until you went to the boys school?"

"My mother taught me reading and writing," Mr. Hartley said. "I learned about tracking, hunting, and the woods from my father. He was a very good woodsman."

They passed a bookshop with a bright red sign hanging so low that it nearly brushed Mr. Hartley's tricorne. Emeline cleared her throat. "I see."

"Do you?" he asked softly. "My world back then is a far cry from this." He nodded at the noisy London street. "Can you imagine a forest so quiet you can hear the leaves fall? Trees so big a grown man cannot wrap his arms about their girth?"

She shook her head. "It's difficult to picture. Your woodlands sound very strange to me. But you left those woods, didn't you?"

He was watching the flow of the crowd about them as they walked, but now he glanced down at her.

She drew in a breath, staring into his dark eyes. "That must have been quite a change, leaving the freedom of the forest for a school."

One corner of his mouth tilted up, and he looked away. "It was, but boys are adaptable. I learned how to follow the rules and which boys to stay away from. And I was big, even then. That helped."

Emeline shuddered. "They seem so savage, boarding schools."

"Boys are savage little beasts, by and large."

"What of the teachers?"

He shrugged. "Most are competent. Some are unhappy men who dislike boys. But there are others who truly love their profession and care for the children."

Emeline knit her brows. "What a very different childhood you and your sister must have had. You said she grew up in the city of Boston?"

"Yes." For the first time, his voice sounded troubled. "Sometimes I think our childhoods were too different."

"Oh?" She watched his face. His expressions were so subtle, so fleeting, that she felt like a diviner when she caught them.

He nodded, his eyes hooded. "I worry that I don't give her all that she needs."

She stared ahead as she tried to think of a reply. Did any of the men she knew worry about the women in their lives this way? Had her own brother cared about her needs? She thought not.

But Mr. Hartley took a breath and spoke again. "Your son is a spirited boy."

Emeline wrinkled her nose. "Too spirited, some would say."

"How old is he?"

"Eight this summer."

"You employ a tutor for him?"

"Mr. Smythe-Jones. He comes in daily." She hesitated, then said impulsively, "But Tante Cristelle thinks I should enroll him in a school like the one you attended."

He glanced at her. "He seems too young to leave home."

"Oh, but many fashionable families send their sons away, some much younger than Daniel." She realized that she was twisting a bit of ribbon at her throat in her free hand, and she stopped and carefully smoothed the piece of silk. "My aunt worries that I will tie him to my apron strings. Or that he will not learn how to be a man in a house of women." Why was she telling a near stranger these intimate details? He must think her a ninny.

But he only nodded thoughtfully. "Your husband is dead."

"Yes. Daniel—my son is named for his father—passed away five years ago."

"Yet, you have not married again."

He leaned closer, and she recognized the scent she smelled on his breath. Parsley. Strange that such a domestic scent would seem so exotic on him.

He spoke softly. "I don't understand why a lady of your attraction would be left to languish for so many years alone."

Her brow creased. "Actually—"

"Here is a tea shop," Tante Cristelle called from behind them. "My bones ache most terrible from this exercise. Shall we rest here?"

Mr. Hartley turned. "I am sorry, ma'am. Yes, indeed we'll stop here."

"*Bon*," Tante said. "Let us compose ourselves for a time, then."

Mr. Hartley held open the pretty wood and glass door, and they entered the little shop. Small, circular tables were placed here and there, and the ladies settled themselves while Mr. Hartley went to purchase the tea.

Tante Cristelle leaned forward to tap Rebecca's knee. "Your brother is very solicitous of you. Be grateful; not all men are so. And those who are do not often stay in this world overlong."

The girl knit her brows at Tante's last remark, but she chose to reply to the first. "Oh, but I am very grateful. Samuel has always been kind to me when I saw him."

Emeline smoothed a lace ruffle on her skirt. "Mr. Hartley said that you were raised by your uncle."

Rebecca's eyes dropped. "Yes. I only saw Samuel once or twice a year, when he came to visit. He always seemed so big, even though he must've been younger than I am now. Later, of course, he enlisted and wore a magnificent soldier's uniform. I was quite in awe of him. He walks like no other man I know. He strides so easily, as if he could keep up his pace for days on end." The girl looked up and smiled self-consciously. "I describe it badly."

But oddly Emeline knew exactly what Rebecca meant. Mr. Hartley moved with a graceful confidence that made her think he knew his own body and how it worked better than other men did theirs. She turned to watch Mr. Hartley now. He waited for his turn to buy the tea. In front of him, an older gentleman frowned and impatiently tapped his toe. There were other customers as well, some tapping their feet, some shifting their weight restlessly. Only Mr. Hartley was perfectly still. He looked neither impatient nor bored, as if he could stand thus, one leg bent, his arms crossed at his chest, for hours. He caught her eye, and his eyebrows slowly rose, either in question or in challenge, she couldn't tell. Her face heated and she looked away.

"You and your brother seem very close," she said to Rebecca. "Despite your childhood apart."

The girl smiled, but her eyes seemed uncertain. "I hope we're close. I think that we are close. I admire my brother greatly."

Emeline watched the girl thoughtfully. The sentiment

was correct, to be sure, but Rebecca phrased the words almost as a question.

"My lady," Mr. Hartley said, suddenly at her side.

Emeline started and glanced at the man in exasperation. Had he crept up beside her on purpose?

He smiled that maddeningly cryptic smile of his and held out a plate of pink sugared sweets. Behind him, a girl brought the tray of tea things. Mr. Hartley's coffee-brown eyes seemed to chide Emeline for her pettiness.

She took a breath. "Thank you, Mr. Hartley."

He inclined his head. "My pleasure, Lady Emeline."

Humph. She tasted a candy and found that it was tart and sweet at once. Just right, in fact. She glanced at her aunt. The older lady had her head close to Rebecca's, talking intently.

"I hope my aunt is not lecturing your sister," she commented as she poured the tea.

Mr. Hartley glanced at Rebecca. "She is made of sterner stuff than she looks. I think she will survive whatever travails your aunt may throw at her."

He was leaning casually against the wall not two feet away from her, all the chairs having been already taken. Emeline sipped at her tea as her gaze fell to his strange footwear.

Without thinking, she voiced her thoughts. "Wherever did you come by those slippers?"

Mr. Hartley extended one leg, his arms still crossed at his chest. "They're moccasins, made from American deerskin by the women of the Mohican Indian tribe."

The ladies at the next table got up to leave, but he made no move to sit down. The bell rang over the shop door as more people came in.

She frowned at Mr. Hartley's moccasins and the leggings above them. He'd gartered the soft leather just below his knees with an embroidered sash and let the ends hang down. "Do all white men wear this attire in the Colonies?"

"No, not all." He crossed his legs again. "Most wear the same shoes or boots as gentlemen wear here."

"Then why do you choose to sport such strange footwear?" She was aware that her voice was sharp, but somehow his insistence on unconventional clothing was unbearably irritating to her. Why did he do it? If he wore buckle shoes and stockings like every other gentleman in London, no one would notice him. With his wealth, he could perhaps become an English gentleman and be accepted into the ton. He'd be respectable.

Mr. Hartley shrugged, patently unaware of her inner turmoil. "Hunters wear them in the woods of America. They're very comfortable and much more useful than English shoes. The leggings protect against thorns and branches. I'm accustomed to them."

He looked at her, and in his eyes she somehow saw that he was aware that she wished he was conventional and more like the usual English gentleman. He understood and it made him sad. She stared into his warm, brown eyes, not knowing what to do. There was something there, something they communicated between them, and she didn't quite understand the subtleties.

Then a male voice spoke from behind her. "Corporal Hartley! What are you doing in London?"

Sam tensed. The man hailing him was slender and of average height, perhaps a little below. He wore a dark green coat and brown waistcoat, perfectly respectable and ordinary. In fact, he would've looked like a thousand other London gentlemen if it weren't for his hair. It was a bright, orangey-red and clubbed back. Sam tried to place the stranger and couldn't. There'd been several redheaded men in the regiment.

The man grinned and stuck out his hand. "Thornton. Dick Thornton. I haven't seen you in, what? Six years at least. What're you doing in London?"

Sam took the proffered hand and shook it. Of course. He could place the other man now. Thornton had been one of the 28th. "I'm here on business, Mr. Thornton."

"Indeed? London is a long way for a backwoods tracker from the Colonies." Thornton smiled as if to take the insult from his words.

Sam shrugged easily. "My uncle died in sixty. I mustered out of the army and took over his import business in Boston."

"Ah." Thornton rocked back on his heels and glanced inquiringly at Lady Emeline.

Sam felt an odd reluctance to make the introduction, but he shook it off. "My lady, may I present Mr. Richard Thornton, an old comrade of mine. Thornton, this is Lady Emeline Gordon, Captain St. Aubyn's sister. Also, this is my sister, Rebecca Hartley, and Lady Emeline's aunt, Mademoiselle Molyneux."

Thornton bowed showily. "Ladies."

Lady Emeline held out her hand. "How do you do, Mr. Thornton?"

The other man's expression sobered as he bent over Lady Emeline's hand. "It's an honor to meet you, my lady. May I say that we were all grieved when we heard of your brother's death."

No distress showed on Lady Emeline's face, but Sam felt her stiffen, even though several feet separated them. He could not explain how this was possible, but it was as if there was a change in the very air between them.

"Thank you," she said. "You knew Reynaud?"

"Of course. We all knew and liked Captain St. Aubyn." He turned to Sam as if for confirmation. "A gallant gentleman and a great leader of men, wasn't he, Hartley? Always ready with a kind word, always encouraging us as we marched through those hellish woods. And at the last, when the savages attacked, ma'am, it would've done your heart proud to see the way he stood his ground. Some were fearful. Some thought to break ranks and run—" Thornton suddenly stopped and coughed, looking guiltily at Sam.

Sam stared back stonily. Many had thought he had run at Spinner's Falls. Sam hadn't bothered explaining himself then, and he wasn't about to start doing so now. He knew that Lady Emeline was looking at him, but he refused to meet her eyes. Let her damn him like the rest, if that was what she wanted.

"Your memories of my nephew are very welcome, Mr. Thornton," Mademoiselle Molyneux said, breaking into the awkward silence.

"Well." Thornton straightened his waistcoat. "It was a long time ago, now. Captain St. Aubyn died a hero's death. That's what you should remember."

"Do you know of any other veterans of the 28th here in London?" Sam asked the other man softly.

Thornton blew out a breath as he thought. "Not many, not many. Of course, there were few survivors to begin with. There's Lieutenant Horn and Captain Renshaw—

Lord Vale, he is now—but I hardly move in the same exalted circles as they." He smiled at Lady Emeline as if to acknowledge her rank. "There's Wimbley and Ford, and Sergeant Allen, poor blighter. Terrible what he's become. Never recovered from losing that leg."

Sam'd already questioned Wimbley and Ford. Sergeant Allen was harder to track. He mentally moved his name to the top of the list of people he needed to speak to.

"What about your comrades from the regiment?" he asked. "I remember that there were five or six of you who used to share the same fire at night. You seemed to have a leader, another redheaded man, Private..."

"MacDonald. Andy MacDonald. Yes, people used to have trouble telling us apart. The hair, you know. Funny, it's the only thing some people remember about me." Thornton shook his head. "Poor MacDonald took a ball to the head at Spinner's Falls. Fell right beside me, he did."

Sam kept his gaze steady but could feel a drop of sweat slide down his backbone. He didn't like thinking of that day, and the crowded London street had already made him uneasy. "And the others?"

"Dead, all dead, I think. Most fell at Spinner's Falls, although Ridley survived for a few months after—before the gangrene finally took him." He grinned ruefully and winked.

Sam frowned. "Do you—"

"Mr. Hartley, I believe we still have the shoemaker's to visit," Mademoiselle Molyneux cut in.

Sam broke eye contact with Thornton to look at the ladies. Rebecca was watching him with confusion in her eyes, Lady Emeline's face was blank, and the old lady merely appeared impatient. "My apologies, ladies. I didn't mean to bore you with the reminisces of long-ago events."

"I apologize as well." Thornton made another beautiful bow. "It was most pleasant meeting you—"

"Might I have your address?" Sam asked hastily. "I'd like to talk to you again. Few remember the events of that day."

Thornton beamed. "Yes, of course. I, too, enjoy reminiscing. You may find me at my place of business. It's not too far from here. Only continue down Piccadilly to Dover Street and you will find me. George Thornton and Son, Bootmakers. Founded by my father, don't you know."

"Thank you." Sam shook hands once again and watched as Thornton made his farewells to the ladies and walked off. His red hair could be discerned in the crowd for some time before he disappeared.

He turned to Lady Emeline and offered his arm. "Shall we?" And then he made the mistake of looking into her eyes. There was no way she wouldn't have figured it out. She was an intelligent woman, and she'd heard the entire conversation. But he still felt a sinking in his chest.

She knew.

MR. HARTLEY WAS in London because of the massacre at Spinner's Falls. His questions to Mr. Thornton had been too pointed, his attention to the replies too intense. Something about the massacre of the 28th Regiment bothered him.

And Reynaud had died at Spinner's Falls.

Emeline placed her fingertips on his forearm, but then couldn't restrain herself. She gripped the muscle of his arm in clenched fingers. "Why didn't you say anything?"

They had started walking, and his face was in profile to her. A muscle in his cheek twitched. "Ma'am?"

"No!" she hissed at him. Tante and Rebecca were right behind, and she didn't want them to hear. "Don't pretend to misunderstand. I'm not a fool."

He glanced at her then. "I would never think you a fool."

"Then don't treat me like one. You served in the same regiment as Reynaud. You knew my brother. What are you investigating?"

"I..." He hesitated. What was he thinking? What was he hiding from her? "I don't want to bring up unpleasant memories. I don't want to remind you—"

"*Remind* me! Mon Dieu, can you believe that I have forgotten the death of my only brother? That I would need a word from you to make me think of him? He is with me every day. *Every* day, I tell you." She stopped because her breath was coming too roughly, and her voice was beginning to tremble. What idiots men were!

"I'm sorry," he said quietly. "I did not mean to make light of your loss—"

She snorted at that.

He continued over her interruption. "But credit me with some sensitivity. I didn't know how to speak about your brother. About that day. My sin is one of stupidity, not deliberate maliciousness. Forgive me, please."

Such a pretty speech. She bit her lip and watched as two young aristocrats sauntered by, dressed in the height of fashion. Lace spilled from their wrists, their coats were made of velvet, and their wigs were extravagantly curled. They probably hadn't yet attained their twentieth year, and they walked with all the arrogance of money and privilege, confident in their place in society, confident that the woes of the lesser classes would never touch them. Reynaud had walked like that once.

She looked away, remembering black, laughing eyes. "He wrote about you."

He glanced at her, his brows raised.

"Reynaud," she clarified, although she could hardly be speaking of anyone else. "In his letters to me, he wrote about you."

Mr. Hartley stared straight ahead. She saw his Adam's apple dip as he swallowed. "What did he say?"

She shrugged, pretending interest in the window of a lace shop as they passed. It had been years since last she'd pored over Reynaud's letters, but she knew the contents of every single one by heart.

"He said that an American corporal had been assigned to his regiment, that he admired your tracking ability. He said that he trusted you above all the other scouts, even the native Indians. He said that you showed him how to discern the difference between the native tribes. That the Mohicans wore their hair in a bristle at the top of their head and that the Wy-Wy—"

"Wyandot," he said softly.

"Wyandot were fond of the colors red and black and favored a long piece of cloth worn in front and back—"

"A breech clout."

"Just so." She looked down. "He said he liked you."

She felt the movement of his chest against the back of her hand as he inhaled. "Thank you."

She nodded. There was no need to ask what he thanked her for. "How long did you know him?"

"Not long," he said. "After the Battle of Quebec, I

was attached to the 28th informally. I was only supposed to march with them until they reached Fort Edward, help scout the way. I knew your brother for a couple of months, maybe a little more. Then, of course, we came to Spinner's Falls."

He had no need to say more. Spinner's Falls was where they had all died, caught in the cross fire from two groups of Wyandot Indians. She'd read the accounts that were written in the newspapers. Few survivors of the massacre actually wanted to talk of it. Fewer still were willing to discuss it with a woman.

Emeline inhaled. "Did you see him die?"

She felt him turn to stare at her. "My lady—"

Emeline twisted a ruffle at her waist until she felt silk tear. "Did you see him die?"

He blew out a breath, and when he spoke, his voice was tight. "No."

She let the bit of fabric go. Was it relief she felt?

"Why do you ask? Surely it does no good to hear—"

"Because I want—no, I *need*—to know what it was like for him at the last." She glanced at Mr. Hartley's face and knew from the slight indent between his brows that he was puzzled. She gazed sightlessly ahead as she tried to find the words for her thoughts. "If I can understand, perhaps feel, just a little of what he went through, I can be closer to him."

He was frowning harder now. "He's dead. I doubt that your brother would want you to brood thus over his death."

She chuckled, but it came out a dry exhalation of air. "But as you say, he is dead. What he would or would not want no longer matters."

Ah, now she had shocked him. Men were sure that ladies were to be shielded from life's harsh realities. Men, poor dears, were so naive. Did they think childbirth was a stroll before luncheon?

But he rallied fast, this strange colonialist. "Please explain."

"I do this for myself, not Reynaud." She puffed out a breath. Why did she even bother? He wouldn't understand. "My brother was so young when he died, just eight and twenty, and there were many things left undone in his life. I have only a finite number of memories of him. There will never be any more."

She stopped, still gazing sightlessly at the street ahead. He didn't speak. This was a personal matter. She shouldn't talk about it to a comparative stranger. But he'd been there in that foreign place where Reynaud had died. If only in a small way, he was part of Reynaud.

She sighed. "There was a book of fairy tales we used to look at together as children. Reynaud loved those stories. I can't remember what they were about exactly, but I keep thinking if only I could read it again..." She was suddenly conscious that her conversation was meandering. She glanced up at him.

Mr. Hartley stared back, his head tilted in interest toward her.

She waved a hand impatiently. "But the book is neither here nor there. If I can find out how his last hours were, then he lives just a little longer in my memory. It doesn't matter that they are awful moments, do you see? They are Reynaud's moments, and thus precious. They bring me closer to him."

He bowed his head as his brows drew together. "I think I understand."

"Do you? Do you truly?" If he did, he would be the first to understand her. Not even Tante Cristelle could fully comprehend her need to find out everything that had happened to Reynaud in his last days. She watched him in amazement and with a dawning awareness. Maybe he truly was unlike other men. How odd.

He looked up then and caught her eye. That sensuous lower lip curved. "You're a frightening woman."

And Emeline realized to her horror that she could come to like Samuel Hartley. Come to like him too much. She hastily looked straight ahead and took a deep breath. "Tell me."

He no longer pretended that he didn't know what she asked. "I'm trying to find out why Spinner's Falls happened. The Wyandot didn't find our regiment by accident." He turned to look at her, and she saw that his eyes had hardened to iron—strong, determined, and resolute. "I think we were betrayed."

Chapter Four

*The old man was dressed in dirty rags. It hardly
seemed likely, so Iron Heart thought, that such a one
would hold the key to marrying a princess.*

*But as he started to turn aside, the old man caught
his arm. "Listen! You will live in a marble castle
with Princess Solace as your bride. You will have silk
clothes to wear and servants to wait upon your every
need. All you must do is follow my instructions."*

*"And what are your instructions?"
Iron Heart asked.*

*The old wizard grinned—for naturally he
was a wizard to know so much. "You must not
speak for seven years."*

Iron Heart stared. "And if I am unable to do this?"

*"If you utter one word—even one sound—you will
be returned to rags and Princess
Solace will die."*

*Now, this may not seem such a wonderful bargain
to you or me, but remember that Iron Heart was
presently employed as a street sweeper. He looked
down at his feet, shod in tattered leather, then over*

at the gutter where he would make his bed that night,
and in the end he did the only thing he could.
He agreed to the wizard's price....
                                        —from *Iron Heart*

Tonight the moon was curtained by clouds. Sam glanced at the sky as he paused beside a dark doorway. The moon was waning, anyway, so even when it came out from behind the clouds, its light was thin. He welcomed the thick shadows. It made the night perfect for hunting.

Sam slid now into an alley, moving swiftly past a bundled shape hunched against a wall. The bundle didn't stir, but a cat sitting by its side paused in her bath to watch Sam with glowing eyes. There was a row of fine stables farther on, nearly twice the size of the ones behind his own rented house. Sam snorted. What did one man need with so many beasts?

A light appeared at one of the stable doors, and a short, sturdy man holding a lantern emerged. Sam froze, drifting back into the shadows. The man set his lantern down on the cobblestones in the mews while he dug in a pocket; then he withdrew a long clay pipe and lit it from the lantern's flame. Puffing contentedly, he picked up his lantern again and disappeared around the corner of the stables.

Sam grinned. He waited a moment more and then followed in the man's wake. There was a wall here with a gate, separating the mews from the back garden of the house, that was his target. He passed by the gate. It was too exposed, too likely to have a guard or a lightly sleeping groom nearby. He continued into the shadows beneath a tree that overhung the wall. Eyeing the bricks, he backed a pace and then leapt. The wall was about eight feet tall, and he was just able to fling his arms over the top. Swiftly, he levered himself up, rolled over the top, and landed in a crouch on the other side. He didn't pause but used his jump's momentum to run along the wall and duck under a bush several paces away. Here he dropped to the ground and lay on his belly, carefully watching the dark garden.

It was a large, rectangular town garden, planted with small ornamental trees and bushes in a severely geometric pattern. A gravel path led from the mews wall to the back of the house, where no doubt there would be separate servant and master entrances. At the moment, nothing moved in the garden.

Sam got to his feet and made his way to the back of the house, eschewing the graveled walk for fear of the sound. As he approached the house, he saw that the servant's entrance was partly belowground; there was a well with steps leading down to the door. Above was a kind of balcony or terrace with a low, ornamental wall and French doors. A light flickered behind the French doors. Sam crept up the curving granite stairs and close to the glass doors. The man within had not bothered to draw the curtains, and he was as well lit as if he stood on a stage.

Jasper Renshaw, Viscount Vale, half sat, half lay on a great red velvet wing chair. One long leg draped over the chair's arm and swung absently as he turned a page in the great book on his lap. A large buckle shoe lay overturned beside the chair; the foot on the swinging leg was clad only in a stocking.

Sam snorted softly and crouched by the window, enjoying the fact that the man never knew he was being watched from without. Vale had commanded the Light Company of the 28th. Where the other former soldiers he'd talked to had aged and changed in the six years since he'd seen them, Renshaw—now Viscount Vale—was the same. His face was long and thin, with deep lines bracketing a wide mouth and a too-large nose. He wasn't a handsome man, and yet his face was impossible to dislike. The eyes drooped at the corners, rather like a hunting dog's, appearing always slightly sad, even when he was in good cheer. The rest of Vale looked like he'd never outgrown the lankiness of adolescence. His arms and legs were long and bony, his hands and feet overlarge as if he still waited for his limbs to fill out. Yet Vale was the same age as Sam. As Sam considered him, Vale licked his thumb and turned another page in his book; then he picked up a crystal glass with ruby liquid and sipped from it.

Sam remembered Vale as a good officer, though not as commanding as Reynaud. He'd been too relaxed to bother instilling respect in the men. Instead, he'd been the one who others had gone to with their problems and their petty arguments. Vale was as likely to dice with the common soldiers as dine with the officers. He'd always been in a good mood, always ready to tell a joke or play a prank on his fellow officers. It'd made him a favorite of the troops. He wasn't the type of man anyone would think could betray an entire regiment.

And yet if Sam's information was true, someone had. He patted his pocket, feeling the paper within. Someone had alerted the French and their Wyandot Indian allies, told them exactly where the 28th would be. Someone had conspired to massacre an entire regiment of his fellow soldiers at Spinner's Falls. That possibility had driven Sam to England. He had to find the truth. Find if there was a reason for so many to have died that fall day six years ago. And when he found the man responsible, maybe then he could reclaim his soul, reclaim the life he'd lost at Spinner's Falls.

Was Vale the right man? The viscount had been in debt to Clemmons, and Clemmons had died in the massacre. But Vale had fought bravely, *gallantly,* at Spinner's Falls. Could such a brave officer murder an entire regiment just to get rid of one man? Wouldn't he be marked? Wouldn't he bear the scars of his depravity on his face? Or would he, six years later, be sitting contentedly in his library reading a book?

Sam shook his head. The officer he thought he'd known six years ago would never have done such a thing. But he'd only been with the 28th for a little over a month. Maybe he'd never really known Vale. His instinct was to confront Vale, here and now, but he would get no answers that way. Better to approach him obliquely at a social gathering. That was why he'd sought the services of Lady Emeline. On the thought of that lady, Sam withdrew, making his way back through the dark garden. What would Lady Emeline think if she found out his true reason for asking for her help? She still grieved for her brother, but would she want to upset her social standing to accuse a peer? He grimaced as he went over the mews wall again.

Somehow he thought that Lady Emeline would not be happy with the course he'd set.

"No! No! No!" Emeline exclaimed the next morning.

Rebecca froze, her foot half lifted, her expression terrified. They were in Emeline's town house ballroom where she was attempting to teach the American girl a few of the newer dance steps. Tante Cristelle assisted at the harpsichord, which had been especially carried into the room by two burly footmen. The ballroom floor was parquet, polished to a high gleam, and mirrors lined one entire wall. Rebecca, with her raised foot and terrified expression, was reflected countlessly in the mirrors. Emeline took a deep breath and tried to modify her own expression, pasting on a smile.

Rebecca didn't look reassured.

Emeline sighed. "You must move easily. Gracefully. Not like a...a..." She searched for a phrase that would not involve the word *elephant*.

"Drunken sailor." Samuel Hartley's voice echoed in her ballroom. He sounded amused.

Rebecca lowered her foot with a thump and glared at her brother. "Thank you very much!"

Mr. Hartley shrugged and strolled into the room. He was neatly turned out in brown and black, but the bruise on his chin was turning yellowy-green, and he had dark circles beneath his eyes.

Emeline narrowed her own eyes. What activities were keeping the colonial from sleeping at night? "Was there something you needed, Mr. Hartley?"

"Indeed," he replied. "I find I have an urgent need to come supervise my sister's dancing lesson."

Rebecca *harrumphed* at his words, but a shy smile crept over her lips. She was obviously pleased at her brother's attention.

Emeline was not. Merely the presence of the man in her ballroom disrupted her concentration. "We are very busy here, Mr. Hartley. There are only two days remaining before Rebecca's first ball."

"Ah." He bowed with ironic precision. "I understand the gravity of the situation."

"Do you?"

"Ahem!" Tante cleared her throat with a horrible grinding noise. Both Emeline and Mr. Hartley turned to stare at her. "The child and I need a short rest from our exertions. A walk about the garden, perhaps? Come, *ma petite,* I will instruct you on elegant conversations when strolling in so boring a garden." She held out her hand to Rebecca.

"Oh, thank you, ma'am," Rebecca replied weakly as she followed the older lady.

Emeline waited, her foot tapping, as her aunt and Rebecca walked to the door and exited the room; then she whirled on Mr. Hartley. "You've interrupted this morning's lesson. What are you doing here?"

He raised his eyebrows and stepped so close, his breath brushed her cheek. "Why do you care?"

"Care?" She opened her mouth, closed it, and then opened it again. "It isn't that I *care;* it's simply—"

"You're in a bad mood." He pursed his lips and tilted his head as if he were examining a suspect piece of fruit. "You're often in a bad mood."

"That's not true."

"You were in a bad mood yesterday."

"But—"

"You were in a bad mood when first I met you at Mrs. Conrad's salon."

"I was *not*—"

"And while your mood was not precisely *bad* when we came to tea, it certainly could not be termed *good.*" He smiled kindly at her. "But perhaps I have the case wrong. Perhaps you're usually a lady with a sunny disposition, and it's only my advent into your life that has turned you sour."

She gaped at him—actually gaped, her mouth hanging ajar like the greenest debutante. How dare he? No one spoke to her in this manner! He had turned away now and was idly plinking the harpsichord in a very annoying manner. She caught him glancing slyly at her, his mouth curving at the corner; then he went back to watching his fingers abuse the harpsichord.

Emeline took a deep breath and twitched her skirts straight. She hadn't been the belle of innumerable balls for nothing.

"I hadn't realized my voice was so sharp, Mr. Hartley," she said as she wandered closer to where he stood. She kept her eyes downcast and worked to look woebegone— not a very familiar expression. "Had I known the distress my unladylike surliness would cause you, I would have died a thousand deaths rather than acted so. Please accept my apology."

She waited. It was his turn. Now he would be covered in shame because he'd made a lady apologize so abjectly. Perhaps he would even stutter. She tried not to smirk.

Instead there was only silence. His long fingers played on the harpsichord keys without any notion of music. If he continued much longer, she would go mad.

Finally, she looked up.

Mr. Hartley wasn't even paying attention to his hands. Instead he was watching her with a faintly amused expression. "When was the last time you apologized to a man?"

Oooh! He was the most provoking oaf!

"I don't know," she said sadly. "Years, perhaps." She stepped closer and placed her hand on the keys beside his. Then she looked up at him and slowly let her mouth curve into a very small smile. "But I do know he was most satisfied with my apology."

His hands stilled, the room suddenly hushed. His eyes were intent in an almost frightening way. For the life of her, Emeline could not look away from him. She watched as his gaze drifted over her face, coming finally to rest on her mouth. Without even thinking, her lips parted. His eyes narrowed and he took a step toward her, closing the space between them and raising his arms—

The door to the ballroom opened.

"We are ready now, yes?" Tante Cristelle said. "Another hour, I think, no more. My hands, they will be crippled if I play longer at that instrument."

"Yes, of course," Emeline gasped. Her face was probably as red as a boiled beet. Out of the corner of her eye, she saw that Mr. Hartley had somehow contrived to place himself on the other side of the harpsichord—a distance that was more than respectable. When had he done that? She hadn't even seen him move.

"Are you all right, Lady Emeline?" the girl asked innocently. "You look hot."

Oh, these terrible colonials with their blunt ways! Emeline saw the horrid man smirk, though she doubted anyone else caught his expression.

"Quite." Emeline twitched her left sleeve forward. "Shall we begin again with those dance steps? Mr. Hartley, this will no doubt bore you to tears. We give you leave to go about your business."

"I would, Lady Emeline, had I any." Mr. Hartley settled into a chair and crossed his leg at the ankle as if he planned to stay into the night. "Business, that is. I'm afraid I'm quite free all afternoon."

No sane person could expect her to actually smile at this news.

"Ah. Then we will naturally enjoy your company," she replied stiffly.

Tante glanced at her sharply, eyebrows raised in either question or censure; it was hard to tell. Reprimanded, Emeline schooled her features, and her aunt began to play. Emeline watched Rebecca practice the steps for nearly a second before her mind turned to her embarrassing exchange with Mr. Hartley.

What in the world had possessed her? Everyone knew that gentlemen liked a lady to be soft and gently spoken. Wasn't that the one lesson that was drummed into a girl's head right from the cradle? Well, that and preserving one's virginity for marriage, but that hardly applied in her case. She couldn't even claim intoxication from the wine at luncheon as an excuse. It had been regrettably overwatered, as Tante had been sure to point out.

And the insidiously suggestive words she'd spoken to Mr. Hartley at the last! She blushed again just thinking of them. But perhaps he hadn't understood the double entendre? Emeline glanced at Mr. Hartley. He was watching her, his eyelids half lowered and a smile playing about his mouth. He caught her look and quirked one eyebrow upward. Emeline hastily looked away. Quite obviously, he had *indeed* understood.

"Oh, I just can't!" Rebecca suddenly stopped in mid-turn. "These steps are so slow. I feel like I'll overbalance and fall."

"Perhaps you need a partner," Mr. Hartley said. He rose and made a lovely bow to his sister. "May I?"

The girl blushed very prettily. "You don't mind?"

"Not unless you stomp on my toes." He grinned down at Rebecca.

Emeline blinked. Mr. Hartley was exceedingly handsome when he smiled. Why hadn't she noticed it before?

"The only problem," he continued, "is that I'm in as much need of tuition as you." He looked expectantly at Emeline.

Devious. Emeline nodded briskly and stepped forward so that she and Rebecca now flanked Mr. Hartley in a line. She held out her hand to him. He took her fingertips, quite properly, but his hand felt hot on hers.

Emeline cleared her throat. She raised their joined hands to shoulder height and faced forward. "Very well." She pointed her right toe. "We begin on three. One and two and *three*."

For the next quarter hour, they practiced various dance steps together. Mr. Hartley sometimes partnered his sister, sometimes her. And Emeline, though she would never have admitted it even if put on the rack, rather enjoyed herself. She was amazed that such a big man could be so light and graceful on his feet.

Then somehow, Rebecca made a false step, and she and her brother ended up tangled. He caught his sister about the waist as Emeline hastily stepped away from the mess. "Careful there, Becca, or you'll have your partner on the floor."

"Oh, I'm terrible at this!" the younger girl cried. "It

isn't fair! You never danced this way as a boy and yet *you* can follow the steps."

Emeline looked between brother and sister. "In what way did Mr. Hartley dance as a boy?"

"Badly," he said.

While at the same time his sister said, "He jigged."

"Jigged?" Emeline tried to imagine Mr. Hartley's tall form bouncing up and down in a country jig.

"The peasants about the château where I grew up used to dance so," Tante remarked.

"I would like to see you jig," Emeline mused.

Mr. Hartley shot her an ironic look. Emeline smiled back. For a moment, their gazes were locked and she couldn't quite discern the look in his brown eyes.

"He was wonderfully fast," Rebecca said, warming to her theme. "But then he got old and stiff, and he doesn't jig anymore."

Mr. Hartley broke eye contact with Emeline to mock frown at his sister. "A challenge if I ever heard one."

He took off his coat and, in shirtsleeves and waistcoat, struck a pose, hands on hips, head held high.

"You'll really do it?" Rebecca was laughing openly now.

He sighed theatrically. "If you'll keep time."

Rebecca began clapping and Mr. Hartley leapt. Emeline had seen men jig before—peasants celebrating or sailors on shore leave from their ships. Usually such dancing was characterized by the clumsiness of the movements, legs and heels kicking everywhere, hair and clothing flying in the air like a puppet on a string. But when Mr. Hartley jigged, it was different. He was contained, for one thing, his movements precise and intentioned. And he was graceful. It was extraordinary. He was jumping about, his moccasined feet stomping on the parquet floor, and yet somehow he contrived to be graceful and quick. He grinned at her, a wholly joyful look, his strong, white teeth flashing against his brown skin. Emeline clapped to the beat along with everyone else, including Tante.

He darted forward and drew Rebecca into his wild dance, spinning her in a circle until she staggered away, laughing and out of breath. Then he caught Emeline. She found herself whirled in strong, sure hands. The mirrored walls and the faces of Rebecca and Tante flew past, and she felt her heart speed until she thought it might burst from her chest. Mr. Hartley grasped her about the waist and lifted her high over his laughing face, and she found that she was laughing, too.

Laughing with joy.

THAT NIGHT, SAM wore black, the better to slide into the shadows between the buildings. It was well past midnight, and the moon hung high overhead, casting a colorless glow on the earth below. He was on his way home, having already been to see Ned Allen—or what was left of the man. The ex-sergeant had been incoherent with drink. Sam hadn't been able to get any information from him; he'd have to try again later, perhaps catch the man earlier in the day. Trying to question Allen had been a waste of time, but stalking the shadows was invigorating nevertheless.

He carefully watched the street. A carriage was rumbling closer, but there was no other sign of life. Visiting Ned's crib had made Sam remember Scarlet Coat. Had his follower given up the chase? He'd not seen the big man again. Strange. What had the man been—

"Mr. Hartley!"

Sam closed his eyes for a moment. He knew that voice.

"I say, Mr. Hartley! What are you doing?"

He'd been the best tracker in the Colonies during the war. It wasn't vanity that said so; his commanders had told him. Once, he'd snuck right through a camp full of sleeping Wyandot warriors and not a one had been the wiser. And yet one small woman found him out. Could she see in the dark?

"Mr. Hartley—"

"Yes, yes," he hissed, emerging from the dark doorway he'd been lurking in. He approached the grand carriage. It was stopped in the middle of the road, the horses blowing impatiently. Lady Emeline's head appeared disembodied, sticking out from the dark curtains that covered the carriage's window.

He bowed. "Good evening, Lady Emeline. Fancy meeting you here."

"Come inside," she said impatiently. "I can't think what you're doing out alone so late. Don't you know how dangerous London can be for a man by himself? But perhaps you are used to the more benign streets of Boston."

"Yes, that's probably it," he said wryly as he climbed inside her elegant carriage. "And may I ask what you're doing out late, my lady?" He rapped at the roof before taking the seat across from her.

"I'm returning from a soiree, of course," Lady Emeline said. She smoothed the shawl that covered her knees. The carriage lurched forward as they started again.

It was dim inside the carriage, the only light a single lantern by her face, but he could see that she was dressed very grandly. She wore a flame-red frock with some type of pattern in yellow. The skirt had been drawn aside to reveal a petticoat in yellow and green. Above, her bodice was square and very low, her breasts pushed up until they formed two soft, white mounds that nearly glowed in the lamplight. Heat seemed to radiate off her, warming his bones.

"It was rather dull, so I came away early," the lady continued. "You won't believe, but the punch was gone by ten, and there was hardly much for a midnight supper—only a few meat pies and fruit. Quite scandalous. I can't think what Mrs. Turner was about, serving such poor refreshments to everyone who matters. But the woman always has been a wigeon. The only reason I attend her parties is in the hope of seeing her brother, Lord Downing. *He* is a terrible gossip."

She paused, probably because she'd run out of breath. Sam stared at her, trying to figure out why she was speaking so fast. Had she been drinking spirits at her party? Or was she...? He felt a smile forming and worked to suppress it. No, it couldn't be. Was Lady Emeline nervous? He'd never thought to see the sophisticated widow out of sorts.

"But why were you about so late?" Lady Emeline asked. Her hands, which had been busy playing with the lace that trimmed her bodice, stilled. "Or, perhaps that is none of my business." Even in the dim light, he could see the blush that stained her cheeks.

"No, it isn't your business," he replied. "But not for the reason you think."

If she'd been a little black hen, her feathers would've ruffled. "I don't know what you mean to imply by that, Mr. Hartley. I am sure—"

"You think I've been to see a whore." He smiled and slid lower in the carriage seat, canting his legs to the side so that he might cross them. He slipped his fingers into his waistcoat pockets, enjoying himself. "Admit it."

"I will do no such thing!"

"But that blush on your cheeks says otherwise."

"I...I—"

He tutted. "Your thoughts are very lewd. I am shocked, my lady, quite shocked."

For a moment, all she could do was sputter; then her eyes narrowed as she recovered. Sam braced himself. God, he liked sparring with this woman.

"I couldn't care less how you conduct yourself after dark," she said primly. "Your affairs are of absolutely no importance to me."

She'd made an entirely proper statement and was obviously uncomfortable on this ground. If he was a gentleman, he'd let it—*her*—go, turn the conversation to something dull and polite such as the weather. The problem was that once the prey was within his grasp, it was so very difficult to let go.

Not to mention that polite conversation had always bored him. "My affairs should be of no importance to you, but they are, aren't they?"

Her brows drew together as she opened her mouth.

"Ah. Ah." He held up a finger to forestall her denial. "It's past midnight, and we're alone in a dark carriage. What's said here will never see the light of day. Humor me, lady, and be frank."

She inhaled deeply and sat back, her face entirely hidden by shadows now. "What difference does it make to you if I do find your affairs to be of interest, Mr. Hartley?"

He smiled wryly. "Touché, my lady. I'm sure a sophisticated gentleman of your society would deny it to his death if he was moved by your interest, but I am made of simpler stuff."

"Are you?" The words were whispered in the dark.

He nodded slowly. "So I tell you: I am moved by your interest. I am moved by you."

"You are frank."

"Can you admit the same?"

She gasped and for a moment, he thought he'd gone too far and that she'd retreat from this dangerous game. She was a lady of standing, after all, and there were rules and boundaries in her world.

But she slowly leaned forward, her face emerging into the small pool of light cast through the window. She looked him full in the face and arched one black eyebrow. "And if I did?"

And he felt something within his chest leap that she dared to pick up his gauntlet—something like joy. He grinned at her. "Then, my lady, we have a point of mutual interest that bears further discussion."

"Perhaps." She sat back against her plush red cushions. "What were you doing out on the streets this late at night?"

He shook his head, smiling slightly.

"You're not going to tell me." The carriage was slowing now.

"No." He glanced at the window. They were outside her town house. It blazed in the night with lit lanterns. He looked back at her. "But I wasn't with a woman; I give you my word."

"It shouldn't matter to me."

"But it does, doesn't it?"

"I think you presume too much, Mr. Hartley."

"I think I don't."

A footman opened the carriage door. Sam stepped down and then turned to offer her his hand. She hesitated a moment, as if considering whether to let him help her or not. She was surrounded by the dark interior of the carriage, her pale face and bosom glowing as if lit by a fire from within. She placed her small gloved hand in his. He tightened his fingers over hers as he drew her into the light by the walk.

"Thank you," she said, and tugged at her hand.

He stared down at her dark eyes, aware that he didn't want to let her go. But in the end, he opened his hand and let hers slip away. There was no other choice.

He bowed. "Good night, my lady."

And he walked away into the darkness.

Chapter Five

The wizard winked once, and Iron Heart found
himself within the castle's walls. He was dressed as
the king's own guard, and there, not two paces away,
sat the king himself on his golden throne! Well,
you can imagine how surprised he was. He opened
his mouth to exclaim when he remembered the
wizard's words. He must not speak, else he would
return to rags and the princess would die. So Iron
Heart shut his mouth and vowed not to let a sound
pass his lips. His vow was soon tested, for what
should happen next but seven burly knaves rushed
into the throne room, bent on killing the king.
Iron Heart leapt forward into battle, swinging his
sword left and right. The other guards shouted,
but by the time they drew their swords, all seven
assassins lay dead on the floor....
—from *Iron Heart*

"Samuel Hartley is the most irritating man," Emeline said late the next morning.

She was in the little sitting room with Melisande Fleming. This room was one of her favorites; the walls were papered in yellow and white stripes with a thin scarlet line that occasionally repeated. The furnishings were not as new as the ones in her formal sitting room, but they were done in lush reds and oranges in lovely damasks and velvets. One felt just like a cat in the room, as if it would be easy to stretch out on the rich fabrics and purr. Not, of course, that she would do anything so uninhibited, but still, the feeling was there. In actual fact, she and Melisande sat quite properly by the windows. Or rather, Melisande sat and Emeline paced as her friend calmly drank tea.

"Irritating," Emeline muttered, and straightened a tasseled pillow on the settee.

"So you've said before," Melisande replied. "Four times since I arrived."

"Have I?" Emeline asked vaguely. "Well, but it's true. He doesn't seem to have the first idea of social manners—he danced a *jig* in this very house just the other day—he always has a bit of a smile on his face, and his boots have no heels."

"Horrors," Melisande murmured.

Emeline shot Melisande, who had been her very good friend since nearly the beginning of time, an exasperated look. She sat as she always did, as if she strove to occupy as little space as humanly possible. Her back was straight and prim, her arms almost clapped to her sides, her hands folded in her lap—when she wasn't drinking tea—and her feet placed neatly side by side on the carpet. She probably never felt an urge to lounge in the pillows piled up on the flame settee. Also—and this was something of a point of contention between the friends—Melisande always wore brown. Sometimes, it was true, she strayed from brown and was seen in gray, but that could hardly be called an improvement, could it? Today, for instance, she was in an impeccably cut sack dress that was an awful shade of dirt brown.

"Why ever did you have that gown made in that fabric?" Emeline asked.

Another lady might look down at herself. Melisande picked up the teapot and calmly poured herself more tea. "It doesn't show dust."

"That's because it's the same color as dust."

"There you are."

Emeline stared at her friend critically. "With your fine, blond hair—"

"It's dust-colored, too," Melisande murmured wryly.

"No, it's not. It's just that you have very subtle coloring."

"Dust-colored hair, dust-colored eyes, dust-colored complexion—"

"Your complexion is not dust-colored," Emeline said sternly, then winced when she realized her gaffe. She hadn't meant to imply that the rest of her friend was dust-colored.

Melisande shot her an ironic look.

"If you would just wear more vibrant colors," Emeline said hastily. "A lovely dark plum, for instance. Or crimson. I long to see you in crimson."

"Then you shall have to pine away," her friend said. "You were telling me about your new neighbor."

"He's quite irritating."

"You may have mentioned that before."

Emeline ignored that. "And I don't know what he does at night."

Melisande looked at her. One eyebrow rose almost imperceptibly.

"That's not what I meant!" Emeline fluffed a pillow rather overhard.

"I am relieved," Melisande replied. "But I'm wondering what Lord Vale thinks of this colonial."

Emeline stared. "Jasper has nothing whatsoever to do with Mr. Hartley."

"Are you sure? Would he approve of your association with the man?"

Emeline wrinkled her nose. "I don't want to discuss Jasper."

"I must say, I'm outraged on Lord Vale's behalf," Melisande said without heat as she plunked a spoonful of sugar into her tea.

"I'm sure Jasper would be flattered if he only knew." Emeline sat on the edge of a beautiful gold velvet chair. Her mind immediately reverted to her original theme. "It's just that I ran across Mr. Hartley last night quite late. I was coming home from Emily Turner's soiree—you were right; I never should have gone—"

"Told you."

"Yes, and I've just *said* so." Emeline bounced a little in her chair. Melisande could be so didactic sometimes. "Anyway, there he was, skulking in a quite suspicious manner in a dark alley."

"Perhaps he makes his living as a footpad," Melisande said. She was examining the tray of sweets that the maid had left them.

Emeline frowned. It was very hard sometimes to tell when her friend was jesting and when she was not. "I don't *think* so."

"How reassuring," Melisande said, and chose a tiny pale yellow cake.

"Although he does seem to move very quietly," Emeline mused, "which I would think would be most helpful if one was a footpad."

Melisande had popped the cake into her mouth, and she merely raised her eyebrows now.

"But no. No." Emeline shook her head decisively. "Mr. Hartley isn't a footpad. So that leaves the question, What was he doing walking about so late?"

Melisande swallowed. "The most obvious answer is an assignation."

"No."

"No?"

"No." Emeline didn't know why her friend's suggestion so nettled her. It was, as she said, obvious. Emeline took a steadying breath. "I asked and he said most explicitly that he had not been to see a lady."

Melisande coughed dryly. "You asked a gentleman if he was returning from a tryst with a female."

Emeline blushed. "You always make things sound so awful."

"I merely repeated your words."

"It wasn't like that at all. I made an inquiry; he replied most properly."

"But, dearest, don't you see that he would deny an assignation to you in any case?"

"He didn't lie to me." Emeline knew she spoke too vehemently. Her face and neck were hot. "He didn't."

Melisande looked at her with eyes that were suddenly weary. This was a sore point for her friend. Melisande was nearly eight and twenty and had never married, despite having a very respectable dowry. She'd been engaged once, nearly ten years ago, to a young aristocrat whom Emeline had never really liked. And her dislike had proven well founded. The cad had thrown Melisande over for a dashing titled widow, leaving Melisande with an unnaturally cynical view of gentlemen in general.

Yet, despite her own views, Melisande merely nodded now at Emeline's rather silly assertion that a gentleman she hardly knew would tell her the truth about so private a matter.

Emeline smiled in gratitude. Brown or not, Melisande was the dearest friend imaginable.

"If he wasn't returning from an assignation," Melisande said thoughtfully, "then perhaps he'd been to a gaming hell. Did you ask him where he'd been?"

"He wouldn't tell me, but I really don't think it was anything as prosaic as a gaming hell."

"Interesting." Melisande stared out the window. The little sitting room was at the back of Emeline's town house and overlooked the garden. "What does your aunt think of him?"

"You know Tante." Emeline wrinkled her nose. "She is worried that his sister might not wear shoes."

"*Does* she wear shoes?"

"Of course."

"What a relief," Melisande murmured. "Tell me, is your Mr. Hartley a tall gentleman with lovely brown hair, unpowdered and clubbed back?"

"Yes." Emeline stood and moved to the window. "Why do you ask?"

"Because I believe he is doing something gentlemanly in his back garden." Melisande nodded out the window.

Emeline looked and felt an odd little nervous jolt when she saw Mr. Hartley's form just over the wall that divided the gardens. He was handling a very long gun.

At that moment, a small form catapulted down her own garden path, followed more slowly by a thin little man. Daniel had come out for his morning walk.

"What do you think he is about with that great gun?" Melisande asked idly.

Mr. Hartley had put down his gun again and now seemed to be peering into the barrel—a position that appeared inherently dangerous.

"Lord knows," Emeline muttered. She had a great desire to abandon her very good friend and find some pretext to go into her garden. Wigeon! "Something masculine, no doubt."

"Mmm. And Daniel out there so near to him." Melisande looked at her over a cup of tea, her eyes amused. "A concerned mama might very well go out to see what her neighbor was doing."

SAM WAS AWARE of the boy well before he actually saw him. The brick wall between the gardens was six feet tall, but the sounds of a boy could easily be heard—a skipping run in dry leaves, a panting cry to "come see!" and finally the scrabbling of boots on tree bark as the lad scrambled up a tree. There was a relative silence then, broken only by the sound of heavy breathing as the boy watched him.

Sam sat on a marble bench beneath the wall, his Kentucky rifle laid across his knees. He took a long piece of wire from his pocket and threaded it through the touchhole, working it back and forth to scrape out any corrosion. Then he blew into the tiny hole and sighted down the barrel.

The boy broke. "What are you doing?"

"Cleaning my gun." Sam didn't look up. Sometimes an animal was braver when it didn't think the tracker was interested.

"I have a gun." There was the sound of rustling leaves as the boy shifted.

"Oh?"

"Belonged to my uncle Reynaud."

"Mmm." Sam got up and stood the gun on its butt. He slid the ramrod out from under the barrel.

"M'man says I can't touch it."

"Ah."

"Can I help you clean your gun?"

Sam paused at that and squinted up at the boy. Daniel lay on a branch two feet over his head, arms and legs dangling. He had a scratch on one cheek and a streak of dirt on his white shirt. His blond hair hung over his forehead, his blue eyes sparkling with excitement.

Sam sighed. "Would your mother mind if I let you help me?"

"Oh, no," the boy said instantly. He began inching out on the limb, closer into Sam's yard.

"Whoa, there." Sam set aside his rifle and went to stand underneath the boy in case he fell. "What about your tutor?"

Daniel craned his neck, looking back into his own garden. "He's sitting on the bench under the rose arbor.

He always falls asleep there when we take our walk." He inched forward again.

"Hold it there," Sam said.

The boy froze, his eyes wide.

"The branch won't bear your weight if you go much farther out. Swing your legs down and I'll help you."

Daniel grinned in relief and let both legs dangle off one side of the branch, holding on by his arms. Sam caught the boy by the waist and lowered him to the ground.

Immediately, Daniel ran to the gun. Sam watched carefully, but the boy didn't touch the weapon; he merely examined it.

Daniel whistled through his teeth. "'Pon my word, that's the longest gun I ever did see."

Sam smiled and hunkered down next to the boy. "It's a Kentucky rifle. Settlers use it on the frontiers of Pennsylvania in the Colonies."

Daniel glanced sideways at Sam. "Why's it so long? Don't that make it hard to carry?"

"Not much. It's not that heavy." Sam picked up the gun and sighted down the barrel again. "Aim's better. Shot's better. Here, take a look."

Daniel eagerly stood beside him as Sam held the gun. "Zounds!" the boy whispered. He squinted down the barrel, one eye shut, breathing through his mouth. "Can I shoot it?"

"Not here," Sam replied. He lowered the gun. "Hop on the bench and you can help me."

The boy scrambled to stand on the bench.

"Take this." Sam handed him a thick rag. "Now hold the gun steady and don't drop it. The water's hot. Ready?"

The boy grasped the barrel of the rifle in both hands,

the rag underneath to keep his hands from burning. His brow creased with concentration. "Ready."

Sam picked up a steaming kettle of water from the ground and carefully poured a thin stream of boiling water down the barrel. Dirty black water bubbled out of the touchhole.

"Zounds," Daniel breathed.

Sam glanced at him and smiled. "Hold it there a minute." He set down the kettle and picked up the ramrod, wrapping a bit of rag around the end. He inserted the ramrod into the barrel and shoved it halfway down. "Want to do it?"

"Coo! Would I?" The boy grinned at him, and Sam saw that although his coloring must come from his father, his smile was all his mother's.

"Then go ahead."

Sam held the barrel while the boy worked the ramrod.

"Good. Push it up and down. We need to get every bit of powder out of there."

"Why?" The boy frowned as he labored to shove the ramrod.

"A dirty gun isn't safe." Sam watched, but Daniel was doing a good job. "Might not fire. Might misfire and take the shooter's nose off. A man should always keep his gun clean."

"Huh," the boy grunted. "What do you hunt with it? Eagles?"

"No, it's too big for birds, even one as large as an eagle. The woodsmen hunt game—deer, mostly—but it comes in handy if a man comes across a bear or a catamount."

"Have you ever come across a catamount?"

"Only once. I walked around a bend in a trail and there stood one, big as you please, in the middle of my path."

Daniel stopped his ramming motion. "What did you do? Shoot it?"

Sam shook his head. "Didn't have the chance. That big cat took one look at me and ran the other way."

"Huh." Daniel seemed a little disappointed at his answer.

"That's good," Sam said, indicating the rifle. "Now let's pour in more water."

Daniel nodded, eyes intent and serious on the gun.

Sam withdrew the ramrod with the rag, now black, and picked up the kettle of water again. "Ready?"

"Ready."

This time the water bubbled out gray.

"How many times must we do the water?" Daniel asked.

"Until it runs clear." Sam handed the boy the ramrod with a new rag on the end. "Remember to always use boiling water, too, so that the barrel dries well and doesn't rust."

Daniel nodded as he drove the ramrod into the barrel of the gun.

Sam nearly smiled. What for him was an easy chore took quite a bit of effort on the boy's part, but Daniel never complained. He simply put his back into working the ramrod up and down. Sam became aware of a rustling over the wall. The scent of lemon balm drifted in the air. He didn't look up, but his entire body was suddenly on the alert, anticipating when the woman would make herself known.

"How much more?" Daniel asked.

"That should do it." Sam helped him withdraw the ramrod.

Daniel watched him handle the metal rod. "Did you fight in a war?"

Sam hesitated for a moment and then continued unwrapping the dirty rag from the ramrod. "Yes. I fought the French in the Colonies. Ready?"

The boy nodded. "My uncle Reynaud fought in that war."

"I know." Sam was silent as he poured the steaming water into the barrel.

"Did you kill anyone in the war?"

Sam looked at the boy. He was watching the water stream from the touchhole. The question had probably been an idle one. "Yes."

"The water's clear."

"Good." Sam wrapped a dry rag around the ramrod and gave it to Daniel.

Daniel started working the ramrod. "Did you shoot them with this gun?"

The rustling on the other side of the wall had long since stopped. She might've wandered away again, but Sam didn't think so. He had the feeling that Lady Emeline waited, breathless, just out of sight, for his answer.

He sighed. "Yes. At the battle of Quebec, when we seized the city. A French soldier ran at me. He had his bayonet fixed to the end of his rifle. It was already stained with blood."

Daniel's little body froze. He looked at Sam.

Sam held his gaze. "So I shot him dead."

"Oh," the boy whispered.

"Take the ramrod out and we'll oil the barrel."

Lady Emeline's voice floated from over the wall. "Daniel."

Sam took care not to spill the oil he was pouring on a clean rag. What did she think of his tale? It wasn't filled with the glory so many expected in stories told about war. Then, too, she must've heard the rumors about him. Did she think him a coward because of Spinner's Falls?

Daniel twisted around. "M'man, come look! Mr. Hartley has the longest gun in the world, and I'm helping him to clean it."

"So I see." Lady Emeline's head appeared at the top of the wall. She must have been standing on a bench on the other side. Her eyes didn't meet his.

Sam wiped his fingers carefully on a clean rag. "Ma'am." Perhaps he'd disgusted her.

She cleared her throat. "I don't see how I am to examine this wonderful gun. There is no gate in the wall."

"Climb over," Daniel said. "I'll help you."

"Hmm." Lady Emeline looked first at her son and then the wall. "I don't think—"

"Would you allow me?" Sam asked Daniel's permission gravely.

The boy nodded.

He turned back to Lady Emeline who was now eyeing him with an inscrutable expression. "Can you climb higher?"

"Naturally." She glanced down at her side of the wall and then climbed on something so that now she was visible from the waist up.

Sam raised his eyebrows and stepped onto the bench on his side. He looked over the wall. Lady Emeline stood quite primly on a tree branch. He suppressed a grin and reached for her. Her eyes widened as he placed his hands about her waist, and he felt his own breath catch. "If I may?"

She nodded jerkily.

He lifted her over the wall. The old wound in his side ached as his muscles pulled under her weight, but he didn't let his discomfort show on his face. He brought her down slowly, letting her slide a little against his chest. He was taking advantage of the situation, but he enjoyed her warmth and the scent of lemon balm, anyway. Her gaze met his as he held her for a fraction of a second with her face level with his own. Her black eyes were heavy-lidded, her color heightened. He was conscious of her quickened breath against his lips. Then he set her down.

She bent her head as she fussed with her skirts. "Thank you, Mr. Hartley." Her voice was husky.

"My pleasure, ma'am."

It was a good thing he'd kept his face straight, because she glanced at him sharply. She flushed a deeper pink and bit her lip. He watched her, wondering what it would be like to feel those sharp little teeth on his bare skin. She was an ornery creature. He'd wager she'd like to bite.

"Come see, M'man," Daniel repeated impatiently.

Lady Emeline walked over to the gun and eyed it. "Very nice, I'm sure."

"Would you like to help us oil it?" Sam asked innocently.

She shot him a warning look. "I think I'll simply observe."

"Ah." Sam took the oily rag and wrapped it about the ramrod. "Shove it down the barrel good, Danny. Every inch must be oiled."

"Yes, sir." Daniel took the ramrod and did as instructed, his brows knit seriously.

Sam wet another rag with the oil and began rubbing it over the outside of the barrel. "My sister says that you'll accompany us to a ball tomorrow evening, my lady."

Out of the corner of his eye, he saw her nod. "The Westerton soiree. Quite a grand event, usually. It took a bit of work to get an invitation for the two of you. Luckily, you're something of a novelty, Mr. Hartley. Quite a few hostesses have indicated their interest on that basis alone."

Sam ignored that. "Will Rebecca be ready for this ball in your estimation?"

"Of course." She leaned closer, apparently peering down the barrel. Daniel still worked the ramrod. "But a smaller event would certainly be easier for her first introduction to London society."

Sam was silent. He concentrated on the brass cheekplate on the butt of the rifle and tried to ignore the guilt worming in his stomach.

"Rebecca mentioned that you were the one to insist on that particular ball." Her deep pink skirts brushed his knee. "I wonder why?"

EMELINE WATCHED MR. Hartley's back stiffen. He knelt at her feet, head bent down as he gently stroked a cloth over his extraordinary gun. It was a long weapon but oddly light-looking, the barrel very narrow. The wood was a beautiful pale burl, the grain swirling all along the stock. She pursed her lips. Only a man would make a weapon so lovely. On the base was a brass plate, cut out in curls and polished to a high gleam. Mr. Hartley's hands were large and brown against the white cloth, but they moved with a gentle, almost loving rhythm.

She looked away. The feeling of irritation—an almost physical itching on her skin—had started the moment she'd heard his voice. And the irritation had only intensified when she'd watched him over the wall. He'd taken off his coat and waistcoat—very improperly, even in the privacy of his own garden. Gentlemen never, *never* took off an article of clothing, except in the most extreme of circumstances. Emeline refused to believe that the rules could be any different even in the wilds of America.

So now he worked in only his shirt. The crisp, starched linen was stark white against his tan. He'd rolled up the sleeves, revealing the dark hairs on his forearms, and even though Emeline knew she was being ridiculously sensitive, she was terribly aware of those bare forearms. She longed to touch his arm, run her finger along the lean muscle there and feel the brush of those dark hairs.

Damn him!

"Was there a particular reason you chose the Westerton soiree?" she asked now in a voice that was shrewish, even to her own ears.

"No." He still didn't look up. His queue swung over his shoulder as he shifted to rub a different part of the gun. That, too, was annoying. The sunlight showed lighter streaks of brown in his dark hair.

Emeline narrowed her eyes at him. He gave no outward sign, but she knew he was lying to her.

"That's enough," Mr. Hartley said, and for a moment she thought he spoke to her.

But Daniel straightened and grinned. "Is it clean now?"

"Well and truly clean." The colonial stood, rising so close to her that they nearly touched.

Emeline checked an impulse to step back. He was so tall. It was really quite rude of him to tower over her in such a manner.

"Now may I try it?" Daniel asked.

She opened her mouth to give a resounding *No!*, but Mr. Hartley spoke first. "This isn't the place to shoot a gun. Think of all the things—and people—we might accidentally hit."

Her son's lower lip puckered out in a pout. "But—"

"Daniel," Emeline said in warning, "you mustn't badger Mr. Hartley when he has been so kind as to let you help him with his gun."

Mr. Hartley frowned as if she'd said something wrong. "I was very pleased to have Danny's help—"

"His name is Daniel." The words were out before she could check them. Her tone was too sharp.

He stared at her, his mouth thinning.

She glared back, thrusting out her chin.

He said slowly, "Daniel worked well today. He isn't bothering me."

Her son beamed as if he'd been given the most extravagant praise. She should be grateful that Mr. Hartley was so kind, that he knew exactly what to say to a small boy. Instead, she was vaguely peeved.

Mr. Hartley smiled back at Daniel and then bent to pick up the cloths and oil. "You'll probably be busy tomorrow morning, preparing for the ball."

Emeline blinked at the abrupt change of subject. "Why, no. There are many preparations if one is throwing a ball, but as we are simply attending—"

"Good." He glanced up, his brown eyes laughing, and Emeline suddenly realized she'd walked straight into a trap. "Then you'll be able to accompany me to view Mr. Wedgwood's pottery. I should like a feminine perspective on what to order."

She opened her mouth to say something that she'd no doubt regret later but was saved by the voice of Mr. Smythe-Jones.

"My lord? Lord Eddings?"

Daniel hunched his shoulders and whispered, "Don't tell him I'm here."

Emeline frowned. "Nonsense. Go to your tutor at once, Daniel."

"But—"

"Best to do as your mother says," Mr. Hartley said quietly.

And miraculously, her son shut his mouth. "Yes, sir." He went to the wall and called over, "I'm here."

They heard the thin voice of the tutor. "Whatever are you doing over there? Come down at once, Lord Eddings!"

"I—"

Mr. Hartley leapt onto the marble bench that sat against the wall. For such a big man, he moved lithely. "Danny was visiting me, Mr. Smythe-Jones. I hope you don't mind."

Startled murmuring came from over the wall.

"Come on, Danny." Mr. Hartley made a step with his hands. "I'll give you a leg up."

"Thanks!" Daniel stepped into the big hands and Mr. Hartley gently lifted him up. The boy scrambled to the top of the wall and then onto the big crab-apple branch that lay just over it. In a moment he was gone.

Emeline looked at the toes of her shoes as she listened to the tutor remonstrating with her son, his voice fading as they walked back to the house. She twisted a bit of ribbon on her overskirt. Then she looked up.

Mr. Hartley was watching her from atop the bench. He jumped lightly to the ground, landing just a little too close to her, his coffee-brown eyes intent. "Why don't you want me to call your son *Danny*?"

She pursed her lips. "His name is Daniel."

"And Danny is the nickname for Daniel."

"He's a baron. He will sit in the House of Lords one day." The ribbon was digging into the soft pads of her fingers. "He doesn't need a nickname."

"Need it, no." He stepped even closer to her so that she was forced to look up in order to continue meeting his eyes. "But what harm does a nickname do a little boy?"

She inhaled, realizing as she did so that she could smell him, a combination of gunpowder, starch, and gun oil. The scent should have been repulsive, but she found it strangely intimate instead. And the intimacy was arousing. How awful.

"It was his father's name," she blurted. The ribbon broke.

He stilled, his big body poised as if to pounce. "Your husband?"

"Yes."

"It reminds you of him?"

"Yes. No." She waved the suggestion away. "I don't know."

He began a slow prowl around her. "You miss him, your husband."

She shrugged, fighting down the urge to twist and face him. "He was my husband for six years. It would be very odd if I didn't miss him."

"Even so, it doesn't follow that you would miss him." He had meandered behind her and now spoke over her shoulder. She imagined that she could feel his breath against the spot behind her ear.

"What do you mean?"

"Did you love him?"

"Love is not a consideration in a fashionable marriage." She bit her lip.

"No? Then you do not miss him."

She closed her eyes and remembered laughing blue eyes that had teased. Soft, pale hands that had been unbearably gentle. A tenor voice that had talked and talked about dogs and horses and phaetons. Then she remembered that pale face, unnaturally drawn, all the laughter gone, lying against black satin in a casket. She didn't want those memories. They were too painful.

"No." She turned blindly to the house and a way out of this too-close garden and the man who stalked her. "No, I do not miss my husband."

Chapter Six

❦

*Well! The king was very grateful to the guard who
had saved his life single-handedly. All hailed Iron
Heart as a hero, and he was immediately made the
captain of the king's guard. But though everyone
asked the valiant captain his name, he would not say
a word. This stubborn refusal to speak rather vexed
the king, who was a man used to having his own way
in such matters. However, even that little worry was
put aside when one day the king was out riding and
a terrible troll decided to make the king his lunch.
Clang! Thump!* Iron Heart *charged forward and soon
separated the troll's head from his body....*
—from *Iron Heart*

Emeline awoke to the curtains being pulled back on her
bed. She blinked sleepily up into the face of Harris, her lady's maid. Harris was a wooden-faced woman of at least
five decades with a large, bulbous nose that dominated the
rest of her more-petite features. Emeline knew of many

ladies who complained that their personal maids spent too much time gossiping and flirting with the menservants in the household.

Such was not the case with Harris.

"There is a Mr. Hartley waiting in the downstairs hall for you, my lady," Harris said stonily.

Emeline glanced blearily at her bedroom window. The light seemed quite pale. "What?"

"He says that he has an appointment with you, and he will not leave until he sees you."

She sat up. "What time is it?"

Harris pursed her lips. "A quarter of eight, my lady."

"Good Lord. Whatever is he about?" Emeline threw back the covers and searched for her slippers. "He must be mad. No one comes calling at eight o'clock."

"Yes, my lady." Harris bent to help her with her slippers.

"Not even nine o'clock," Emeline muttered, thrusting her arms into the wrapper Harris held for her. "Really, anything before eleven is suspect, and I myself would never bother before two o'clock. Quite, quite mad."

"Yes, my lady."

Emeline became conscious now of tuneless whistling. "What is that noise?"

"Mr. Hartley is whistling in the downstairs hall, my lady," Harris said.

For a moment, Emeline stared at her maid, speechless. The whistling crested on a particularly horrific note. Emeline rushed from her room and out into the upper hall. She marched down the hall and to the banister that overlooked the downstairs entry. Mr. Hartley was standing with his hands behind his back, holding his tricorne.

As she watched, he idly rocked back on his heels and whistled through his teeth.

"Hist!" Emeline leaned over the banister.

Mr. Hartley whirled and looked up at her. "Good morning, my lady!" He gave a little bow. The man looked fresh and alarmingly alert for so early in the morning.

"Have you gone stark, raving mad?" Emeline demanded. "What are you doing in my hall this early?"

"I've come to take you to Wedgwood's business offices to help me order pottery."

She scowled. "I never—"

"You'll need to dress." His gaze wandered to her chest. "Not that I mind your present attire."

Emeline slapped a hand to her bosom. "How dare—"

"Wait here, shall I?" And he began that awful whistling again, this time even louder.

Emeline opened her mouth, realized that he wouldn't be able to hear anything over the noise coming out between his lips, and shut it again. She gathered her skirts and stomped back to her room. Harris had already laid out a flame-colored watered silk, and Emeline was clothed and coiffed in scandalously little time. Even so, Mr. Hartley was peering at the hall clock when she descended the stairs.

He glanced at her rather perfunctorily. "Took you long enough. Come on, I don't want to be late to see Mr. Bentley—Mr. Wedgwood's partner."

Emeline frowned as he hustled her out the door. "When is your appointment?"

"Nine o'clock." Mr. Hartley handed her into the waiting carriage.

She narrowed her eyes at him when he sat across from her. "But you came for me before eight o'clock."

"I thought it might take you a while to get ready." He smiled at her, his coffee-brown eyes crinkling at the corners. "And I was right, wasn't I?" He rapped on the roof.

"You take too much for granted," Emeline said frostily.

"Only with you, ma'am. Only with you." His voice was low and soft and disconcertingly intimate.

Emeline glanced out the window so she wouldn't have to meet his eyes. "Why is that?"

There was a silence and for a moment she thought he might avoid the question.

"I don't know why you affect me like this," he said finally. "I think you'd as well ask a catamount why it runs after a fleeing deer as ask me why I quicken when you're near."

Her gaze jerked around to his. He watched her with a purely male gaze, frank and assessing. It should've made her afraid, being the subject of such a perusal. Instead it thrilled her. "Then you admit it."

He shrugged. "Why not? It's purely instinctive, I assure you."

She twitched at a ribbon on the front of her gown. "You must be quite at a loss if your *instincts* cause you this problem whenever you're near a lady."

"I already told you, remember?" He leaned forward and wrapped his hand around her fingers, stilling her agitated teasing of the ribbon. "This happens only with you."

Emeline looked down at their fingers. She should snap at him. Set him down properly and let him know that he'd gone too far with his familiarity. But the sight of his brown fingers wrapped around and cradling her own smaller, white ones was mesmerizing somehow. The carriage bumped around a curve, and he withdrew his hand.

She smoothed out the ribbon. "Haven't you a man of business?"

"Yes, Mr. Kitcher. But he's a rather dry old man. I thought you'd be better company."

She snorted softly at that. "Where are these offices?"

"Not far," he said. "They've rented part of a warehouse."

Her hands were trembling, and she clasped them together in her lap. "Mr. Wedgwood and Mr. Bentley haven't showrooms?"

"No. They're relatively new to the trade. Part of the reason I hope to get a bargain from them."

"Mmm." Emeline looked at him curiously. Mr. Hartley's eyes were narrowed and alert as if he were readying for battle. "You like this."

His eyebrows shot up. "What?"

She waved a hand vaguely. "Trade. Doing business. The hunt of finding a good bargain."

His sensuous lips curved. "Of course. But I trust you won't give me away to Bentley."

Then the carriage was drawing up next to a warehouse. Mr. Hartley jumped down as soon as the steps were set and turned to help Emeline.

She looked at the plain brick and wood building doubtfully. "What do you want me to do?"

"Simply give me your opinion." He tucked her hand into his elbow as a gentleman in curled wig and rust-colored coat came out of one of the warehouse's doors.

"Mr. Hartley?" the man exclaimed in a Northern accent. "An honor, sir, an honor to meet your acquaintance. I am Thomas Bentley."

Mr. Hartley took Mr. Bentley's hand and shook it. This close, Emeline could see that Mr. Bentley was younger than she had thought—probably not much above thirty years. His face was florid and his middle just a little stout. Mr. Hartley introduced her, and the pottery merchant's eyes widened when he heard her title.

"*Lady* Emeline. Why, this is an honor, ma'am; it is indeed. Won't you take a dish of tea? I've just purchased some from India that's quite nice."

Emeline smiled at the man, murmuring her assent, and Mr. Bentley showed them into the warehouse. The building soared overhead, dark and cool. She could smell sawdust and damp bricks. Half the space was packed with barrels and crates, but Mr. Bentley led them into a smaller office off the main room. The office was just large enough for a wide desk, some chairs, and a stack of boxes against the wall. In one corner was a small hearth with a kettle already steaming.

"Here we are, then," he said cheerfully as he held a chair for Emeline. "I'll just get the tea, shall I?"

"Will Mr. Wedgwood be joining us?" Mr. Hartley asked. He had chosen to remain standing.

"Ah, no," Mr. Bentley said as he squinted over the pot of tea. "Mr. Wedgwood is the master potter, whilst I am the businessman. He is presently overseeing the making of the pottery in Burslem. There we are." Mr. Bentley said this last as he set the tea on the desk. He'd had to stack several ledger books on the floor to make room. The man blinked nervously at Mr. Hartley.

But the American merely nodded and raised a brow

at her. Emeline sat forward to pour the tea. She wasn't sure, exactly, of the undercurrents of this meeting, and she didn't want to upset Mr. Hartley's position. At the same time, she was intrigued by how he would act in this, his own world. Right now he seemed very still, his expression relaxed but giving nothing away. Mr. Bentley, in contrast, was beginning to look worried. Emeline hid a smile as she sipped her tea. She had the feeling that Mr. Hartley was deliberately making his opponent unsure of his position.

For the next several minutes, the two gentlemen and Emeline took tea and made small talk. She knew that Mr. Hartley must be impatient to see the pottery he wanted to buy, but he didn't let his impatience show on his face. He leaned on a corner of the desk and sipped his tea as pleasantly as if he were visiting a maiden aunt.

Mr. Bentley shot him several worried looks and then finally put down his teacup. "Would you like to see some of our pottery, sir?"

Mr. Hartley nodded and set aside his own teacup. The pottery merchant went to one of the wooden boxes against the wall and opened the lid, revealing a mass of straw.

Emeline couldn't help but lean forward. She'd never before thought much about the plates she used—save that they be of the newest design—but now pottery seemed a most important affair. Mr. Hartley shot a glance at her behind Mr. Bentley's back. He almost imperceptibly shook his head once. Emeline wrinkled her nose at him, feeling as if she'd been reproved like a small child. However, she sat back and smoothed her features into an expression of ennui. Mr. Hartley's mouth twitched as if he found her enthusiasm amusing, and he winked at her. Emeline tilted her nose away from him. She'd have to set the man down. Later.

Meanwhile, Mr. Bentley had carefully removed a layer of straw. Underneath was a lidded jar in the shape of a pineapple with a dark green glaze. Mr. Bentley handed the jar to Mr. Hartley, who took it and examined it without speaking. He brought the jar over and stood it on the desk in front of Emeline, watching as she bent to examine it.

Mr. Bentley was unearthing more pottery, teapots, dishes, cups, bowls, and tureens. Indeed, all manner of pottery soon filled the desk, most glazed a deep green and many in the shapes of cauliflowers or pineapples.

Mr. Hartley cocked an eyebrow at Emeline while Mr. Bentley's back was turned. She elevated her own eyebrows in return. The fact was that the pottery was all very nice and well made, but nothing out of the ordinary.

Mr. Hartley gave a slight nod and turned to the other man. "I believe that Mr. Wedgwood has some newer pieces?"

Mr. Bentley paused, still bent over the crate. "Ah, I'm not sure...."

"I was told that he is working on some very fine creamware." Mr. Hartley met the pottery merchant's eyes and smiled.

"Well, as to that..." Mr. Bentley darted a look at a small crate by itself in the corner of the office. He cleared his throat. "Mr. Wedgwood is indeed experimenting with a creamware, but he is not yet ready to show it publicly. He hopes, in fact, to present it to the queen first."

Emeline clapped her hands. "Really, Mr. Bentley, how exciting!"

The merchant's face became even ruddier. "Thank you, ma'am. It is indeed."

"But won't you let us see this wonderful pottery?" Emeline leaned a little forward, letting her bosom swell over her square-cut bodice. "Please?"

The man turned red, and Emeline nearly grinned. She would never admit it in a million years, but she was enjoying this whole exchange enormously. Who knew trade could be such a battle of wits?

"Ah..." Mr. Bentley took out a handkerchief and swiped it nervously over his glistening brow. He shrugged. "Why not? If it pleases you, my lady."

"Oh, it does."

Having made up his mind, the merchant went to the small box in the corner and pried off the lid. He reached inside and took out something with great care before turning with it in his hands. Emeline held her breath. The teapot was very plain. As its name proclaimed, it was a rich cream color, almost yellowish, with straight classical lines and a pretty little spout.

Emeline held out her hands. "May I?"

The merchant placed it in her hands, and Emeline felt the lightness of the piece; the clay was thinner than she was used to. She turned it over to look at the maker's mark. *Wedgwood* was stamped on the bottom.

"This is quite elegant," she murmured softly.

She looked up in time to see Mr. Hartley watching her, and her breath caught. His eyes were hooded, his lips straight, but he had a possessive air about him. Somehow she knew: It pleased him that she shared in the discovery of the creamware teapot. Just as much as it pleased her. She and Mr. Hartley made an extraordinarily well-matched team. The thought made her uneasy. She shouldn't enjoy bargaining. She shouldn't like knowing that he valued her opinion.

She shouldn't care at all.

Mr. Hartley's eyes had narrowed. There was no pity there. Not one trace of compassion. It was as if a tame tomcat suddenly showed the catamount that lurked always beneath the purring facade. As if she was his prey.

He nodded once and turned to discuss terms with Mr. Bentley. The civilized veneer was back in place, but Mr. Bentley was having to marshal all his wits to keep up with the American's hard bargaining, and the sums of money that Mr. Hartley so casually mentioned were enough to raise even Emeline's eyebrows. She had no doubt that this was the man who had made a fortune out of his uncle's business in only four years.

As the men haggled, Emeline bent over the teapot, tracing its elegant lines, and thought about the ladies of the Colonies who would pour tea from the pretty little spout. And she wondered: Why exactly had Mr. Hartley brought her here?

What had he meant to show her besides a beautiful teapot?

"IT'S JUST THAT I'm not sure about the neckline." Rebecca stared into the mirror and tried without success to tug up the material at her bodice. There seemed to be a vast amount of her own skin revealed in the mirror.

"It's quite all right, miss." Her maid, Evans, didn't even glance up as she bustled about the room, collecting the debris from Rebecca's toilet.

Rebecca tugged one more time at her bodice and then

gave up. Evans had been personally recommended by
Lady Emeline, and if the maid said it was required that
Rebecca go to her first London ball nude, Rebecca would
follow her suggestion. She'd been to many dances and
social events in Boston, of course, but Lady Emeline had
made it quite clear that a London ball was an entirely different matter.

All this trouble over her only served to make Rebecca
feel guilty. It'd been she who had badgered Samuel into
taking her on this trip. Now, he apparently felt obliged to
spend great sums of money on her so she'd be entertained
in London. It wasn't exactly what she'd had in mind when
she begged to accompany him. All she'd wanted was to
spend some time with him. Perhaps learn to know her
older brother just a little better. Rebecca wandered over to
a chair as she thought.

"No," the maid called.

Rebecca froze in an unladylike half-crouch over the
chair.

Evans gave a strained smile. "We don't want to wrinkle
our skirts, do we?"

Rebecca straightened. "But when I sit in the carriage,
surely—"

"Can't be helped, can it?" the maid chirped. "More's
the pity, really. I don't know why these clever gentlemen
don't invent a method for a lady to travel to a ball standing up."

"Oh, yes?" Rebecca murmured faintly.

Evans was a small, dark-haired woman who was
dauntingly fashionable. Her panniers were so wide, she
could hardly do her duties as maid. Actually, Rebecca was
rather terrified of her.

Although the maid seemed to be trying to be friendly. "Perhaps we can go downstairs and rest in the small sitting room? *Not* in the hallway, of course. A lady should never be seen to hang about waiting for her carriage to arrive."

"Of course." Rebecca turned to the door, feeling rather relieved.

"Remember, we mustn't sit!" her maid caroled after her.

"I wonder if *we* will be allowed to use the necessary," Rebecca muttered to herself as she negotiated the stairs in her wide skirts.

She looked about guiltily to see if anyone had overheard her crass remark. The only person she could see was a single footman—the black-haired one—in the downstairs hall, and he stared straight ahead, apparently deaf to all that went on around him. Rebecca blew out a breath of relief. She continued down the stairs without incident until she came to the last step. There she somehow caught her heel on her hem and had a bad moment when she teetered ungracefully until she caught the banister with both hands. She froze, still clutching the wooden ball at the end of the stair banister, and glanced over at the footman. He was now looking at her, one foot forward as if he'd been about to leap to her rescue. When their gazes met, he withdrew his foot and resumed staring forward woodenly.

Oh, how embarrassing! She couldn't even walk in her own skirts without falling down the stairs in front of the servants. Rebecca carefully placed both feet on the marble hallway and released the banister. She took a moment to smooth her skirts and then walked determinedly toward the doors to her right. The doors were tall and made of dark wood, and the handles were proportionately large. Rebecca grasped one and pulled.

Nothing happened.

Sweat broke out at her hairline. The black-haired footman would think she was an absolute ninny. Why did the man have to be so lovely? It was one thing to make an ass of oneself in front of an old, balding man, and quite another—

He cleared his throat directly behind her.

Rebecca yelped and swung around. The footman's beautiful green eyes were wide and startled, but he merely said, "If I might, miss?"

He reached around her and pushed open the door.

Rebecca stared past the open door and into the library. Oh, Lord. "Actually, I believe I've changed my mind. I'd like the sitting room, please." And she pointed behind him like a small, slightly backward child.

Fortunately, he didn't seem to find her at all odd. "Aye, mum." He pivoted and opened the door across the hall.

Rebecca held her head high and swanned across the hallway, but as she neared the footman, she could see quite plainly that his gaze was not where it should be. She stopped dead and slapped her hands over her bosom.

"It's too low, isn't it? I knew I shouldn't have listened to that maid. She might not mind her boobies hanging out for all to see, but I just can't—" Her brain suddenly caught up with her mouth. She removed her hands from her bosom and slapped them over her awful, awful, *awful* mouth.

And then she just stared at the gorgeous black-haired footman, who was staring back at her. There really wasn't anything else to do, except possibly die right here in her brother's London town house hallway, and that option, unfortunately, seemed very unlikely at the moment.

Finally, he cleared his throat again. "You're the fairest lass I've ever seen, mum, and in that gown, you look just like a princess, you do."

Rebecca blinked and cautiously removed her hands. "Really?"

"Swear on me mam's grave," he said earnestly.

"Oh, is your mother dead, too?"

He nodded.

"That's a pity, isn't it? My mother died when I was born, and I never knew her."

"Me mam died two years ago this Michaelmas," he said in a soft kind of burr.

"I'm sorry."

He merely shrugged. "After me youngest sister was born. Eldest of ten, that's me."

She smiled up at him. "You don't sound like the other servants."

"That's because I'm Irish, mum." His green eyes seemed to twinkle at her.

"Then, why—"

But she was interrupted by her brother's voice. "Are you ready to leave, Rebecca?"

She jumped and spun for the second time that night. Samuel stood three risers above her on the stairs.

"I wish you'd make some sort of noise when you move," she said.

He raised his eyebrows, his gaze flicking to the footman. Rebecca followed his look and found that the black-haired footman stood against the wall again, his eyes straight ahead. It was as if he were a magical creature who'd turned back into wood.

"O'Hare, will you get the door?" Samuel asked, and for a moment Rebecca wondered to whom he spoke.

Then the black-haired footman jumped forward. "Sir." He opened the door and held it as they walked outside.

Rebecca looked into his face as they passed, but his expression was perfectly blank, and the twinkle was gone from his green eyes. She sighed and laid her hand on Samuel's arm as he led her down the steps to the carriage. If she didn't know better, she'd think that she'd imagined her conversation with O'Hare the footman.

They settled into the carriage, and she noticed her brother's attire for the first time. He wore a perfectly respectable dark green coat and breeches with a gold brocade waistcoat. Unfortunately, he'd chosen to wear his usual leggings and moccasins over his breeches.

"Lady Emeline will not approve of your leggings," she remarked.

He glanced at his legs, and his lips quirked. "No doubt she'll make her opinion known."

She stared at his face, and a funny thought entered her head. Samuel smiled the same way O'Hare the footman did: with his eyes.

LADY EMELINE CONTAINED herself for fully a minute after entering the carriage, which was a minute longer than Sam had estimated.

"What are you thinking to wear such things?" She scowled at his feet and legs.

"I believe I've told you before that they're comfortable." Probably she would scowl harder if she knew that he thought the expression was adorable. She wore an elaborately embroidered pale red gown with a yellow underskirt. The colors were gentler than those she usually employed, and although they became her, he preferred the flame reds and bold oranges.

She was an elegant lady of the London ton tonight, far removed from the woman who had accompanied him to a warehouse to inspect pottery. What had she thought of their outing? She'd seemed interested in his business transaction, but was it merely the novelty? Or did she perhaps feel the same communion of mind as he did?

Lady Emeline shook her head at him now, oblivious to the direction of his thoughts. Maybe she was beginning to realize the futility of arguing over his leggings. She turned on Rebecca instead. "Now, remember that you must not dance with anyone I have not expressly approved. Nor may you talk to anyone that I have not introduced you to. There will be men—I do not call them gentlemen—who have been known to break these rules, but you must not let them."

Sam wondered if she was thinking of himself. She turned a gimlet eye on him, and he was made certain. He grinned back at her, his little ruffled hen. Lady Emeline sat beside her aunt, both ladies ramrod straight, although the older woman was nearly a head taller than her niece. The carriage rattled around a corner, making everyone inside sway. Beside him, Rebecca had wrapped her arms about herself.

He leaned close. "You look splendid. I hardly recognized you when I came down the stairs."

Rebecca bit her lip and peeked up at him, and he was suddenly reminded of her as a little girl. She had looked at him thus when he'd visit her at their uncle's house in Boston. He remembered her in a white cap and apron, standing shyly in Uncle Thomas's dark hallway, waiting to greet him. He'd never known what to say to her when he'd visited—he'd come to Boston once or twice a year. His little sister had seemed such a foreign creature, a girl child brought up in the prim civilization of Boston society. All the things he knew—the forest, hunting and trapping, and eventually the army—were completely strange to her.

He blinked now, realizing that Rebecca had spoken to him. "What?"

She leaned close, her brown eyes vulnerable. "Do you think anyone will dance with me?"

"I'll have to beat them off with a stick."

She giggled and for a moment that little girl in the white cap shone in her eyes.

Mademoiselle Molyneux cleared her throat. "We are almost there, *ma petite*. Compose yourself so that you may present an appearance of gentility." The old lady sent a sharp look at Rebecca's skirts. "You have remembered to wear the shoes, yes?"

Rebecca blinked. "Yes, ma'am."

"*Bon*. And here is the mansion."

Sam looked out the window and saw a line of carriages creeping toward the Earl of Westerton's town house. Lady Emeline was right: This was too grand a ball to be Rebecca's first. But introducing his sister to society was only part of the reason he'd chosen this particular ball tonight. The other, more important half, was that he was on the hunt.

He waited patiently as their carriage crawled forward

in line, listening with only a fraction of his attention to the female chatter within the carriage. Even now, when his entire being strained toward his goal, he was aware of Lady Emeline in particular. Without turning his head, he followed the cadence of her speech, the pauses and dips in tones. He knew when she glanced his way and could feel her puzzled curiosity in her gaze. She still wanted to know why he'd chosen this particular ball. He could tell her. It involved her brother as well. But something within him shrunk from revealing his true purpose.

The carriage door was flung open by a footman he didn't know, and Sam's eyes narrowed at the servant. That was a matter he must watch as well. He hadn't missed how close O'Hare had stood to Rebecca earlier in the hallway. Sam met the footman's gaze. This man immediately lowered his eyes, something O'Hare had failed to do. Sam admired courage, but he wondered how long a man could last as a servant with such a spirit.

Sam stepped down onto the cobblestones in front of the Westerton house and turned to help his sister and Mademoiselle Molyneux out. Only Lady Emeline remained in the carriage. She hesitated in the doorway, eyeing him suspiciously.

He smiled and held out his hand. "My lady."

She pursed her lips. "Mr. Hartley."

But she laid her hand in his, and Sam had the pleasure of wrapping his fingers around hers. She descended the steps regally and attempted to withdraw her hand. Instead, he bowed over her hand, brushing his lips against fine kid, the scent of lemon balm bathing his face.

Then he straightened. "Shall we?"

But her expression had softened somehow in the interval

that he'd bent over her hand. He stilled, the people around him, his sister, even the hunt, fading into the background as he stared at Lady Emeline. Her lips were parted, red and wet, as if she'd just licked them, and her eyes were uncertain. Had they been alone, he would have caught her, drawn her into his arms until her body met his, and lowered his head to—

"Samuel?"

He jerked his head and his attention to his sister. Rebecca. God! "Yes?"

She looked confused. "Are you all right?"

"Yes." He held out his arm to Mademoiselle Molyneux, who took it with a thoughtful look at him. He braced himself and turned to Lady Emeline, his voice deepening. "Shall we?"

His words were the same as moments before, but their meaning had changed fundamentally. Her eyes widened, and he saw her sweet breasts expand as she inhaled.

Then she met his eyes and her chin lifted. "Of course."

Which left him to ponder, as he escorted the ladies up the steps, what exactly Lady Emeline had meant by those two innocuous words.

Inside the great double doors, Westerton House was ablaze with hundreds, perhaps thousands, of candles. Even the entry hall was warm, giving an unpleasant taste of the heat that would lurk in the ballroom itself. Why anyone would voluntarily attend an event such as this was truly a puzzle to him. He felt sweat start at the base of his spine. He hated crowds. He'd always had, but since Spinner's Falls...He pushed the thought from his mind, concentrating on his reason for being here.

The ladies surrendered their wraps to a footman, and the articles of clothing were whisked away. Then they were at the entrance to the ballroom itself, and a footman with a magnificent wig was announcing them. The room was cavernous, but that didn't help the heat, for it was overflowing with people. They literally stood shoulder to shoulder so that one had to wait for an opening to move forward.

Sam caught his arms twitching and had to consciously still the movement. This was his idea of hell. The heat, the shuffle of bodies against bodies, the noise of scores of voices laughing, talking, complaining. He felt a bead of sweat slide down his back. Mademoiselle Molyneux had already found a crony and slipped away into the mass of bodies. Someone bumped against Lady Emeline, still on his right arm, and he found himself baring his teeth at the man. He saw a startled look on a reddened face and then that man, too, was lost. Sam closed his eyes for a moment to try to control the panic that rose in his chest, but with his eyes shut, the worst part nearly overwhelmed his senses.

The *smell*.

Oh, God, the smell of burning wax, foul breath, and sweating bodies. Male sweat. That strong acid stink, that rank musk, that rotten armpit odor. They shoved around him, trying to get past, trying to run away. Some old enough to be grandfathers, some too young to shave, all fearing for their lives, all wanting just to live another day. That was what he smelled: the terror of death. He gasped, but all the air had been sucked into babbling lungs, and he inhaled only the fear of battle and the smell of sweat and blood.

"Mr. Hartley. *Samuel.*"

Her voice was near, and he felt a cool hand on his cheek. With an effort, he opened his eyes.

Her black eyes were staring into his, and he latched on to the sight, trying to focus on only her.

"Are you all right?" she asked.

He opened his mouth and formed the word carefully, speaking the truth because that was all he could do. "No."

Her eyes left his for a moment, and he grasped her shoulders to keep his balance. "What is wrong with him, do you know?" she asked.

"I don't know. I've never seen him like this," Rebecca said.

Her black eyes returned to his, and he felt relief. "Come with me."

He nodded, his throat working convulsively, and stumbled after her like a drunken man. Their progress was slow, and he knew that sweat was running down his cheeks. He kept her constantly in his vision, a guideline to sanity. Then, suddenly, there were doors, and he tumbled out into cool, fresh air. It was a veranda with a low rail. He made it to one end before spewing over the rail and into the bushes.

"He's ill," Sam heard Rebecca say as he gulped great breaths of air. "Maybe he ate something spoiled. We should send for a doctor."

"No." His voice emerged a strangled rasp. He cleared his throat, fighting to sound normal. "No doctor."

Behind him, Rebecca made a sound of distress. He wished he could face her, reassure her that nothing was wrong.

"Mr. Hartley," Lady Emeline murmured very close to him. She laid her hand on his shoulder. He hunched it. Shameful for any woman to see him like this, let alone *her.* "You're ill. Please satisfy your sister's worry and let us send for a physician."

Sam closed his eyes, willing his body to stop shaking, to stop betraying him with phantom fears. "No."

Her hand fell away. "Rebecca, can you wait with your brother whilst I fetch some wine? Perhaps that will revive him."

"Yes, certainly," Rebecca replied.

And then Lady Emeline started to leave him. He heard a low groaning and realized dimly that it was himself, but he couldn't stop the sound, nor the urge to make her stay by his side. He turned, meaning to keep her there, but instead he was brought up short by what he saw.

Lord Vale stood in the doorway to the ballroom.

JASPER SHUT THE French doors behind him, smiled his careless, charming smile, and said, "Emmie! Godsblood, hadn't expected to see you here."

All Emeline could think was, *How am I to get him out of the way?* Hardly a kind sentiment for a man she'd known all her life, but there it was. It was imperative to get Samuel away before Jasper saw how bad his condition was. Somehow she knew that Samuel would hate to have another man see him like this.

It had happened so suddenly in the ballroom. She'd felt him stiffen as they'd entered the house but thought nothing of it. Many would be nervous at such a gathering of the ton. But he'd slowed as they'd advanced into the ballroom. Even allowing for the awkwardness of moving through the crowd, Samuel had walked oddly. Until she had at last looked up into his face and had seen he was in agony. What kind of agony—whether mental or physical—she did not know, but everything about him, from the closed eyes to the pale and sweating face to the way he suddenly clutched her hand bespoke great pain. The idea that this strong man was in pain made her almost paralyzed. It was as if she'd felt a corresponding pain deep within her own being. She'd led him out of the ballroom as quickly as possible, the whole time aware of his silent agony.

And now she must deal with Jasper.

Emeline squared her shoulders and assumed her most haughty expression—the one she'd learned in the nursery growing up the daughter of an earl. But as it turned out, there was no need. Jasper wasn't even looking at her. His eyes were fixed behind her, presumably on Samuel.

"Hartley? I say, it is Corporal Hartley, isn't it?" Jasper asked.

"Yes." The single word was clipped out from behind her.

Emeline turned and saw that Samuel was upright now, no longer leaning against the railing, although his face was still pale and shone with sweat. He was unmoving, as though waiting for something. Beside him, Rebecca hovered hesitantly, looking from one man to the other, her expression clearly confused.

Jasper took a step closer. "I haven't seen you since…" His voice trailed off as if he couldn't bring himself to say the name.

"Since Spinner's Falls."

"Yes." All the usual amusement was gone from Jasper's face, and without it, Emeline saw the lines carved beside his long nose and too-wide mouth.

"Did you know we were betrayed?" Samuel asked softly.

That startled Jasper. He drew his hairy brows together. "What?"

"Someone betrayed the regiment. Do you know anything about that?"

"Why would I?"

Samuel shrugged. "You were in debt to Clemmons."

"I beg your pardon?"

"Deeply in debt. Every veteran of the regiment that I've talked to since my arrival in England remembers that fact clearly. You were in danger of being drummed out of the army, stripped of your rank, disgraced."

Jasper's head reared back as if he'd been hit. "That's—"

"The massacre at Spinner's Falls saved you from having to pay that debt."

Jasper slowly flexed his fingers, and Emeline felt a prickle on the back of her neck at the aggression in the air. "What exactly are you implying, Hartley?"

"You had a reason to betray us," Samuel stated softly.

"You think I sold my men to the French?" Jasper's tone was almost casual, but his face was graven.

"Perhaps," Samuel said in a voice so low it was nearly a whisper. He swayed slightly where he stood—he wasn't as recovered as he'd like them to think. "Or to the Wyandot Indians. The same result in either case. They knew we would be there at Spinner's Falls. They knew and they waited, and when we came, they killed us all—"

Jasper's big fists balled, and he took a step toward Samuel.

Emeline knew she had to intervene before the men came to blows. "Stop it, Samuel! Stop saying these things."

He never took his eyes from the other man. "Why?"

"Please, Samuel, come away from Jasper."

"Why?" Samuel finally turned his eyes, glancing quickly from her to Jasper. "Who is he to you?"

She bit her lip. "A friend. He's—"

But Jasper spoke for himself. "I'm her fiancé."

Chapter Seven

All lauded the captain of the guard for his bravery,
strength, and loyalty, although many wondered why
such a man would stubbornly refuse to speak even
one word. But what really put the feather in Iron
Heart's cap was when he saved the king's life a third
time. The castle was attacked by a fire-breathing
dragon, and Iron Heart fended off the loathsome
beast with great swings of his sword. After this, the
king pronounced that there was only one award fit for
such a gallant man. He must guard the king's most
precious possession—the princess royal herself....
—from *Iron Heart*

"*Fiancé?*" Sam felt as if he'd taken a fist to the gut.

His lungs deflated, the breath leaving his body with a
whoosh as he slowly turned his head and met Lady Emeline's sweet black eyes.

"We haven't formally announced it yet, but we've had
an understanding for ages," she whispered.

How could this woman be engaged to another man and he not know it? It was as if he'd suddenly lost something that he'd not fully been aware of wanting in the first place. Which was lunacy. She was a titled aristocrat, the daughter, sister, mother, and widow of titled aristocrats. Her world was so far outside of his that he might as well be a child trying to grasp the moon in the night sky.

Impossible.

But he had no more time for further thoughts on Lady Emeline. This was the wrong place, anyway. If he'd not been made ill by the smell of other men's bodies, if he'd not had that overpowering memory of the massacre, he never would've chosen to accuse Vale here. But having done it, there was no point in regrets.

"I didn't betray us," Vale said. He was standing casually now, yet the man looked as if he were ready to attack.

Sam tensed.

At the same time, Rebecca touched his shoulder. "Come away, Samuel. Please come away." And he saw that she was trying not to cry. God, what had he done?

"You didn't seem insane six years ago when I knew you," Vale said conversationally. "What makes you think we were betrayed?"

Sam eyed him. Vale had the type of face that one instinctively trusted, a funny, open countenance habitually wrapped in a smile. Of course, Sam had known several men who smiled when they killed. "You were in debt to Lieutenant Clemmons. Everyone knew that."

"So?"

"So, Clemmons died in the massacre, effectively nullifying the debt."

Vale gave an incredulous bark of laughter. "You think

I killed two hundred and forty-six men so I wouldn't have to pay my debt to Clemmons? You *are* mad."

Maybe he was. Rebecca stood crying behind him, and Lady Emeline was watching him warily as if he might suddenly try to climb the walls. Vale stared at him with no fear in his eyes.

Sam remembered how the viscount had looked that day, astride his horse, trying to reach Colonel Darby through the mess of fighting men. The bay had been shot out from under Vale, and Sam had seen him jump clear of the falling horse. Stand and open wide his mouth in a battle cry Sam hadn't heard, swing his sword savagely, and watch in despair as Darby was pulled from his own horse and killed. And then Vale had continued fighting even as the battle was clearly lost.

Sam should be apologizing to Vale and backing away. This man couldn't be the traitor. But something inside whispered, *A brave man isn't necessarily an honest man.* MacDonald had been a brave soldier, too, before his arrest. Deep in his belly, Sam needed to find out the truth of Spinner's Falls.

Lady Emeline shook herself as if coming out of a trance and marched to the doors, her small back militantly straight. A footman was lingering there, gawking at the spectacle, and she pointed at him. "You. Bring some wine and biscuits, please. Thank you." And she firmly closed the doors on his face.

"Is that all you have?" Vale asked. "My gambling debts led you to believe that I'd betrayed our regiment, then had myself captured by Indians and Reynaud killed?"

Lady Emeline flinched. Vale didn't seem to notice.

Sam hadn't wanted to speak of this in front of her, but

now it was inevitable. "There was a letter detailing our plans to march to Fort Edward. It included a map with drawings that could be deciphered by the Indians."

Vale leaned against the rail. "How do you know about this letter?"

"I have it."

Rebecca had stopped crying and now said wonderingly, "That's why you wanted me to attend this ball, isn't it? It had nothing to do with me at all. *You* wanted to meet Lord Vale."

Damn. Sam stared at his younger sister. "I—"

"Why didn't you tell me?" she asked.

"Or me," Lady Emeline said. Her words were quiet, but Sam knew not to take that as a sign she wasn't angry. "Reynaud was killed because of that battle. Didn't you think I had a right to know?"

Sam frowned. His head hurt, his mouth tasted like acid, and he didn't want to deal with the women in his life. This was man's business, although he wasn't such a fool as to say that aloud.

Apparently, Vale had no such qualms. "Emmie, this will only open old wounds for you. Why don't you and Miss..." He looked uncertainly at Rebecca.

"This is Miss Hartley," Lady Emeline said coolly. "Mr. Hartley's sister."

"Miss Hartley." Vale nodded, urbane even when accused of treason. "Why don't you two go back into the house and enjoy the ball?"

Sam nearly groaned. Didn't Vale know anything about women?

Lady Emeline smiled tightly, her lips pressed into a thin line. "I believe I will stay here."

Vale opened his mouth again, the fool.

"I'll stay, too," Rebecca said before Vale could speak.

Everyone swung in her direction. Rebecca's cheeks pinkened, but she tilted her chin defiantly.

Lady Emeline cleared her throat. "We'll just sit here."

She marched to a marble bench set against the railing. Rebecca followed her. Both ladies sat down, crossed their arms, and assumed nearly identical expressions of expectation. In any other circumstances, it would've been funny. *Damn.* Sam raised an eyebrow at Vale.

Who shrugged helplessly. God only knew where the man got his reputation as a rake.

The footman returned with a glass of wine on a tray. Samuel took it and sipped. He spat the first mouthful over the rail into the bushes before downing the rest of the glass, feeling marginally better.

Vale cleared his throat when the footman had left. "Yes, well. Where did this letter you have come from? How are we to know it wasn't forged?"

"It's not forged," Sam said. He felt more than saw Lady Emeline purse her lips. How dare she sit in judgment of him? "I received it from a Delaware Indian—he's part English on his mother's side. The man is a friend I've known for many years."

"That strange little Indian who came to visit you at your place of business last spring!" Rebecca exclaimed. "I remember now. He was in your office when I went to bring you your luncheon."

Sam nodded. His offices were near the docks in Boston, a place his sister didn't usually visit. But that day he'd forgotten the basket that Cook had packed for his luncheon, and Rebecca had fetched it for him.

"You were so distracted afterward," Rebecca murmured. She looked at him as if seeing him for the first time. As if he were a stranger. "And angry. You were in a black mood for days. Now I know why."

Sam frowned, but he couldn't address his sister's worry right now. He looked at Vale. "Coshocton—the Indian—obtained the letter from a French trader who had been living among the Wyandot. It was the Wyandot who attacked us."

"I know that," Vale retorted. "But how do you know it was someone from our side who wrote the blamed thing? It could've been a Frenchie or—"

"No." Sam shook his head. "It was written in English. And besides, whoever wrote it knew too much. You remember that our march to Fort Edward was secret. Only the officers and a few of the trackers knew we marched instead of taking canoes down Lake Champlain."

Vale stared. "The lake passage was the more usual way, I remember."

Sam nodded. "Anyone hearing where we were headed would assume we went by water, not land."

Vale pursed his lips, then seemed to come to a decision. "See here, Hartley. My debt was high, I don't deny it, but I was quite able to pay it."

Sam narrowed his eyes. "Were you?"

"Yes. In fact, I did."

Sam stared. "What?"

"I quietly paid the debt to Clemmons's estate." Vale glanced away as if embarrassed. His voice was gruff. "Least I could do, don't you know, under the circumstances. Doubt any of the men you talked to knew that, but you can contact my solicitors if you wish. I've got the papers to prove it."

Sam closed his eyes. His head was pounding, and he felt like an idiot.

"Who else had reason to betray the company of soldiers besides Jasper?" Lady Emeline asked quietly. "Because I've known Jasper all my life, and I cannot believe he would do something that would end in Reynaud's death."

Viscount Vale grinned. "Thank you, Emeline, although I notice you don't acquit me of treason."

She merely shrugged.

"But she's right." Vale sobered. "I didn't betray the regiment, Hartley."

Sam stared at the aristocrat. He didn't want to believe him; he'd come all the way to England because he'd been looking for answers. He'd hoped Vale would be the key to everything. That he could finally put Spinner's Falls to rest. But any motive for Vale to have betrayed the regiment seemed to have evaporated. Besides, he knew now in his gut that Vale wasn't the traitor. And if he hadn't had his gut telling him Vale was innocent, there was Lady Emeline. She trusted the man, damn him.

Lady Emeline got to her feet and shook out her skirts. "I believe that means someone else is the traitor, doesn't it?"

"YOU SHOULD RETURN to the festivities," Emeline told Jasper. "Rebecca and I are more than ready to return home."

She didn't include Samuel in her words, but he was the one she was most worried about. He no longer wavered as he stood, but his face was still pale and shining with sweat.

But she made sure not to look at him as she addressed Jasper. She knew that Samuel wouldn't welcome her solicitation in front of another man. "I don't think it wise to go through the ballroom again—Rebecca has had enough excitement for the night. I'll send word to Tante Cristelle to meet us in front of the house, and we can walk around by the mews."

"*Non.*"

Emeline jumped and whirled at the single word. Her nerves were obviously more ragged than she'd thought.

Tante Cristelle stepped from the shadows near the doors. "Inside they whisper of two gentlemen arguing." She scowled at the gentlemen, though only Jasper had the grace to look ashamed. "Therefore, I shall remain and put the gossip to rest. I shall have a footman summon the carriage to the mews."

"But how will you return home?" Emeline asked.

Tante gave an expressive shrug. "I have many of the friends, do I not? It will not be so hard to find a carriage." She darted a glance at Rebecca, who had begun to look wilted. "You go and put all right at home, *ma petite.*"

Emeline smiled in weary gratitude at the old lady. "Thank you, Tante."

Tante Cristelle snorted. "It is you who have the harder part, I think, to manage these two bulls." She nodded and slipped back inside the ballroom.

Emeline squared her shoulders and turned back to her *bulls.*

"I'll escort you to your carriage." Jasper was already holding out an arm for her, and she took it, chiding herself not to feel hurt that Samuel did not do the same.

She was quiet as Jasper led her down the Westerton

garden and out into the mews, conscious all the while that Samuel trailed her with his sister. As they made a streetlamp on the side road, she glanced up at Jasper. "Thank you. Make sure you don't stay out too late."

"Yes, ma'am." Jasper grinned down at her. "I'll be sure to be tucked into bed before midnight. Wouldn't want to turn into a pumpkin."

Emeline wrinkled her nose in exasperation at Jasper's careless reply. That only made him smile wider. The carriage came rattling around the corner.

Emeline said hastily, "I'd like you and the Hartleys to come to tea tomorrow at my house so we can discuss all of this further." It wasn't a very graceful invitation; she didn't even look at Samuel or Rebecca, though they must have heard.

Jasper quirked an eyebrow at her. He might act comical at times, but that didn't mean he took orders from her. For a moment, she held her breath.

Then he smiled again. "Of course. Sleep well, my sweet."

He leaned down and brushed his lips over her temple. Jasper had kissed her like this dozens, perhaps hundreds of times, in the years they'd known each other. But this time, Emeline was conscious that Samuel was standing somewhere behind her in the dark, watching. She felt strangely flustered, which was nonsense. She owed the colonial nothing—less than nothing since it appeared that Jasper had been his target all along.

"Good night, Jasper."

He nodded and then turned to Samuel. "Tomorrow, then?"

Samuel didn't smile, but he inclined his head. "Tomorrow."

Jasper gave an ironic salute and then strolled off down the street. Despite her admonition to return to the ball, apparently he had other plans. But that was none of her business. Emeline shrugged and turned, only to find that Samuel was much closer behind her than she'd expected.

She pursed her lips. "May we leave now?"

"As you wish." He stepped aside and gestured to the waiting carriage steps.

Emeline was forced to brush against him to climb the steps. Which was what he intended, no doubt. Men could be so transparent when they wanted to show mastery. As she mounted the first step, she felt his hand grasp her elbow. His body was right behind hers, almost indecently near. She darted a look at him, and his mouth twitched.

Awful man.

Emeline settled herself in the carriage seat and watched as he knocked on the roof and sat down next to his sister.

She looked thoughtfully at the fading bruises on his jaw. "You were in a fight recently."

He merely raised his eyebrows.

She pointed with her chin. "Those marks on your jaw. Someone hit you."

"Samuel?" Rebecca was staring at her brother, too, now.

"It's nothing," he said.

"You keep so much of yourself hidden from me, don't you?" Rebecca whispered. "Most of yourself, in fact."

His eyebrows drew together. "Becca—"

"No." She turned her face to the window. "I'm too tired to argue tonight."

"I'm sorry," he said.

Rebecca gave a great sigh as if the weight of the world rested on her shoulders. "I didn't even get to dance."

Samuel looked at Emeline as if for help, but she was no more in sympathy with him than his sister. She stared out the black window, watching her own reflection. She noticed that the small lines about her mouth made her look particularly old tonight.

They traveled the remainder of the journey home in silence, the carriage rocking and swaying as it rattled through the nighttime London streets. By the time they pulled up in front of her house, Emeline felt stiff and sore and as if she'd be quite happy never to attend another ball in her life. The carriage door opened, and the footman pulled down the metal steps. Samuel got out and helped his sister descend. Rebecca didn't wait but immediately ran up the steps to her brother's town house and disappeared inside. Samuel stared after her, frowning, but didn't move to follow. He held out his hand to Emeline.

She inhaled and carefully placed her fingertips in his. Despite her precaution, he pulled her close as she stepped down.

"Ask me in," he murmured as she passed him.

Cheek! She made the cobblestones in front of her own home and attempted to withdraw her hand. He wouldn't let her. She raised her head and met his eyes. His were slightly narrowed, his mouth a determined horizontal line.

"Mr. Hartley," she said coldly. "Will you come inside for a moment? I have a painting in my sitting room that I would like to have your opinion on."

He nodded and released her hand. But he followed her

closely as she mounted the steps to her house, as if he suspected a trick.

Inside, Emeline gave her wrap to Crabs. "Prepare the sitting room, please."

Crabs had been with her since before her marriage, and in all those years, Emeline had yet to see him surprised. Tonight was no different.

"My lady." The butler snapped his fingers, and two footmen ran to begin lighting candles and setting the fire.

Emeline glided after them. She went straight across the dark room and stood by the window, pretending to look out, although of course all she could see was her own ghostly reflection. After a while, the bustling behind her died and she heard the door shut. She turned.

Samuel was stalking toward her, his face quite grim in the candlelight. "Why Vale?"

"What?"

He continued coming, his footsteps disconcertingly silent on the sitting room carpet. "Vale. Why marry him?"

She clutched the fabric of her overskirt in her right hand and tilted her chin up. "Why not? I've known him since childhood."

He halted in front of her finally, much, much too close, damn him, and she was forced to crane her neck up in order to meet his eyes.

His angry eyes. "Do you love him?"

"How dare you?" she breathed.

His nostrils flared, but that was his only reaction. "Do you love him?"

She swallowed. "Of course I love him. Jasper is like a brother to me—"

He gave a nasty bark of laughter. "Would you make love to your brother?"

She slapped him. The sound echoed in the room, and her hand stung. She drew back in appalled shock at her own violence, but before she could say anything—even *think* to say anything—he'd grasped her.

He pulled her close and lowered his head until she felt his breath brush her cheek. "He kisses you like a brother. As if you meant no more to him than the maid who brings his tea in the morning. Is that what you really want from your marriage?"

"Yes." She glared up at him, so intimately close. Her hands had nowhere to go but his shoulders, and she clutched him as if they embraced. As if they were lovers. "Yes, that's what I want. A civilized man. An Englishman who knows the rules of society, an aristocrat to help me with my son and my lands. We are perfectly suited, Jasper and I. We are as alike as two peas in a pod."

She saw the hurt in his eyes. It was very subtle, few other people, perhaps no other person, would understand it, but she saw and comprehended. She was hurting him.

So she drove the knife home. "We will be married soon, and I will be very, very happy—"

"Goddamn you," he growled, and then he kissed her.

His mouth ground down over hers, smashing her lips against her teeth until she tasted blood. She tried to twist away, but he clutched her harder and lifted her from the ground so she had no purchase. She arched her head and he followed, walking with her until her back was against the wall. And then she truly had nowhere to go. She should've given up then—she knew he would never really hurt her—but something inside her refused to admit defeat. She opened her mouth, and when he hesitated for a fraction of a second, she took advantage.

She *bit* him.

He reared back and grinned at her, his beautiful lower lip bloody. "Cat."

She would've hit him then—*again*—if he didn't already have control of her arms.

And then it was too late. He'd bent his head to hers. This time his lips were soft, brushing over hers delicately, lightly. Teasing, as if he had all the time in the world. She pushed her face forward, to deepen the contact, but he moved aside. Perhaps he was afraid she'd bite him again. Perhaps he was merely toying with her. She couldn't think anymore, and it didn't seem to matter, anyway. He returned, like a moth alighting on her lips. Softly, sweetly, as if she were made of spun glass, a delicate, fragile creature instead of the cat he'd just called her.

In the end, she couldn't hold out. She parted her lips as shyly as a virgin, as if she'd never been kissed before. Maybe she hadn't—not like this, anyway. The tip of his tongue darted into her mouth and out again, and her tongue followed. She pursued him into his mouth, and he sucked at her, gently, oh, so gently, biting. His entire weight was pressed against her, holding her upright against the wall. And she wished, desperately, that there were not so many layers of fabric between them. That she could feel that hardness—feel him. She moaned, a whispering, light sound, entirely unlike herself, and he stilled.

He lowered her gently to the ground and took his mouth, his hands, and himself away from her. She stared at him, completely at a loss for words.

He bowed. "Good night." And he left the room.

Her legs were shaky, and for a moment she simply leaned against her sitting room wall, not even attempting to walk to the settee for fear her legs would collapse beneath her. As she leaned there, she licked her lips and tasted blood.

Whether his or hers she could not tell.

A CIVILIZED MAN. Sam shouldered past the gawking footmen and out of Emeline's town house. *A civilized man.* He ran down the steps and continued running, the familiar feel of his muscles lengthening and warming a comfort.

A civilized man.

Of all the words that could be used to describe him, *civilized* was the last anyone would use. He rounded a corner and had to dodge a group of drunken riffraff. The men scattered apart in surprise at his appearance. By the time they started yelling insults, Sam was yards away. He continued down the street, ducking on a whim into a dark alley. His feet pounded rhythmically against cobblestones, each footfall a silent jolt to the body. With every step, his body grew looser, more well oiled, until he ran almost without volition, almost without effort. The momentum built until he flew. He could run like this for miles, hours, *days* if he had to.

There was no point in lusting after a woman who didn't want him. In Boston he was a well-respected figure, a leader of the trading community, thanks to his uncle's business and the wealth he'd amassed since inheriting it. In only the last year he'd been approached twice by keen fathers, making it known that Sam would be a welcome son-in-law. The ladies in each case were pleasant enough, but there'd been no spark. Nothing to make him single them out as special. He'd begun to think that his standards were too high. That a man in his position should settle on good family and a pretty face as adequate for a contented marriage.

Sam cursed and quickened his pace, leaping over a pile of trash. And now he felt a stupid, wholly uncontrollable yearning for a woman he simply could not have. A woman who wanted a *civilized* man. Why her? Why this prickly aristocrat who didn't even like him?

He halted, placing his hands on the small of his back to stretch it. It was all a joke of the cosmos, it must be, for it all to come together at once as it had tonight. His nightmares about the massacre, made real and terribly tangible in the ballroom. His confrontation with Vale. The horrible revelation that *she* was engaged to that aristocratic prig. He threw back his head and laughed at the night and the black sky and his world that was trembling around him, about to fall. A cat startled and scurried into the shadows, howling its displeasure.

And then he ran again.

EMELINE TOUCHED ONE finger to the green baize book cover. A fine dusting of rot fell to the tabletop. She'd found the fairy-tale book that Reynaud and she had spent so many hours poring over as children. It had necessitated an extensive search of the attics all this morning, accompanied by much sneezing and filth, and she'd had to take a hot bath afterward, but she'd found the book. Now she'd placed it on a table in her sitting room as she contemplated her find.

What she hadn't expected was that it would be in such terrible condition. In her memory, the book was pristine and new, Reynaud's long, slim fingers deftly turning the pages. In truth, the worms and moths had evidently been at the book. The binding was warped, the pages yellowed and falling out. Quite a few were stained from damp and mold. Emeline frowned as she traced the embossing on a corner of the cover. It depicted a pike or staff laid against a worn soldier's pack, as if a soldier home from war had set the items by his front door.

She sighed and turned back the cover to reveal the other unfortunate surprise. The book was in German—something she's completely forgotten from her youth. She'd barely begun to read when she and Reynaud looked at the book, and she'd spent most of the time examining the illustrations.

At least she thought the language was German. On the frontispiece was the title in ornate, nearly illegible letters and beneath was a crude woodcut illustration. It showed four soldiers in tall métier hats and gaiters marching side by side. Nanny had been a Prussian émigré, having crossed the Channel when she was a little girl. The book must have originally been hers. Had Nanny told the stories from memory or had she translated them into English as she turned the pages?

Voices came from the hallway outside the sitting room door, and Emeline straightened away from the table, walking several paces from it. For some reason, she didn't want to share her find just yet with her guests.

The door opened to reveal Crabs. "Lord Vale and Mr. Hartley are here, my lady."

Emeline nodded. "Show them in."

She struggled to hide her surprise. She'd invited them to tea this morning, but it had never occurred to her, after last night's disagreement, that they'd arrive together. Yet here they came, Jasper first in a striking scarlet coat with yellow trim and a cobalt blue waistcoat that caught the color of his eyes. His dark mahogany hair was clubbed back in an unpowdered queue that no doubt had been quite neat when he'd left his valet this morning. Now, however, curling locks rioted about his temples. Emeline knew quite a few girls who'd cheerfully kill their nearest and dearest for hair like Jasper's.

"My sweet." Jasper advanced and caught her a careless kiss somewhere near her left ear. Emeline, looking over Jasper's shoulder, met Samuel's enigmatic gaze. The colonial was in brown again today, and, although the handsomer man, standing next to Jasper, he appeared like a crow in the shadow of a peacock. The viscount stepped back and threw himself into one of her setting-sun orange chairs. "Hartley and I have come hat in hand like petitioners before a queen. What would you have with us? Do you mean to broker a peace?"

"Perhaps." Emeline smiled quickly at Jasper and then turned to Samuel, bracing herself for the contact. "Will your sister join us?"

"No." Samuel laid his long fingertips against the back of a chair. "She sends her apologies and pleads a migraine."

"I'm sorry to hear that." Emeline gestured to a chair. "Please. Won't you sit, Mr. Hartley?"

He inclined his head and sat. His hair was tightly braided in a military queue today, every strand contained and controlled, and the sight made her perversely want to take it apart. To let his hair stream round his shoulders and run her fingers through it until it pulled at his scalp.

The maids bustled in with tea at that moment, and Emeline was glad to take the chance to calm herself. She sat and oversaw the placement of the tea things and kept her eyes down, away from the wall and away from *him*. Just last night he'd kissed her in this very room. He'd pressed her against the wall beside the window, and he'd traced her lips with his tongue, and she'd bit him. She'd tasted his blood.

Her teaspoon clattered as Emeline's hand trembled. She glanced up, right into Samuel's dark stare. His face looked carved from stone.

She cleared her throat and glanced away. "Tea, Jasper?"

"Yes, please," he replied cheerfully.

Was he completely oblivious to the undercurrents between her and Samuel? Or perhaps he was aware and chose not to notice. They had a very civilized understanding, after all. She didn't expect him to live like a monk before marriage—or indeed afterward, if it came to that—and perhaps he was equally tolerant.

She handed the teacup to Jasper and asked without looking up, "Mr. Hartley?"

There was a silence. Jasper noisily stirred sugar into his tea—he had a horrible sweet tooth—and took a sip.

"Tea, Mr. Hartley?"

She stared at her fingers curled around the teapot handle until she couldn't stand it any longer. Jasper must surely know something was wrong. She looked up.

Samuel still watched her. "Yes. I'd like some tea." But that wasn't what his deep voice said.

She shuddered, actually felt the tremor run through her, and knew she was embarrassingly hot. The teapot rattled against the cup as she poured. Abominable man! Did he want to humiliate her?

Meanwhile, Jasper had his dish of tea balanced precariously on one knee. He seemed to have forgotten it after a couple of sips, and now the cup sat, just waiting for a sudden movement to crash to the floor.

"Sam said something earlier about a Dick Thornton, Emmie," he said. "I don't recall a Thornton. 'Course with over four hundred men in the regiment originally, one didn't know them all by name. Most by sight, but not by name."

Samuel had placed his own cup on a side table next to his chair. "After Quebec, there were less than that."

Emeline cleared her throat. "Mr. Thornton was a common soldier? I never would have guessed from meeting him the other day. His speech was quite clear."

"Thornton was a private when we knew him in the war," Samuel said. "He was great friends with another soldier, MacDonald—"

"The redheaded twins!" Jasper exclaimed. "Always together, always up to a bit of mischief."

Samuel nodded. "That's right."

Emeline looked from one man to the other. They'd seemed to have made some strange male accord without any help from her. "You know this MacDonald as well?"

Jasper sat forward, nearly upsetting the cup of tea. "Damn me, now I remember. Bad business, that. Weren't MacDonald and his friend Brown brought up on charges of murder and—*ahem!*" He cut off the rest of his sentence with a cough and an embarrassed glance at Emeline.

She raised her eyebrows. From the look the gentlemen exchanged, whatever the *bad business* was about, it must be horrible enough that they deemed it unsuitable for her ears. She sighed in frustration. Men were so silly sometimes.

"Did MacDonald survive the massacre?" Jasper asked.

Samuel shook his head. "No. Thornton said he saw Mac-Donald fall, and Brown must've died in the assault as well. We would've heard of his court-martial if he had survived."

"But we don't know for certain about Brown."

"No."

"We ought to ask Thornton, see if he knows," Jasper mused.

Samuel elevated his eyebrows. *"We?"*

Jasper looked like a little boy embarrassed—an expression Emeline was familiar with from childhood. It was one he often used to get his own way without too much argument. "I thought I might help you in your inquiries, since I'm not the traitor."

"I'm relieved you have acquitted yourself," Samuel began rather stiffly, "but I'm not so sanguine—"

"Oh, come, Samuel!" Emeline burst out. "You know Jasper isn't the traitor. Admit it." She glared at him, only belatedly realizing that she'd used his Christian name.

Samuel made a pretty, overshowy bow to her. "As my lady wishes." He turned to Jasper. "I admit your innocence, if only to appease *your* fiancée."

"Kind of you, I'm sure." Jasper smiled with exposed teeth.

Samuel bared his teeth back.

Emeline straightened determinedly. "So it is decided, then. You will investigate the massacre and its aftermath. Together."

Jasper raised his eyebrows at Samuel.

Who nodded grimly. "Together."

Chapter Eight

*Day after day and night after night, Iron Heart
guarded Princess Solace. He stood behind her as
she ate her meals. He followed her as she paced the
royal gardens. He rode beside her as she hunted with
her falcons. And he listened with a grave face as she
told him her thoughts, her feelings, and the deepest
secrets that lay hidden in her heart. It is a strange
fact, but a true one nonetheless: a lady may come to
love a man though he speak not a word....*
—from *Iron Heart*

Rebecca cracked the door to her room and peered out. The
hall outside seemed deserted. Moving quietly, she tiptoed
into the hall and shut the door behind her. She was supposed to be lying down with an aching head. Evans had
already supplied her with a scented cloth and the instructions to keep it on her forehead for the next half hour. But
since the headache had only been an excuse in the first
place, Rebecca didn't feel any guilt about not following

orders. What she did feel was a sneaking fear of her own maid. Hence her furtive movements.

She crept down the stairs and headed toward the back of the house, to the door that led out to the garden. She'd been so frightened when Samuel had had that fit in the ballroom the night before. Her elder brother always seemed so solid, so strong and in control. To see Samuel suddenly shivering and white had terrified her. Samuel was the rock she leaned on. Without him, who would be her support?

Voices came from above, and Rebecca paused. The voices coalesced into two maids arguing over the cleaning of the fireplace grates, and she relaxed. The back passage was dark, but the door was just ahead. It was ridiculous, after the fear she'd felt for her brother in the ballroom, to then feel betrayed when he revealed his real reason for coming to England. She had been the one to beg to come on this trip. She'd been so happy—so *grateful*—when he acquiesced to her pleas. Now, her disappointment was in proportion to her initial happiness.

Rebecca pushed open the door that led into the back garden and fled into the sunlight. Perhaps because the true owners rented the town house out, its garden had a dismal air of neglect. There were no flowers, at least none in bloom. Instead, there were a few gravel paths bordered with shoulder-height hedges. Here and there, an ornamental tree grew, and sometimes the hedges parted to reveal a square or circle with miniature hedges cut into intricate patterns. Benches lined the path at frequent intervals in case the walker became tired of this monotonous scenery.

Rebecca wandered down one of the paths, letting her

hand idly brush the scraggly hedges as she passed. Her emotions for Samuel were overwrought, she knew. She felt as if she were always nagging him for his attention, like a little child, instead of a grown woman. Why she should feel this way, she wasn't clear. Perhaps—

"Good afternoon."

Rebecca started at the voice and swung around. The hedge parted to her right to reveal another one of the little square openings, and a man rose from the bench inside. He was red-haired, and for a moment she couldn't place him. He stepped forward, and she realized that it was Samuel's army friend, the one they'd met in the street. She couldn't remember his name.

"Oh! I didn't see you there."

He smiled, revealing lovely white teeth. "I'm sorry, I didn't mean to startle you."

"That's all right." There was a pause, and she glanced around the otherwise deserted garden. "Um . . . why . . . ?"

"You must be wondering what I'm doing in your lovely garden."

She nodded gratefully.

"Well, actually I came to call upon your brother," he said with a wry, confiding smile. "But he isn't in, so I came out here to wait for his return. I'd hoped we could catch up a bit, your brother and I. I don't see many men from the old regiment anymore. Most died, you know, in the massacre, and the ones who didn't were scattered to other regiments immediately afterward."

"Spinner's Falls," she whispered.

The name of the battle was engraved on her brain now. Samuel had never mentioned it to her. She'd had no inkling how important the event was to him until the ball last night.

Impulsively, she leaned toward the man. "Can you tell me about Spinner's Falls? What happened there? Samuel doesn't talk of it."

His eyebrows shot up, but he nodded. "Of course, of course. I understand exactly."

He clasped his hands behind his back and began strolling, his chin against his chest as he thought.

"The regiment was marching back from Quebec," he began. "After taking the fort from the Frenchies. Quebec was well fortified, and there'd been a long siege all that summer, but we'd prevailed in the end. Then it was autumn, and it was thought best by those in command to retire before the weather became inclement in winter. We began marching south, toward Fort Edward. None but the officers knew our route. The Indians lurked in the woods all around us. Our commander, Colonel Darby, wished to make the fort without alerting the savages to our presence."

"But that didn't happen," Rebecca said softly.

"No." He sighed. "No, it didn't. The regiment was attacked in the second week. We were marching only two abreast, and the line was strung out over almost half a mile when we were ambushed." He stopped talking.

Rebecca waited, but he didn't resume. They'd come to the far end of the garden by the back gate that led into the mews. She stopped and looked at Samuel's friend. What was his name? Why was she so terrible at remembering names?

"What happened then?"

He tipped his head up to squint at the sky, then darted

a look at her from the corner of his eye. "They attacked from both sides, and most of the men were killed. You know that the savages liked to cut off the scalps of their victims with their hatchets, as a kind of war trophy. You can imagine my dismay"—he patted his hair ruefully—"I actually heard one fellow shout to another that he wanted my scalp, it was so pretty."

Rebecca looked at the tips of her shoes. She wasn't sure if she was happy now to have finally heard something of what her brother had endured. Perhaps it would've been better to remain in ignorance.

"'Course," Samuel's friend was still speaking, "Mac-Donald wasn't so fortunate."

Rebecca blinked and glanced up. "What?"

He smiled a friendly smile and patted his hair again. "MacDonald. Another soldier, a friend of mine. His hair was as gingery as mine. The Indians took his scalp clean off, poor sod."

"YOU NEVER TOLD her how St. Aubyn died, did you?" Sam asked that afternoon. They rode in Vale's carriage, heading into the east end of London. Thornton hadn't been at his place of business, and so now they had decided to try Ned Allen, the surviving sergeant. Sam only hoped he was sober.

Vale turned from the window. "Emmie?"

Sam nodded.

"No. Of course I didn't tell her that her beloved brother was crucified and then burned alive." Vale flashed a grim smile. "Would you?"

"No." Sam held the other man's gaze, feeling a reluctant gratitude that Vale had stood firm against what had probably been a determined assault by Lady Emeline for information. He'd seen how the lady worked. Once she set her mind to it, only a very strong man would be able to hold out against her. Vale obviously was such a man. Damn him.

The viscount grunted and nodded. "Then we don't have a problem."

"We might."

Vale raised his eyebrows.

The carriage lurched around the corner, and Sam grabbed the leather strap hanging by his head. "She wants to know what happened. How Reynaud died."

"Christ." Vale closed his eyes as if in pain.

Sam looked away. He realized now that a craven part of him had been hoping the other man didn't care about Lady Emeline. That their engagement was a purely practical matter. Obviously that wasn't so.

"You mustn't tell her," Vale was saying. "There's no need for her to live with that image in her mind."

"I know that," Sam growled.

"Then we're in accord."

Sam nodded once.

Vale looked at him and started to say something, but the carriage lurched to a stop. He glanced out the window instead. "What a lovely part of London you've brought me to."

They were in the East End stews. The crumbling buildings were packed so closely together that sometimes only a walkway wide enough for a man separated them. They'd have to make the rest of the journey on foot.

Sam raised his eyebrows politely. "You can stay behind in the carriage if you're afraid."

The other man snorted.

The door opened and a footman set the step. The servant watched them with a knitted brow as they descended. "Shall I come with you, my lord? 'Tisn't safe hereabouts."

"We'll be fine." Vale clapped the man on the shoulder. "Stay and guard the carriage until our return."

"Yes, sir."

Sam led the way down a dark alley.

"He's right," Vale said behind him. "Do we really need to visit Ned Allen?"

Sam shrugged. "I don't have many others to question. There weren't a lot of survivors, as you know. And Allen was an officer."

"Hardly any survivors at all," Vale muttered. There was a splash and he swore.

Sam hid a grin.

"What happened to your lieutenant? Horn, wasn't it?"

"Matthew Horn. He's traveling the continent, last I heard."

"And the naturalist?"

"Munroe?" Vale's voice was casual, yet Sam knew he'd somehow won the other man's complete attention.

They entered a tiny courtyard, and Sam cast a swift glance around. The buildings here looked like they'd been erected hastily after the great fire and were already in the process of decaying. They leaned ominously into the small courtyard, which, judging from the smell, was also the local privy.

"The man who survived with you," Sam said. There had been a civilian naturalist attached to the 28th, a quiet

Scotsman who had been one of the men taken captive by the Wyandot.

"Alistair Munroe's up in Scotland, last I heard. He has a great drafty castle and doesn't go out much."

"Because of his wounds?" Sam asked softly. They ducked into the alley that led to the house Allen had a room in. Vale hadn't answered. Sam looked back.

Vale's eyes held demons, and Sam had the uneasy feeling that they might mirror his own. "You saw what those savages did to him. Would you want to go out with scars like that?"

Sam looked away. It had taken almost a fortnight for the rescue party to track the Wyandot Indians back to their camp, and in that time, the captured soldiers had been tortured. Munroe's wounds had been particularly gruesome. His hands...Sam pushed the thought aside and kept walking, keeping a keen eye on the doorways and shadows they passed. "No."

Vale nodded. "I haven't seen him in years."

"Still," Sam said. "We ought to write him a letter."

"I've tried. He never writes back." Vale quickened his steps until he was breathing down Sam's neck. "Who are you watching for?"

Sam glanced at him. "I was followed the other day."

"Really?" Vale sounded cheerful. "Why?"

"I don't know." And that fact disturbed him.

"You must've stirred something—or someone—up. Who had you been to see?"

Sam stopped beside a low lintel. "Ned Allen lives through here."

Vale merely looked at him and raised his shaggy eyebrows.

"I'd talked to three soldiers," Sam said impatiently. "Barrows and Douglas—"

"Don't remember them."

"You wouldn't. They were just foot soldiers and probably spent most of the massacre cowering under one of the supply wagons. They didn't seem to know anything. The third soldier was a pioneer in the army—"

"One of the fellows who cleared trees and such to make way for the marching column."

"Yes." Sam grimaced. "He described how he used his ax to decapitate one of the attacking Indians. He was quite proud of himself. He didn't tell me much beyond that. And I'd tried to talk to Allen, but he was too drunk the first time I tracked him down. I doubt either Allen or the pioneer sent my follower."

Vale smiled. "Interesting."

"If you say so." Sam ducked to enter the building. Inside, it was cold and dark. He made his way mostly by feel and memory.

Behind him, Vale swore.

"All right back there?" Sam drawled.

"Fine. Enjoying the quaint scenery," the viscount shot back.

Sam grinned. They climbed a series of stairs, and then he led the way to Allen's room. It was much as it had been before—smelly and small. Ned Allen lay in a corner, reduced to a bundle of rags.

Sam sighed and approached the man. The smell grew worse as he neared.

"Good God," Vale muttered as he followed. He toed Allen. "Stinking drunk."

"I don't think so." Sam hunkered by the prone man and

rolled him to his back. The man turned all of apiece, as if he were made of wood. A knife stuck out of his chest, the handle made of white bone. "He's dead."

Vale crouched beside him and stared. "Damn me."

"No doubt." Sam rose swiftly and wiped his hands against his breeches.

The room was suddenly too small, too close, too smelly. He turned, stumbling, and nearly ran from the room. He tumbled ungracefully down the stairs and out into the light. Even this grimy courtyard was better than the death room upstairs. Sam took deep breaths, trying to still the rolling nausea in his belly, aware as he made his way back into the narrow alleyway that Vale clattered behind him.

"He could've been killed by anyone, living in this cesspit," the viscount panted.

"Maybe." Sam felt a grudging gratitude that the other man didn't mention his ignoble retreat. "Or perhaps I was followed here before. The man who was trailing me had a bone-handled knife."

Vale sighed. "Then Sergeant Allen must've known something."

"Christ." Sam stopped. "I should've come back sooner."

Vale looked at him a moment and then tipped his head back to stare at the small patch of blue overhead. "There were so many."

Sam stared. "What?"

"Do you remember Tommy Pace?"

A memory of a young lad—too young to have told the truth about his age—came to Sam. Freckled cheeks, dark hair, a small wiry frame.

"He used to pretend to shave," Vale said dreamily. "Did you know that? He probably had all of three whiskers on his chin, and every morning he'd be stropping his razor, so proud."

"He won the razor off Ted Barnes."

"No." Vale looked at him. "I didn't know that."

Sam nodded. "In a card game. It was part of the reason Tommy was so proud of the thing."

Vale chuckled. "And Barnes had such a heavy beard. That's irony for you."

There was silence as they both contemplated this old gossip. A rodent scurried into the shadows near a doorway.

"And now they're both dust in the ground," Vale said softly, "along with all the rest."

There was nothing to say to that, so Sam pivoted and resumed walking back to the carriage.

Vale strolled a little behind him. The alley wasn't wide enough for two men to walk abreast.

"If they were betrayed, we'll avenge them. All of them," Vale said conversationally.

Sam nodded, keeping his eyes straight ahead.

"Where do we go now?" Vale asked.

"Dick Thornton. Perhaps he's returned to his place of work. We need to question him."

"Glad you agree." The viscount whistled a few merry notes and then cut himself off. "Did you see MacDonald's body, by the way?"

"No." They rounded the corner, and the carriage came into view, the footmen and driver standing around it looking nervous. "I never went back. I was too busy running to Fort Edward and then guiding the detachment with the ransom. That was one of the things I wanted to ask Allen: who among the regiment survived?"

Vale nodded, probably busy with his own terrible memories as they made their way back to where the carriage waited.

The footmen looked relieved when they came into sight. Vale nodded to his men, and Sam entered the carriage and settled into the seat across from the viscount. The carriage lurched forward.

"Did I ever thank you?" Vale asked. He was watching out the window, apparently engrossed in the dismal neighborhood.

"Yes," Sam lied. In fact, Vale had been in shock by the time the rescue party had ransomed the surviving officers at the Wyandot Indian camp. All of the captured men had run the gauntlet—a double line of whooping Indian men and women who had pummeled the victim as he ran by. Then, too, from what Sam heard, Vale had been made to watch St. Aubyn's death and the torture of Munroe and the others. Vale had been in no condition to thank anyone when they'd eventually rescued him.

Vale was frowning now. "So we only have Thornton's word that MacDonald is dead."

Sam looked at him. "Yes."

"Look here, if anyone had a reason to make sure the regiment never got to Fort Edward, it was MacDonald." Vale sat forward. "The man was in chains as we marched."

"He would've been hung at the fort," Sam said. "Rape and murder. His court-martial would've been very short."

MacDonald had been a nasty piece of work. He and another soldier named Brown had looted a French settler's cabin, raping and killing the settler's wife when she surprised them. Unfortunately for MacDonald and his companion, the French settler's wife had turned out to be an Englishwoman—and the sister of a British colonel. Looting and rape were hanging offenses, but ones that some officers might turn a blind eye to, as long as they weren't wholesale. The rape and murder of an Englishwoman was a crime that couldn't be swept under the rug. There had been a hunt within the British army, and soon soldiers had come forward with the information that Brown had drunkenly boasted of the crime. Once under arrest, Brown had soon betrayed MacDonald, and both men had been marching in chains when the 28th Regiment of Foot had been attacked.

That thought made Sam grimace. "Brown might also be the traitor."

Vale nodded. "MacDonald seemed to be the leader of that little gang, but you're right; Brown had just as much reason to stop the march as MacDonald."

"Or they might've been in it together." Sam shook his head. "But in either case, how would they have known the route we'd take?"

Vale shrugged. "Wasn't Brown friends with Allen?"

"Yes. They often shared their fire with Ned Allen."

"And as an officer, Allen would've known the route."

"He might've carried a message, if they'd bribed him."

"Surely not to a Frenchie?" Vale's eyebrows had shot up.

"No. But all they needed was an intermediary who could take a message to a neutral Indian, and as you know, there were plenty who either switched sides or dealt with both French and English."

"If Allen talked to someone about the route the regiment took, it would certainly be a motive to kill him."

Sam thought of the pathetic bag of bones they'd just found, and grimaced. "Yes, it would."

Vale shook his head. "There're holes to that theory, but in any case, we need to talk to Thornton again and determine what he remembers."

Sam frowned. Thornton had made him uneasy from the first. "Do you think that's wise? Bringing Thornton in on this? For all we know, he's the traitor."

"All the more reason to confide in him. If he thinks we trust him, he's more likely to slip." Vale touched his lips with a long, bony finger. Then he smiled, almost sweetly. "Keep your friends close, but your enemies closer."

EMELINE PAUSED JUST inside Samuel's town house garden. What was Rebecca doing with Mr. Thornton—alone?

"You may go now," she said absently to the butler who had shown her the way through the town house and into the garden.

She'd come calling in the hopes of finding Rebecca better. Perhaps they could go hunting for a pair of dancing slippers. New slippers always cheered Emeline up, and she felt the poor girl might need some reviving after the events of last night.

It seemed Rebecca was already revived.

Emeline squared her shoulders. "Good afternoon."

Rebecca jumped back from Mr. Thornton and turned a woefully guilty face toward Emeline.

Mr. Thornton, in contrast, pivoted smoothly. "Lady Emeline, how pleasant to meet you again."

Emeline narrowed her eyes. It was a point in the man's

favor that he'd been properly introduced to Rebecca, but it still didn't excuse his tête-à-tête with an unattended maiden. And in any case, it seemed odd to find Mr. Thornton in the garden with Rebecca so soon after talking about him with Samuel and Jasper. Very odd.

"Mr. Thornton." Emeline inclined her head. "How...*unexpected* to meet you here. Do you have business with Mr. Hartley?"

He smiled wider at her pointed question. "Yes, but it seems Mr. Hartley isn't at home. I was waiting here in the garden when Miss Hartley joined me and made my wait so much easier." He finished his pretty speech with a courtly little bow in Rebecca's direction.

Humph. Emeline linked her arm with Rebecca and began to stroll. "I believe you said you were in trade, Mr. Thornton."

The garden path was narrow, and the man was forced to trail behind the ladies. "Yes, I make boots."

"Boots. Ah, I see." Emeline didn't bother looking around. The town house garden was mediocre, but she kept her pace slow as if she might actually be interested in dying foliage.

"Boots are very important, I'm sure," Rebecca said, coming to Mr. Thornton's defense, which was not at all what Emeline had intended.

"I supply them to His Majesty's army," Mr. Thornton called from in back.

"Quite." It occurred to Emeline that Mr. Thornton might very well be rich. She had so little knowledge of the workings of the army, but she could imagine the piles of boots that would be ordered from Mr. Thornton.

"Are they made here in London?" Rebecca asked. She craned her neck a little to try to see him.

"Oh, yes. I have a workshop on Dover Street and employ thirty-two fellows there."

"Then you do not make the boots yourself?" Emeline inquired sweetly.

Rebecca gasped, but Mr. Thornton replied cheerfully enough, "No, my lady. I'm afraid I wouldn't even know where to start. Father used to, of course, when he began the business, but before long he'd hired other fellows to do the work for him. I might've learned when I was young, but I had a falling-out with Pater—"

"Is that why you joined the army?" Rebecca interrupted. She stopped and turned to face Mr. Thornton, and Emeline was forced to halt as well.

Mr. Thornton smiled, and Emeline realized that he was rather handsome in a bland sort of way. He wasn't the type of man one would notice in a crowd, but perhaps that made him all the more dangerous.

"Yes, I'm afraid I took the king's shilling in a fit of callow pique. Left Pater and my wife—"

"You're married?" Emeline cut in.

"No." Mr. Thornton's expression sobered. "Poor Marie died not long after I returned home."

"Oh! I am so sorry," Rebecca murmured.

Emeline looked back down the path. Someone was coming.

"It was a terrible blow," Mr. Thornton said. "She—"

"Emmie! Ah, there you are." Jasper was striding up the path, his long, horsey face beaming.

Mr. Thornton stopped and turned at the sound of Jasper's voice, his features going curiously blank. But Jasper wasn't who she had expected. Confusion and a kind of disappointment shot through her, and then she saw him. Behind Jasper, Samuel followed, his eyes hooded, his expression sober.

Emeline held out her hands. "Why, Jasper, I did not expect you back until nightfall, if at all. Have you been successful in your investigations?"

Jasper took her hands and bent over them, brushing a kiss against her knuckles. "We lost the trail, alas, and went hunting Mr. Thornton instead. Except he wasn't at his business, and we retired here in defeat only to find you have supplied the man we looked for."

By this time, Samuel had caught up to Jasper. "Lady Emeline, Rebecca." He nodded at them and then held out a hand to his guest. "Mr. Thornton, it is good to see you, although I confess some surprise at finding you at my house."

Mr. Thornton grasped Samuel's hand in both of his. "You are no more surprised than I, Mr. Hartley. I had not intended to presume upon your hospitality, but I was in the area, and my feet led me to your house whether I willed it so or not."

"Indeed?" Samuel cocked his head, watching the other man.

"Yes. Maybe it was our reminiscences of the war the other day. I..." He hesitated a moment, looking down before raising his gaze to stare frankly in Samuel's eyes. "You will think me an imaginative fellow, but I had the sensation when we talked that you did not think what happened at Spinner's Falls occurred by happenstance."

There was a silence as both men looked at each other. Samuel was fully a head taller than the other man, but there were certain similarities otherwise that were hard to overlook. They were both self-made men who worked in trade. They both carried themselves with a certain raw confidence, an ability to look a higher-born gentleman in the eye and dare him to make comment. And, Emeline sensed, to have succeeded in what they did, both men would have had to be daring. They were men who could see a chance and seize it, knowing the consequences might very well be dangerous.

At last, Samuel glanced sideways at her and Rebecca. He cleared his throat. "Perhaps if the ladies permit, we gentlemen should retire to my study inside to discuss this in private."

Emeline arched an eyebrow. Did he really think she could be fobbed off that easily? "Oh, I'm most interested in what you have to say to Mr. Thornton. Please. Continue."

"I say, Emmie," Jasper began rather nervously.

She didn't look at Jasper, her eyes holding Samuel's gaze. "It's the least you can do, don't you think?"

She saw a muscle in his jaw flex, and he certainly didn't look happy, but he nodded before turning to Mr. Thornton. "We were betrayed."

Emeline felt a flicker of satisfaction. Samuel treated her as an equal, and that kind of trust was curiously heady.

Then Mr. Thornton blew out a breath. "I knew it."

"Did you?" Samuel asked softly.

"At the time, no." Mr. Thornton looked grim now. "But there were so many circumstances that had to align correctly for us to have been attacked at that point, and the fact that the Indians numbered so many"—he shook his head—"the thing must have been planned by someone."

"That's what it looks like," Jasper finally spoke. "We had meant to ask you if you were certain that MacDonald and Brown were dead."

"MacDonald?" For a moment, Mr. Thornton looked confused; then he glanced quickly at the ladies and nodded. "Oh, of course. I see where your thoughts lie, but I'm afraid both men were quite dead. I helped bury them."

Emeline pursed her lips, wondering for a moment what the men weren't saying about MacDonald. She'd have to ask Samuel later, in private.

"Damn," Jasper muttered. "If it'd been MacDonald, it would've wrapped this up neatly. Nevertheless, we have a few more questions to make of you."

"Perhaps we should adjourn inside," Samuel said. He held his arm out to his sister, but Rebecca ignored it and took Mr. Thornton's instead. Samuel's lips thinned.

Emeline hated to see him hurt. She laid her hand on Samuel's sleeve. "What a good idea. I'd enjoy some tea."

Samuel glanced from her eyes to her hand and back again. His brows rose almost imperceptibly. She tilted her chin at him. But the others were moving toward the back of the town house now.

"I don't know if I can be of any use," Mr. Thornton was saying ahead of them. "The man you really ought to talk to is Corporal Craddock."

"Why is that?" Samuel called to him.

Mr. Thornton looked over his shoulder. "He gathered the wounded after Spinner's Falls, after you'd... Well, you'd run into the woods. I guess you could say he was the officer in charge."

Emeline felt Samuel's arm stiffen under her fingers, but he didn't say anything.

Jasper seemed not to have noticed that Mr. Thornton had nearly called Samuel a coward to his face. "Is he here in town?"

"No. I believe he retired to the country after the war. I could be wrong, of course; one hears so many things. But I think he's in Sussex, near Portsmouth."

Emeline thought she hid it well, but Samuel must've felt her start nonetheless.

"What is it?" he murmured without taking his eyes from the path ahead.

She hesitated. She'd just sorted her stack of invitations this morning, trying to determine the social events that would be best to attend in the upcoming month.

He looked at her, his brows drawn. "Tell me."

Really, what choice did she have? It was almost as if the Fates had arranged the trap, and she was the unlucky hare that had run straight into it. Was there any point in struggling at all?

"We've been invited to the Hasselthorpe estate in Sussex."

"What's this?" Jasper had halted and turned.

"Lord and Lady Hasselthorpe, dear. Remember? They invited us weeks ago, and their house isn't far from Portsmouth."

"Damn me, you're right." The furrows next to Jasper's nose and mouth stretched into arcs as he grinned. "What a stroke of luck! We can all go to this house party and then call on Craddock. That is..." He looked worriedly at Mr. Thornton. Rebecca and Samuel were easily included in the invitation as friends of Emeline's. A bootmaker— even a very rich one—was a different matter.

But Mr. Thornton grinned and winked. "Never fear, I

can continue our inquiries here in London whilst you talk to Craddock."

And like that, Emeline knew that it was all decided. Her breath seemed to grow short as if her chest were being squeezed. Oh, they would argue and discuss the details back and forth, and she would need to petition Lady Hasselthorpe for invitations for the Hartleys, but in the end, it would all work out. She would be attending a house party with Samuel.

She looked up, knowing that he was watching her, and as her eyes met his warm coffee-brown ones, she wondered, Did he know what went on at house parties?

Chapter Nine

*Now, of all the things in the world that the king loved,
he loved his daughter most of all. He so doted on
her that whenever she asked for a thing, he did his
utmost to see that she received it. Which is why,
when Princess Solace begged the king for permission
to marry her own guard, instead of being a trifle
tetchy as most royal parents might, he simply
sighed and nodded. And that is how Iron Heart
came to marry the most beautiful maiden in
the land and a princess to boot....*
—from *Iron Heart*

"Will you be gone a *very* long time?" Daniel asked a week later.

He was lying on Emeline's bed, head hanging off one end, both feet in the air, completely in the way of Harris, who was packing.

"Probably a fortnight," Emeline said briskly. She sat at

her pretty little dresser trying to decide which jewelry to bring to the Hasselthorpe house party.

"A fortnight is fourteen days. That's a terrible long time." Daniel swung a foot and got it tangled in the bed curtains.

"Lord Eddings!" Harris exclaimed.

Really, one ought not to miss one's own offspring. She knew that. Many mothers of her rank hardly saw their children at all. Yet she hated leaving him. It was just so heart-wrenching to say good-bye.

"That will be all," Emeline told her lady's maid.

"But, my lady, I haven't half finished."

"I know." Emeline smiled at Harris. "You've been working so hard, you must be in need of refreshment. Why don't you take some tea in the kitchen?"

Harris pursed her lips, but she knew better than to contradict her mistress. She set down the pile of clothes she'd been holding and marched out of the room, closing the door behind her.

Emeline got up and went to the bed, shoving aside the mound of petticoats laid out on the surface to make a space. Then she sat, her back against the great oak headboard, her legs straight in front of her on the bed. "Come here."

Daniel scrambled toward her like an eager puppy. "I don't want you to go."

He squirmed against her, smelling of little boy sweat, his knobby knees digging into her hip.

She stroked his blond curls. "I know, darling. But I shan't be gone overlong, and I shall write you every day."

More silent squirming. His face was hidden against her breast.

"Tante Cristelle will stay here with you," Emeline whispered. "I don't suppose you shall have any currant buns or sticky sweets or pies at all whilst I'm gone. You'll have quite wasted away by the time I return and look like a stick boy and I shan't recognize you."

Breathy giggles came from her side until his blue eyes surfaced once again. "Silly. Tante will give me lots of sweets."

Emeline feigned shock. "Do you think so? She's very severe with me."

"I'll be fat when you come back." He puffed out his cheeks to show her.

She laughed appreciatively.

"I can talk to Mr. Hartley, too," he said.

Emeline blinked, startled. "I'm sorry, darling, but Mr. Hartley and his sister will be at the house party as well."

Her son's lower lip protruded.

"Have you been talking to Mr. Hartley often?"

He darted a look at her. "I talk to him over the wall, and sometimes I go to visit him in his garden. But I don't bother him, really I don't."

Emeline was skeptical about this last. Right now, though, her mind was more taken up with the notion that Daniel and Samuel seemed to have formed a bond without her even knowing it. She wasn't sure how she felt about that.

Her thoughts were interrupted by the squirming imp beside her. "Can you sing me my song?" he asked in a small voice.

So she stroked his hair and sang "Billy Boy," changing the name to Danny as she had since he was a baby, making it his song.

Oh, where have you been,
Danny Boy, Danny Boy?

> *Oh, where have you been,*
> *Charming Danny?*

And as she sang, Emeline wondered what the next fort-night would bring.

THE RENTED CARRIAGE was not as well-sprung as Lady Emeline's vehicle, and Sam was beginning to regret decid-ing to ride inside with Rebecca instead of renting a horse for himself. But he and Becca had hardly talked in the week since the disastrous Westerton ball, and he'd hoped that the enforced time together would break the spell.

So far, it hadn't.

Rebecca sat across from him and stared out the window as if the view of hedges and fields were the most fascinat-ing in the world. Her profile wasn't a classic one, but it was very pleasing to him. Sometimes, when he caught sight of her out of the corner of his eye, he'd have a flash of recog-nition. She looked a little like their mother.

Sam cleared his throat. "There'll be a dance, I think."

Becca turned and wrinkled her brow at him. "What?"

"I say, I think there'll be a dance. At the house party."

"Oh, yes?" She didn't seem particularly interested.

He'd thought she'd be delighted. "I'm sorry I ruined the last one for you."

She blew out a breath as if exasperated. "Why didn't you tell me, Samuel?"

He stared at her a moment, trying to understand what she meant. Then a horrible chill crept through his belly. Surely she wasn't talking about..."Tell you what?"

"You know." Her lips crimped in her frustration. "You never talk to me; you never—"

"We're talking right now."

"But you're not saying anything!" She spoke the words too loudly and then looked chagrined. "You never say anything, even when people make terrible accusations about you. Mr. Thornton came close to calling you a coward to your face when we were in the garden last week, and you never said a word to him. Why can't you defend yourself at least?"

He felt his lip curl. "What people like Thornton say isn't worth replying to."

"So you'd rather remain silent and let yourself be condemned?"

He shook his head. There was no way to explain his actions to her.

"Samuel, I'm not those people. Even if you won't justify yourself to them, you must talk to me. We are the only family we have left. Uncle Thomas is dead, and Father and Mother died before I could ever know them. Is it so wrong that I want to be closer to you? That I want to know what my brother faced in the war?"

It was his turn to stare out the window now, and he swallowed bile. There seemed to be the smell of men's sweat in the close carriage, but he knew that it was his brain playing abominable tricks on him. "It isn't easy to talk of war."

"Yet I've heard other men do so," she said softly. "Calvary officers bragging of charges and sailors talking of battles at sea."

He frowned impatiently. "They're not..."

"Not what?" She leaned forward over her knees as if she would will the words from him. "Tell me, Samuel."

He held her gaze, although it caused him physical pain to do so. "The soldiers who have seen close action, the soldiers who have felt another man's breath before taking it from him…" He closed his eyes. "Those soldiers hardly ever speak about it. It's not something we want to remember. It hurts."

There was a silence, and then she whispered, "Then what can you talk about? There must be something."

He stared at her, and a rueful smile curved his lips at a memory. "The rain."

"What?"

"When it rains on a march, there's nowhere to hide. The men and their clothes and all the provisions get wet. The trail turns to mud beneath your boots, and the men begin to slip. And once one falls, it's a rule, it seems, that half a dozen will fall next, their clothes and hair all over mud."

"But surely you can pitch a tent when you stop for the night?"

"We can, but the tent will be wet as well by then and the ground underneath a sea of mud, and in the end, one wonders if it would be better to simply sleep in the open."

She was smiling at him, and his heart lightened at the sight. "Poor Samuel! I never dreamed you spent so much time in the mud as a soldier. I always imagined you performing heroic feats."

"My heroic feats mostly involved a kettle."

"A kettle?"

He nodded, relaxing against the carriage seat now. "After a day's march in the rain, our provisions were always wet, including the dry peas and meal."

She wrinkled her nose. "Wet meal?"

"Wet and sticky. And sometimes we'd have to make it last another week, wet or no."

"Wouldn't it mold?"

"Very often. By the end of that week, the meal might be mostly green."

"Oh." She covered her nose as if she could smell the rotten meal. "What did you do?"

He leaned forward and whispered, "Ah, this is quite the secret. Many in the army wanted to know what I did with my little kettle."

"You're teasing now. Tell me what you did with a kettle that was so heroic."

He shrugged modestly. "Only fed my entire camp with rotten meal. I found that if I rinsed the meal three times and then threw it in with a kettle full of water, it made a nice soup. Of course, it was better on the days I'd caught a rabbit or squirrel."

"How absolutely awful," his sister said.

"You did ask." He grinned at her. She was talking to him, and he'd bore her to death with silly stories of army life if it made her happy.

"Samuel…"

"What, dear?" His heart squeezed at her uncertain expression. She was right; they were their only family left to each other. It was important that she not grow distant. "Tell me."

She bit her lip, and he was reminded of how young she was. "Do you think they will converse with me, all these titled English ladies?"

He wished in that moment that he could smooth the way for her, make sure that she was never hurt for the rest of her life. But he could only tell the truth. "I think most will. There's bound to be a girl or two who will have their noses in the air, but those are the sort who aren't worth talking to, anyway."

"Oh, I know. It's just that I'm so nervous. I never seem to know what to do with my hands, and I wonder if my hair has been properly done."

"You've that maid Lady Emeline found for you. I'll be there and Lady Emeline as well. She at least will not let you go out with your hair improperly done. And I think you perfect in any case."

She blushed, her cheeks tinting a delicate pink. "Do you really?"

"Yes."

"Well, then I shall remember that my brother was the best rotten meal soup maker in His Majesty's army, and I shall hold my head high."

He laughed and she grinned back. The carriage bumped over something in the road, and Sam looked out the window to see that they were crossing a narrow stone bridge, the carriage's sides nearly scraping the walls.

Rebecca's gaze followed his. "Are we coming to a town?"

He pushed aside the curtain to peer farther ahead. "No." He let the curtain drop and looked at her. "But it won't be much longer now, I think."

"Thank goodness. I am sore." She shifted restlessly in her seat. "It's a pity poor Mr. Thornton could not come."

"I don't think he minds."

"But…" She wrinkled her brow. "It does seem hypocritical, doesn't it? I mean, that he's not been invited just because he makes boots? You're in trade, too."

"True."

"In the Colonies, I don't think we would make such a fine distinction." She frowned down at her hands.

Sam was silent. The fact was, these kinds of distinctions between men's rank bothered him as well.

"It seems so much harder, here in England, for a man to raise himself purely by merit alone." Rebecca was nibbling her lip now, still staring down at her hands. "Even Mr. Thornton had his father's business, small though it might have originally been. A man who hadn't even that—who was perhaps a servant—could he ever become respectable?"

Sam narrowed his eyes, wondering if she was thinking of a particular servant. "Perhaps. With a bit of luck and—"

"But it's not likely, is it?" She looked up.

"No," he said softly. "It isn't very likely that a man who labors as a servant will become a man of means in England. Most will live and die a servant."

Her lips parted as if she would say something further. Then she closed them firmly and gazed out the window instead. They were silent again, but this time the silence was a companionable one. Sam closed his eyes and leaned his head back against the seat. He wondered sleepily just how much his sister's questions were prompted by O'Hare the footman.

He dozed a bit, and when he next woke, the carriage was turning into an enormous drive.

"It's very large, isn't it?" Rebecca said in a small voice.

Sam had to agree. The Hasselthorpe home was more a rolling mansion. It squatted complacently at the end of the gravel drive, in the middle of a vast field of mown grass, all the better to reflect its glory. Several generations had obviously been at work on the gray stone structure. Here were gothic windows, there, Tudor chimneys; the different styles jumbled together only gave notice that the family that lived here had been in residence for centuries. In front, the drive circled and there were already four carriages there, depositing gentlemen and ladies of the ton.

Samuel straightened and gave a reassuring smile to Rebecca. "We've arrived."

IT WAS A perfect day for an outdoor picnic, Emeline reflected the next morning. The sun shone and the sky was bright blue with fluffy white clouds. There was a tiny little breeze, just enough to play with the ribbons on the ladies' hats, but not so much that it blew their hats off. The gentlemen looked handsome and manly. The ladies pretty and delicate. The grass was still green and the view lovely: rolling hills with a few sheep to give it interest. One couldn't ask for more.

Or rather one *shouldn't* have to ask for more, because unfortunately, Lady Hasselthorpe had forgotten the wine. To be fair, the lack of drink was technically the fault of the housekeeper, but every lady knew that the servant reflected the mistress. A good chatelaine hired a competent housekeeper. An absentminded chatelaine made do with a housekeeper who forgot to pack the wine.

Emeline sighed. It was funny how thirsty one became the moment it was discovered that there wasn't anything to drink. The first footman had already sent back several of his fellows for the wine, but as the luncheon party had walked over half an hour to find this lovely spot, it would take some time.

Lady Hasselthorpe flitted about her guests, her cheeks pink, her hands fluttering helplessly. She was a great beauty with golden hair, a wide, smooth forehead, and a tiny rosebud mouth, but alas, her intellect did not nearly match her looks. Emeline had once spent an excruciating twenty minutes in her company at a ball, trying to make conversation, only to realize that her companion was incapable of following her thoughts to a logical conclusion.

Emeline wished very much that Melisande were here, but Melisande wouldn't arrive until tomorrow. A burst of overloud laughter drew her gaze. Jasper was in the midst of a group of gentlemen, and as she watched, he set them all roaring with laughter again with something he said. In contrast, Lord Hasselthorpe stood in grave conversation with the most illustrious guest, the Duke of Lister. Both Hasselthorpe and Lister were important members of Parliament, and Emeline suspected that their host had even higher political ambitions. She watched Lister send Jasper an irritated glance, which her fiancé never even noticed. The duke was a tall, balding man of middling years well known for his ill humor.

"Will you stroll with me?" Samuel's deep voice came by her side.

Emeline turned, unsurprised. She'd known the moment he started walking toward her. It was strange but she found that she always seemed to be aware of his movements. "I thought you were angry with me, Mr. Hartley."

Where another man might have prevaricated, Samuel met her head-on. "Not angry so much as disappointed that you plan to marry for convenience instead of passion."

"Then I don't understand why you would wish to stroll with me, if you're so insulted by my choice."

It was the first time they'd been able to speak alone since the argument with Jasper, over a week ago now, and that disastrous kiss afterward. She glanced at Jasper. Her fiancé was in the midst of some sort of story, his long face animated, and he wasn't looking their way at all.

Samuel bent his head toward hers. "Don't you? I think you're quite sophisticated enough to understand my reasons."

"Nevertheless, I don't like to stroll with a gentleman insufficiently in control of his temper."

He leaned close, his eyes searching hers, and while there was a small smile playing about his lips for the benefit of the other house party guests around them, she knew that he wasn't at all amused. "Quit attempting to start an argument and walk with me."

Lady Hasselthorpe turned in their direction at that moment. For some reason, their hostess had chosen to wear exceedingly wide panniers draped with lavender and orange satin for a ramble in the countryside. Now her fashionable skirts swayed incongruously, the hem sweeping against the grass.

"Oh, Lady Emeline, do say you aren't disappointed in me! I can't think what became of the wine. I shall have to dismiss Mrs. Leaping immediately on our return. Except"—she twisted her hands at her waist in a pretty, confused, and altogether useless way—"I don't know where else I'll find a housekeeper. They are so dear about these parts."

"Finding a good housekeeper is always a problem," Emeline murmured.

"And look, *that* woman is all by herself." Lady Hasselthorpe indicated a strikingly handsome blond woman in a green frock that showcased an amazing bosom. "She's the duke's *special friend,* you know. He insisted we invite her, and naturally no other lady will speak to her." Lady Hasselthorpe knitted her brow fretfully. "And with no wine! Whatever am I to do?"

"Shall we investigate the progress of bringing back the wine?" Samuel asked gravely before Emeline could say anything.

"Oh, will you, Mr. Hartley, Lady Emeline? I'd be ever so grateful." Lady Hasselthorpe glanced about vaguely. "I suppose I'll have to be the one to talk to Mrs. Fitzwilliam. Won't that just be daring?"

"Indeed, my lady." Samuel bowed. "Meanwhile, we'll seek out your wine. Lady Emeline?" He held out his arm to her.

Which made it impossible to refuse.

"Of course." Emeline smiled and rested her fingertips on the diabolical man's forearm, too aware of the heat emanating from his body. She only hoped that the heat wasn't reflected in her face.

As they walked over the downs, he paced his longer strides to hers, and they soon left the picnickers behind. Now that he had his way and they were strolling together, she'd expected him to immediately start a conversation, but instead he was silent. She peered at him out of the corner of her eye. He had a slight frown on his face as he watched the path. What was he thinking? And why in the world should she care?

She huffed out a breath of air and turned her own eyes forward again. It was a beautiful day, after all. Why let a surly companion spoil—

"Who's that young man talking to Rebecca and the other girls?" Samuel's voice cut into her thoughts.

And how silly to feel a twinge of disappointment that he'd begun the conversation with his sister. Had he forgotten all about the kiss he'd given her the week before? Perhaps he had. Well, then, so would she. "Which one?"

Samuel waved a hand impatiently. "The one with the idiot laugh."

She smiled. Unfortunately, that described the young man rather too well. "Mr. Theodore Green. He has a very nice annual income and an estate in Oxford."

"Do you know anything else about him?"

She shrugged, feeling contrary. "What else is there to know? I don't believe he gambles."

He glanced at her with something like disappointment in his eyes. "Is that the only way in which you judge a man? His income?"

"And rank, of course," she drawled.

"Of course."

"He's the nephew of a baron. A very nice catch for Rebecca, if she can overlook the idiot laugh," she said as if considering. Something seemed to drive her to provoke this man. "Really, I don't think we can aim any higher for her. Your colonial money will only buy her into a certain level of society and no further. I'm afraid your family can be of no consequence in the matter."

His lip curled. "You aren't as shallow as you pretend."

"I don't know what you mean." She was glad she faced forward, for she wasn't sure she could control her expression. The wind picked up the hem of her skirts playfully, and she batted them down.

"All this talk of money and rank. As if that was all that made a man."

"We are discussing your sister and prospective husbands, are we not? How would you have me judge a gentleman?"

"Character, intellect, kindness to others," he listed rapidly. His tone was low and intense. They'd crested a little hill, and golden fields demarcated by hedges and low stone walls lay before them. "How he fulfills his duty and looks after those who depend on him. There are any number of points I'd place above income in a man I would wish Rebecca to marry."

Emeline pursed her lips. "So, then, if I found a kind, intelligent beggar in the street, you would immediately want to draw up a marriage contract?"

"Don't pretend to be obtuse." His arm was hard as rock under her fingers. "It doesn't become you, and you know perfectly well what I mean."

"Do I?" She gave a short laugh. "I beg your pardon, but perhaps I am obtuse. Here in England, we like to marry our daughters and sisters to gentlemen who can properly keep them—"

"Even if the man is a rakehell or a half-wit or—"

"Yes!" He was striding so fast now that she had to skip to keep up. "We think only of money and rank because we're such greedy wretches. Why, if I could find an earl with twenty thousand a year, I'd marry him even if he were riddled with disease and senile to boot!"

He stopped short and grabbed her by the upper arms, which was just as well, as she would've fallen otherwise. When she looked up into his face, she knew that she ought to be afraid. He was pale with rage, his mouth twisted in a sneer. Fear, however, was the last thing she felt.

"Cat," he hissed at her, and then he lifted her nearly off her feet to bring her mouth to his.

The word *kiss* did not adequately describe their embrace. His mouth ground down on hers, forcing her lips apart, forcing her to accept his tongue. And she gloried in it. She met his rage with her own fury. She gripped at his shoulders and dug her fingernails into the fabric of his coat. Had she access to his bare skin, she would've scored him, marked him with her despair and been glad. She was panting, almost crying, her mouth working under his, their teeth scraping against each other inelegantly. There was no finesse, no pretty caress in their kiss. This was a display of lust and anger.

She could smell his skin. He wore no powder or pomades or perfume, it was purely him, and she was driven mad by his scent. She wanted to tear the coat from his shoulders, rip off his shirt and neckcloth and bury her nose in his naked neck. The desire was animalistic and nearly out of control and that was what finally made her stop. She pulled her head back and saw that he watched her almost analytically. His eyes were far more calm than she felt.

Damn him! How dare he not be as affected as she?

He must've seen the anger in her eyes. His mouth curved, though not into a smile. "You do it apurpose."

"What?" she gasped in real confusion.

He studied her face. "You argue with me, enrage me, until I can't stand it anymore and kiss you."

"You say that as if I plan to make you kiss me." She pulled at his grip, but he wouldn't let her go.

"Don't you?"

"Of course not."

"I think you do," he whispered. "I think you feel you can only accept my touch when it is forced upon you."

"That's not true!"

"Then prove it," he murmured as his head lowered to hers again. "Sheath your claws and kiss me."

He brushed his lips softly over hers, a caress that was

almost reverent. She gasped, parting her lips, and he kissed her openmouthed. Lushly. Sweetly. She could drown in a kiss like this; it was much more dangerous than their near-violent sparring of before. This kiss spoke of yearning, of *need*. She shook at the possibility that this man could want her so much. And that she wanted him in return. She knew she shouldn't, but she pressed her mouth back at his. She kissed Samuel, all her hopeless yearning caught in the whisper of breath between them. If only she—

He suddenly raised his head, and she opened her eyes dazedly, missing his mouth.

He was looking over her shoulder. "The footmen Lady Hasselthorpe sent back are about to join us. Are you all right?"

"Yes." Her hands were trembling, but she buried them in her skirts and turned, pasting a bored expression on her face. The footmen were indeed trudging up the little hill, carrying a basket of wine bottles between them. They didn't look particularly interested, so perhaps the footmen had missed their explosive embrace.

"Will you take my arm?" He held it out.

She took it, trying to steady her shaking senses. When had she become so impulsive? The effect Samuel Hartley had on her was not one she relished. He seemed to tear the veil of civilization from her limbs. He left her naked and exposed. She was an unsophisticated creature all emotion and nerves, crouching without a mask at his feet, unable to control her basest compulsions. She ought to refuse his arm and run as fast as she could away from him. She needed to find her old self, to soothe her raw nerves with the rituals of polite society.

Instead, as she laid her fingers on his arm, she felt when

he threw a triumphant look at her, as if she had conceded something.

LADY EMELINE'S TOUCH soothed him, even if it was given reluctantly, and the scent of lemon balm drifted close to his face. Sam closed his eyes for a second, trying to regain control of himself before the footmen were upon them. He'd been a soldier, had faced down screaming native warriors and not broken rank. Yet, place him with Lady Emeline and in seconds he was sweating. He whispered a curse as the footmen tramped closer. This had to stop. She was an aristocrat and not for him.

He let his face relax and hailed the footmen. "We were sent to look for you. May I help you carry that?" He indicated the full basket of wine.

"No, sir. Thank you, sir," the elder man replied. His breath was short, and his companion's face was red, but there was an undertone of shock to his voice. Obviously a gentleman was not supposed to offer to help a servant.

Sam sighed and turned with Lady Emeline to lead the way back to the picnic. "Your people revere divisions between men."

She peered up at him, a little frown creasing her brows. "I beg your pardon?"

He gestured to the footmen panting behind them. "Every little detail of rank, every little opportunity to separate one fellow from another. You English worship the tiniest difference between men."

"Are you saying there are no differing classes in the Colonies? Because if you are, I won't believe you."

"There are differences, but take my word that station is

not nearly so idolized there as here. In America, a man can raise himself above the rank he was born with."

"As has your friend, Mr. Thornton." She tapped his arm for emphasis. "An *Englishman*."

"Thornton wasn't invited to this pretty house party, was he?" He watched her face flush a becoming dark pink and suppressed a smile. She hated to lose an argument. "He may've raised his standing and wealth, but obviously he is still not considered good enough for the gentlefolk in your society."

"Come, Mr. Hartley," she snapped. "You served in the army. Don't try to tell me that you weren't aware of rank there."

"Aye, we had ranks," he replied bitterly. "And some of the worse fools were placed above me, made generals even, solely on the basis of their birth. You needs must find a better argument than that, if you're to convince me of the good in ranks."

"Was my brother a bad soldier?" she asked stiffly.

He damned himself for a cad. God! How could he be so thoughtless? Naturally she would think of her brother first. "No. Captain St. Aubyn was one of the best officers I ever knew."

Her head was down bent, her lips thinned. For such an argumentative woman, she could be very vulnerable sometimes. It hurt him, somewhere in his chest, to see her so. It was odd, her vitriolic tongue made him feel alive, made him want to seize her and kiss her until she moaned beneath his mouth. But when she revealed a rare weakness, she crushed him. Pray she only let show her vulnerability with him. He couldn't stand the thought of another man seeing that part of her. He wanted to be the only one to protect that softness.

"And Jasper?" she asked now. "Was he a good officer as well? Somehow I cannot see him leading men. Playing cards and jesting with them, yes. Ordering them about, no."

"Then perhaps you do not know your fiancé very well."

Her head came up and she scowled at him. "I've known Jasper since I was in leading strings."

He shrugged. "I don't think you ever know a man until you see how he faces death."

They'd come within sight of the picnic spot now. Lady Emeline looked over to where Jasper remained in the midst of a group of laughing gentlemen. He'd doffed his coat for some reason—most improperly—and stood gesturing in his waistcoat and shirtsleeves, long arms flapping in the air like a great gander. As they watched, another wave of laughter went through the group.

"Lord Vale was the most courageous man in battle I ever knew," Sam said thoughtfully.

Lady Emeline turned to stare at him, her eyebrows raised.

He nodded. "I've seen him fall from a horse shot out from underneath him. Seen him get up bloodied and keep fighting, even when all around him were dying. He faced battle—faced death—as if he had no fear. Sometimes he smiled as he fought."

She pursed her lips, watching Jasper caper about. "Maybe he didn't have any fear."

Sam slowly shook his head. "Only fools have no fear at all in battle, and Lord Vale is no fool."

"Then he is an accomplished actor."

"Perhaps."

"Our rescuers!" Lady Hasselthorpe flew at them, her pale hands fluttering helplessly. "Oh, thank you, Mr. Hartley and Lady Emeline. You've saved my little alfresco party from disaster."

Sam smiled and bowed.

"And you?" Lady Emeline asked quietly as their hostess flitted about, getting in the footmen's way.

Sam glanced at her in question.

"How do you face death?" she clarified, her voice so low only he could hear.

He felt his face freeze. "As well as I might."

She shook her head gently. "I think you must've been just as much a hero as Jasper in battle."

He looked away. He could not meet her eyes. "There are no heroes on the battlefield, my lady; there are only survivors."

"You're modest—"

"No." His voice was too intense, he knew. He was in danger of drawing attention. But he could not banter about this subject, of all things. "I am not a hero."

"Emmie!" Lord Vale hailed them. "Come have some pigeon pie before it is all devoured. I have risked my very life to save you a slice or two. I fear the roast chicken is already disappeared."

Sam nodded to Vale, but he leaned down and whispered in Lady Emeline's ear before he led her there, because it was important she not have any illusions about him.

"Don't ever think me a hero."

Chapter Ten

So all of the things that the old wizard had promised
came to pass. Iron Heart lived in a wonderful castle
with Princess Solace as his bride. He had purple
and crimson clothes to wear, and there were servants
everywhere to wait upon him. Of course, he still could
not speak, for that would break the promise
he'd made the wizard, but Iron Heart found that
silence was not such a very bad hardship. After all,
a soldier is rarely asked his opinion....
—from *Iron Heart*

"That scowl on your face does not become you," Melisande
murmured the next morning.

Emeline tried to smooth her forehead, but she had a
feeling her irritation still showed through. She was watching Samuel, after all. "I wish you had come down yesterday instead of today."

Melisande raised an eyebrow fractionally. "Had I

known that you would pine for my company, I would've, dear. Is that why your mood is so gray?"

Emeline sighed and interlocked her arm with her friend's. "No. My mood has nothing at all to do with you except as you make me feel calmer."

They stood on the long mown lawn at the back of Hasselthorpe House. Half of the house party had assembled here for target shooting, the other half having chosen to go into the nearby town to see what sights there were. Painted canvas targets were being erected at the far end of the lawn by footmen. Behind the targets were straw bundles to catch the balls that were fired. The gentlemen who intended to participate were standing about showing off their weapons to admiring ladies who were, of course, to be the audience.

"Mr. Hartley's gun is awfully long," Melisande commented. "No doubt that is why you are glaring at him so ferociously."

"Why does he have to stand apart?" Emeline muttered. She picked fretfully at her rose and green striped skirts. "It's as if the man goes out of his way to be different from the other gentlemen. I declare he does it just to aggravate me."

"Yes, that's probably the first thing he thinks about when he wakes in the morning. 'How shall I go about aggravating Lady Emeline today?'"

Emeline looked at her friend, who was staring back with innocent wide brown eyes. "I'm being a ninny, aren't I?"

"Now, dear, I didn't say ninny—"

"No, but you didn't have to." Emeline sighed. "I brought something that I want to show you."

Melisande looked at her, brows raised. "Oh?"

"It's a book of fairy tales that my old nanny used to read to us. I found it recently, but I think it's written in German. Can you translate it for me?"

"I can try," her friend said. "But I won't promise anything. My German is only fair, and there are many words I don't know. A product of learning it from my mother and not a book."

Emeline nodded. Melisande's mother had been a Prussian who had never entirely learned English, despite marrying at the age of seventeen, and Melisande had grown up speaking both German and English. "Thank you."

The targets in place, the last footman began to walk toward the shooting party. The gentlemen bent their heads together in a grave manner, evidently deciding in what order they should shoot.

"I don't know why he causes all intelligent thought to flee my mind." Emeline realized she was glowering at Samuel again.

Unlike the other gentlemen, he didn't make a show of aiming his weapon and such. He held his rifle with the butt resting on the ground as he stood casually, one hip cocked. He caught her eye and nodded, unsmiling. Emeline looked quickly away, but she could still see in her mind's eye his plain brown coat, the now-familiar dull leather leggings, and the wind ruffling the hair on his bare head. Nothing about his dress recommended him. Even with the other gentlemen attired for shooting in the country, Samuel could've been a servant, so much more plain were his clothes. And yet, she had to exert her will to refrain from looking at him again.

She tugged at a bit of lace at her throat. "He kissed me yesterday."

Melisande stilled. "Mr. Hartley?"

"Yes." She could feel his eyes on her, even though she had not looked at him again.

"And did you kiss him back?" her friend asked as if she inquired the price of ribbons from a vendor.

"God." Emeline choked on the word.

"I'll assume that means yes," Melisande murmured. "He is a handsome man, in a rather primitive way, but I wouldn't've thought that he'd attract you."

"He doesn't!"

But her heart knew she lied. This was like a horrible fever. She actually grew flushed whenever he was near. She was quite unable to control her body—or herself— when around the awful man. Emeline had never felt this wild in her life, not even with Danny, and that thought made her bite her lip. Danny had been so young, so gay, and she had been young and gay with him. It didn't seem right to have stronger feelings now for another man—a man not even her husband.

Melisande glanced at her skeptically. "Then you will avoid him in the future, no doubt."

Emeline turned her head so that Samuel wasn't in her line of sight at all. Instead, she stared at an ornamental pond behind the targets. It looked like it was filled with reeds. Lady Hasselthorpe should've had the pond cleared before the house party. Mrs. Fitzwilliam stood by herself near the bank, poor woman. "I don't know what I'll do."

"A wise lady would seek out her fiancé's company, of course," Melisande murmured.

Jasper was part of the shooting party, naturally. He loved anything to do with physical exertion. Unlike Samuel, though, he was in constant movement—one moment crouching on the ground for some reason, the next bounding up to the footmen to help with straightening the targets. For a moment, Emeline remembered what Samuel had said about Jasper: that he fought as if he'd had no fear. That was certainly not the man she knew. But then again, maybe a woman never really knew the men in her life.

Emeline shook her head. None of that mattered. "This has nothing to do with Jasper. You know that."

"You do have an understanding with him," her friend reminded her neutrally.

"An understanding, yes. That's exactly what it is. Jasper's heart is not involved."

"Isn't it?" Melisande glanced at her toes, pursing her lips. "I think he has a certain fondness for you."

"He sees me as a sister."

"That can be the basis for a loving union—"

"He has other women."

Melisande didn't say anything, and Emeline wondered if she'd shocked her friend. It was to be expected that an aristocratic gentleman would have affairs, both before and after a marriage, but it was considered gauche to speak of such things aloud.

"You had no quarrel with that before," Melisande said. The gentlemen were beginning to order themselves as to who would shoot first. "Come, let us go watch the target shooting."

They strolled toward the shooters.

"I still have no quarrel with Jasper's feelings for me," Emeline said low. "In fact, I believe a kind regard toward one's spouse is for the best in marriage. Far better than desperate passion."

She felt Melisande's sharp glance, but her friend did not comment. They had neared the group of gentlemen shooters now. The Duke of Lister stepped forward and made a show of preparing to shoot. No doubt he'd been given the first shot as a badge of his rank.

"Nasty man," Melisande muttered.

Emeline raised her eyebrows. "The duke?"

"Mmm. He drags his mistress about like a little dog on a chain."

"She doesn't seem to mind." Emeline glanced at Mrs. Fitzwilliam again. She was shielding her eyes to watch the shot, her golden hair glinting in the sunshine. She appeared perfectly relaxed.

"She can't show any vexation, can she, if she's to keep her position?" Melisande frowned at her, and Emeline suddenly felt rather dim-witted. "But all the same, it must be wretched. None of the ladies will talk to her and yet *he* is perfectly respectable."

The duke raised the gun to his shoulder.

Melisande covered her ears with her hands as he fired, and she winced when the sound of the shot echoed off Hasselthorpe House. "Why do guns have to be so loud?"

"So that we ladies can be duly impressed, I expect," Emeline said absently.

A footman advanced ceremonially toward the target and painted a black circle around the bullet hole so that all could see where it had hit. Lister's shot was near the edge of the target. He scowled, but the watching ladies clapped enthusiastically. Mrs. Fitzwilliams started forward as if to congratulate her protector, but the man didn't notice her and turned away to talk loudly with Lord Hasselthorpe. Emeline watched as the woman halted uncertainly before smiling and strolling back to the edge of the lake. Melisande was right. Obviously it wasn't an easy job being a mistress.

"Don't the gentlemen look manly!" Lady Hasselthorpe fluttered toward them. Today their hostess was dressed in pink-dotted dimity over wide panniers. Many pink and green ribbons decorated her elaborately draped skirts, and she held a white shepherd's crook in one hand. Apparently she fancied herself a rustic shepherdess, although Emeline doubted many shepherdesses wore panniers whilst tending sheep. "I do so love to watch the gentlemen show off their prowess."

She was interrupted by another loud *bang!*

Melisande started at the sound. "Lovely," she said with a strained smile.

"Oh, and Mr. Hartley is next with his odd gun." Lady Hasselthorpe squinted toward the gentlemen—she was notoriously nearsighted but refused to wear spectacles. "Do you think it will fire properly with such a long barrel? Perhaps it will explode. That would be most exciting!"

"Quite," Emeline said.

Samuel stepped up to the mark and stood for a moment simply looking at the target. Emeline frowned, wondering what he was doing. Then, almost faster than her eye could follow, he lifted the rifle to his shoulder, aimed, and fired.

There was a stunned silence from his audience. The footman with the paintbrush started toward the target. Samuel had already turned aside even as everyone else waited to see where the ball had hit. Solemnly, the footman painted a black circle at the very center of the target.

"My God, he's hit a bull's-eye," one of the gentlemen finally murmured.

The ladies clapped, the gentlemen crowding around Samuel to examine his gun.

"Lord, I hate the sound of a gun firing," Melisande muttered as she lowered her hands.

"You should have brought lint for your ears," Emeline said absently.

Samuel hadn't blinked as he shot. Not as he'd raised the gun to his shoulder, not at the sound of the shot, and not as the smoke from the flintlock had wafted over him. The other gentlemen handled a gun easily; they probably went hunting and target shooting fairly often at country parties like this one. But none of them had shown the absolute familiarity that Samuel displayed. She could imagine that he'd know how to shoot that gun in the dark, while running, or while being attacked. In fact, he probably had.

"Yes," Melisande muttered, "that would certainly improve my appearance if I had lint growing out of my ears like a rabbit."

Emeline laughed at the image of her friend with rabbit ears, and Samuel turned as if he could hear her amusement. She caught her breath as his eyes met hers. He stared for a moment, his dark eyes intense even across the distance that separated them, and then turned away as Lord Hasselthorpe said something to him. Emeline could feel the blood pulsing in her head.

"Whatever am I to do?" she whispered.

"Damn good shot, that," Vale murmured from behind Sam.

"Thanks." Sam watched as their host prepared to shoot.

Hasselthorpe stood with his feet too close together and was in danger of falling or at least staggering when he fired.

"But then you always were a good shot," Vale continued. "Remember that time you got five squirrels for our dinner?"

Sam shrugged. "Not that it did much good. They still hardly filled the stew pot. Too scrawny."

He was aware that Lady Emeline stood not twenty feet away, her head close to her friend's, and he wondered what the ladies were talking about. She was avoiding his gaze.

"Scrawny or not, they were welcome fresh meat. I say, Hasselthorpe's going to blow over, isn't he?"

"Might."

They were silent as their host squinted down the barrel, squeezed the trigger, and then inevitably couldn't keep the gun from jerking as it fired. The shot went wide, missing the target altogether. Lady Emeline's friend covered her ears and winced.

"At least he didn't fall down," Vale murmured. He sounded a little disappointed.

Sam turned to look at him. "Have you asked about Corporal Craddock yet?"

Vale idly rocked back on his heels. "I've got the address Thornton gave us, and I found out where Honey Lane is—Craddock's house is there."

Sam eyed him a moment. "Good. Then we shouldn't have problems finding it tomorrow."

"None at all," Vale said cheerfully. "I remember Craddock as a sensible sort. If anyone can help, I'm sure he can."

Sam nodded and faced ahead again, although he didn't notice who stepped up to shoot next. He hoped to hell that Vale was right and Craddock could help them.

They were running out of survivors to question.

EMELINE SMOOTHED THE coral silk draped over her panniers that night as she stepped into the Hasselthorpe ballroom. The cavernous room had been recently redecorated, according to Lady Hasselthorpe, and it appeared as if no expense had been spared. The walls were shell pink with baroque gilt vines outlining ceiling, pilasters, windows, doors, and anything else the decorators could think of. Medallions along the walls, also rimmed in baroque gilt leaves, were painted with pastoral scenes of nymphs and satyrs. The whole was like a sugared flower—overpoweringly sweet.

Right now, though, Emeline was less concerned with the Hasselthorpes' grand ballroom than with Samuel. She hadn't seen him since the shooting party this afternoon. Would he attempt the dance, even after his problem at the Westerton ball? Or would he forgo the experience altogether? It was silly, she knew, to worry so much over a matter that was none of her business, but she couldn't help hoping that Samuel had decided to stay in his rooms tonight. It would be awful if he were overcome again here.

"Lady Emeline!"

The high voice trilled nearby, and Emeline turned, unsurprised, to see her hostess bearing down on her. Lady Hasselthorpe wore a pink, gold, and apple-green confection, belled out so extravagantly that she had to sidle sideways to make her way through her guests. The pink of her skirts exactly matched the pink of her ballroom walls.

"Lady Emeline! I'm so glad to see you," Lady Hasselthorpe cried as if she hadn't just seen Emeline not two hours before. "What do you think of peacocks?"

Emeline blinked. "They seem a very pretty bird."

"Yes, but carved in sugar?" Lady Hasselthorpe had reached her side and now leaned close, her lovely blue eyes genuinely concerned. "I mean, sugar is all *white,* is it not? Whereas peacocks are just the opposite, aren't they? *Not* white. I think that's what makes them so lovely, all the colors in their feathers. So if one does have a sugar peacock, it isn't the same as a real one, is it?"

"No." Emeline patted her hostess's arm. "But I'm sure the sugar peacocks will be marvelous nonetheless."

"Mmm." Lady Hasselthorpe didn't appear convinced, but her eyes had already wandered to a group of ladies beyond Emeline.

"Have you seen Mr. Hartley?" Emeline asked before her hostess could flit away.

"Yes. His sister is quite pretty and a good dancer. I always think that helps, don't you?" And Lady Hasselthorpe was off, singing about turtle soup to a startled-looking matron.

Emeline blew out a frustrated breath. She could see Rebecca now, pacing gently with the other dancers, but where was Samuel? Emeline began to skirt the dancers, working her way to the far end of the ballroom. She passed Jasper, who was whispering something in a girl's ear that made the child blush, and then Emeline was blocked by a phalanx of elderly men, their backs toward her as they gossiped.

"I saw the book of fairy tales you left in my room," Melisande said from behind her.

Emeline turned. Her friend was wearing a shade of gray-brown that made her look like a dusty crow. Emeline raised her eyebrows but didn't comment. They'd had this discussion before, and it hadn't changed her friend's attire a wit. "Can you translate it?"

"I think so." Melisande opened her fan and waved it slowly. "I only looked at a page or two, but I could decipher some of the words."

"Oh, good."

But her voice must've been distracted. Melisande looked at her sharply. "Have you seen him?"

Sadly, there was no need to explain who *him* was. "No."

"I thought I saw him go out onto the terrace."

Emeline glanced to where glass doors had been opened to let in the night breeze. She touched her friend's arm. "Thank you."

"Humph." Melisande snapped her fan shut. "Be careful."

"I shall." Emeline was already turning away, moving through the crush.

A few steps farther and she was at the doors leading to the garden. She slipped through. Only to meet disappointment. There were several couples outside, strolling the stone terrace, but she didn't see Samuel's distinctive silhouette. She glanced around as she advanced, and then she felt him.

"You look lovely this evening." His breath brushed her bare shoulder, raising goose bumps on her skin.

"Thank you," she murmured. She tried to look in his face, but he'd caught her hand and tucked it in his elbow.

"Shall we stroll?"

The question was rhetorical, but she nodded anyway. The night air was a relief from the hot ballroom. The chatter of the guests faded as they crossed to wide steps leading into a gravel path. Tiny lanterns hung from the branches of fruit trees in the garden, and they sparkled like fireflies in the autumn dusk.

Emeline shivered.

His hand tightened on hers. "If you're cold, we can go back in."

"No, I'm fine." She glanced at his shadowed profile. "Are you?"

He gave a soft snort. "More or less. You must think me an idiot."

"No."

They were silent then, their steps crunching on the gravel. Emeline had thought he might try to lead her off the path into the dark, but he kept to the proper, lighted ways.

"Do you miss Daniel?" he asked, and for a moment she misunderstood him, thinking he meant her dead husband.

Then comprehension flooded her. "Yes. I keep worrying that he might be having nightmares. They sometimes trouble him, as they did his father."

She felt him glance at her. "What was his father like?"

Emeline looked down blindly at the dark path. "He was young. Very young." She glanced at him quickly. "You must think that a silly thing to say, but it's true. I didn't realize it at the time because I was young, too. He was only a boy when we married."

"But you loved him," he said quietly.

"Yes," she whispered. "Desperately." It was almost a

relief to admit it, how terribly she'd been in love with Danny. How prostrate with grief she'd been at his death.

"Did he love you?"

"Oh, yes." She didn't even have to think about it. Danny's love had been easy and natural, a thing she'd taken for granted. "He said he fell in love with me at first sight. It was at a ball, like this one, and Tante Cristelle introduced us. She knew Danny's mother."

He nodded, not speaking.

"And he sent me flowers and took me for drives and did everything that was expected. I think our families were almost surprised when we announced the engagement. They'd forgotten that we weren't already engaged." Those days were golden but a little blurry now. Had she ever been that young?

"He was a good husband?"

"Yes." She smiled. "He drank and gambled sometimes, but all men do. And he used to give me presents, pay me the loveliest compliments."

"The marriage sounds ideal." His voice was even.

"It was." Was he jealous?

He stopped and faced her, and she saw it wasn't jealousy in his eyes at all. "Then why, after an ideal, loving first marriage, do you want a loveless second one?"

She gasped, feeling as if he'd hit her. She raised her own hand, almost without realizing it, either in defense or to strike him back, but he caught her fist and pulled it aside, leaving her unshielded.

"Why, Emeline?"

"That's none of your business." Her voice shook no matter how hard she fought to control it.

"I think it is, my lady."

"Someone will come," she hissed. The path was deserted, save for themselves, but she knew it wouldn't stay that way for long. "Let me go."

"You lied to me." He ignored her plea, pushing his face with his analytical eyes toward her. "You did love him."

"Yes! I loved him and he died and left me." Her breath caught on the traitorous words. "He left me all alone."

He still looked at her as if he could see inside her head to pick apart her very soul. "Emeline—"

"No." She tore away from him and ran.

Ran up the garden path and away from Samuel as if she were fleeing from demons.

THE DAY HAD turned gray by the time Sam and Lord Vale rode out early the next afternoon. Sam shivered atop his borrowed horse and hoped that there wouldn't be rain on the trip home. He hadn't been able to talk to Emeline all morning. Whenever he saw her, she'd made sure to be in the company of someone else. Her refusal to let him talk out their troubles bothered him. He'd touched a raw spot the night before in the garden, he knew. She had loved her first husband. In fact, Sam had the feeling that Emeline was capable of deep, unwavering love.

And maybe that was the problem. How many times could she give that kind of love and lose it without eventually feeling the effect? He imagined her a fire, banking itself, conserving its embers by burning low so that it might not go out altogether. It would take a determined man to stir those flames again.

Sam's horse shook its head, jingling the bridle, and he returned his thoughts to the present. He and Vale were riding to the nearby town of Dryer's Green where Corporal

Craddock lived. Vale had been uncharacteristically silent as they'd procured their horses and jogged up the long drive to the main road.

When they reached the wrought-iron gate that stood at the drive's end, Vale spoke. "Your aim was impressive all day yesterday. I think you hit a bull's-eye on every shot."

Sam looked at the other man, wondering at the choice of subjects. Perhaps Vale was only making small talk. "Thank you. You didn't shoot yourself, I noticed."

A small muscle jerked in Vale's jaw. "I had enough of guns and gunfire in the war."

Sam nodded. That he could understand. Aristocrat or common soldier, there had been far too many experiences in the war that didn't bear repeating.

Vale glanced at him. "I expect you think me a coward."

"Far from it."

"Kind of you." The other man's horse shied at a leaf, and for a moment, he tended to the reins. Then he said, "It's odd; I don't mind hearing gunfire or smelling the smoke. It's just holding a gun in my hands. The weight and the feel. Somehow it brings it all back, and the war is real again. Too real."

Sam didn't reply. How could one reply to such an observation? At times the war was too real for him, too. Maybe the war still lived for all the soldiers who had returned home—the wounded and the ones who only seemed whole.

They'd turned into the road now, following an ancient hedge along one side, the other side bordered by a dry-stone wall. Beyond these barriers, the brown and golden fields rolled away into the distance. A party of haymakers was working one field, the women with their skirts gathered to their knees, the men in smocks.

"Did you know Hasselthorpe was in the war, too?" Vale asked suddenly.

Sam glanced at him. "Indeed?" Hasselthorpe didn't have a particularly military bearing about him.

"Was an aide-de-camp to one of the generals," Vale said. "Can't remember which one now."

"Was he at Quebec?"

"No. I'm not sure he saw any action at all. I don't think he was in the army very long, anyway, before he inherited."

Sam nodded. Many aristocrats sought soft commissions in His Majesty's army. Whether or not they were suited to army life had very little to do with their choice of career.

Their conversation ceased until they'd entered the outskirts of Dryer's Green some minutes later. It was a bustling little town, the kind that would have a thriving market every week. They passed the smithy and a cobbler's shop, and an inn came into sight.

"I'm told Honey Lane is just here." Vale indicated a small road just past the inn.

Sam nodded and turned his horse down the lane. There was only one house here—a mean little cottage, the thatching blackened with age. Sam looked at Vale, his brows raised. The viscount shrugged. Both men dismounted their horses and tied them to low branches near the stone wall that separated the cottage from the road. Vale unlatched the wooden gate, and they marched up the brick walk. The place might've once been nice. There were signs of a garden, long neglected now, and the cottage, while small, was well proportioned. Evidently Craddock had fallen on hard times. Or he'd lost the ability to tend to the house.

On that uneasy thought, Sam knocked at the low door.

No one came. Sam waited a moment and then knocked again, this time more forcefully.

"Perhaps he's out," Vale said.

"Did you find where he's employed?" Sam asked.

"No, I—"

But the door creaked open, interrupting Vale. A woman of middling years peered at them through a hand-span crack. She wore a white mobcap but otherwise was all in black, a shawl wrapped across her bosom and tied at the waist. "Aye?"

"Pardon us, ma'am," Sam said. "But we're looking for Mr. Craddock. We were told that he lives here."

The woman gasped softly and Sam tensed.

"He did live here," she said. "But not anymore. He's dead. He hung himself a month ago."

Chapter Eleven

Six years went by in wedded happiness—for what man wouldn't be happy to be rich and married to a beautiful woman who loved him? In the sixth year, Iron Heart's happiness reached a new peak, for the princess found she was expecting their child. What rejoicing there was in the Shining City! The people danced in the streets, and the king showered the populace with gold coins the night the princess gave birth to a son. This small baby was the heir to the throne and one day would wear a king's crown on his head. On that night, Iron Heart smiled down on his son and his wife and knew that soon he would be able to speak aloud their names. For this was the third day before the end of his seven years of silence....

—from *Iron Heart*

"Capers," Lady Hasselthorpe said.

Emeline swallowed a bite of goose and glanced at her hostess. "Yes?"

"That is to say…" Lady Hasselthorpe looked down her long, elegant supper table at her guests, all of whom had paused to look at her. "Where do they come from?"

"From the cook! Ha!" a young gentleman exclaimed. No one paid him any heed, save the young lady at his side who giggled appreciatively.

Lord Boodle, an elderly gentleman with a thin, pale face under a rather stringy full-bottomed wig, cleared his throat. "I believe they are buds."

"Truly?" Lady Hasselthorpe widened her lovely blue eyes. "But that seems most fanciful. I rather thought they might be related to peas, only more *sour,* if you understand my meaning."

"Quite, quite, my dear," Lord Hasselthorpe rumbled at his spouse from the other end of the table. One wondered sometimes how Lord Hasselthorpe, a thin, dour gentleman without an ounce of humor, had ever come to marry Lady Hasselthorpe. He cleared his throat ominously. "As I was saying—"

"Very, *very* sour peas," Lady Hasselthorpe said. She was frowning down at the puddle of sauce that surrounded the slice of goose on her plate. A scatter of capers swam there. "I don't know that I like them, really, sour little things. There they lurk in a perfectly plain sauce, and when I bite into one, it quite startles me. Doesn't it you?" She appealed to the Duke of Lister, sitting on her right.

The duke was known for his oratory in Parliament, but now he blinked and seemed at a loss for words. "Ah…"

Emeline decided to rescue the conversation. "Shall we have the footman remove your plate?"

"Oh, no!" Lady Hasselthorpe smiled charmingly. Her blue eyes were exactly matched by the blue in her gown tonight, and she wore a tight necklace of pearls at her throat that highlighted her long, slim neck. She really was extraordinarily beautiful. "I shall just have to watch out for the capers, shan't I?" And she popped a piece of goose into her mouth.

"Brave woman," the duke muttered.

His hostess beamed at him. "I am, aren't I? Braver than Lord Vale and Mr. Hartley, I think. They didn't even come back from the village for supper. Unless"—she glanced inquiringly at Emeline—"they are hiding in their rooms?"

Actually, this was a subject that Emeline had been rather worrying about. Where could Samuel and Jasper have got to? They'd left directly after luncheon and had been gone for hours now.

But Emeline feigned a careless smile for her hostess. "I'm sure they've simply stopped at the village tavern or something similar. You know gentlemen."

Lady Hasselthorpe widened her eyes as if uncertain whether she did know gentlemen or not.

"Actually." Lister unexpectedly cleared his throat. "I believe Lord Vale is in the conservatory."

Lady Hasselthorpe stared. "Whatever is he doing there? Doesn't he know supper isn't served in the conservatory?"

"I believe he is, ah"—the duke's face reddened—"*indisposed.*"

"Nonsense," their hostess said roundly. "The conservatory is a silly place to be indisposed. Surely he'd pick the library?"

The duke's rather hairy eyebrows shot up at this statement, but Emeline only vaguely noticed. What was Jasper doing in the conservatory *indisposed*? He'd have to have been back to the house for some time to be in that condition, yet she hadn't seen him. More importantly, where was Samuel?

"Have you seen Mr. Hartley?" she asked His Grace, interrupting his convoluted explanation as to why a gentleman might choose to indispose himself in the conservatory.

"I'm sorry, no, ma'am."

"Well, they shall both have to miss their suppers," Lady Hasselthorpe said merrily. "And go to bed without."

Emeline tried to smile at this witticism, but she thought the smile didn't quite come off. The supper lasted nearly another hour, and for the life of her, she had no idea how she replied to the conversation of her neighbors. Finally, after a course of cheese and pears that she could hardly bear to look at, the meal ended. Emeline lingered only long enough to be polite; then she hurried in the direction of the conservatory. She traversed a series of halls before her heels tapped on the slate floor that heralded the entrance to the room. A pretty glass and wood door kept the moist heat within the room.

Emeline pushed open the door. "Jasper?"

All she could hear was the tinkle of water. She grimaced in exasperation and closed the door behind her. "Jasper?"

Something clattered up ahead, and then she heard a male curse. Definitely Jasper. The conservatory was a long, keyhole-shaped building, the sides and ceiling made of glass. Here and there a few green plants in buckets gave the room its purpose, but mostly it was an ornamental folly. Emeline gathered her skirts to walk down the slate aisle. Near the end, she rounded a stone Venus and found Jasper lounging on a bench. Behind him a fountain was centered in the round space at the end of the conservatory.

"There you are," she said.

"Am I?" Jasper's eyes were closed. He was tilted to the side, his hair and clothes disarranged, and frankly, she didn't see why he hadn't toppled over yet.

Emeline placed a hand on his shoulder and shook him. "Where's Samuel?"

"Stop that. Makin' me dizzy." He batted at her arm without opening his eyes and naturally missed by a mile.

Lord! He must be completely soused. Emeline frowned. Gentlemen did like to drink too much, and Jasper in particular seemed to be rather overfond of spirits, but she'd never seen him actually drunk. Merry, yes. Drunk, no. And in public, no less. Her worry intensified. "Jasper! What happened in the village? Where is Samuel?"

"He's dead."

A thrill of pure horror coursed through Emeline before she realized that this simply could not be. Surely they would've heard if Samuel had met with an accident of some sort? Jasper's head had fallen forward, his chin resting on his chest. Emeline knelt at his feet to try to see his face. "Jasper, darling, please tell me what happened."

His eyes suddenly opened, shocking turquoise blue and so sad that Emeline gasped. "That feller. Killed himself. Oh, Emmie, it'll never end, will it?"

She had only a dim idea of what he babbled about, but it was obvious that something terrible had happened in the village. "And Samuel? Where did Samuel go?"

Jasper flung an arm wide and nearly went over backward into the fountain. Emeline caught him about the waist to steady him, although he didn't seem to notice either his near fall or her help. "Out there somewheres. Took off the moment we got off our horses. Running. Grand runner, Sam is, jus' grand. Ever seen him run, Emmie?"

"No, I haven't." Wherever Samuel was, at least he was alive. Emeline sighed. "Let's get you to bed, dear one. You shouldn't be out like this."

"But I'm not out." Jasper's comical bloodhound face contorted in confusion. "I'm with you."

"Mmm. Nevertheless, I think you'd be far better abed." Emeline gave an experimental tug at Jasper's waist. To her surprise, he stood easily. Once upright, he towered over her, swaying slightly. Good Lord, she hoped she could manage him by herself.

"Whatever you wish," Jasper slurred, and placed a wide pawlike hand on her shoulder. "Wish Sam was here. Then we could have a party."

"That would be lovely," Emeline panted as she guided Jasper up the walk. He stumbled slightly and leaned into an orange tree, breaking off a branch. Oh, dear.

"He's a wonnerful feller, did I tell you?"

"You did mention that." They were at the door now, and Emeline had a moment of worry, trying to puzzle out how to open it without letting go of Jasper. But he solved the problem by opening the door himself.

"He saved me," Jasper muttered as they entered the hallway beyond. "Brought back the rescue party jus' when I thought those savages might cut off me baubles. Oops!" He stopped and looked at her in chagrin. "Not 'spose to say that in front of you, Emmie. D'you know, I think I might be tight."

"Really, I never would've guessed," Emeline murmured.

"I didn't know Samuel was the one who brought back help."

"Ran for three days," Jasper said. "Ran 'an ran 'an ran, even wi' a knife wound in his side. He's a grand runner, he is."

"So you've said." They'd come to the stairs, and Emeline tightened her grip on him. If he fell, he'd bring her down as well; there was no way that she'd be able to hold his weight. And it was a miracle no one had seen them so far.

"It bloodied him, though," Jasper said.

Emeline had been concentrating on the treads. "What?"

"All that running. His feet were bloody stumps by the time he got to the fort."

Emeline drew in her breath sharply at the awful image.

"How do you thank a man for doing that?" Jasper asked. "He ran until his feet blistered. Ran until the blisters broke and bled. An' then kept running."

"Dear Lord," Emeline whispered. She'd had no idea. They were at Jasper's rooms now, and she knew that it wasn't proper for her to go in, but she couldn't very well leave him in the hallway. And it was *Jasper,* for goodness' sake. He was as close a thing to a brother that she had in this world anymore.

Emeline reached for the doorknob but was saved by the door opening. Pynch, Jasper's burly valet, stood in the doorway, absolutely expressionless. "Might I assist you, my lady?"

"Oh, thank you, Pynch." Emeline gratefully handed over her inebriated fiancé. "Can you see to him?"

"Of course, my lady." If Pynch had shown an expression, it might have been affront, but really it was impossible to tell.

"Thank you." Emeline was indecently relieved to leave Jasper to Pynch's care. She flicked a smile at the valet and then hurried back down the stairs.

It was imperative that she find Samuel.

NIGHT WAS FALLING. The sky had taken on that shade of pewter that heralded the end of the day's light.

And still Sam ran.

He'd been running for hours. Long enough to have reached exhaustion. Long enough to have passed exhaustion into a second wind. Long enough to have lost that wind and simply be enduring now. His body moved in the repetitive rhythm of a machine. Except that machines did not feel despair. However long he ran, he could not outrun his thoughts.

A soldier dead by suicide. To have made it through all the battles, the marching, the rotten food, the cold of winter with inadequate clothing, the diseases that periodically swept the regiment. To make it through all that alive and whole, a near miracle, one of the few to survive the massacre intact. To come home to a neat little cottage and a loving wife. It should've all been over. The soldier come home, the war lost to history, and stories by a winter fire. And yet Craddock had stood on a stool, looped a rope about his neck, and kicked the stool away.

Why? That was the question that Sam couldn't outrun. Why, when you'd already cheated death, why go willingly into her withered arms? Why now?

His breath caught as he crested a hill, his legs trembling

with fatigue, his feet slicing with pain with each step. Dark had settled now on the fields he ran through, and he didn't like it. With each footfall there came the real possibility that he might step wrong. Hit a rabbit hole or rock and fall. But he must not fall. He had to keep running because others depended on him. If he stopped, then his reason for running in the first place would be false. He'd be a coward, merely fleeing a battle. He wasn't a coward. He'd survived battle. He'd killed men, both white and Indian. He'd come through the war and become a gentleman, a man of means and respect. Others depended on him; others nodded gravely at his opinions. Hardly anyone accused him of cowardliness anymore—at least not to his face.

Sam stumbled, his left foot catching. But he didn't go down. He didn't fall. Instead, he half whirled, sobbing with pain, the stars overhead blurring.

Keep running. Don't give up.

Craddock had given up. Craddock had succumbed to the blackness that seeped into his mind in odd moments, the nightmares that tore apart his sleep, the thoughts that he could not keep away. Craddock slept now. Peacefully. Without nightmares or fear for his own soul. Craddock was at rest.

Don't give up.

EMELINE DIDN'T KNOW what woke her late that night. Certainly Samuel moved without a sound, silent and secretive like a cat returning home from the hunt. But she woke nevertheless when he entered his room.

She straightened in the chair by the fireplace. "Where have you been?"

He didn't seem startled to see her in his room. His face was pale and unreadable in the candlelight as he walked toward her, oddly stiff. She looked down. Dark stains on the carpet followed his footsteps. She almost took him to task for not wiping the mud from his feet, but then she understood. And in that moment came fully awake.

"Oh, dear Lord, what have you done?" She stood and grabbed his arm, thrusting him urgently into the chair she'd occupied. "You stupid, stupid man!" She whirled to pile more coal on the fire, then brought a candle closer. "What have you done? What could have possessed you?"

She closed her mouth because what she saw in the candlelight nearly made her ill. He'd run through his moccasins. They were merely tattered leather strips about his feet. And his feet, dear God, his *feet*. They were nothing more than bloody rags, the stumps that Jasper had told her about only hours ago. But now they were real and in front of her. She looked wildly about the room. There was water, but it wasn't hot, and where could she find cloth to use as bandages? She started for the door, but his hand flashed out to catch her arm.

"Stay."

His voice was guttural, raspy with exhaustion, but his eyes had focused on her. "Stay."

How many miles had he run? "I need to get water and bandages."

He shook his head. "I want you to stay."

She pulled away from him roughly. "And I don't want you to die of infection!"

Emeline was scowling down at him, and she knew the fear showed in her eyes. But despite her harsh tone and unlovely face, he smiled. "Then come back to me."

"Don't be silly," she muttered as she went to the door. "Of course I will."

She didn't wait for an answer but took the candle and almost ran into the hallway. She paused there only long enough to verify that no one was about; then she made her way as quickly and as quietly as possible to the kitchens. House parties were notorious for clandestine assignations. Most of her fellow guests would turn a blind eye if they saw her scurrying about the place in the wee hours of the night, but why chance the gossip? Especially as she was quite innocent.

The Hasselthorpe House kitchens were vast, with a great vaulted main room that probably dated back to medieval times. Emeline was satisfied to note that the cook obviously was a competent woman: She kept the fire banked at night. Emeline hurried across the room to the great stone fireplace and nearly stumbled over a small boy sleeping there.

He uncurled from a nest of blankets like a little mouse. "Mum?"

"I'm sorry," Emeline whispered. "I didn't mean to wake you."

There was a huge earthenware jar in the corner, and she lifted the lid to peer inside. She nodded in satisfaction. It contained water. As she dipped some out into an iron kettle, she heard the boy rustle behind her.

"Can I help you, mum?"

She glanced at him as she set the kettle on the fire and stirred up the coals. He sat on his blankets with his dark hair standing on end. He was probably all of Daniel's age.

"Does Cook have a salve for burns and cuts?"

"Aye." The boy got to his feet and went to a tall cupboard and pulled out a drawer. He rummaged inside and brought back a small jar to hand to her.

Emeline lifted the lid and looked inside. A dark, greasy substance filled half the jar. She sniffed it and identified the odors of herbs and honey.

"Yes, this will do. Thank you." She recovered the jar and smiled at the boy. "Go back to bed now."

"Aye, mum." He settled on his pallet and watched her sleepily as she waited for the water to boil and then poured it into a metal pitcher.

There was a pile of neatly folded cloths in a basket on the cupboard. Emeline took several and grasped the pitcher with one. She smiled at the boy. "Good night."

"'Night, mum."

His eyes were already drooping as she left the kitchen. She hurried from the kitchens and back up the stairs, the heavy pitcher in one hand, the jar of salve in the other, and the cloths over her arm. The candlestick was left behind. She knew the route now, anyway, even in the dark.

She thought Samuel might be asleep, but his head turned alertly at her entrance, although he didn't say anything as she crossed the room. She poured the hot water into a basin, added just a little of the cold water from the pitcher on the dresser, and brought the basin over to him.

Emeline knelt at his feet and frowned. "Have you a knife?"

In answer, he pulled a small blade from his waistcoat pocket. She took it and carefully cut away what remained of his moccasins. Some of the leather stuck to the drying blood, and careful as she was, there were bits that pulled and started the bleeding afresh. It must have hurt, yet he didn't make a sound.

She rolled up the embroidered edges of his leggings and placed the basin under him. "Put your feet in here."

He complied and hissed softly as his feet met the hot water. She glanced up, but his face merely showed weariness as he watched her.

"How long did you run?" she asked.

She half expected him to deny it, but he didn't. "I don't know."

She nodded and frowned at the basin of water. It was clouding with blood.

"Vale told you?" he asked.

"Jasper said something about the man you went to see being dead," she murmured absently. If he'd run through the soles of his moccasins into bare feet, there would be dirt and debris in the wounds. She'd have to clean them thoroughly or infection would set in. It was going to be terribly painful.

"Where's Vale?" he asked, interrupting her distressed thoughts.

She looked up. "In his rooms in the care of his valet. He drank himself nearly into a stupor."

Samuel nodded but didn't comment.

She pulled a cloth across her lap and tapped his left leg. "Lift."

He complied, holding out a dripping foot. She guided it to rest on her lap so she could examine the sole. It was raw-looking, reddened and scraped, but in better condition than she would've thought. There were several broken blisters but only one cut. She was conscious, too, that it was a rather elegant foot for a man, which was a silly thought. His feet were large and bony, but with a high arch and long toes.

"He had hung himself," Samuel murmured.

Emeline glanced at him. His eyes were closed, his head resting against the back of his chair. The flickering firelight cast the planes of his face into stark lines and shadows that gleamed a little from old sweat. He must be completely exhausted. It was a wonder that he was still awake.

She inhaled and looked back at the foot. "The soldier you and Jasper went to see?"

"Yes. His wife was there at the cottage. She said that he came home after the war and seemed fine for a while."

"And then?" She had taken another cloth and ripped it until she had a rag the size of her palm. Now she dipped it into the salve and began to wash the bottom of his foot. Emeline frowned to herself. She should've brought some type of scrub brush from the kitchen.

She heard him sigh. "He stopped living."

She glanced up at him. He must be in pain—she was handling his foot quite roughly to get the grit out—but his face was smooth and calm. "What do you mean?"

"Craddock went out less and less until he never left the cottage at all. He'd lost his job long before that point; he'd been a clerk in the village dry grocer's store. After that, he stopped talking. His wife said he'd sit by the fire and simply stare into it as if mesmerized."

Emeline set his left foot on a clean rag by her side and tapped his right foot. "This one, please."

She watched as he lifted the dripping foot onto her lap. She didn't want to listen to this. Didn't want to hear about old soldiers who couldn't come home and live normally. Would Reynaud have been like Mr. Craddock had he lived? Would she have had to watch him slowly eat himself alive? And what about Samuel?

She cleared her throat and picked up a fresh rag. "And?"

"And then he stopped sleeping."

She frowned and glanced quickly up at him. "How can that be? Everyone must sleep; one has no control over it."

He opened his eyes and looked at her with such a well of sorrow in his face that she wanted to glance away. Wanted to flee the room and never have to think about wars and the men who had fought in them.

"He suffered from nightmares," Samuel said.

The fire popped from behind her. He held her gaze. She stared into his eyes, turned black by the firelight, and felt her breasts push against her stays as she breathed in, filling her lungs with air. She didn't want to know; she truly didn't. Some things were too awful to imagine, too awful to hold in her soul for the rest of her life. She'd been fine all these years since Reynaud's death. She'd grieved and railed against fate, and then she'd accepted because she'd had no other choice. To find out now what the war had been like, what it was still like for the men who returned, alive but not whole... It was too much.

Samuel held her gaze. Emeline inhaled again for fortitude and asked, "Do you have nightmares?"

"Yes."

"What..." She had to stop and clear her throat. "What do you dream about?"

The lines about his mouth grew deeper, more grim. "I dream about the stink of men's sweat. About bodies— dead bodies—crushing me, their wounds still open, still flowing with bright, red blood even though they are dead. I dream that I am already dead. That I died six years ago and never knew it. That I only think I'm alive, and when I look down, the flesh is rotting from my hands. The bones show through."

"Oh, God." She couldn't bear hearing of his horrible pain.

"That's not the worst," he whispered so low she almost didn't hear.

"What is the worst?"

He closed his eyes as if bracing himself, then said, "That I've failed my fellow soldiers. That I'm running through the woods of North America, but I'm not running to fetch help. I'm merely running away. That I'm the coward they call me."

It was horribly inappropriate, ghastly, really, but she couldn't help it. She laughed. Emeline stuffed her fist into her open mouth like a little child, trying to stifle the sound, but it broke forth, anyway, loud in the room.

"I'm sorry," she gasped. "I'm sorry."

But one side of his mouth moved upward as if he almost smiled. He reached down and pulled her into his lap, her skirts dragging through the basin of bloody water. She didn't care. All she worried about was this man and his hellish nightmares.

"I'm sorry," she murmured again, dropping the bloody rag. She placed her palm against his face. If she could only absorb his pain into herself, she would. "Oh, Samuel, I'm sorry."

He stroked her hair. "I know. Why did you laugh?"

She caught her breath at the tenderness in his voice. "It's so ludicrous, the thought that you could ever be a coward."

"But it isn't," he murmured as his face drew close to hers. "You don't know me."

"I do. I—" She had meant to say that she knew him

better than any man alive, even Jasper, but his lips covered hers.

He kissed her tenderly, his mouth soft, and she swallowed sorrow from his kiss. Why this man? Why not some other man of her own rank, of her own country? She took his face in between her hands and pushed her mouth on his, and her mouth wasn't soft or gentle. What she wanted from him wasn't a gentle thing. She licked across his lips, tasting salt, then forced her tongue into his mouth. She turned her upper body and pressed herself against him without any artifice, a wanton woman. He broke then. His arms wrapped about her back, and he pulled her fully into his chest, holding her tightly as his tongue slid against hers. She felt the drying tears on her face, she felt the ridge of his organ, even through all the intervening clothes, and she felt an answering feminine thrill.

And then she felt him push her away.

She grasped his shoulders to keep from falling in the basin of water. "What—?"

"Go."

His face was dark, working with some emotion. Had she misunderstood his interest? But, no, looking at his lap, it was all too evident that he'd been fully engaged in their kiss. Then why...?

"Go!"

He picked her up, placed her on her feet, and shoved her unceremoniously toward the door. "Go."

And Emeline found herself outside Samuel's room. She fled down the hall, her skirts dripping bloody water and her heart overflowing with pain.

Chapter Twelve

That night, when all was quiet in the castle, Iron Heart woke on the stroke of midnight. He felt a nameless fear, and leaving his marital bed and the princess asleep, he grasped his sword and went to find his baby son. When he reached the nursery, the guards were asleep outside the door. Quietly, he cracked the nursery door open, and what he saw inside froze the blood in his veins. For a giant wolf, its fangs glittering in the dark, stood over his son's crib....

—from *Iron Heart*

Oddly, he'd slept well. That was Sam's first thought the next morning. It was as if Lady Emeline had laid a balm not only on his feet, but also on his soul. Which was a strange thought. She'd laugh if she'd heard it; she was such a prickly little thing.

His second thought was that his feet throbbed with pain. He groaned and sat in the huge bed the Hasselthorpes had provided for him. The entire room—like the house itself—was magnificent. Red velvet curtains hung from the bed, the walls were paneled with dark carved wood, and a thick carpet lay on the expansive floor. The cabin he'd grown up in might almost fit in the bedroom. If this was what they'd given him, probably the least important of their guests, what had they given the others?

He grimaced. The thought left Sam disgruntled. He didn't belong here in a house of velvet and antique wood. He was from the New World, where men were judged by what they achieved in their own lifetimes, not by what their ancestors had gained. And yet he couldn't dismiss England altogether. This was Lady Emeline's home, and she fit in as only one who was born into this country and class could. That fact alone should've been reason enough to stay away from her. Their worlds, their experiences, their lives, were too far apart.

But that hadn't been why he'd pushed her off his lap the night before. No, that had been an instinctive move, one that had gone against his body's own wishes. He'd been throbbingly hard, had been thinking of nothing save putting his body within hers, and then he'd known it wasn't right. He'd not wanted her capitulation if it was because of pity. Pity wasn't the emotion he wanted from Lady Emeline. Not at all. 'Course, maybe that made him a fool, because his cock certainly didn't seem to care why she'd lain across his lap like butter melting on toast. It only knew that the lady had been willing, and like a hound set to a scent, it was already proudly awake and ready for the chase.

First things first. He smelled like a pigsty, the result of running the night before until the sweat streamed from his body. Sam limped to the door and called for hot water. Then he sat and examined his feet. Lady Emeline had done a good job. The bottom of both feet were covered with broken blisters, and he had a rather nasty cut on the right one, but the wounds were clean. They'd heal properly; he knew by experience.

His bath was in a tin tub that barely fit Sam's body, but the warmth and steam felt good to his aching muscles. Then he dressed, grimacing as he laced his older pair of moccasins, and went down to break his fast. The hour might be late for him, but for an English aristocrat, it was still early and when he limped into the breakfast room, it was only half full.

The room was long, running across a portion of the back of the house. Diamond-paned windows lined the outer wall, letting in the morning light. Instead of one long table, smaller ones had been set here and there for the diners. Sam nodded to a gentleman whose name escaped him and tried to correct his limp as he made his way to the dishes laid out on a sideboard on the far end of the room. Rebecca was already there, peering at a plate of fried gammon.

"There you are!" his sister muttered at him.

Sam glanced sideways at her. "Good morning to you, too."

She scowled at him, then cleared her brow when she saw Lady Hopedale staring at them. "Don't do that."

"Do what?" He placed a slice of gammon on his plate. He'd noticed the other day that it was particularly good here.

"Pretend you don't know what I'm talking about," his sister said in palpable exasperation.

Sam looked at her. In fact, he had no idea what she was talking about.

Rebecca blew out a breath of air, then said slowly as if talking to a very small child, "You were gone all day yesterday. No one knew where you and Lord Vale were. You were missing."

Sam opened his mouth, but she leaned into him and continued in a whisper, "I was *worried* about you. That's what happens when you suddenly disappear and no one can find you and people start wondering if you've fallen into a ditch and are lying dead somewhere. Your sister starts to worry about you."

Sam blinked. He wasn't used to accounting for his movements to anyone. He was a grown man and in the peak of health. Why would anyone worry about him? "There's no reason to worry. I can take care of myself."

"That's not the point!" Rebecca hissed loud enough to make a matron with pendulous jowls look back at them. "You could be the strongest, most well-armed man in the world, and I would still worry if you disappeared for no reason."

"That doesn't make any sense."

Rebecca slapped a salted herring onto her plate. "What doesn't make any sense is *you*." She turned and marched off with her fish.

Sam was still staring after her, trying to understand where he had gone wrong in the conversation, when Vale spoke beside him. "Your sister's feathers seem to be ruffled."

Sam glanced at the other man and winced. Vale's face was ashy-gray, and he swayed almost imperceptibly as he peered at the plate of gammon. "You look like a pile of horseshit."

"Most kind." Vale swallowed. His gray face was taking on a greenish undertone. "I don't believe I'll have anything to eat just now."

"Good idea." Sam heaped buttered kidneys on his own plate. "Maybe some coffee?"

"No." Vale closed his eyes for a second. "No. Just some barley water."

"As you think best." Sam called a footman over and asked for a glass of barley water.

Vale winced. "I think I'll sit in the corner where it's quiet."

Sam smirked and piled two pieces of toast on his plate before following the other man to a small, round table. He ought to be sympathetic. The devils that plagued Vale were the same as his, although the symptoms they evoked were different.

"Have you seen Emmie this morning?" Vale asked as Sam sat across from him.

Sam looked down at his plate as he set it carefully on the table. "No." God, he hated the familiarity of that nickname. He wanted to punch Vale each time he used it.

Vale smiled weakly. "'Fraid I was an ass to her last night."

"Were you?" Sam stared at the other man, feeling hostility well in his chest. "She was with you?"

"Not for long." Vale squinted. "At least I think not. I was a bit tight."

Sam cut into the gammon in a vicious, controlled motion. Had Lady Emeline been in Vale's rooms as well? Had she undressed him and readied him for bed? Cared for him with as much tenderness as she had Sam? He pushed too hard and his knife skidded across the plate with a screech, pushing the gammon onto the table.

"Whoops," Vale said with an imbecilic smile.

Lady Emeline walked into the room.

Sam watched her with narrowed eyes. She was wearing a demure white and pink dress today, and the sight provoked him. Pink made her look like a silly society lady, a woman who would never be able to make a decision for herself, when he knew that the opposite was the truth. She was a strong woman, the strongest he'd ever met.

"There's Emmie," Vale exclaimed.

Had her fiancé ever looked at the grown woman? Evidently not, or he'd never call her such a girlish name as Emmie. Sam felt his hostility grow. She was like a sister to Vale, nothing more. And while love for a sister might be true and deep, it wasn't passion. Emeline was a strong woman with intense emotions. She needed more than brotherly love.

She'd seen him. He knew that, although she pretended otherwise, her head turned away as she talked to their hostess. Emeline was always aware of where he was. He should've taken that as a sign. He should've known, just from that one fact: he couldn't hide from her, even if he wanted to.

"Emmie!" Vale called to her and winced at the sound of his own voice. "Damn me, why doesn't she see us?"

But she looked toward them then, though she was careful not to meet Sam's eyes. She made a last comment to Lady Hasselthorpe and squared her shoulders before walking toward their table.

"Good morning, Jasper. Mr. Hartley."

Vale reached for her hand, and Sam's fingers fisted under the table. "Can you ever forgive me, Emmie? I'm ashamed I was such a drunken oaf last night."

She smiled sweetly, making Sam immediately suspicious. "Of course I can forgive you, Jasper. *You* are always so appreciative."

Sam was sure he'd not imagined her emphasis on the second *you*. He cleared his throat, trying to draw her attention, but she was resolute in her determination not to look at him. "Please. Sit with us."

She couldn't ignore him speaking directly to her without drawing attention. Emeline smiled tightly at him. "I don't think—"

"Yes, yes! Have a seat," Vale cried. "I'll go get you a plate."

A flicker of pure exasperation crossed Emeline's face. "I—"

But she was too late. Vale was already up and bounding over to the sideboard. Sam smiled and pulled out the chair between his and Vale's seat. "He's left you no choice."

"Humph." She flounced into the chair, pointedly tilting her chin away from him.

Strangely, this made him come achingly erect. He leaned toward her, hoping to catch her scent. "I'm sorry I pushed you away last night."

Her cheeks flushed a lovely shade of pink, and she finally looked at him. "I don't know what you're talking about."

He watched her dark eyes. "I refer to you sitting on my lap, my lady, and sticking your tongue in my mouth."

"Are you mad?" she asked low. "You cannot speak about that here."

"Not that I didn't appreciate sucking on your sweet tongue."

"Samuel," she protested, but her gaze fell to his mouth.

God, she made him feel alive! He wanted her. Damn their differences, damn Vale, damn the whole goddamn country. She'd been eager last night. "And I liked the feel of your rump on top of my cock."

Her eyes flared wide. "Stop it! It's too dangerous. You can't—"

"Here we are," Vale said happily. He plunked down a laden plate in front of Emeline and sat with a tall glass of what must be barley water for himself. "I wasn't sure what would tempt you, so I got some of everything."

"You're too kind," Emeline said weakly, picking up a fork.

"Quite the gallant," Sam murmured. "I shall have to take lessons from him, don't you think, Lady Emeline?"

She pursed her lips. "There's no need—"

"But there is." He'd lost all control. It was the sight of her being cared for by Vale, a man who didn't even know her. He was aware that his face had tensed, that he was revealing too much, but he couldn't seem to stop himself. "My manners are too rough, my speech too blunt. I need to learn to smooth my ways so that I can have proper congress with a lady."

On the word *congress,* Emeline dropped her fork.

Vale choked on the sip of barley water he'd taken and started coughing.

Sam looked at him. "Don't you think so, Lord Vale?"

"I'm sorry, I just remembered..." Emeline's face was pale with anger as she searched for an excuse. "I don't know. I have to go." And she got up and walked quickly from the room.

"Congress, old man, is really not the word you were looking for," Vale said. "Conversation, maybe, or—"

"No? I stand corrected," Sam murmured. "Excuse me."

He didn't wait for Vale's reply or look to see what the other man thought. He didn't care anymore. She'd fled, and she must know by now the reaction that that would provoke in a predator.

EMELINE GATHERED HER skirts as she quickened her pace down the hallway. Awful, awful man! How dare he—after rejecting her the night before, actually pushing her away from himself—act as if he were the one wronged? She rounded a corner, nearly cannoning into the Duke of Lister and barely muttering an apology before continuing. The worst part was that her attraction to the horrible man was completely undimmed. How mortifying. To have offered herself to him, have him reject her in no uncertain terms, and then be unable to kill the animal lust her body felt for him.

She'd been so worried when she'd first seen him in the breakfast room. How were his feet? Had she properly cleaned them? How had he been able to walk this morning? And then he'd begun stalking her with his words, not caring who overheard or that he'd already rejected her. It was because of Jasper, she was sure. Samuel was reacting with a kind of male territorial instinct like a hound guarding its dinner. Well, she wasn't some moldy bone to be fought over.

The stairs were in front of her, but her vision was blurred

by rage and frustration. She didn't care for him; she *re-fused* to care for him. He was a colonial without manners or sophistication. She hated him. On that thought, she nearly slipped on a tread and prayed she could make her room before she broke down altogether. That would be the final straw—to be found wandering the Hasselthorpe hallways out of her mind because of a man. She nearly ran the last distance to her room, wrenching open the door and falling inside before slamming it behind her.

Or at least she tried to slam the door. It met with resistance. She looked over her shoulder and found to her utter horror that Samuel stood there, one palm flat against the wooden door.

"No!" Emeline pushed against the door with all her might. "Get out! Get out, you whore-mongering, son of a bitch, arsehole!"

"Hush." His eyebrows were drawn down sternly. He took her shoulder and effortlessly pulled her away from the door before shutting it.

Which only enraged her further. "No, you don't!"

She was writhing, trying desperately to get out of his grasp, slapping at his hands, snaking her head to bite him.

"Yes, I do," he retorted.

And he pulled her roughly against his chest. He slammed his mouth onto hers. Immediately, she bit him. Or tried to. He yanked his head back and, amazingly, grinned down at her, although the expression held no amusement. "I remember that trick."

"Bastard!" She flung up a hand to hit him, but he caught that as well.

He shoved her bodily against the wall and pinned her there like some unfortunate moth. Then he bent his head and, avoiding her mouth, bit her neck, just under her ear. And her body—her *idiot,* traitorous body—responded, going all soft and warm. He nipped and tongued her neck, and her head arched back even as something close to a growl slipped from her lips. He chuckled.

"Don't you laugh at me!" she screeched like a harpy.

"I'm not," he murmured against her throat. "I'd never laugh at you." He pulled at her bodice, ripping something. Then he was licking across the mounds of her breasts above her stays.

She sobbed and his mouth softened, whispering against her flesh.

Damnable man. "Don't you dare do this out of jealousy."

He raised his head, his cheeks flushed, his mouth reddened from kissing her. "This doesn't involve anyone else. This is purely between you and me." He yanked her hand down and thrust it crudely against his breeches.

And she felt him, long and hot, waiting behind his clothes just for her. It was a kind of triumph that she could make his body hard for her. She wanted that. She wanted him. She pressed the palm of her hand against his length.

He groaned and then spun her to face the wall, reaching around her to tear at the ties in the front of her stays. She placed her hands flat against the wall, scraping her nails against the paint; her fevered cheek lay on the cool plaster. This was madness, insanity, and she didn't care. He wrenched down the sleeves of her gown, more fabric ripping, and she felt cool air on her shoulders. He trailed his hands, large and warm, down her spine. She could feel his calluses, male against her soft, feminine skin. He nipped at the back of her neck, and she closed her eyes. It had been so long. So very long. She was melting. There was no need for him to do any more; she was quite ready for him now, but he seemed in no hurry. Or maybe he was just enjoying her naked and vulnerable. He was kissing her spine now, and she felt the touch of his lips, each moist stroke of his tongue.

She moaned.

He reached her hips, where her gown, chemise, and underskirts were tangled. He must've done something truly awful to her clothing then, because there was a prolonged tearing sound, and yards of fabric were at her feet and her bottom was bare. He placed his mouth on the small of her back and kissed her there before moving downward to kiss, actually *kiss,* her buttocks. This wasn't mannerly. This was animal and crass and she shouldn't like it. She shouldn't.

"Samuel," she moaned.

"Hush," he muttered.

He was urging her legs apart, and one part of her mind was thinking that his position relative to hers did not put her in the most attractive angle. Then she forgot any doubts, for he was running his thumb along her crease.

"You're wet," he said, his voice deep and dark with male satisfaction.

She lifted her head from the wall and almost pulled away at that. How dare he take her for granted?

But he tilted her hips and then...

Oh, God! And then he licked her. Her cheek fell back against the wall. It didn't matter anymore, her ungraceful position, his feral nature. She wanted him to continue this forever. His tongue worked between her folds, nudging and licking, and she thought she had never felt anything

like it in her life. He pulled his mouth away and blew on
the place where it had been, cooling and exciting her at
once. Then he was pulling apart her folds with his thumbs
and tonguing his way to the very center of her being. She
was moaning now, her hips pushing back at his face, and
if she thought too hard about what she was doing and
what he was doing, she would be completely mortified.
So she drove any thoughts from her mind and simply
concentrated on the sensation, his mouth against her most
intimate flesh. His tongue seeking out and finding her clitoris. She moaned as he found her. Moaned again when
he licked delicately.

She felt him wrap one hand about her hip and stroke
through her curls. She gasped and opened her eyes to
look down. The sight was unbearably erotic. His dark
fingers tracing across her white skin and into the black
curls above her thighs. He slid his middle finger into her
cleft, and she was forced to close her eyes as that finger
replaced his tongue on her knot. She felt him lick back,
and then he thrust his tongue into her, and she convulsed
violently. Her body shuddered and she gasped, scraping
the wall with her fingernails, moving her hips mindlessly
as pleasure streamed through her. Spasms wracked her as
he thrust and thrust again his tongue into her body, while
his finger worked over her bud. Her climax seemed end-
less, a hard, shimmering river of light that went on and
on and on.

Finally she subsided, weak and shivering, her knees
threatening to give beneath her, her arms shaking as she
held herself up.

His mouth left her and she tried to turn, but he held her
still. "Bend over."

She was dazed, her mind in a fevered sexual haze, and she could do naught but obey him, bending at the waist and grasping at the wall with outstretched arms to keep from falling.

His fingers nudged against her wet flesh, and then his cock. She sighed. So sweet, so beautiful. That hard, hot flesh parting her folds, beginning to enter her. This was the best part, the part of discovery. When he was a man stripped to his essentials and she was a woman receiving him. Exploring him and holding him. Discovering how this was with him.

He should be at the end of his rope by now, nearly frantic with delayed lust, but he went slowly. She felt each inch of his flesh enter hers, widening her until the fabric of his breeches met her bare bottom. He inhaled and thrust once, and he was fully seated. She could stay like this forever, she thought dreamily, holding his hardness within herself, reveling in the feeling of fullness, of connection.

But he drew back, as slowly as he'd entered her, and her inner muscles pulled at him, as if reluctant to let him leave. He thrust suddenly, and her arms bent with the force of the impact.

"Hold still," he grunted, the words almost unintelligible.

She locked her elbows. And then he gripped her hips and began thrusting into her, hard and fast, the slide of his cock tormenting and wonderful. She angled her hips to more fully receive him.

"Jesus!" he growled.

His fingers were suddenly in her bush again, tunneling and seeking, finding that part of her that ached for his touch. He pressed down firmly in front even as his cock ravished her from behind. She felt a scream build in her throat. It was too much, the pummeling, the pressure of his knowing finger, the ache of her arms holding her up.

He swore suddenly, and then he caught her against himself, her bare back pressed to his waistcoat as his cock buried itself in her and began to spurt. It was an odd angle—and erotic—her feet on tiptoe, her legs wide apart, her breasts and belly bare and displayed, impaled on his cock. She heard him groan and reveled in his loss of control. He worked insistently at her bud, splaying his hand possessively over her cunny as he came inside her.

And then she did scream. Waves of almost painful pleasure coursed through her as she convulsed on his cock. He placed his hand over her mouth to muffle the sound, and she bit him, relishing the taste of his skin on her tongue.

Behind her, he caught his breath. "Little cat."

He withdrew his flesh from hers and grasped her about the waist, lifting her from behind and dumping her on her back on the bed. Emeline only had time to brace herself and then he was in the bed beside her, the mattress dipping with his weight.

"You'll probably bite me again, but it might just be worth it," he said before bringing his mouth down on hers. He kicked her legs apart and shoved himself into her again. And then he just lay there, heavy and hot, kissing her hungrily.

He hadn't even undressed, she thought hazily as she opened her mouth beneath his. He was still wearing coat, waistcoat, breeches, and leggings, probably even had his moccasins on the covers of her bed. But then that thought fled, and she gave herself over to his tongue, courting and seducing hers. She felt the press of the cold metal buttons of his waistcoat on her bare breasts as he leaned into her.

Someone knocked on the door. Emeline froze. Samuel lifted his head.

"Are you all right, my lady?" Harris, her maid, called.

He arched his eyebrow at her.

Emeline cleared her throat, conscious of his flesh still in hers. "Perfectly fine. You may leave."

"Of course, my lady." They heard receding footsteps.

Emeline exhaled and pushed at his chest. "Get off."

"Why?" he asked lazily. "I like it here."

But she was feeling a suffocating sense of panic. "My maid will return."

He pulled back and searched her face. "I find that hard to believe. I'm sure you demand only the best-trained servants."

She pushed again, and this time he yielded, withdrawing his penis from her as abruptly as he'd placed it there. He rolled to the side. She scrambled off the bed before she could regret the loss of his flesh. "You should go."

How terribly awkward to stand nude in front of the man she'd just made wanton love to. He should have the common decency—a *gentleman's* decency—to leave quietly after the act. But apparently he did not. She could feel his silent gaze as she bent over her pile of discarded clothes, rummaging for something, anything, to cover her nakedness. She pulled out her chemise and held it over her front, but then discovered that it was more rag than cloth. It was too much.

Emeline threw the shredded chemise down and whirled to the man on the bed. "You must go!"

He was lounging on his side, propped on one elbow,

watching her as she knew he'd be. His hair was still tightly braided, his clothes rumpled but otherwise the same. But his mouth had relaxed into a sensuous, wide curve, his eyes half-lidded and sleepy-looking. He hadn't even the tact to button the flap of his breeches. Her gaze was drawn helplessly to his manhood, shining and thick, and the only nude part of him. His cock should've been limp and little by now, a thing to be pitied, but it wasn't. Quite the contrary, it lay arrogant and half-erect as if willing to do the whole thing over.

The sight enraged her. "Why haven't you left?"

He sighed and sat up. "I had hoped to lie with you a time, my lady, but evidently that does not meet with your pleasure."

She flushed. Emeline actually felt the heat invade her cheeks and neck. She knew she was being surly and unreasonable. She knew she should display grace and perhaps an indifferent sophistication, but she couldn't.

She simply couldn't.

"Please go." She crossed her arms over her breasts in an inadequate defense and glanced away.

He stood and buttoned the flap of his breeches without hurry. "I'll go now, but this is not over."

She looked up in horror. "Of course it's over! You got what you wanted; there's no need to...to..." She trailed away because she really didn't know how to voice the thought. Oh, if she'd only been one of those sophisticated widows! The ones who took discreet lovers and made liaisons where both parties knew the rules of behavior. But she'd had to care for Daniel and Tante Cristelle and then Reynaud had died and, well, she'd never felt the urge before.

While she'd been thinking about her woeful lack of experience, he'd finished putting himself to rights and strolled over to where she stood like a rather aged dryad. He bent and brushed his lips against hers, softly, tenderly, the touch almost making her weep.

And then he stepped back. His eyes were narrowed and thoughtful. "Yes, I got what I wanted—and what you wanted as well—but I'm not quenched. I'm coming to you again, and you can either let me in quietly, or I will knock your door down and in the process summon the whole household." The corner of his mouth quirked upward, but he didn't look amused. "I may not be fully aware of all the niceties of your society, but I think that you won't want that."

Her mouth had fallen open during this arrogant speech, but now as he turned away, she found her voice. "How dare you presume—"

He caught her by the shoulders, making her indignant sentence end on a squeak. He bent his head and spoke fiercely into her ear. "I dare because you welcomed me into your body not a quarter of an hour ago. Your body rained your pleasure all over my cock, and I want that again."

He covered her mouth. But this time his kiss wasn't gentle or soft. It spoke of a man's desire. He thrust his tongue into her mouth and angled his head so that his lips all but enveloped hers, and her silly body arched into him. She wanted this. She craved this. Intellect and reason fled her brain.

He stepped back so suddenly she nearly fell. His face was hard and flushed. "Let me in tonight, Emeline."

He left her room before she could reply.

As she sank into her pile of ruined clothes, she had a blinding realization. She'd lost whatever control she'd ever had over this affair.

"CRADDOCK HUNG HIMSELF a month ago," Lord Vale said later that afternoon.

Sam dragged his thoughts away from Emeline—her skin, her breasts, the fact that she didn't want to see him again—and focused on the problem of the 28th. "You'd think that Thornton would've known that Craddock was already dead."

Vale shrugged. "Thornton didn't say when he'd last seen the man."

"True."

"Who's next on your list to question?"

Sam grimaced. "No one."

It was raining outside, which had sent their hostess into a flurry of despair. Apparently, Lady Hasselthorpe had planned an afternoon expedition to view the ruins of an abbey, a famous local sight. Sam was privately relieved at the rain. He would never have been able to hike over the hills today, not at least without a good deal of pain, and making an excuse would've drawn Rebecca's attention. He was beginning to realize that his sister saw much more than he'd given her credit for. Having to explain to her why his feet were in ribbons would've been awkward indeed.

But instead the majority of the house party had retreated to a large sitting room at the back of the house. Emeline was noticeably absent, of course—she was obviously avoiding him—but most everyone else was in attendance. Some of their number amused themselves playing cards; others were reading or talking in small groups.

Like Vale and Sam.

"You don't have anyone else to question at all?" Vale looked incredulous.

Sam grit his teeth. "I'm happy to take suggestions."

Vale pursed his lips. "Ah…"

"Assuming you have any ideas of your own?"

"Well…" Vale found a sudden interest in the rain-drenched windows.

"Thought not," Sam muttered.

Both men gazed at the windows as if transfixed by the terrible weather. Vale drummed his fingers on the arm of his chair in an incredibly annoying manner.

Finally, the viscount inhaled. "If Thornton was the traitor, he'd have to have a reason to betray the 28th."

Sam didn't take his eyes from the window, strangely unsurprised that the other man's thoughts had run along the same lines as his. "You definitely suspect him, then?"

"Don't you?"

Sam thought of the unease he'd felt since meeting Thornton again in London. He sighed. "I might suspect him, but I can't think why he'd betray the entire regiment. Any ideas?"

"Haven't a clue," Vale said. "Perhaps he was growing weary of all the peas porridge we had to eat on that wretched march."

The viscount seemed to like him. There was something villainous in pretending friendship with a man when you'd just made love to that man's fiancée. Sam would've avoided him, but Vale had sought him out as soon as he'd entered the sitting room.

"There's always money, I suppose," Vale mused, "but I don't see how killing an entire regiment would benefit Thornton unless he was paid by the French."

"Does Thornton speak French?" Sam asked idly.

"Haven't a clue." Vale drummed his fingers for a moment, apparently considering Thornton's linguistic abilities. "Not that it matters—the note was written in English, you said. And besides, plenty of French speak English."

"Was he in debt?" Sam watched as Rebecca tilted her head to listen to another girl. She'd found at least one lady to talk to.

"We should find out. Or rather I should find out. Haven't been much help to this investigation so far. Ought to lend more of a hand, what?"

Sam looked over at Vale. The other man was watching him with his earnest, hangdog eyes. What kind of a man would betray a friend like this?

"Thank you," Sam said gravely.

Vale made one of those mercurial transformations that he was sometimes capable of. He grinned and his funny, homely face lit up, his almost iridescent blue eyes sparkling. "Don't mention it, old man."

And Sam looked down, no longer able to meet the other man's eyes. He should in all honor resolve to never see Lady Emeline again. Which must make him the most dishonorable man alive.

For he fully intended to find her and make love to her again tonight.

Chapter Thirteen

*The giant wolf leapt for the baby's cradle, its jaws
gaping wide. But Iron Heart ran at the beast, his
sword upraised to protect his son. Then what a battle
commenced! For Iron Heart must remain silent—he
could not call for help—and the monster wolf was
a test of all his strength and skill. Back and forth
across the room the combatants raged, smashing the
furniture to splinters. The babe's cradle
was overturned and he began to wail. Iron Heart
gave a mighty blow and struck the wolf's hind leg.
The beast howled with pain and lashed out,
flinging the man against the wall with a crash
that shook the castle. Iron Heart's head hit the
stone wall and he knew no more....*
—from *Iron Heart*

She'd argued with herself all day, even as she'd been careful to keep to her rooms for fear that she might see him.
The reasons were well worn by now. They were of differ-

ent classes, different worlds. She had a son and a family to think of. He was too intense, a man not easily led. She wouldn't be able to hold the upper hand with him. And yet...

And yet...

Maybe it was because she'd spent all day debating and redebating herself. None of the arguments seemed to hold sway anymore. She shrugged them aside because they paled in comparison to her need. She needed to feel him inside her once again. Shocking, how animal she'd become. She'd never done this before—pushed reason aside, let her physical self rule. It was a frightening thing, to give herself solely over to the sensual. Frightening, and exhilarating at the same time. She'd always held herself in strict control, *been* the one in control. Someone had had to—all the men who were supposed to hold the family together had left. First Reynaud, then Danny, then six months later, Father, leaving her alone.

So terribly alone.

She tensed as she heard a footstep outside the door. She was ready for him, nude and already in bed, and she felt excitement shoot through her. Then he was opening the door. He closed it behind him, not bothering to disguise his limp once inside the room. In that moment before he saw her, she noticed the lines that carved furrows into his cheeks, the slump of his broad shoulders. He was weary, she could tell, probably not yet recovered from his punishing one-man race of the day before. And she didn't care. She would have him tonight, would use him as he used her.

She saw the moment he noticed her. He paused, his coat half off, and she sat up in the bed. *His* bed. The coverlet slipped to her waist, revealing her bare breasts. "I've been waiting for you."

"Have you?" He pulled off his coat. His tone was casual, but his eyes were on her breasts.

She leaned a little back on the pillows, which had the effect of thrusting out her breasts. She didn't have to look down to know that her nipples had tightened in reaction to the night air—and to him. "Hours, it seems."

"I'm sorry." He unbuttoned his waistcoat, his fingers working nimbly, although he never took his eyes off her. "I would have hurried had I known."

"I'd prefer you not hurry, actually." She made a moue, as if displeased at the thought.

His fingers paused. "I shall keep that in mind."

He flung aside the waistcoat and pulled off his shirt in a flurry of activity, then prowled toward her, bare-chested. He had a lovely chest, broad and muscled, the dark hair curling over nipples and in a line down his belly. Just the sight of him was making her wet, but she must not lose her advantage.

"Yes, you should." Her gaze flicked downward, toward the breeches, leggings, and moccasins he still wore. "Yet you seem to be approaching me prematurely."

His eyes narrowed, and for a moment she thought she'd gone too far. His mouth thinned and he didn't look particularly pleased. But then he grabbed a wooden chair and set it facing her, only a few feet from the bed. He placed a foot on the chair and began unlacing the moccasin. It was different from the ones he'd ruined; he must have more than that one pair. She watched tiny muscles in his arms and back work as he untied the laces. He pulled the first one off, glanced at her, and began on the other.

She swallowed. He was only taking off his shoes, yet she knew he was preparing himself, undressing himself, solely for her. The thought made her breath catch, and she was aware that her body was ready for him.

He took off the second moccasin and revealed that he'd wrapped his feet in linens. What she could see of his bare feet looked to be healing well, though. He straightened and untied a lace at his side. She saw that his leggings were held up by leather laces tied to a strip of leather about his waist. He untied the lace at his other side and stripped the leggings off. Then he placed his hands on the buttons of his breeches, and she quite forgot about his leggings. He looked at her, holding her eyes as he unbuttoned himself, the flick of his fingers precise and controlled. She thought about what those long, nimble fingers would soon be doing to her and nearly moaned. But she didn't break the silence, and the rustle as he pushed down his breeches and smallclothes was loud in the room.

He stepped out of his garments and was gloriously nude, except for that band of leather riding below his navel. She held her breath and watched him unwind that as well and toss it atop his leggings. He was long and lean, his skin tanned where it had met the sun and naturally swarthy where it had not. She could've spent years just looking at him. He had dark hair on his calves, bony knees, and thighs that were thick and strong. There was that beautiful, secret male spot where hip met belly, just next to his groin. A muscle arched into his hip there. Above that a thin white scar cut across his belly, and another scar, small and puckered, marred his upper right chest. For a moment, her eyes lingered on the thin scar on his belly, and she remembered how Jasper had said he'd run for days with a knife wound in his side. How hard that must have been. How proud she was to have such a brave man want her.

Her eyes wandered down again—saving the best for last—to his manhood. She'd forgotten how wondrous a man's genitals were. His penis pointed nearly upright, thick and hard, wrapped about with veins that bulged with his arousal. Below, his bollocks were tight and round, and the dark hair that curled at his lower belly merely served to emphasize all. She swallowed and had trouble catching her breath.

"Will I do?" he asked quietly, breaking the silence. He'd stood still, letting her take her time to examine him fully.

Her eyes rose to his and she inhaled unsteadily. "I think so."

His eyebrows shot up, an arrogant male insulted. "*Think?* If you are unsure, my lady, let me help you make up your mind."

He was at the bed in a second, a rushing pounce that made her jump with nervous feminine alarm. He crawled up and over her on all fours, like an animal, and when she thought he would kiss her, instead he dipped his head to her left nipple. And sucked. She arched, a sigh escaping her throat. He touched her nowhere else, just that single nipple, and he sucked strongly. Was it possible to feel so much from such a small bit of flesh? She reached up and wound her arms about him, reveling in what she'd been unable to do before. Touch him. Feel the heat of his skin beneath her palms, run her hands over the ridges of his ribs, smooth the broad expanse of his lovely back. She wanted to feel every inch of him, to taste him, and to take him into herself until she knew his body as well as her own.

He lifted his head, but his gaze remained on her breasts. "I've been thinking of this all day—your nipples, bare to me and what I would do with them. I could hardly walk for the cockstand in my breeches." His eyes flicked to hers, and she saw that his expression was almost angry. "That's what you do to me—turn me into a mindless, hungering cock."

She squirmed at the words, so crude and explicit.

His nostrils flared at her movement and she froze. "Hold them for me. Offer your breasts to me so I can suck them until you come."

Oh, Lord! She *mustn't* let him talk to her this way. He would assume too much if she allowed him to order her about. But at the same time, she felt the moisture seep at her center from just his words. She wanted to offer herself to him. She wanted to let him suck her nipples. So she placed her palms under her breasts and lifted them, like a sacrifice to a half-animal god.

He growled low in his throat, a sound of approval, and attacked her breasts. Nipping and licking, grasping the rosy tips gently between his teeth, moving back and forth from one breast to the other, his day's growth of beard scraping against her sensitive skin. Then he took a nipple into his mouth and sucked at it, worrying the opposite nipple with his fingers. And the two points of pleasure lit within her until she arched helplessly, gasping. It was too much. He would hurt her. She couldn't stand anymore.

She shuddered, a light blinding her behind her closed eyes as warmth flooded her limbs. Her hands fell away, but he continued to lick, his tongue gently soothing on her breast, each rasp a separate spark. She felt the soft brush of his lips as he kissed her nipple.

She opened her eyes. She met his coffee-brown gaze, for he was right there, her breast under his mouth. His look was intense and not kind.

"I can't wait any longer," he muttered, and jerked the coverlet from her legs.

He pushed her thighs apart unceremoniously and sank between them, guiding his penis with one hand. He found her entrance and pushed, parting and breaching her. He pushed again, entering her and entering her until his entire length lay inside. His eyelids fell helplessly and he groaned, still and hard and in her.

She smiled. How could she not? He took such pleasure in her flesh, seemed so powerless to stop himself from enjoying her. She touched the side of his face with her palm, and he opened his eyes, shockingly bright.

"You're laughing at me," he growled.

She shook her head, opening her mouth to explain, but he'd levered himself up so that he was braced on straight arms, his hips pressing hers down into the mattress. And then he moved. He withdrew and jolted back into her, hard and fast. She closed her eyes, forgetting what she was about to say, not caring if he was offended or even angry with her, as long as he kept moving. His hardness was thrusting in her, rubbing against her sensitive flesh, relentless in its purpose—to pleasure him and her.

"Will this do?" he grunted.

She didn't answer, lost in a sea of bliss.

He slammed into her and held still. "*Will* this do, my lady?"

Her eyes flew open and she glared at him. "Yes!" She

clutched at his buttocks, trying to get him to move again. "Yes! Yes! Yes! Just *move,* damn you!"

And he complied, either chuckling or growling low in his throat; it was impossible to tell, because her eyes had fallen closed again. Besides, she just didn't care anymore. All she cared about was the movement of his body in hers. The relentless pistoning, the relentless pleasure. His hardness and drive and the fact that she never, never, *never* wanted him to stop.

Until she came in wave after crashing wave. She felt his hand cradle the side of her face. She opened her eyes in time to see him arch, his pelvis grinding against hers, and she watched Samuel Hartley convulse as he came deep inside of her.

HE WAS GASPING, more out of breath than when he ran. She'd wrung him dry and it felt wonderful.

Sam collapsed onto Emeline, careful to keep most of his weight off of her but still wanting to feel her fully beneath him. Her breasts against his chest, her belly under his, and her legs tangled about his knees. Somewhere at the back of his brain, he knew that this was a primitive urge to dominate the woman—*his* woman—and that it was not a kind urge or one he should be proud of. But he pushed the thought away because he was too tired to reason; besides, the position was perfect.

Although maybe not to her.

"Get off me," she mumbled.

He didn't think he'd ever heard the so-proper Lady Emeline mumble before and he was delighted. "Am I crushing you?"

"No." She was quiet for a bit, and he thought she

might've fallen asleep. But then she spoke again. "But you should get off me, anyway."

"Why?" He'd placed his head on the pillow beside hers and was enjoying lying face-to-face and watching her expression.

She wrinkled her nose without opening her eyes. "Because it's the polite thing to do."

"Ah. But I'm very comfortable where I am, so I'm not that interested in politeness at the moment."

Her eyes snapped open, and she scowled at him in an utterly adorable way. Not that he would ever tell her, but he found her anger arousing.

"Isn't my comfort of any importance?" she demanded in a haughty, upper-crust accent.

"No," he told her kindly. "None at all."

"Humph," was her not-very-eloquent retort, and he smiled at that as well. He loved having reduced her to monosyllables.

She'd closed her eyes again, and now she said sleepily, "You're very sure of yourself."

"That's because"—he leaned close enough to kiss her cheek and then whisper in her ear—"my cock is in your cunny."

"Self-satisfied," she mumbled.

"Yes, and so are you."

She grunted. "Go to sleep, you vain man."

He smiled to himself since she could no longer see and pulled the coverlet over them both. And then, still interlocked with her, he followed her orders and let himself sleep.

EMELINE CAME FULLY awake all at once early the next morning. She immediately knew that she had stayed the

night in Samuel's room. He still lay beside her. In fact—
she tried an experimental wiggle—he still lay *in* her.
Which made a discreet exit rather awkward.

She watched him. He lay prone, his face turned toward
her. His hips covered hers, but most of his upper body was
off her chest, except for an arm, thrown possessively over
her breasts. The lines beside his mouth had smoothed,
and he looked young, his brown hair tousled like a boy's.
Had he looked this way before the war?

He opened his eyes and focused on her, and his gaze
darkened with awareness. He was silent, his gaze traveling over her face. It was early morning, she'd just woken
up, and she must look terribly disheveled, but she couldn't
turn away. She let him inspect her, his gaze more intimate
than when he had looked at her nude body the night before. What did he see when he looked at her? She couldn't
fathom, and at any other time she'd be cross with her own
uncertainty, her own exposure. But right now, with the
morning light softly revealing the room, she didn't let her
own vulnerability spoil the moment.

He raised his palm to cradle the back of her head and
brought his face nearer slowly so he could examine her
as he approached. He only closed his eyes at the last minute. And then he was kissing her. His mouth was softer
in the morning, more relaxed and lazy. He opened it over
hers but made no attempt to engage her tongue. Instead
he kissed her lushly, his lips moving slowly, erotically,
on hers. She could feel his morning stubble, scraping her
face in contrast to the softness of his lips. He seemed in
no hurry, even though she could feel him, large and incredibly hard, within her.

He levered himself over her on his elbows, never

breaking the kiss, his palms cradling her face, and he surrounded her, male and hard, protective and possessive.
She'd never felt so cherished. Never felt so wanted. He'd
widened her legs and settled his hips more fully on hers.
She could feel the tickle of his chest hairs on her nipples.
It was all so intimate. She wasn't sure she could bear this,
this too-close lovemaking. It exposed her, left her open
to reveal things she'd rather keep hidden. But she was
caught in the moment, seduced by her own yearning and
by the man above her.

His hand traveled from her face to her throat, caressing
over her shoulder and side. He paused at her hip, seem-
ingly distracted by their kiss; he'd licked his way into her
mouth and she was sucking him. Then his hand continued,
reaching one knee and grasping it. He pulled that knee up
and over his hip and left it draped there as he pressed his
pelvis down into hers.

She gasped into his mouth. She was open and vulnerable in this position, and when he pressed, she could feel
all of him against her mons. She wasn't sure she liked it,
this leisurely, *thorough* lovemaking. He was laying bare
her soul, whether that was his intention or not. She didn't
even think he was aware of what he did to her. But when
she would've pushed him away, she was beguiled all over
again by the sure thrust of his hips. He broke their kiss,
raising his head to watch her as he ground slowly down
on her exposed flesh. She gasped at the sensation and then
frowned at him. How rude to stare at her in this moment!
Didn't he know that this simply wasn't done? That what
they did was only a fleeting pleasure of the flesh, nothing
more.

Nothing more...

When he shifted and pressed again, his body hard and insistent within hers, it didn't feel like only a physical act. It was more. Much more. She panicked, the weight of him, the emotions suddenly overwhelming. She tried to turn her head, raising her arms to push him off, but he caught her quickly, effortlessly, and trapped her wrists on the pillow on either side of her head.

She sobbed, helpless and angry, and more angry that she let her innermost feelings show. "Stop."

He shook his head slowly, pressing into her again, his hard body causing hers to flower open, vulnerable to all the sensations he was making her feel. His eyelids dropped for a second as if he, too, were overwhelmed by what he did. Then he raised them and looked into her eyes. "No."

He bent his head to lick the sweat at her hairline. She felt the gentle abrasion of his tongue and at the same time, the pressure of his cock inside her as he hitched his hips higher, grinding with devastating accuracy onto the one spot that could not withstand his ravishment. He withdrew a fraction of his length, but she felt the friction as his cock pulled against her oversensitive flesh. Then he was bearing down again, grinding, grinding, grinding against her exposed clitoris, and she couldn't stand it anymore.

She came apart, all the secrets, doubts, worries, and hopes that she had kept tightly bound to herself flying outward, free and unharnessed, exposed to the chill morning air and to him.

To him.

And she looked up in time to see him grit his teeth and tremble, undone as much as she, as he released his seed within her.

*   *   *

HER TEACUP SHOOK as Emeline raised it to her lips later that morning. She frowned at this outward manifestation of her inner turmoil and sternly made her fingers stop trembling. Around her, no one else in the breakfast room seemed to notice. Except for perhaps Melisande, sitting across from her at the little round table they shared and sending her a too-perceptive look. It really wasn't something to be valued in a friendship, sensitivity to others. It only led to awkward questions and overly sympathetic glances.

Emeline pointedly looked away from her dearest friend in the world and tried to focus her mind on something other than the overwhelming lovemaking she'd experienced just that morning. And the night before. And the morning before that. She frowned at her teacup, now perfectly still. Perhaps an overabundance of sex was curdling her brain. That would certainly explain her inability to think of anything else. It couldn't be healthy to be thinking, brooding, *obsessing* over a man and his long legs and wide chest and hard, hard, hard *penis*. Emeline coughed on her tea and looked guiltily at Melisande.

Who said, "I've translated the title of the first fairy tale in that book you gave me. It's called *Iron Heart*."

"Really?" For a moment, Emeline was diverted from her troubles. She remembered the fairy tale. *Iron Heart*. It had been about a man who was brave and strong and true. A man like Samuel, she suddenly realized. How strange.

Across from her, Melisande cleared her throat. "Lord Vale was asking about you last night."

Emeline nearly spilled her tea. Hastily, she set down her teacup. Obviously she just wasn't cut out for this type of subterfuge. Her nerves were overwrought. "What did you tell him?"

Melisande raised her mouse-brown eyebrows. "Nothing. He wouldn't have noticed me, anyway."

Emeline was distracted from her own worries by her friend's cynical self-assessment. "Don't be silly. Of course he'd notice you."

"He doesn't know my name."

"What?"

Melisande nodded, no trace of self-pity in her steady brown eyes. "He hasn't a clue who I am."

Emeline looked over to where her fiancé sat among a bevy of young ladies. He was gesturing widely, evidently in the midst of some story, and his right hand nearly clipped the cap of the lady sitting nearest to him. She again wanted to snap at Melisande not to be silly, but the truth was, Jasper probably did indeed have no clue what Melisande's name was. He'd always paid more attention to the most beautiful ladies in their circle. That was only to be expected, she supposed. Men were rather shallow that way, caring more for a lady's looks than her feelings or mind. Most men, anyway. Samuel sat in the opposite corner, flanked by his sister and Mrs. Ives—a rather plain lady of advanced years. He had his head tilted to the lady as she said something, but his eyes caught hers just as she looked at him.

Emeline looked away, feeling heat invade her cheeks. Damn the man. It wasn't enough that he'd used her body until it ached this morning in a terrible, pleasurable way; now he must invade her every waking thought.

"...do hope you used a preventative," Melisande was saying across from her.

"What?" Emeline asked too sharply.

Her friend glanced at her as if she could tell that Emeline's mind was elsewhere. "I said I hoped that you used a preventative last night."

Emeline stared. "What are you talking about?"

"Something to prevent a baby—"

Emeline choked.

"Are you all right?" her bosom beau asked as if she hadn't just shot a cannon into the conversation.

Emeline waved at her as she took a drink of tea. Briefly, she contemplated denying that she'd spent the night with Samuel, but the conversation seemed well past that point. Instead, she settled on the more pressing matter. "Quite. How...how—?"

Melisande stared at her sternly. "I can't think how you can embark upon an affair without taking appropriate measures. There are sponges that fit in the female body—"

"How in the world do you know of such things?" Emeline asked in real wonder. Melisande was unmarried and presumably a maiden.

"There are books if one is interested."

Emeline's eyes widened. "Books about...?"

"Yes."

"Good Lord."

"Pay attention," Melisande said sternly. "Have you taken the appropriate measures?"

"I think it's too late for that," Emeline muttered.

Her hand crept to her laced belly before she caught herself and snatched it away. How could she not think about such a fundamental thing, even in the heat of passion? The possibility of a baby was a real concern, and one she could not afford. Jasper was very sophisticated, but no man wanted his heir to be someone else's get. If she was with child, she'd have to marry Samuel. The mere thought turned her stomach. There would be nowhere to hide, living with such a man. She'd be constantly exposed, her feelings, her worst traits, open to him. He saw her, really *saw* her as no man had ever done before, and she didn't like it. He would demand things of her, emotions she didn't want to feel, and she wouldn't be able to hide behind a fraudulent facade.

Her horror must've shown on her face, for Melisande leaned forward and placed her hand on hers. "Don't panic. It's too soon to know; there may be no cause for worry. Unless"—she frowned—"this affair has been going on longer than I've thought?"

"No," Emeline moaned. "Oh, no. It's just been…" But she couldn't finish the thought. What must Melisande think of her? She'd been cavorting with a man she'd known only a little while at the same party that her fiancé attended.

Her friend patted her hand. "Then there's no point in worrying. Enjoy the rest of the party and don't go back to him without prevention."

"Of course not." Emeline drew a steadying breath. "I won't even look at him again. I'm certainly not going to…" She waved away the rest of the sentence and straightened her shoulders. "I'll just avoid him. There won't be another time."

"Hmm." Melisande's murmur was noncommittal, but her look was skeptical.

And Emeline really couldn't blame her friend. She'd tried, but her voice sounded uncertain even to herself.

Against her will, her gaze wandered back to the corner where Samuel sat. He was watching her, his eyes narrowed. To anyone else, his expression was casual, she was sure. But to her it was not. In his eyes she saw lust, possession, and certainty of his own strength. This man wouldn't give her up without a fight.

Dear Lord, what had she gotten herself into?

Chapter Fourteen

*Iron Heart woke on the next dawn—the day before he
was to be released from his silence—to the scream of
a woman. The wet nurse stood in the doorway to the
plundered nursery, and she screamed and screamed.
For every stick of furniture was broken, the walls
were splashed with crimson blood, and worse, far,
far worse, the baby was gone. Soon the nursery was
crowded with the people of the palace—guards,
servants, cooks, and maids. All stared at Iron Heart,
covered in blood in the nursery where his son had
once slept. But his heart did not ache until Princess
Solace pushed to the front of the crowd and beheld
her husband, and her eyes filled with sorrow....*
—from *Iron Heart*

She was avoiding him. This much was obvious to Sam
as he and Emeline moved through an odd, furtive dance
that morning. He would enter a room and she would turn
aside, giving him her shoulder. He would make his way

slowly, casually toward her; she would voice an excuse and exit the room before he ever got close to her. Over and over again they played this game, and each time he grew more frustrated. He no longer cared if his attempts to catch her were observed by the other members of the party. His only focus was on cornering her. And each time she eluded him, he became more determined.

They were in the library now, the house party confined to the indoors again today since the rain continued relentlessly outside. He was biding his time, making no move toward her, simply watching for an opening. She sat in the corner with her friend, Miss Fleming. The other woman was plain beside Emeline's dark beauty, but her eyes were sharp, and she was aware of his every move. Either Emeline had confided their involvement to her friend or the woman had guessed. Not that it mattered. Miss Fleming might be a fierce watchdog, but he wouldn't let her stand between him and his prey.

Sam grimaced at the thought and looked away. His emotions had never been this primitive, this ungentle, with a woman he wanted before. He knew he was losing control—had perhaps already run past the point of self-control—and yet he could not help himself. He wanted her. Her rejection was like ice held against his bare skin too long. Painful. Unacceptable. She'd let him make love to her; she could not withdraw herself from him now. And underneath all that, there was a layer of hurt that he didn't want to acknowledge. She'd hurt him, both his pride and something else within him that was basic to his being. It was agonizing, this hurt, and he needed it to stop.

He needed her.

"Won't you come play cards?" Rebecca asked beside him. He'd not even seen her approach.

"No," he said absently.

"Well, then you must at least stop looking at Lady Emeline like a dog at a sausage."

"Am I?"

"Yes," she said with exasperation. "I expect you to start drooling at any moment. It's not nice."

He turned his head and focused on her face. "Is it that bad?"

"Probably not to others, but I'm your sister. I see things."

"Yes, you do." He studied her a moment. The yellow of her gown seemed to make her shine. He suddenly realized that his sister was probably among the most lovely of the ladies assembled here. "Are you enjoying the party? I haven't asked."

"It's...interesting." She looked down, avoiding his eyes. "I was afraid at first that no one would talk to me, but that hasn't been the case. The other ladies have been nice. Mostly."

He frowned. "Who hasn't been nice to you?"

She flicked her hand impatiently. "No one. It doesn't matter. Don't fuss."

"I'm your brother; I'm supposed to fuss," he said, trying to make it a jest.

His words must not have come off well, because she didn't smile. Instead she just gazed at him quizzically.

He inhaled and tried again. "I've noticed that you've been keeping company with Mr. Green."

"Ye-es." Rebecca drew the word out, her voice cautious. Her head was down-bent, but she darted a glance at that gentleman now. Mr. Green was among the card players in the corner.

Sam felt like an ass. Rebecca had asked him to play cards. She must want him to give her an excuse to approach Green. He smiled down at her and extended his arm. "Shall we go play cards?"

But she squinted up at him. "I thought you didn't want to play?"

"Perhaps I've changed my mind."

She sighed as if he'd said something incredibly simple-minded. "Samuel, you don't want to play cards."

"Yes, but I thought you wanted to play cards," he said slowly. He felt as if he were searching for a hidden path. Or perhaps that he'd wandered off the path altogether.

"I did, but not for the reason you think. Have you heard Mr. Green's laugh?"

"Yes."

"Well, then," she said as if that decided the matter. She clasped her hands together as if bracing herself. "I heard Mr. Craddock was dead when you went to question him?"

He looked at her warily. "He was."

"I'm sorry. I suppose his widow knew nothing?"

"No. We'll have to wait until our return to London to continue the quest." And then he'd corner Thornton. Over Rebecca's shoulder, he saw Emeline turn and stroll from the room. Dammit! "Excuse me."

"She's fled again, I suppose," Rebecca said without even looking over her shoulder.

He bent and brushed a kiss across her temple, just where her dark hair was pulled back. "You are much too perceptive for a sister."

"I love you, too," she muttered.

He paused and looked at her, startled. She was a grown woman, his sister, and he didn't always understand her, but he did love her. He grinned down into her worried eyes.

And then he was out the door, on the hunt.

THIS WAS THE problem with engaging in an *affaire de coeur* with a colonial: he obviously didn't know when the thing was over.

Emeline darted a glance over her shoulder as she scurried into a dim servant's passage. She couldn't see the dratted man, but she could feel him somewhere behind her. Any other gentleman would know by now that he'd been given his conge. She'd been careful to not look at him, to not engage him in any conversation all this morning. She'd all but cut him dead, and still Samuel would not give up. And the terrible part was that something inside her thrilled at his determination. How he must want her to pursue her like this! She couldn't help but be flattered.

In a very exasperated way, of course.

Emeline rounded a corner, completely lost now, and shrieked when a large hand shot out of the darkness to grab her. Samuel pulled her behind a dusty curtain. There was a little alcove here in the passage that was used as a storage space—she could make out the shapes of barrels stacked against the wall. Nevertheless, it was a very small space, and she was forced up against his chest, which made her squeak.

"Hush," he murmured into her hair in the most provoking manner, "you are so loud."

"You nearly gave me apoplexy," she growled at him.

Pushing at his chest was having no discernible effect at all, so she gave up and peered at him in the gloom. "What do you think you're doing?"

"Trying to talk to you," he muttered. There was an edge to his voice, and she could feel, even through the miles of fabric between them, that he was quite hard. He sounded frustrated, and a small, not very nice feminine part of her rejoiced. "It's not been easy."

"That's because I haven't *wanted* to talk to you." She shoved at his chest, despite her vow not to, but he didn't give an inch.

"You're such a prickly little thing," he said.

"I don't want to see you anymore. I don't want to talk to you anymore." Her frustration boiled over, and she slapped him on the chest. "Let me go!"

"No."

"We can't go on like this." She set her jaw, making her voice hard. "It was pleasant while it lasted, but it's over now."

"I don't think so."

"This was nothing but a country affair. We will be going back to the city soon, and then all shall be as it was before. You must be on your way."

"Does that often work?" He sounded amused, not at all put out by her hurtful words.

"What?" she asked irritably.

"Ordering men about." His voice was low, but in the dim alcove it sounded loud to her ears. "I bet it does. They probably creep off, their tail between their legs to lick the wounds your sharp tongue cuts into them."

"You're impossible!"

"And you're spoiled by getting your own way all the time."

"I am not." She reared back, trying to see his features. "You don't know a thing about me."

She felt him still against her, and there was a sudden silence in the alcove.

When next he spoke, his voice was grave and horribly intimate in the dark. "I know that you have a cutting tongue and a quick mind that doesn't always think pleasant thoughts. And I know that you try to hide all that, as if you were like every other lady, a pretty thing made of meringue—sugary sweet and nothing but air."

"A lady should be sweet," she whispered. Awful that he knew such things about her. Worse than the intimacies revealed by sex. She maintained the facade with most, or at least she thought she did. A lady should be sweet, not sharp-tongued with mean thoughts flying through her mind all the time. She was too strong, too self-sufficient, too masculine. He must be repulsed.

"Are there rules for how a lady should be, then?" he asked her temple. "So many things you must do properly in this country, I don't know how you stand it."

"I—"

"I like a tart lady." Was that his tongue on the lobe of her ear? "I like the taste of sour, a sharp surprise, like an apple picked too green."

"Green apples give you a stomachache," she muttered against his chest. She felt a welling in her throat, as if tears threatened. How dare he do this again? Push past her defenses. Destroy her walls like so much papier-mâché?

He chuckled, the vibration rumbling against her neck. "Green apples never give me a stomachache. And they make the best pie. Other apples are too sweet; they turn to bland mush when cooked. But a green apple"—his hand was on her skirts, lifting and bunching them—"is brought to life by the sugar and spice. Just right on my tongue."

He brought his mouth down on hers, and she was lost all over again. The taste of him was intoxicating. She might be sour to him, but to her he was coffee, rich, darkly sweet, and pure male. She gasped, widening her mouth, wanting to drink him in. This would be the last time; she must stop this insanity soon. She pushed that thought away and simply felt, drifting in a sea of sensation, his arms about her, his tongue in her mouth, the sheer bulk of him over her.

The scrape of a shoe came from the hallway. Emeline broke the kiss and would've gasped, but Samuel covered her mouth with his hand.

"Has she lost her mind?" an ill-humored voice grumbled directly outside the curtain they hid behind. "To try tennis in the great hall. Jaysus!"

Emeline glanced down and saw a huge pair of buckle shoes just below the hem of the curtain. She looked up at Samuel in mute horror. His lips were trembling as he watched her, his hand still over her mouth. The dreadful man was amused! She narrowed her eyes at him. If she could've hit him without alerting the man standing not two feet away, she would've.

"Not much else they can do, is there?" A second man was speaking now, his voice higher and almost slurred, as if the servant had been drinking. "Toffs gotta have amusements, don't they?"

"Yeah, but tennis?" The first man's tone was rich with

disgust. "And in the house? Why can't they just do their cards or maybe dice or somethin'?"

"Dice? Don't be daft, man. Toffs don't dice."

"Well, why not? Whatsa matter with dice, I asks you?"

Emeline could feel Samuel shaking against her as he tried to contain his laughter. How he could find this amusing was beyond her understanding. She was nearly petrified with the fear of discovery. She glared at him as she lifted her foot and brought the heel of her shoe down on his moccasin. For a moment, she thought he'd lose his self-possession altogether. Instead of sobering him as she'd meant to do, apparently the feel of her heel digging painfully into his foot only amused him further. His eyes sparkled with silent laughter. She stood mutely glaring at him, and then he took his hand from her mouth and re- placed it with his own mouth. He kissed her deeply, thor- oughly, and altogether silently.

From without the curtain came a sigh. "Have you some of that good 'bacco?"

"Aye, right here."

"Ta."

Dear God, they were settling in to smoke a pipe! The thought sent horror spiking through Emeline, but at the same time, Samuel thrust his tongue into her mouth and the horror became mingled with pleasure, heightening both. He'd begun working on her skirts again, drawing them stealthily up. The fabric rustled as it moved over her thighs and she froze.

Outside the curtain, one of the men coughed. She could smell the fragrant scent of tobacco smoke now. They must have both lit pipes. Then that thought fled as Samuel brushed the bared curls at the top of her thighs.

"Why tennis, d'you 'spose?" the lower voice asked.

Samuel was threading through her maiden hair, his long fingers drawing nearer to that special spot. She clutched at his shoulders, distracted, confused, and incredibly aroused.

"I dunno," Higher Voice replied meditatively. "Better than lawn bowls, surely? At least indoors it is."

Samuel drew back his head and met her eyes. He grinned like the devil himself as his hand reached the apex of her slit. She had to consciously keep from moaning as he slid one finger over her clitoris. Gently he shook his head and at the same time circled that delicate bud.

"What about the windows?"

"What windows?"

"The windows in the great hall."

"Well, what about them?" High Voice sounded peeved.

Samuel bit his lip as if to still a laugh, but Emeline was riding a wave of terrified bliss. If the footmen outside opened the curtain now, they'd discover her nearly naked from the hips down and with Samuel's large hand working at her pussy. He inserted a thick finger into her core slowly, carefully, watching her face all the while. At the same time, his thumb pressed firmly down on that special bit of flesh. She opened her mouth in a silent gasp, glaring at him.

"Tennis balls would break them, won't they?" Low Voice said.

Whatever was the man babbling about? Not that it mattered, as long as the servant was engaged. Samuel slowly withdrew his finger and then quickly thrust it in again, making her hips jerk in reaction. She couldn't stand this much longer; she would give them away. She did the only thing she could do. She wrapped her hands about Samuel's neck and drew his mouth down to her own. He began a rapid thrusting of his finger, and she opened her mouth and invited his tongue in. She needed him. The feelings, the emotions, were intense. She wanted to climb his body, she wanted to suck his tongue, she wanted to bring him to his knees as he'd brought her to hers. Why did this man, of all the men she knew, have power over her? She turned into a puddle of yearning want around him, and only he seemed able to fill the void at her center. Her breath caught because he was indeed filling her. A second finger had joined the first, and he plunged them into her together, then spread them, widening her. She was wet, and even that thought couldn't bring her embarrassment right now. She was emotion and pleasure and never wanted this to stop.

"Best be back to work," Low Voice said. A shoe scraped against the passageway's stone floor as the man evidently put away his pipe. "Haven't looked in the cellar yet, have we?"

"Don't be daft, man." The footsteps were receding now. "The tennis things won't be in the cellar."

"You're such a clever one, tell me where they are, then." Low Voice's words floated back down the hall to them, and then there was silence.

Oh, Lord. Samuel had never stopped moving his fingers within her or kissing her open mouth all this time, and now she felt the first tremors start. She broke away and gasped, biting her lip, so that she wouldn't cry out loud.

But he withdrew his hand from her suddenly, catching her about the waist and lifting and shoving so that her rump balanced precariously on a barrel. Then he was between her legs, and she opened her eyes to watch him frantically rip at his breeches.

"God!" It was a groan. He freed himself and thrust into her, huge and hot, in the same movement. "God!"

She sank her nails into the cloth covering his shoulders and hung on for dear life, wrapping her legs high over his hips. He jerked rapidly in her, thrusting again and again and again. Her orgasm had not fully crested and now it began anew on a higher, sweeter, almost painful note. He had one hand braced flat against the wall by her head, one at her hip, and his cock buried deep in between her spread legs. She tore at his coat, ripping it off his upper arm, and filled her mouth with clean linen and his shoulder. Her eyes closed in bliss as she bit him. She clung to him while his cock took his pleasure of her. He rode her hard, rode her until she wanted to scream, rode her until he grabbed the back of her head and kissed her, his mouth wide and gasping as he came, his great body shaking. She could feel the heat of his seed flooding within her. And she knew, even as she crested the wave herself, she knew.

This must be the last time.

"MAY I TALK to you?" Emeline asked Jasper that afternoon. She'd caught him in an upper hallway. The guests were beginning to linger by the dining room in anticipation of a late luncheon.

"Of course." He smiled his wide, slightly lopsided

smile, and she could tell that he wasn't really paying attention to her.

"Jasper." She touched his sleeve.

He stopped and turned to her, his bushy eyebrows knit. "What?"

"It's important."

His eyes searched hers. So often they were vague or camouflaged behind the fool he liked to play. It was rare for him to look clearly, for her to see the man who lurked beneath the mask. Now, though, he was looking at her. Really looking at her. "Are you all right?"

She took a breath, and to her own astonishment, the truth escaped her lips. "No."

He blinked, then raised his head to glance around the hallway. They were at the back of the house, but there were still people about, footmen and maids bringing in the luncheon, guests assembling in the next room. He took her hand and pulled her through a doorway into another passage. Several doors lined the hall here, and he seemed to pick one at random. He opened it and stuck his head in.

"This'll do." He pulled her inside and shut the door behind them. It was a small sitting room or office, evidently unused because the fireplace was empty and sheets covered most of the furniture. He folded his arms. "Tell me."

Oh, how she wanted to! The urge to simply spill all her secrets was nearly overpowering. What a relief it would be if she could tell him everything and he would pat her shoulder and say, "There, there."

Except he wouldn't. Jasper might be the closest thing she had to a brother, he might be scandalously liberal

about love affairs and matters of the flesh, but when you
came right down to it, he was a viscount. He was expected
to sire an heir to a very old and very respected family.
The knowledge that his fiancée had been meeting secretly
with another man would not bring him joy. He might hide
it, but in the end, Emeline very much feared that he would
care.

So she pasted on a smile and lied. "I can't stand it here
anymore. I really can't. I know I should be more patient
and bear with Lady Hasselthorpe and her awful conversation and this dreadful house party, but I can't. Do you think
you could take me back to London, Jasper? Please?"

His face as he watched her make this speech was disconcertingly blank. Odd that such a manic man, a man
with many comical expressions should, when he chose, be
utterly impossible to read. But when she came to the end
and there was an awful dead silence, he suddenly sprang
forward, his face animated once more as if a toymaker
had turned the key on a very clever windup toy.

"Naturally, dear Emmie, naturally! I shall have my bag
packed in a thrice. Can our flight wait for the morning,
or...?"

"Today, if you don't mind. Now, please." Emeline
nearly wept with relief when he simply nodded.

He leaned forward and bussed her cheek. "I'd best alert
Pynch." And he strode off.

Emeline paused a moment to gather her sensibilities.
Horrible, this constant feeling of losing control over her
emotions. She'd always thought of herself as a level-
headed woman. The unemotional one, the one who others
leaned on. She'd hardly wept when Father had died; she'd
been too busy packing up Tante Cristelle, overseeing

the succession of the estate to the next earl, and settling their decimated family in London. Then people had been admiring, almost awed by her good sense and stoicism. Now she was like an infant—shook by whatever emotion stormed over her.

She made her way back to her room, always alert like some woodland animal afraid of the hunter. And that was quite apropos, wasn't it? Samuel was a hunter—a good one, too. He'd hunted her down this morning, chased her into a corner, and had had his way with her. She grimaced. No, that wasn't exactly right. Samuel might've chased her, but she'd been thrilled to be caught; and while he'd had his way with her, she'd been having her way with him. That was the real problem. She had no defenses against the man. She'd never thought of herself as being a slave to the flesh, but here she was fleeing a man because she could not withstand his advances. Evidently she'd been a wanton all these years and not even known it. Either that, or it was the man involved.

But she pushed that thought away as she entered her room. Harris was supervising the packing of all her things with the help of two maids from the house.

The lady's maid looked up as Emeline entered. "We shall be ready in a half hour more, should it please your ladyship."

"Thank you, Harris."

Emeline peeked out the door, scanning the hallway before venturing forth again. She'd rather spend that half hour hiding in her room where it was relatively safe, but her presence would only impede Harris's well-organized packing campaign. Besides, she couldn't in all conscience leave so abruptly without talking to Melisande.

Her friend's door was only a few down in the same hallway, and Emeline swiftly crept to it. Melisande should be downstairs already, waiting with the other guests, but she had a habit of arriving late to a gathering. Emeline had long suspected that her friend's tardiness was a ruse to keep from having to engage in conversation. Melisande was rather shy, although she hid her affliction well beneath a carapace of aloofness and sarcasm.

Emeline scratched at the door. There was a rustle within, and then Melisande cracked the door. She cocked an eyebrow at the sight of her friend and held the door wide in silent invitation.

Emeline hurried inside. "Close the door."

Her friend's eyebrows winged higher. "Are we hiding?"

"Yes," Emeline replied, and went to warm her hands by the fire.

She heard Melisande's skirts rustling behind her. "I think it's a Germanic dialect."

"What?" Emeline turned to find Melisande seated in a wingback chair.

Her friend gestured to the book spread on her knees. "Your nurse's book. I think it's some type of Germanic dialect, probably spoken only in a small area, maybe only a village or two. I can try to translate it for you, if you like."

Emeline stared at the book. Somehow it didn't seem as important as it once had. "I don't care."

"Really?" Melisande fingered a page. "I've already figured out the title: *Four Soldiers Returned from War and Their Adventures.*"

Emeline was distracted. "But I thought it was a book of fairy tales?"

"It is, that's the funny thing. These four soldiers all have the strangest names, like the one I told you about, Iron Heart, and—"

"It doesn't matter anymore," Emeline said, and then felt awful when her friend's face, unusually animated, shuddered. "I'm sorry, dear, I'm a beast. Do go on."

"No. I think what you have to tell me is more important." Melisande closed the old book and laid it aside. "What is it?"

"I'm leaving." Emeline dropped into the chair opposite her friend. "Today."

Melisande relaxed her rigid posture to lean back into her chair. Her eyes were hooded. "Has he hurt you?"

"Samuel? No!"

"Then why the haste?"

"I can't...I can't..." Emeline threw her hands up in frustration. "I can't seem to resist him."

"Not at all?"

"No!"

"That is interesting," her friend murmured. "You're usually so controlled. He must be a very—"

"Yes, well, he is," Emeline said. "And what do you know of such matters? You're supposed to be a maiden."

"I know," Melisande said. "But we're discussing you. Have you thought what you'll do if you're increasing?"

Emeline's heart seemed to stop dead at her fear spoken aloud. "I'm not."

"Do you know that?"

"No."

"So, if you are?"

"I shall have to marry him." She said the words with dread, but inside her chest, something traitorous leapt with a forbidden joy. If she was pregnant, she'd have no choice, would she? Even with all her doubts and fears, she'd have to embrace the catamount.

"And if you're not?"

Emeline thrust aside the traitorous emotions. She could not marry a colonial. "I'll do what I'd always planned to do."

Melisande sighed. "Will you tell Lord Vale about what happened during this house party?"

Emeline swallowed. "No."

Melisande was looking down now, her face closed and impossible to read. "That is probably best if you want to make a life with him. A man often cannot take the truth."

"Do you think me awful?"

"No. No, of course not, dear." Melisande glanced up, a flicker of surprise crossing her face. "Why would you think that I'd judge you?"

Emeline closed her eyes. "So many would. I think I would, if I only heard the facts and not the people involved."

"Well, I am not such a Puritan as you," her friend said with pragmatic flatness. "But I do have one question. How will leaving here help your problem with Mr. Hartley?"

"The distance, don't you see? If I'm not in the same house, or county, as he is, well, then I won't be as susceptible to his...his..." Emeline waved her hands. "You know."

Melisande looked thoughtful—and not altogether convinced. "And when he returns to London as well?"

"It'll be all over. I'm sure time and distance will make

a great difference." Emeline said the words sturdily, as if she completely believed them, but inside she was not so certain.

And no matter her words, Melisande must've sensed the doubt. Her eyebrows were up almost to her hairline again. But her friend didn't comment. She simply stood and gave one of her rare signs of affection.

Melisande drew Emeline into her thin chest and hugged her tightly. "Good luck, then, dear. I hope your plan works."

And Emeline laid her head against her friend's shoulder and prayed, eyes squeezed shut, that her plan would work. If it didn't, she had nowhere else to run.

Chapter Fifteen

Murder! cried the guards. Murder! cried the lords and ladies of the court. Murder! cried the people of the Shining City. And all Iron Heart could do was clasp his head in his bloodied hands. The princess cried and begged, first to her mute husband that he might break his silence and explain what he had done, and then to her father for mercy, but in the end, it was no use. The king had no choice but to sentence Iron Heart to death by fire, the execution to be carried out before the next dawn....
—from *Iron Heart*

"It was a lovely party, wasn't it?" Rebecca broke an hour's silence with her tentative question.

Sam tore his gaze from the gloomy scenery rolling past and tried to focus on his younger sister. She was sitting across from him in their rented carriage, looking forlorn, which was his fault, he knew. It had been three days since Emeline had quit the house party so abruptly. He hadn't even known she was gone until long after she hadn't shown for luncheon on the day they'd made love in the corridor. By the time he discovered her flight, she'd had a two-hour start.

Still, he would've followed her if Rebecca hadn't talked some sense into him. She'd begged him to stay, pointing out the scandal he'd create if he pursued Lady Emeline so soon after she'd left. Personally, he didn't care two figs about possible wagging tongues. But Rebecca was a different matter entirely. She'd been spending quite a bit of time with several of the young ladies from good English families. Scandal would kill any budding friendships.

Sam had tamped down his raging need to hunt Emeline, catch her, and hold her until she came to her senses and stayed by him. He'd sat on his hands and made polite conversation with giggling girls and insipid matrons. He'd dressed in his best clothes, played idiot games, and ate overly rich foods. And at night he'd dreamed of her snapping tongue and her soft, warm breasts. For three days, he'd restrained himself, until finally members of the house party had begun to leave and Rebecca deemed it appropriate for them to depart Hasselthorpe House as well. It had been three days of hell, but that was hardly Rebecca's fault, and he was a cad to be such a boring traveling partner.

He tried to make up for the hours of silence she'd endured. "Did you enjoy the party?"

"Yes." She smiled at him in relief. "At the end, many of the other young ladies were talking to me and the Hopedale sisters have invited me to come have tea with them some afternoon in London."

"They should've been talking to you at the beginning of the party."

"They had to get to know me, didn't they? It's really not all that different from people at home."

"Do you like it here in England?" he asked softly.

She hesitated, then shrugged. "I suppose so." She looked down thoughtfully at her hands in her lap. "And what about you? Do you like England enough to stay here with Lady Emeline?"

He hadn't expected such a blunt query, although he should have. Rebecca was a very perceptive girl. When they'd arrived in London, he'd planned on staying only long enough to do his business with Mr. Wedgwood and look into the Spinner's Falls massacre. Now his business was finished, and soon he hoped to talk to Thornton and clear up Spinner's Falls as well. What then? "I don't know."

"Why not?"

He glanced at Rebecca impatiently. "She hasn't stood still long enough for me to talk to her, for one thing."

Rebecca watched him for a moment, then asked hesitantly, "Do you love her?"

"Yes." He answered without considering the matter, but he found that it was true. Somehow, without his even realizing it, he'd fallen in love with his prickly Emeline. The thought was strange and at the same time perfectly natural, as if he'd known all along that she was the woman he needed. It was a joyous feeling, as if he'd been waiting all his life for this missing piece.

"You should tell her, you know."

He looked at his sister in exasperation. "Thank you for

tutoring me in love. I'll tell her as soon as the lady permits me to catch her."

She giggled. "And then what will you do?"

He thought of Lady Emeline and how she argued with him every chance she got. He thought of how far apart they were in rank. He thought about the fear she tried to hide, successfully with everyone, it seemed, but him. He thought about how startled she looked when she fell apart in his arms, as if she couldn't fathom not being in control of everything around her, including her body. And he thought about the sadness he sometimes saw in her eyes. He wanted to hold that sadness, cradle it and comfort it until it turned to happiness. He wanted to feel her hands on him again, like the night she'd bound his broken feet, soothing him, laying her balm on his soul. She'd warmed him. She'd healed him.

And he knew what he would do. He grinned at his sister. "I'll marry her, of course."

"WHY ISN'T MR. Hartley home yet?" Daniel asked.

Emeline looked up in time to see her only child poke a piece of paper into the fire in her room. The paper caught and Daniel dropped it just before the flame reached his fingers. The burning sheet fluttered down, fortunately landing in the hearth rather than on her carpet.

She paused in writing out a series of last-minute instructions for the party tonight. "Dearest, would you mind not setting Mother's room afire? I don't think Harris would be particularly pleased."

"Aww."

"And I'd rather you not burn up your fingers. They are

quite useful, you know, and you might need them in later life."

Daniel grinned at this silliness and came over to climb into a chair near her desk. She winced as his shoes scraped against the satin chair cushion but decided not to comment. It was nice to have him here with her again after being separated so long.

He leaned on her desk, his chin in his crossed arms. "He must come back soon, mustn't he?"

Emeline looked back at her writing, struggling to maintain a composed expression. She didn't have to ask who Daniel was referring to; he was a tenacious child and obviously wouldn't give up the subject of their neighbor—her lover—easily.

"I don't know, dear. I'm not privy to Mr. Hartley's plans."

Daniel scratched one finger across her blotter, wrinkling his nose as he made an indent in the paper with his fingernail. "But he is coming back?"

"I assume so." Emeline inhaled. "I believe Cook was making pear tarts in the kitchen today. Perhaps you should go see if they are done."

Usually the mention of freshly made tarts would be an immediate distraction for her son.

Not today. "I hope he comes back. I like him."

And her heart contracted. Three simple words and she was reduced to near tears. Carefully, she laid aside her pen. "I like him, too, but Mr. Hartley has his own life to lead. He can't be always around to entertain you, to entertain us."

Daniel was still watching his fingernail, his bottom lip beginning to protrude now.

She tried to make her voice cheerful. "There's always Lord Vale. You like him, too, don't you? I can see if he'd escort us to Hyde Park." Her son's lip protruded farther. "Or...or to a fair or perhaps even fishing."

Daniel cocked his head to look at her skeptically. "Fishing?"

Emeline tried to picture Jasper with a fishing pole, standing beside a rushing river. Her imaginary Jasper immediately slipped, flailed wildly, and fell into the river.

She winced. "Maybe not fishing."

Daniel was back to pressing half-moon shapes into her blotter. "Lord Vale's all right, but he doesn't have a big rifle."

Faint praise indeed.

"I'm sorry, darling," she said softly.

She looked down at the papers scattered on her desk, at the instructions she'd been writing, and her vision blurred. She felt as if her heart were breaking. Damn Samuel for ever coming into their lives. For seeking her out at Mrs. Conrad's salon that first day, for talking to her son so gently, for making her feel again.

She gasped at the thought. That was the real problem. He'd made her feel again, cracked the shell that had hardened around her emotions and left her defenseless and vulnerable. She was too raw now, her skin too soft. How long would this feeling last? How long before she could grow another shell? She looked at Daniel, her beautiful boy. He was growing so fast. It seemed like he'd been a tender little babe only yesterday, and today she worried for her furniture with his big shoes. Did she even want to shield herself from emotion again?

Impulsively, she leaned forward, her head nearly

touching his. "It'll be all right. It really will. I'll make sure it is."

One side of his face scrunched up in thought. "But can it be all right with Mr. Hartley?"

"No, dear." She straightened and turned so that he wouldn't see the sadness in her eyes. "I don't think it can."

"But—"

They both looked up as the door opened and Tante Cristelle entered the room. The old lady looked at her with a gaze that had always been too sharp.

Emeline turned back to Daniel. "I must speak with Tante now. Why don't you see if those pear tarts are done yet? Perhaps Cook will let you sample one."

"Yes, ma'am." Daniel wasn't happy at the dismissal, but he'd always been a good boy. He slid off the chair and made a half bow to his aunt before slipping from the room.

"That one missed you most severe while you were away." The lines around Tante Cristelle's mouth became more pronounced in her disapproval. "I do not think it is well that he is so close with you."

This conversation was old, and normally Emeline might argue, but today she didn't have the heart. She gathered her papers silently. Behind her she heard the thump of Tante Cristelle's cane on the Persian carpet and then felt the old woman's frail hand on her shoulder. She looked up into wise eyes.

"It is the right thing that you do tonight; never fear that." Tante Cristelle patted her once—an extreme outpouring of affection—and walked from the room.

Leaving Emeline with eyes once again filled with tears.

*   *   *

BY THE TIME the carriage pulled up outside Sam's town house, it had been dark for hours. A late start combined with a wait for fresh horses at one of the inns had made the journey back to London an overlong one. And then, once they had turned into the street where they lived, there had been an uncommon crush of carriages. Someone must be hosting a ball. As Samuel stepped down and turned to help Rebecca from the carriage, he realized that the lights were blazing in the house next to his. Emeline's house.

"Is Lady Emeline having a party?" Rebecca asked. She hesitated before the steps. "I didn't know she would be throwing one, did you?"

Sam slowly shook his head. "Obviously we weren't invited."

He saw her glance swiftly at him. "Perhaps she planned it before she met us. Or . . . or she might not have expected us back from the country so soon."

"Yes, that must be it," he said grimly.

The little witch was thumbing her nose at him, showing him that he had no part in her London life. He knew that he shouldn't rise to the bait, but his hands had already bunched into fists, his legs twitching, ready to stride into her house and confront her. He grimaced. Now was not the time.

He relaxed his fists and held out his arm to his sister. "Shall we see if Cook can lay out a cold supper for us?"

She smiled up at him. "Yes, let's."

He led her up the front steps and inside, all the while aware of the house next door and the elegantly dressed guests arriving for Emeline's party. He sat his sister in the dining room, ordered a simple supper, and was even able to make polite conversation while they ate. But his mind was elsewhere, imagining Emeline in her most elegant gown, her bosom glowing white and erotic in the light of thousands of candles.

After they ate, Rebecca excused herself, already yawning. Sam went to the library and poured himself a glass of French brandy. He paused and held the glass up to the light. The liquid shown translucent amber. When he was growing up, his father had drunk homemade spirits, bought from a family ten miles away through the woods. Sam had once taken a sip. The drink had been clear like water and hot, burning his throat as he swallowed. Had Pa ever drunk French brandy in his entire life? Maybe once while visiting Uncle Thomas in the big city of Boston. But it would have been an exotic thing, something special to be savored and thought about for days afterward.

Sam sank into a gilt armchair. He didn't belong here; he knew that. There was too wide a gulf between the life he'd led as a boy and the life he led now. A man could change only so much in one lifetime. He would never fully fit into English society, and he didn't really want to. This was the life that Emeline led. The beautiful town houses, the French brandy, the balls that continued until well past midnight. The ocean that yawned wide between her world and his—both metaphorically and physically— was too great a distance. He knew all that, had considered it many times before.

And it didn't matter.

He gulped the rest of the brandy and rose with purpose. He needed to see Emeline. Worlds apart or no, she was a woman and he was a man. Some things were basic.

Outside his town house, he saw that the lights still blazed next door. Coachmen sat huddled on their perches, a few running footmen stood together, passing a bottle between them. He leapt up Emeline's front steps and was confronted with a burly footman. The man made a move as if to block his path.

Sam stared at him hard. "I'm Lady Emeline's neighbor."

This was no invitation, of course, but the footman must've seen the determination in his eyes and decided the point wasn't worth arguing. "Yes, sir." He held the door open.

Sam crossed the threshold and immediately realized his peril. The hall held only a few servants, but the grand, curving staircase was crowded. He began making his way up the stairs, past loudly talking groups. Emeline's ballroom was on the upper floor, and as he neared, the clamor became louder, the air heavier and hotter. He felt sweat start at his neck. He hadn't been in such a crowded space since the Westerton ball, and there he had succumbed to his demons most ignominiously. *Not here,* he prayed.

By the time he made the entrance to the ballroom, his breath was coming fast and short, as if he'd run miles. For a moment, he considered turning back. Emeline had lit thousands of beeswax candles in her ballroom, in mirrored chandeliers overhead. The place was bright, sparkling like a fairyland. Swags of scarlet silk hung from the walls and ceiling, orange and red flowers caught in the knots. The room was beautiful, elegant, but he didn't care. His woman was somewhere in this room, and he meant to catch her and hold her.

Sam inhaled carefully through his mouth and dove into the mass of sweating, milling humanity. He could hear violins faintly playing, but they were all but drowned out by laughter and chattering voices. A gentleman in purple velvet turned and bumped into Sam's chest. *Blood and screaming, eyes wide in a white face below a bleeding scalp.* He closed his eyes, shoving past the man. Ahead was an opening in the crowd where the dancers paced with stately grace. He made the edge of the dance floor and paused, gasping for air. A matron in yellow silk eyed him and whispered behind her fan to her companion. Damn them all, anyway, these overfed, overornamented English aristocrats. When had they ever known fear or felt the splatter of blood from a fellow soldier? *The surprise in a young soldier's face as half his head was blown away.*

The dancers halted, no more out of breath than if they'd sat for the last five minutes. They looked bored and bloodless, as if they could barely take the trouble to keep themselves upright. The crowd shuffled against him, and he had to close his eyes and concentrate to keep from striking out at the nearest person. He breathed deeply and tried to think of Emeline's eyes. In his mind, they were narrowed with exasperation and that made him almost smile.

He opened his eyes, and Lord Vale strode into the middle of the dance floor, now nearly empty. "Friends! Friends, may I have your ear?"

Vale's shout, loud though it was, was swallowed by the mass of bodies. Nevertheless, the conversations began to die.

"Friends, I have something to say!"

A group of young gentlemen moved in front of Sam, obscuring his vision. They looked barely old enough to shave.

"Friends!" came Vale's shout again, and Sam caught a glimpse of scarlet.

His heart galloped. He put out a hand to shove against a padded shoulder, and the young buck in front of him turned to glare. Sam inhaled and caught the stink of sweat. Male sweat, sour and burning, the smell of fear. *The prisoner MacDonald crouching under a wagon as the battle raged all around. MacDonald catching Sam's eye from his hiding place. MacDonald grinning and winking.*

"I have an announcement that pleases me greatly."

Sam started forward, ignoring the stench, ignoring his demons, ignoring the realization that he was already too late.

"Lady Emeline Gordon has consented to be my wife."

The crowd applauded as Sam barreled through the men, those dead and alive, who stood between him and Emeline. He came out on the dance floor and saw Emeline smiling politely beside Vale. Vale had his arms raised, triumphant in this moment. Emeline turned her head and her smile died as she saw Sam.

He started for them with no thought in his head save murder.

Vale caught sight of him. His eyes narrowed and he nodded to someone behind Sam. Sam felt his arms seized and pulled behind him. And then he was being hustled from the ballroom by two burly footmen, a third clearing the way ahead. It happened so fast he didn't even have time to call out to Emeline. At the side of the ballroom, Sam finally came to himself and twisted violently, catching one of the footmen by surprise. He pulled his arm free and swung at the man, but before his fist could connect, he was shoved from behind. The first footman still holding him let go, and Sam half fell into the hall. He straightened and whirled, and Vale's fist slammed into his jaw.

Sam stumbled back, landing on his arse. Vale stood over him, his fists still balled. "That was for Emmie, you whoreson." He turned to the footmen behind him. "Take this rubbish and pitch it—"

But Vale didn't finish the sentence. Sam rose, low and fast, and charged him, catching him about the knees. Vale went down with a thunderous crash, Sam on top. Several women shrieked and the crowd scattered away from them. Sam began to crawl up him, but Vale twisted, and they both went tumbling, rolling toward the stairs. A matron screamed as she fled down the stairs, pushing other ladies ahead of her. Their skirts swept across suddenly cleared steps.

Sam grabbed the top banister to stop the momentum of their roll. He teetered, his shoulders over the first step, until Vale kicked at his undefended stomach and Sam had to let go to shield himself. He slid, head-down, but managed to snatch Vale's arm, bringing the other man with him. They careened without control down the stairs, tangled together in a murderous heap. Each tread raked painfully across Sam's back as they thumped down. He no longer cared if he lived through this encounter or not. He just wanted to make sure he took his enemy with him. Midway down, they slammed into a banister, halting their descent. Sam hooked an arm around a wood pole and kicked viciously at Vale, catching him good and solid, low on the side.

Vale arched under the impact. "Hell!" He twisted and pressed his forearm down on Sam's windpipe, thrusting hard. Sam gagged from the weight. Vale brought his head close to Sam's and spoke low, his face black with rage.

"You stupid, shitty colonial. How dare you put your filthy hands on—"

Sam let go of the railing and slammed both hands against Vale's ears. Vale rocked back, freeing Sam's throat, and Sam gasped painfully for air. But they were sliding farther down the stairs. Vale pummeled him, hitting at face and belly and thighs. Sam jolted with each impact, but strangely, he didn't feel a thing. His entire being was filled with rage and sorrow. Sam punched the other man, striking anything he could hit. He felt his knuckles split against Vale's cheekbone and felt the wet smack as the other man's nose broke. His back jarred into the landing. Vale was on top now, a clear advantage, except that Sam didn't goddamn care. He'd lost everything, and right now this man was the cause of it all. Vale might have righteous anger, but Sam had the rage of despair, pure and simple. There was no match.

Sam lurched up, right through Vale's punches. He could feel their impact on his face, but he plowed through the blows. There was only the need to kill. He caught Vale and threw the bigger man down, and then Sam was hitting him, slamming his fists into Vale's face, and the feeling was glorious. He felt the crunch of bone, saw the splatter of blood, and didn't care. Didn't care.

Didn't care.

Until he caught a movement from the corner of his eye. He swung up and froze, his clenched, bloody fist only inches from Emeline's face.

She flinched. "Don't."

He stared at her, this woman he'd made love to, this woman he'd poured his soul into.

This woman he loved.

She had tears in her eyes. "Don't." She reached out one small, white hand and wrapped it around his bruised and bloodied fist. "Don't."

Below him, Vale wheezed.

Her gaze cut to her fiancé and her tears overflowed. "Please, Samuel. Don't."

He felt, vaguely, the pain begin, both in his body and in his heart. Sam lowered his hand and lurched upright. "Damn you."

He staggered down the stairs and out into the cold night.

Chapter Sixteen

That night, Iron Heart lay chained in the dank, cold dungeon and knew that he had lost everything. His baby son was gone, his princess wife was in despair, the kingdom stood undefended, and before the dawn, he would be put to death. One word from his lips would exonerate him. That same word would send him back to sweeping the streets and kill Princess Solace. He did not care how his life ended, but he could not be the instrument of the princess's death. For a strange and wonderful thing had happened in the six years of his marriage.
He'd fallen in love with his wife. . . .
—from *Iron Heart*

When Rebecca descended the stairs the next morning, she startled two maids. They had been standing, heads bent close together, whispering furiously. At the sound of her footfall, they leapt apart and stared up at her.

Rebecca lifted her chin. "Good morning."

"Miss." The older one recovered first, bobbing a curtsy before hurrying away with her friend.

Rebecca sighed. The servants were naturally excited about the events of the night before. Samuel had awakened the entire household when he'd stumbled in the front door with blood streaming down his face. He'd been adamant that she not send for a doctor, but for once Rebecca had overridden her older brother. The blood and his apathy had frightened her half to death. She hadn't seen Lord Vale, but from bits and pieces she'd gathered from the doctor and the servants, the viscount was in even worse condition.

Rebecca wished desperately that she could tiptoe next door and just talk to Lady Emeline. Sit and commiserate with her. Lady Emeline always seemed to know exactly what should be done in any given situation, and she was the type of woman who could set everything right. Always assuming that this problem could be set right. But Rebecca very much feared that she might never talk to Lady Emeline again. She doubted that there was an etiquette rule that covered this situation. *How to approach a lady whose fiancé your brother has beaten into a bloody pulp.* It was very awkward.

She wandered into the dining room, her brows knit. Samuel had hardly spoken the night before, and she knew from the servants that he hadn't stirred from his bedroom this morning. She had the dining room to herself and her worries. Actually, she felt the most lonely since she'd set foot in England. She rather wished that there was someone she could confide in. But Samuel wasn't talking, and everyone else in the house was a servant.

Rebecca reached for a chair only to find a masculine

hand pulling it out for her. She looked up—far up—into the face of O'Hare the footman.

"Oh, I didn't see you."

"Yes, miss," he said as formally as if he'd never talked to her so casually just a few weeks ago.

There was another footman in the room, of course, and the butler lurked somewhere about. Rebecca sat in her chair feeling a bit deflated. She looked down at the tablecloth in front of her and struggled to hold back sudden tears. Now, that was silly! To go weeping like a baby just because a servant didn't acknowledge one as a friend. Even if one could really use a friend right now.

She watched as O'Hare's big, reddened hand poured her tea. "I wonder . . ." She trailed off, thinking hard.

"Yes, miss?" His voice was so nice, with that bit of a burr softening it.

She looked up and met his green eyes. "My brother's very favorite sweet in all the world is crabapple jelly, and he hasn't had any in ages. Do you think it might be possible to purchase some?"

O'Hare's green eyes blinked. He really did have the most lovely, long eyelashes, almost like a girl's. "I don't know if there's crabapple jelly at the grocer's, miss, but I can go look—"

"No, not you." She smiled sweetly at the other footman, a bowlegged fellow who'd been watching their conversation with wide, not-too-bright eyes. "I'd like *you* to go."

"Yes'm," the second footman said. He looked confused, but he was well trained. He bowed and exited, presumably in search of crabapple jelly.

Which left Rebecca alone with O'Hare.

She took a sip of her tea—too hot, she usually let it sit for a minute to cool off—and set the teacup down precisely on the table. "I haven't seen you since our return from the country."

"No, miss."

She twisted the teacup a bit. "I just realized. I don't even know your name."

"It's O'Hare, miss."

"Not that one." She wrinkled her nose at her teacup. "Your other name. Your Christian name."

"Gil, miss. Gil O'Hare. At yer service."

"Thank you, Gil O'Hare."

She folded her hands in her lap. He stood behind her like a proper footman, ready to serve her anything she might need. Except what she needed wasn't on the table or sideboard.

"Did...did you see my brother last night?"

"Yes, miss."

She looked at the basket of buns in the middle of the table. Really, she wasn't hungry at all. "I suppose they're all talking about it in the kitchens."

He cleared his throat but said nothing more, which she took as a resounding affirmative.

She sighed forlornly. "It was rather spectacular, how he staggered in and collapsed in the hall. I don't think I've ever seen so much blood in my life. I'm sure his shirt is quite ruined."

Behind her, there was a rustle, and then his arm appeared, clothed in a green coat. He reached for the basket of buns. "Would you like a bun? Cook made 'em fresh just this morn."

She watched as he picked one out for her and put it on her plate. "Thank you."

"Yer welcome, miss."

"It's just that I have no one to talk about it with," she said in a rush, staring down at the lone bun on her plate. "For my brother to brawl with Lord Vale like this...It's very confusing."

Gil walked over to the sideboard and brought back a dish of coddled eggs. "You made some fine friends at that house party you went to, didn't you, miss?"

She twisted to look at him as he spooned eggs onto her plate. He didn't meet her eyes. "How do you know that?"

He shrugged. There was a wash of red high on his cheeks. "Talk in the kitchen. Have some o' that." He handed her a fork.

"I expect they were referring to the Hopedale sisters." She absently ate a bite of eggs. "They probably won't ever want to see me again after last night."

"Are you sure?"

Rebecca poked at the mound of yellow eggs and then took another bite. "I doubt anyone in society will be receiving us."

"They'd be right lucky to have you at one of them fancy parties," Gil said from behind her.

She twisted to look at him.

His brow was furrowed, but he smoothed it as she watched. "If you don't mind me sayin' so, miss."

"No, I don't mind." She smiled at him. "It's rather sweet of you."

"Thank you, miss."

She turned back to the table and took a sip of tea. It

was cooler now. "It's just that even if they would see me, I don't know if I could talk to the Misses Hopedale about this. When we converse, it's usually about the weather and types of hats, which I don't know that much about but seems to be a subject they enjoy. And once in a while we discuss which is better, lemon custard or chocolate pudding? It's rather a leap to go from puddings to my brother attempting to murder a peer."

"Yes, miss." He left her side again to walk to the sideboard. "There's a lovely herring here and some gammon."

"But maybe that's what London ladies always talk about." She took her fork and prodded the bun on her plate. "I wouldn't know. I'm from the Colonies, and there's lots that we do different there."

"Is there, miss?" Gil hesitated, then picked up the plate with the herring on it and came over to her.

"Oh, yes," she said. "Why, in the Colonies, a man's birth isn't nearly so important."

"Is that so?" He placed a portion of the herring on her plate.

"Mmm." She ate a bite of fish. "That's not to say that people don't judge other people. I think that happens everywhere. But it's more a matter of what the man has accomplished in his life and if he has money. And you know, anyone can earn money if he works hard enough. I say, this herring is very good."

"I'll tell Cook you said so," Gil said from behind her. "But any man, miss?"

"What?" She was rather enjoying the herring. Maybe all she'd needed was a proper breakfast.

"Can any man become successful in America?"

She paused and glanced over her shoulder. Gil's expression was tense, as if her answer mattered greatly to him. "Yes, I think so. After all, my brother grew up in a one-room cabin. Did you know that?"

He shook his head.

"It's true. And now he's very respected in Boston. The ladies all want him at their parties, and many gentlemen consult him on business. Of course"—she turned back around to fork up a bite of fish—"he started out with Uncle Thomas's importing business, but it was a very small company when Samuel inherited it. Now it's quite the biggest in Boston, I believe, all due to Samuel's hard work and quick wits. And I know many other gentlemen in Boston who had humble beginnings and have become very successful."

"I see."

"I'm not really used to people like the aristocrats here. People who are so bound by the past and expectations. For instance, I don't understand why Lady Emeline has decided to marry Lord Vale."

"They're lords and ladies, miss. Stands to reason that they'd marry one of their own."

"Yes, but what if they fall in love with someone who *isn't* a lord or lady?" Rebecca scowled at her herring. "I mean, love isn't something one can control, is it? That's the wonder of it. That a person might fall in love with someone completely unexpected. Romeo and Juliet, for example."

"Who, miss?"

"You know. Shakespeare."

"Afraid I haven't heard of them people."

She twisted about to peer up at him. "Oh, that's a pity;

it's a very good play up until the ending. You see, Romeo falls in love with Juliet, who is the daughter of his enemy, or rather, his *family's* enemy."

"Doesn't sound very sharp of him," Gil commented practically.

"Well, that's the point, isn't it? He didn't have any choice in who he fell in love with, whether or not it was *sharp* of him."

"Huh," said the footman. He didn't look particularly convinced about the overpowering nature of love. "So, then what happened?"

"Oh, there's several duels and a secret marriage and then they die."

His eyebrows shot up. "They die?"

"I told you the end wasn't particularly good," Rebecca said defensively. "Anyway, it's all very romantic."

"Think living might be better than bein' dead and romantic," Gil said.

"Well, perhaps you're right. Love doesn't seem to have made my brother very happy."

"Is that why he attacked Lord Vale, then?"

"I guess so. He loves Lady Emeline." She glanced at him guiltily. "But you shouldn't tell anyone."

"I won't, miss."

She smiled at him, and he smiled back, his lovely green eyes crinkling at the corners, and she thought about how comfortable he made her feel. With so many people, she spent all her time watching every word she said and constantly worrying over what they thought of her. But with Gil she could just talk.

She turned back to the table to finish her meal, secure in the knowledge that Gil was standing behind her.

* * *

EMELINE WAS IN the small sitting room of her town house, drinking tea, listening to Tante Cristelle, and wishing she could be just about anywhere else.

"You are lucky," her aunt proclaimed. "Very lucky. I do not know how that man could hide his murderous habit so well."

That man was Samuel. Tante Cristelle had decided by a logic understood only by herself that the terrible fight on the stairs the night before was the result of Samuel's true violent nature breaking free from his control.

"Madmen are very cunning, I believe. And he did have very odd shoes," Tante Cristelle said, and took a thoughtful sip of tea.

"I don't think his shoes had anything to do with it, Tante," Emeline muttered.

"But, yes, they must!" Her aunt stared in outrage. "A person's shoes tell so much about them. The drunkard wears the shoes so dirty and worn. The lady of ill-repute has shoes too ornamented. And the so-murderous man, he wears the oddity—the moccasins of an Indian savage."

Emeline tucked her feet beneath her skirts. The slippers she wore today were rather unfortunately embroidered in gold.

Hastily she sought to change the subject. "I don't know how we will survive the gossip. Half of society was crowded into the upper hall last night, the better to see Mr. Hartley throw Jasper down the stairs."

"Yes, and that is very odd."

Emeline raised her eyebrows. "That everyone was staring?"

"No, no!" The older woman waved an impatient hand. "That Lord Vale allowed himself to be tossed so cavalierly."

"I don't think—"

"Mr. Hartley is not so big as milord Vale, and yet he was able to overpower him. It makes one wonder how he came by this strength."

"Perhaps it was the strength of a madman," Emeline muttered with dark humor. She didn't want to think about the fight, the sight of two men she loved trying to kill each other, the look in Samuel's eyes at the last...But it was hard to distract Tante Cristelle off the subject. "The wedding will be ruined, I know. We will be lucky to have more than two guests attend."

Tante Cristelle immediately took the contrary opinion. "It is not so very bad, this gossip and excitement. One would think that gossip is always bad, but this is not so. The talk will cause many to come to your wedding. I think you will have quite the turnout."

Emeline shuddered and looked down at the teacup in her lap. The thought of all those people coming to her wedding just to gawk, hoping perhaps that Samuel would make another appearance and disrupt the wedding, was terribly distasteful. And worse, she knew Samuel had washed his hands of her. The look of disillusionment, of *disgust,* in his eyes last night had felt like a physical blow. He would never want to see her again, she knew. Which was just as well, of course. Far better to make a clean break.

If only she could pick up her spirits a bit so that she could face her future. This path had been laid out for her before she was ever born. She was an aristocrat, the daughter and sister to earls, a woman of family and standing. All that was expected of her was that she make a good match, have children, and conform to society's rules. It was not such a hard task, and until now she had never questioned it. She'd been a good wife and mother. Hadn't she held the remains of her family together against all odds? Hadn't she found a second husband as worthy as the first? And if there would be no fidelity in the marriage, if the love was a fraternal, rather than passionate one, that was only to be expected. Only a fool would balk at her path at this late date.

Only a fool.

Emeline bit her lip and gazed into her cooling tea as Tante Cristelle droned on across from her. Despite all the lectures she gave herself, she couldn't stop mourning for a man not of her world. Samuel had looked at her and really seen her. He was the first and probably the last in her life to ever do so. And what was more miraculous, he'd not recoiled. He'd seen her awful temper, her unwomanly strength of mind, and he'd said they were good. No wonder she still mourned him. Such complete acceptance was intoxicating.

Still, she was a fool.

PEOPLE LOOKED AT Sam as he made his way through the London streets that afternoon. They would peer at him out of the corner of their eyes, then look quickly away again, especially if they met his gaze. He'd seen himself in the mirror this morning and knew what they gawked at: a blackening eye, a cut and swollen lip, and the bruises turning purple on his cheek and jaw. He knew why they looked, but he hated it nevertheless. He'd never been anonymous in a crowd—he wore moccasins, after all—but today they looked at him as if he were a lunatic.

That was the first difficulty. The second was that he wished Vale was making this trip with him. Stupid, he knew, but there it was. He'd become used to Vale's banter and his sardonic view of the world, and even though he loathed the man, he missed him as well. Too, it would've been useful to have another at his back in this.

Sam glanced over his shoulder for followers and ducked into a narrow passageway. He had to pause a moment and lean against a filthy wall, holding his side. Something stabbed there. One or more of his ribs were probably cracked. Rebecca would have a fit if she knew that he was out of bed. His little sister had been surprisingly stubborn last night in her insistence that he see a doctor. In the end, he'd given in to her pleas. What did it matter when the world had fallen in on him?

He peered around the corner of the wall he leaned against and started out again, ignoring the continual pain from his ribs. There was only one thing he had to resolve, and then they could quit this damn island and go home.

This part of London was quiet and mostly clean, the odors assaulting his nostrils kept to a dull roar that hardly disturbed. Sam turned down Starling Lane. The buildings that lined the street were made of newer brick, probably built after the great fire. Small shops were at the street level, tiny, dark windows displaying wares. Above the shops were apartments, presumably for the shopkeepers.

Sam pushed open the door of a small tailor. The shop was dim inside with a low ceiling and a dusty scent. He didn't see anyone else in there. Sam turned and locked the front door behind him.

"A moment's wait, if it please you, sir!" a male voice called from somewhere in back.

The shop was actually quite shallow—presumably the bulk was taken up by the back where the work would be done. Bolts of cloth were stacked on shelves with a single waistcoat displayed on a tree. The waistcoat was well stitched and sturdy enough, but the material wasn't of the finest. This led Sam to think that this tailor probably catered to merchants, doctors, and lawyers, instead of more wealthy gentlemen. There was a tall counter and beyond that an open doorway. Sam slipped behind the counter and peered into the doorway. As he'd suspected, the room behind the shop was much larger. A long table took up much of the space, with odd pieces of cloth, marking pencils, spools of thread, and paper patterns scattered along its length. Two young men sat cross-legged on the table, sewing, while an older, balding man bent over a swath of fabric, swiftly snipping with a pair of shears.

The older man glanced up but didn't stop cutting. "Only a moment, sir."

"I can talk as you work," Sam said.

The man looked puzzled. "Sir?" His hand flew over the fabric as if it had a life of its own.

"I have some questions for you. About a former neighbor of yours."

The tailor hesitated for a second, eyeing him.

The bruises weren't helping his case, Sam knew. "There used to be a cobbler's shop next door."

"Yes, sir." The tailor pivoted the fabric and went back to cutting.

"Did you know the owner, Dick Thornton?"

"Might." The tailor bent over his task as if to hide his eyes from Sam.

"Thornton's father had the place before him, I believe."

"Yes, sir. That was old George Thornton." The tailor threw down his shears, whipped the fabric off the table, and smoothed a new piece of cloth in its place. "A fine man. He'd only opened the shop a year or so before he passed. Even so, he was much missed on this street."

Sam stilled. "The elder Thornton had just opened the shop? He wasn't here before?"

"No, sir, he weren't. Moved from someplace else."

"Dogleg Lane." One of the men sewing piped in suddenly.

The master tailor gave him a gimlet eye under his brows, and the man ducked his head back to his work.

Sam hitched his hip onto the table and folded his arms. "Was Dick home from the war in the Colonies when his father died?"

The tailor shook his head once. "No, sir. It were another year or so before Dick came home. His wife, what was George's daughter-in-law, ran the shop until Dick returned. She was a good lass but not the canniest of women, if you follow my meaning, sir. Wasn't doing too well by the time Dick made it home, but he soon turned it around. Dick were here only a couple of years before he got a bigger shop somewheres else."

"Did you know Dick before he came home from the war? Had you met him?"

"No, sir." The tailor frowned as he deftly snipped a perfect oval in the cloth. "'Twasn't a loss, not knowing Dick Thornton, neither."

"You don't like the man," Sam murmured.

"Not many here did," the sitting tailor muttered.

The master tailor shrugged. "He puts on a nice face, always smiling, but I didn't trust him. And his wife was afraid of him."

"Was she?" Sam looked at his moccasins as he spoke. If what he suspected were true, Mrs. Thornton should've shown much more than fear. "Did she act odd in any other way?"

"No, but it wasn't as if we saw her long after Dick returned."

Sam glanced up sharply. "What do you mean?"

"Died, didn't she?" The tailor met his eyes, his own shrewd, before he looked back at his work again. "Fell down the stairs and broke her neck. That was what her husband said, anyway."

Both of the sitting tailors shook their heads to show what they thought about that.

A savage thrill of triumph went through Sam. This was it, he knew. Dick Thornton wasn't who he said he was. *The prisoner MacDonald crouching under a wagon as the battle raged all around. MacDonald catching Sam's eye from his hiding place. MacDonald grinning and winking.* That was what Sam had remembered the night before as he'd pushed through the crowd at Emeline's party. The way MacDonald used to grin and wink—the same way that Thornton grinned and winked now. Somehow MacDonald the prisoner had taken Thornton's place.

Taken his place and now lived his life.

Ten minutes later, Sam unlocked the door to the little tailor shop and let himself out. It was all but over now. He only had to confront Dick Thornton—or the man who was calling himself Dick Thornton—and then go home.

A year of searching for answers would be over. The dead of Spinner's Falls would finally rest in peace.

Except, as he made his way back to his town house, he knew he would never be at peace again. His body might return to Boston, but his heart would forever remain behind in England.

He was in the mews behind the town house now. He hesitated, then walked past his own gate to the gate that led into Emeline's garden. It was locked, of course, but he scaled the wall, moving a bit slower than he'd have liked because of his ribs. The garden beyond was deserted. Michaelmas daisies bloomed on either side of the path, and the ornamental trees were just beginning to turn color. He could see the back of the house and the windows that lined the upper floors. One of those windows belonged to Emeline. She might at this very moment be looking out.

Sam was conscious of how foolish his actions were— to sneak into the garden of the woman who'd rejected him. He was embarrassed and angry because he was embarrassed. Soon he would need to return home and ready himself for supper with Rebecca, but he lingered a little longer, gazing at her house, his heart aching as it pounded a silent beat: *if only… if only… if only…*

He closed his eyes, coming to a decision. He couldn't leave it like this. He had to speak to her. But now was not the time. For what he wanted, he'd have to wait for nightfall. So he glanced again at that window and then turned and left the garden. He would bide his time. He would wait patiently.

For the fall of night.

Chapter Seventeen

Just past midnight, Iron Heart was dragged from his dungeon cell. Guards marched him up the stairs of the castle, out into the street, and into the square in the middle of the shining city. Crowds lined the streets, clutching torches to light the way, their faces eerily lit by the flames. The people of the Shining City were silent, but one among them was not. For the wizard danced the entire way to the square, crowing his delight at Iron Heart's death sentence and only a little hampered by a limp. And on the wicked wizard's wrist, bobbing as he capered, was a white dove, tethered there with a golden chain. . . .
—from *Iron Heart*

It was late and she was tired, but she still felt him before she saw him. Emeline's heart gave a wild, joyous leap, entirely outside of her control. He was here. Samuel was here. She turned from her vanity table where she'd been brushing her hair in preparation for bed.

He stood by the door that connected her room to a small dressing room. His face was battered, his left eye swollen and black, and he held one hand against his side as if something pained him there. She stared at him, not daring to believe, trying not to breathe in case he evaporated from her sight.

"Your hair is beautiful," he said softly.

It was the last thing she expected him to say. It made her self-conscious and oddly shy. He'd never seen her with her hair down. Never seen her in such a normal, homey setting.

"Thank you." She set her brush down on the vanity table and nearly knocked it to the floor, her hands were shaking so badly.

He glanced at the brush. "I've come to say good-bye."

"You're leaving so soon?"

For some reason, she hadn't expected this, either. She'd thought she would be the one to leave first, after her marriage to Jasper. But that was silly, of course. Samuel had to return to the Colonies some time. She'd always known that.

He nodded slowly at her question. "As soon as I finish my business, Rebecca and I will sail."

"Oh." There were thousands of things she wanted to ask him, thousands of things to say to him, but somehow she couldn't give voice to her real thoughts. She was stuck in this awkwardly formal conversation instead. She cleared her throat. "Is it shipping business? Or the business of finding who betrayed your regiment?"

"Both." He ambled into her room, pausing to pick up a china dish from a side table and turning it over to look at the bottom.

She swallowed. "But surely it will take weeks, maybe months to find out who—"

But he was already shaking his head. "Thornton's the traitor." He replaced the dish.

"How do you know?"

He shrugged, not looking particularly interested in the subject. "He isn't really Thornton. I think he's probably another soldier, MacDonald, who was under arrest when we were attacked. MacDonald somehow took Thornton's place."

She frowned, plucking at her wrap anxiously. She wore only a shift and the silk wrap; her feet were bare. She felt vulnerable with him prowling about her private rooms. Vulnerable, but not afraid. There was something inevitable about this scene, as if she knew all along that Samuel would someday enter her rooms. She only wished she could hold him a little longer. She looked down at her trembling hands in her lap and asked another question, delaying what would come.

"Wouldn't Thornton's friends or family have turned MacDonald in?"

"Most of Thornton's friends were killed at Spinner's Falls. Maybe all of them. As to family"—Samuel fingered the heavy brocade curtains hanging on her bed—"they were dead, too, all except his wife, and she died soon after Thornton, or MacDonald, returned home. I imagine he killed her."

Emeline caught her breath at the casual comment. "Why are you doing this, Samuel?"

He looked up at her tone. "What?"

"Why are you bent on following this trail?" She leaned forward, wanting to cut through his defenses as he had cut through hers. They had so little time left. "Why spend all this effort and money pursuing the man? Why, after all these years?"

"Because I can and the others can't."

"What do you mean?" she whispered.

He dropped the curtain and turned fully to her. There was no artifice, no shield in place to keep her from seeing the desolation in his face. "They're dead. They're all dead."

"Jasper—"

He laughed. "Even the ones who survived are dead, don't you see? Vale may joke and drink and play a fool, but you'll be wedding yourself to a corpse, never doubt that."

She stood to meet his awful despair head-on. "I do doubt that. Jasper may have his demons, but he's *alive.* You saved him, Samuel."

He shook his head. "I wasn't there."

"You ran to bring help—"

"I ran away," he rasped, and she shut her mouth, for she'd never heard him say it aloud. "At the height of the battle, when I knew we were going to lose, when I knew the Indians would overrun us and take scalps from still-living men, I figured there was no longer any point in fighting, so I hid. And when they took Vale, Munroe, your brother, and the other men captive, I ran."

She ventured close to him and grasped his coat in both fists, feeling the wool on her fingertips. She stood on tiptoe and brought her face as near to his as she could. "You hid because you knew that it was pointless to die. You ran to save the lives of the men captured."

"Did I?" he whispered. "Did I? That's what I told myself at the time, that I was running for the others, but perhaps I lied. Perhaps I ran merely for myself."

"No." She shook her head desperately. "I know you, Samuel. I know *you*. You ran to save them, pure and simple, and I admire you for it."

"Do you?" His eyes seemed to focus on her face finally. "Yet your brother died before I could return with the ransom. I failed him. I failed you."

"No," she choked. "Never think that." And she pulled his head down to her own.

She kissed him, trying to instill all her conflicting thoughts and hopes into that simple gesture. Mouth to mouth, lips moving together. A kiss was such a basic thing, a thing easily given, but she wanted this kiss to be more. She wanted Samuel to know that she'd never thought him a coward.

She wanted him to know that she loved him.

Yes, *love*. No matter who she married, no matter if she never again saw him, she would always love this man. Loving him was beyond her control. Even though Samuel was the wrong man to marry, the wrong man to spend the rest of her life with, she couldn't help loving him.

So she kissed him softly, her lips as gentle as she could make them. She moved over his mouth, murmuring incoherent endearments, finally licking so that she could taste him. She would need to remember this moment later, his taste, his lips, what kissing Samuel felt like. She would have to hold the memory in her heart forever. This memory would be the only thing she had of him.

He moved suddenly, grasping her upper arms, and she didn't know whether he sought to push her away or draw her closer. She panicked then. He couldn't leave her before she'd shown him that she loved him.

"Please," she murmured against his lips.

His fingers tightened on her arms.

She pulled back and looked into his eyes. "Please. Let me."

His brows drew together over his beautiful coffee-brown eyes as if he were puzzled. She pressed her palms against his chest. She'd never be able to move him against his will, but he let her. He stepped back, and when she pressed again, he backed again, until his legs hit the side of her bed.

He glanced at the bed behind him and then at her. "Emeline—"

"Shhh." She placed her fingers against his lips. "Please."

He searched her eyes a moment and then must have understood her incoherent plea. He nodded.

She smiled tremblingly at him. For this night, she would put away all thoughts of the future and what would come. Her anxieties, her fears, all the burdens she carried, all the people who depended on her. She would forget them for a few precious hours. Gently she drew his coat from his shoulders, taking care not to jostle his injuries. She folded the garment carefully and placed it on a table; then she began unbuttoning his plain brown waistcoat. She was conscious of her breathing, shallow and quick with nervousness, and his as well, deep and even. He watched her undress him, making no move to either help or hinder, his hands idle by his side.

She glanced up and met his eyes and felt a wash of heat

in her cheeks. What an intimate act this was, to undress a man.

He smiled faintly as he shrugged off his waistcoat. She took a deep breath and started on his shirt. His hands came up to rest on her hips, lightly, but she felt the heat of his fingers even through the layers of cloth. Her hands shook, fumbling with a button. He leaned over her and kissed the top of her head. His body surrounded her, and she inhaled his scent: wool and linen, leather and parsley. She pulled apart the edges of his shirt, looking at his bare chest. His skin was so beautiful; she ran her fingertips over his collarbone and pressed her palm onto his chest. She could feel the wiry hair beneath, and under that the slow beat of his heart. He was here with her, so real. How would she be able to bear it when he wasn't? When he was across a wide, wide ocean?

She pushed that thought away as she urged him onto the bed. He sat and watched her under hooded eyes, waiting for her next move.

She dropped to her knees and began to unlace his moccasins. He made to lift her up.

She looked at him. "Please."

His hands dropped.

The laces were made of some type of leather, and she bent over them, concentrating on discovering how they worked. She was aware, though, of his legs before her and her supplicant position. The pose was humble and at the same time erotic.

The first moccasin came off, and she started on the next. He stroked her hair as she worked, silent, never commenting, and she wondered what he thought of this.

Yesterday he'd been so angry. She looked up and saw only need in his eyes.

He bent and kissed her, thrusting his tongue into her mouth, holding her head now with both hands, and she was lost, forgetting her purpose, forgetting what she wanted. She swayed and placed her hands on his thighs to steady herself as he arched her head back, feeding on her mouth. Oh, Lord, she wanted this man. He brought her forward, and she was enclosed, still kneeling between his thighs, hard and strong, on either side of her. And in front...She smoothed her palms up the leather covering his thighs until they inevitably met where the leather stopped and there was only fabric at the juncture of his legs. She gasped, her inhale lost in his kiss, for he was hard and straining already against his breeches. She cradled his length, tracing him through the cloth.

He caught her hands.

She broke the kiss and glanced up at him. "Let me."

His face was dark, flushed from passion, and he looked in no mood to concede her anything.

"Please," she whispered.

He opened his hands, spreading them palms up on his thighs in a gesture of acquiescence. She squeezed him gently through the fabric and then let go to work on opening the flap of his breeches. She peeled back the cloth and fumbled with his smallclothes until she found him, ruddy and proud underneath. The hair surrounding his cock was almost black, a shockingly private sight. This should only be for her, she knew on a primitive level. This man, this sight, this penis was hers.

She stared for a moment and then looked up at him. "Take them off."

Her tone was probably too commanding, for he half smiled at her, but she didn't care at the moment. She wanted him entirely nude; she wanted to imprint the sight of him on her mind. He shucked his leggings and the rest of his clothes, and she stood to push him back onto the bed, slipping out of her wrap before climbing in next to him, wearing only her chemise. He lay on his back and immediately felt for her, but she slid down his length, out of his reach.

"Emeline—"

"Shhh."

She was at the level of his manhood, and the creature fascinated her. One fingertip traced his length, bumping over his veins. She knew that there were women who found a man's genitals ugly and rude, but she had never been one of them. Had Danny lived longer, had she been a more experienced wife, eventually she would've explored him, but they'd never had that time. Now she was determined not to lose this opportunity with Samuel.

She studied him, beguiled by the way his foreskin pulled back to accommodate his erection, enthralled by the slight curve upward. She flicked her eyes to him and saw that he was watching her intently as she examined him, and a thought occurred to her that, at any other time, she never would've voiced. They didn't have years to overcome shyness and the strictures of polite society. They had only tonight and she would not waste this little time.

So she asked, "What do you do when you're alone?"

He raised his eyebrows, and for a moment she was disappointed. He would pretend not to understand her vulgar question. But, still holding her gaze, he moved his right hand down and wrapped it about his length. Her eyes dropped from his then so that she could watch. He held his penis much more firmly than she would've dared and moved his hand up and down. On the up stroke, the head of his cock nearly disappeared into his fist.

"Doesn't that hurt?" she asked.

She heard him chuckle raspily but couldn't take her eyes from the sight of what he did to look at his face. "Far from it."

And then she did something truly beyond the pale. She leaned forward and licked around the head of his penis.

He paused in his movement, and she heard his inhale before he breathed, "Do that again."

She braced herself on her hands and hovered over him, licking and kissing the head of his cock while he continued to move his fist up and down. It wasn't a sophisticated act; her tongue sometimes hit his hand as well as his penis, her breasts swung free inelegantly under her shift, but she didn't care. She loved the taste of him, salt and spice; she adored the faint gasping sounds he made, and she was aware that she was becoming increasingly wet just from ministering to him. Why such an act should be so erotic, she had no idea, but there it was. His hand moved faster, and she attempted to engulf the entire tip of his cock in her mouth. His hips arched involuntarily off the bed.

"Emeline," he gasped, and the extremity in his voice sent a thrill of sexual triumph through her. "Emeline..."

She looked up just as she sucked strongly on him, flattening her tongue against the underside of his penis. His eyes narrowed, his head arced back, his teeth gritted, and she tasted sweet salt in her mouth.

"Emeline."

She closed her eyes, feeling tears behind her lids and sucked again, and again tasted a gush of salt. Finally, his hips fell, pulling his manhood from her mouth. She wiped her lips on the bed linens. Stupid, stupid tears were running from her eyes, and one splashed on his leg. Helping him do this made her want to sob, and she wasn't even sure why.

She felt more than saw him lift his head. "What—?"

"Shhh," she said again, choking this time.

There was no way to explain her emotions. How could she tell him that she already mourned his loss? That she wished she were a different, more adaptable person? She couldn't, so she didn't. She crawled up his body instead, until she settled herself, straddling his groin.

His hands grasped her hips, comforting and steadying her. "Are you all right?"

"Of course," she whispered, although the tears she could not control gave lie to her reply.

She closed her eyes so she couldn't see the worry and love in his gaze and lifted her shift over her head. She was nude now, just as he was. She didn't wear so much as a hairpin. They were as God had made them, man and woman, without the clothes and trappings that designated rank, relative wealth, and means. They could've been Adam and his wife, Eve—the first humans, unaware of the many gradations that would come to divide their children.

She opened her eyes and leaned forward to place her palm on the center of his chest. "You are mine right now."

"As you are mine," he replied.

It was almost like a vow.

But he didn't demand more. A little part of her died then, even as she reveled in the moment. Samuel had given up on having her in his future, she knew. It'd always been inevitable that they couldn't be together, but for him to have accepted that fact...

She pushed away the thought and bowed over him, smiling as she kissed the spot where her hand had lain. It was wet because her tears had dropped there as well. She kissed across his chest, small wet kisses, until she reached a nipple. Here, she opened her mouth and licked around the tiny point, tasting man, tasting Samuel.

He sighed beneath her and reached up to stroke her hair. She could feel his manhood, still half-erect, under her stomach. She shifted a little, rolling against him, and moved to the other nipple, licking at it with a pointed tongue. Tears were pricking at her eyes again, but she no longer paid attention to them. They were a physical manifestation of her internal turmoil—something completely beyond her control. Tears fell to his chest, and their salt mingled with the salt of his skin, so she couldn't tell them apart as she licked.

She straightened and looked down. His cock was thick, not entirely erect, and lying on his stomach. She wanted to feel that part of him against herself, wanted this last connection. She slid forward until the tip of him lay under the tip of her. She was wet, open and sensitized, and the feeling was so right, so perfect, that she groaned softly. Just a little pressure, just a little shift of her hips. Warmth blossomed at her core. She bit her lip and ground down some more.

Her eyes were closed, so she started a little when large hands palmed her breasts, both at once. She gasped and slid against him. He brought his thumbs together with his fingers and squeezed her nipples. Oh, Lord! He was growing under her, burrowing into her folds. She leaned into his hands, pressing down harder, caught up in the sensation, trying to ignore the tears that still coursed down her cheeks. His cock slid to the side. She whimpered in frustration and grasped him, holding him against her body as she rubbed her clitoris over his cock. So close, so close...

"Put me in you," she heard him say.

She shook her head, wanting to feel him here always. To stay in this moment for eternity as if in a dream. To never wake up. She moved faster over him, frantically, twisting her hips, sobbing, her cheeks wet.

Almost there, almost there...

He squeezed her nipples and still it wasn't quite right. She couldn't complete. She was gasping now, weeping openly, and suddenly she knew that she needed him inside her to reach that point. Quickly, she lifted her hips and placed him at her entrance and bore down. And then...

He was inside her, full and heavy, the feeling exquisite as he stretched her. She paused, savoring the sensation, wanting it to last forever, him filling her. She leaned over him, and in that moment felt his mouth close over one breast, pulling strongly. Her muscles contracted around him, and she came in long, lovely, warm waves. She sobbed aloud in gratitude, in wonderful release. She rubbed herself over and over against his hard body, her head hanging down in surrender, her hair draping over his chest.

He muttered something and released her nipple, catching her hips. He pumped into her in quick, powerful thrusts, grunting with each plunge, his cock hard and hot and long within her. His movements, his obvious desperation, prolonged her pleasure, and when she felt his warmth flood her, she was still in bliss. She fell against his heaving chest, his hand tangling in her hair, his breath rasping against her damp temple. She heard his whisper in her ear.

"I love you."

THE FIRE IN Emeline's hearth had died down long ago, probably some time in the middle of the night when he'd still held her. Sam considered relighting it; her bedroom was chilly in the not-quite-dawn darkness. But she lay under piles of thick blankets in the bed, and he wouldn't be staying long. Besides, he wasn't sure a fire could warm him anymore.

He sat in a chair by the dead fire, fully dressed. There really wasn't anything keeping him from leaving. The servants would be up soon, and he knew that she would be embarrassed and cross if he was discovered in her room. Yet, he still lingered.

He could watch her from the chair. Try to memorize the way two fingers clutched the blanket under her chin. She lay on her side facing him, her mouth relaxed in sleep, her lips half parted. With her sharp eyes closed, she looked much younger, almost sweet.

He nearly smiled at the thought. She wouldn't thank him for the observation. They'd never had time to discuss it, but he thought she might be a little sensitive at her years. He'd like to argue the point, make her confess that a lady of thirty was as beautiful—more beautiful, in his opinion—than a lady of twenty. Then when she continued to argue—for she would, she was so stubborn—he would kiss her into submission and maybe another round of lovemaking. But they were past that now. They would have no more arguments, no more kisses or lovemaking. No time to settle any little problems.

Their time was over.

She sighed and snuggled the blanket over her mouth. He watched the small movement greedily, drinking it in, committing it to memory. Soon. Soon now he would get up and walk to the door, leaving this room and making his way through the silent house. Let himself out into the dawn. Go back to the town house that wasn't truly his. In two days, he would board a ship and spend over a month watching the waves as he sailed back home. And once there? Why, he'd continue his life as if he'd never met a woman named Emeline.

Except, while his life might look the same from the outside, it would be entirely different on the inside. He wouldn't forget her, his warm lady, even if he lived for six decades more. He knew that now, sitting by her cold fire. She would be with him all the days of his life. As he walked the streets of Boston, as he conducted his business or chatted with acquaintances, she would be the ghost beside him. She would sit with him as he ate, she would lie beside him as he slept. And he knew that when his time on this earth was at an end, his last thought as he entered the void would be of her.

The scent of lemon balm would haunt him forever.

So he sat a little longer, watching her sleep. All the days of the rest of his life stretched before him, and he needed to store up these few seconds with her.

They would have to last him a lifetime.

Chapter Eighteen

The guards tied Iron Heart to a great stake and then piled thorny branches about his feet and legs. He looked around and saw his sweet wife standing by her father the king, weeping. Iron Heart closed his own eyes at the sight, and then the thorns were set alight. They quickly caught fire, and the flames leapt into the dark sky. Sparks fled upward as if seeking to join the stars, and the wicked wizard screamed with glee. But an odd thing happened. Although Iron Heart's clothes burned, and indeed were soon reduced to ashes, his body did not. Instead, as he writhed in the flames, his iron heart could be seen beating on his strong, bare chest. An iron heart white-hot from the heat…

—from *Iron Heart*

Samuel was gone when she woke the next morning. A maid was clattering by the hearth, trying to light the fire. It must've been banked badly and gone out during the night.

Emeline closed her eyes for a moment, not wanting to face the day. Perhaps not wanting to face her life without him. And as she did so, she felt liquid seep from inside herself. She thought it was his seed, but when she looked, it proved to be a more familiar stain. Her monthly visitor had come. And this was the truly horrible part: Instead of feeling relief that nothing now stood between her and her marriage to Jasper, she was flooded with wild disappointment. How foolish! How utterly stupid, to *want* to be filled with Samuel's child. To have no choice but to marry him.

Emeline caught her breath then. Her mind—her *sanity*—might know that a marriage to Samuel would be disastrous, but her heart was unconvinced.

"Can I get you something, my lady?" The maid was staring at Emeline, her hand raised over the still-cold fire.

She must've made a sound, done something to reveal her distress, for a servant girl to have noticed. Emeline sat up. "No, nothing. Thank you."

The girl nodded and turned back to the hearth. "I'm sorry I'm taking so long today, ma'am. I can't think why the fire should be so hard to light."

Emeline looked over the side of the bed and found her wrap. She struggled into it while the maid's back was still turned. "It's probably the chill in the air. Here, let me try."

But however many times Emeline stuck a flaming straw into the coals, they refused to light.

"Well, never mind," she finally exclaimed crossly. "Have a hot bath brought into my sitting room. The fire's lit there, isn't it?"

"Yes, my lady," the maid said.

"Then I'll just dress in my sitting room."

An hour later, Emeline's bath had grown cold. Dismally, she stirred the water near her knee. Like it or not, it was past time for her to get out of the bath and face the rest of her life and the choices she'd made.

"Towel," she said, and stood as a maid held out an enormous drying cloth.

Probably they didn't make drying cloths so large in the Colonies. It was lucky she had rejected Samuel and wouldn't have to put up with inferior bath accessories. Emeline stood morosely as her maids dressed her, not even interested when the new wine-red silk was presented. She'd ordered the gown several weeks ago when she'd helped prepare Rebecca's wardrobe. Now she might have been wearing burlap and ashes.

She finally grew restive as Harris fiddled with her coiffure. "That's fine. I won't be receiving visitors today, anyway. I think I'll just go walk in the garden."

Harris glanced doubtfully at the window. "Looks like rain, my lady, if you don't mind me saying so."

"Oh, does it?" Emeline asked in despair.

This seemed the final straw, that the elements should conspire against her as well. She went to the window to peer out. Her sitting room overlooked the street, and as she watched, Samuel descended the steps next door and strode to a waiting horse. She caught her breath involuntarily. The unexpected sight of him sent a jab of pain into her middle, as if she'd been stabbed. Her hand trembled against the cold glass pane. He ought to have looked up then. He ought to have seen her watching him from her window above him. But rather mundanely, he did not. He mounted the horse and rode away.

Emeline let her hand drop from the window.

Behind her, Harris was still talking as if nothing had happened. "I'll just put the new dresses away, then, my lady, unless you need me for anything else?"

"No, that's all." Emeline tore her gaze from the window. "No, wait."

"My lady?"

"Fetch my cloak please. I wish to visit Miss Hartley next door." This might be the only time she'd have to say good-bye to Rebecca. It didn't seem right to let her sail to the American colonies without bidding the girl farewell.

Emeline swung the cloak on and hurried down the stairs, fastening the neck. She didn't know how long Samuel would be gone, but it seemed imperative that she not meet him again. Outside, the sky was heavy and dark with impending rain. If Rebecca was in, she must remember not to stay too long or risk being trapped by a thunderstorm. Inhaling, she rapped on Samuel's door.

The butler's face was ever so faintly shocked when he opened the door. It was too early to be calling, but she was the daughter of an earl, after all. He bowed as she swept past him into the entry hall and then showed her to the small sitting room to wait while he fetched Rebecca. Emeline only had time to nervously glance out the windows before Rebecca came in.

"My lady!" The younger woman seemed startled at her visit.

Emeline held out her hands. "I could not let you go without saying good-bye."

Rebecca burst into tears.

Oh, dear. She'd never quite known what to do with the tears of others. Secretly, Emeline had often thought that ladies who wept in public were desirous of attention. She hardly ever wept, and never in front of others—that is, she realized, until last night with Samuel.

Propelled by that uncomfortable thought, Emeline started forward. "There, there," she muttered as she patted Rebecca's shoulder awkwardly.

"I'm sorry, my lady," Rebecca gasped.

"That's all right," Emeline said gruffly, and handed her a handkerchief. What else could she say? She was almost certain that she herself was the cause of Rebecca's grief. "Shall I ring for tea?"

The girl nodded, and Emeline led her to a chair while she gave orders to the maid.

"I just wish things could be different," Rebecca said when the maid left again. She sat twisting the handkerchief in her hands.

"As do I." Emeline sat on a settee and arranged her skirts with far too much care. Perhaps if she didn't look at the girl, she could get through this. "Have you set a date when you will leave?"

"Tomorrow."

Emeline looked up. "That soon?"

The younger woman shrugged. "Samuel found a berth on a ship just yesterday. He says we will sail tomorrow and leave the bulk of our belongings to be packed and sent on a later vessel."

Emeline winced. Samuel must want to be quit of England—of her—very badly.

"Is it because you don't love him?" Rebecca burst out.

The question was so sudden, so startling, that Emeline answered without thinking. "No." She caught her breath at the near-admission and shook her head. "There are so many things."

"Can you tell me?"

Emeline stood and paced to the fireplace. "There's rank and position, of course."

"But it's more than that, isn't it?"

Emeline couldn't bear to look at the younger woman, so she stared into the glowing fire instead. "You come from a different country, one so far away. I don't think that Samuel would want to make his home here in England."

Rebecca was silent, but her very stillness demanded explanation.

"I have my family to think about." Emeline inhaled. "There's only Daniel and Tante Cristelle now, but they depend on me."

"And you believe that Daniel and your aunt would refuse to sail to America?"

Put like that, her objection was an obvious fabrication. Yes, Tante Cristelle would grumble at a sea voyage, but the old lady need not even leave England if she did not wish to do so. And Daniel would probably be ecstatic at the mere thought of seeing America.

Emeline twisted her fingers into the gathers at her waist. "I don't know . . ." She looked up and met Rebecca's eyes. "They all left me, you see. Reynaud and my husband and Father. I don't think I can do that again—trust in another to keep me safe."

Rebecca frowned. "I don't understand. Samuel would never allow anyone to harm you."

Emeline laughed, although the sound was rusty. "Yes,

that's what I grew up thinking. Even though the matter was never articulated aloud, it was understood that the gentlemen of my family would cherish me and keep me safe. That I would never have to fear for my situation. They would manage the affairs, and I would be a lovely companion and care for their home. But it didn't work out that way, did it? First Reynaud was lost to the war in the Colonies; then Danny died when we were both very young, and then Father"—she caught her breath because she had never said this last to anyone—"then Father died and I was abandoned, don't you see? With Reynaud gone, the title, the estates, everything went to a cousin."

"They left you without money?"

"No." Emeline's hand jerked, and she heard stitches tearing on her gown. "Obviously I have enough money. The Gordon income is quite sufficient. I only chaperone for pin money. But I no longer had anyone to lean on, don't you see? They all left me. Now I make the decisions in my life and the lives of Tante Cristelle and my son. I worry over the investments and whether Daniel should go to Eton soon. I must watch the land stewards to make sure they do not embezzle my monies. There is no one else I trust, no one else I depend upon save myself."

She shook her head, knowing what she was trying to say was intangible. "I can't relax, you see. I can't just...*be*."

How odd that she would confess this to Rebecca now when she'd been entirely unable to talk to Samuel about this.

The younger woman knit her brows. "I think I understand. You can never lay down your burdens. There's no one you trust to carry them for you."

"Yes. Yes, that's it," Emeline exclaimed in relief.

"But…" Rebecca gazed up at her, puzzled. "You plan to marry Lord Vale soon."

"It won't matter. I love Jasper as a brother, but marriage to him won't change a whit the way I live and conduct my life. If he leaves me or dies as the others have, I will be just the same."

Rebecca stared at her silently. Outside the sitting room, voices murmured in the hall.

"You're afraid Samuel will die," Rebecca murmured. "You love him and you're too afraid to commit yourself to him."

Emeline blinked. Fear seemed such a childish, *cowardly* reason to reject Samuel. That couldn't be right. She tried to explain. "No, I—"

The door to the sitting room opened. Emeline turned, frowning, at the interruption. A maid entered, bearing a tray of tea. Immediately behind her was Mr. Thornton.

Dear Lord, what was the man doing here?

The little man advanced into the room, his face wreathed in a smile. He had smiled each time she'd seen him previously, but now the expression seemed twisted, not quite right. It was as if he sought to conceal the terrible thoughts in his brain by hiding behind a cheerful facade. Why had she never noticed it before? Was his self-control slipping, or had her new knowledge colored her perceptions of the man?

"I hope you don't mind my entering unannounced," Mr. Thornton said. "I've come to call upon Mr. Hartley."

"I'm afraid my brother isn't here," Rebecca said. "In fact, I believe that he's gone to see your shop, Mr. Thornton, on Starling Lane. No, I'm sorry." The girl shook her head in irritation. "That's where he went yesterday. Today he's looking for you on Dover Street."

Emeline glanced at the girl sharply. Her face was relaxed and open, the only mar a trace of irritation at being interrupted. Either she was a very good actress or Samuel hadn't confided his suspicions about Mr. Thornton to his sister.

But Mr. Thornton had stilled. "Starling Lane, you say? How interesting. I wonder why Mr. Hartley went there yesterday? I haven't had a shop there since I returned from the war six years ago."

"Really?" Rebecca frowned. "Perhaps Samuel thought you had two shops."

"That may be. In any case, I'm sorry to have missed him." Mr. Thornton looked longingly at the tea being set up by the maid.

"As are we," Emeline said tightly. "Perhaps if you hurry, you will find him at your establishment."

"But then again, we might pass each other as we travel," Mr. Thornton said smoothly. "And wouldn't that be a shame?"

"You can stay here and join us for tea while you wait for my brother's return," Rebecca said.

"Lovely, just lovely." Mr. Thornton bowed and sat. "You are graciousness itself, Miss Hartley."

"Oh, I don't know about that," Rebecca said as she poured. "It's only tea."

"Yes, but many wouldn't be so gracious"—he shot a sly look at Emeline—"to a working man and all. Why, I'm a simple cobbler at heart."

"But you own your establishment," Rebecca objected.

"Oh, indeed, indeed. I have a grand workshop. But it's

all built up by the sweat of my own brow. My father's business was quite small."

"Really?" Rebecca asked politely. "I didn't know that."

Mr. Thornton shook his head ruefully as if at the memory of his father's small business. "I took it over right after I came back from the war in the Colonies. Six years ago, that was. Six long years of hard labor and worry to bring my business to what it is today. Why, I do declare, that I'd kill any man who sought to take my business from me."

Rebecca was looking curiously at Mr. Thornton now. His words, after all, had been far too emphatic for the conversation. Emeline held her breath, watching the man, and as she stared, he did a very strange thing. He cocked his head at her, grinned widely, and winked one eye.

And Emeline felt a thrill of horror shoot through her completely out of proportion to the gesture he'd made.

SAM RODE HOME through the streets of London in a state of angry frustration. Thornton was neither at his home nor his place of business. Some of the information he'd learned today caused him to be anxious that Thornton might try to flee. This together with a kind of animal instinct made urgent the need to find Thornton immediately. Long years of hunting told him that his prey was about to bolt beyond his grasp. If he couldn't find Thornton today, he'd have to give up the berths he'd bought for Rebecca and himself on *The Hopper,* sailing early on the morrow.

Then, too, staying longer in London would mean more days in proximity to Emeline. He wasn't certain he could bear being close to her without going stark, raving mad.

A street urchin ran almost directly under his horse's nose. The horse sidestepped nervously, and Sam had to pay attention to the reins for a moment. The child was long gone, of course. The boy had probably had thousands of such near-misses in his young life, for the streets of London seemed more like a surging river than a thoroughfare. Hawkers screamed their wares at corners and indeed in the middle of the street. Carriages trundled like elephants, inevitably blocking the way with their bulk. Chairmen bearing sedan chairs wove nimbly among the crowd. And people—men, women, children; infants in arms to old men with canes; high, low, and the multitude in between—all crowded round, each on their own business, each in a hurry to get there. It was a wonder that the very air wasn't used up, inhaled by thousands of lungs.

Sam felt his own lungs seize at the thought, the illusion of all the air being sucked from the atmosphere infecting his brain. But that was nonsense. He concentrated on his horse and the path immediately in front of them, trying to block out the rest of the humanity surrounding them. He could breathe. There was plenty of air, though it reeked of sewage, rot, and smoke. There wasn't anything at all wrong with his lungs.

He repeated these thoughts until the town house came into view. Rebecca would still be packing, but perhaps he could entice her to stop long enough for an early luncheon. He swung down from his horse just as one of the lumbering carriages drew up to the house next door—Emeline's house. The crest on the polished black door bore Vale's coat of arms. Sam quickened his step into his own house. There was no point in meeting Vale again; all that could be said had already been said there.

Inside, he gave his hat and cloak to the butler and inquired where his sister was.

"Miss Hartley has just left, sir," the butler replied.

"Indeed?" Sam frowned. Had she gone to do some last-minute shopping? "How long ago?"

"About a half hour."

"By herself? Did she walk or take the carriage?"

"She left in a carriage, sir, with Lady Emeline and Mr. Thornton."

The butler turned away to hang up the cloak and hat, completely unaware of the effect of his words. Sam stared, his gut freezing into ice at the thought that his sister and his heart had somehow climbed voluntarily into a carriage with a rapist and murderer. But of course it couldn't be voluntary. He hadn't told Rebecca of his suspicions regarding Thornton, but Emeline knew of them. Why would she leave with Thornton knowing—

"What have you done with her?"

Sam whirled at the voice in time to be shoved roughly against the wall. A picture crashed to the floor, and Vale thrust his horribly bruised face at him. "Emmie came here over an hour ago. Where is she?"

Sam quelled the urge to simply punch the other man in the face. He'd already done that, and it hadn't made matters any better. Besides, Vale cared for Emeline as well. "Emeline and Rebecca have left with Thornton."

Vale sneered. "What rubbish. Why would Emmie go anywhere with that popinjay? You've got her hidden somewhere." He propelled himself away from Sam and stood, legs spread wide in the hall. "Emmie! I say, Emmie! Come out at once!"

Wonderful. His only ally was a fool. Sam turned away,

starting for the front door. He hadn't time to convince
Vale of what was really going on.

But another voice stopped him. "It's true, my lord."

He swung around to see Vale staring bemusedly at
O'Hare the footman. "Who the hell are you?"

O'Hare gave a bow, sketchy enough to almost be inso-
lent. "Both Miss Hartley and Lady Emeline got into Mr.
Thornton's carriage." He looked past Vale to catch Sam's
eye. "I didn't like the way he stood so close to Miss Hartley, sir. I think something was wrong."

Sam didn't bother asking why O'Hare hadn't stopped
Thornton. In this country, a servant could be turned off
without reference—or worse—for such an act. "Do you
have any idea where they were headed?"

"Aye, sir. Princess Wharf in Wapping. I heard Mr.
Thornton give the direction to the coachman."

Vale looked bewildered. "Wapping? Why would
Thornton take them to a wharf?"

"Wharves mean ships."

Vale's eyebrows shot up. "You think he means to kid-
nap them?"

"God only knows," Sam replied. "But we haven't time
to stand about debating the point. Come on, we'll take
your carriage."

"Hold on, there." Vale grabbed his arm. "What's the
hurry? How do I know that you're not hiding Emmie
here? Or—"

Sam twisted his arm downward, breaking away from
the other man. "Because Thornton is the traitor, and he
must somehow know that I've found him out."

Vale's shaggy eyebrows snapped together. "But—"

"I've told you, we haven't the time," Sam growled. "O'Hare, do you want to help with this?"

The boy didn't even hesitate. "Yes, sir!"

"Come on." Sam was out the door and running down the steps without stopping for Vale's consent. He'd take the waiting carriage even if the other man insisted on staying behind and debating all the possibilities.

But as he made the carriage, he found Vale beside him. "Princess Wharf, Wapping," the viscount called to his coachman. "Fast as you can."

All three men piled into the carriage.

"Now," Vale said as he settled across from Sam and O'Hare. "Tell me."

Sam had his eyes on the window. Thornton's carriage had left long ago, but foolishly he still strained to catch sight of it. "MacDonald took Thornton's place during or shortly after Spinner's Falls."

"You have proof?"

"That a soldier we knew six years ago across the ocean is impersonating a different, dead soldier? No, I don't. He's probably killed any proof there was."

O'Hare shifted beside Sam. The young man hadn't spoken since they entered the carriage, but his face was worried. The carriage slowed to a roll. Shouts came from the street ahead.

Sam barely kept himself from pounding on the carriage's roof. He turned to O'Hare. "There were two redheaded soldiers, you see. One was Thornton; one was MacDonald. No one paid attention to them until MacDonald was put in chains and brought back for trial."

"What had he done, then?" the footman asked.

Sam looked at Vale.

Who pursed his lips and nodded once. "Raped and murdered a woman."

O'Hare's face whitened.

"I can understand how MacDonald could've switched identities with Thornton in the chaos after Spinner's Falls, but what of when he came home to England? Surely Thornton had family?"

"A wife." Sam shook his head. "And she died soon after he came home."

"Ah." Vale nodded thoughtfully.

"But what does he want with the ladies now?" O'Hare burst out.

"I don't know," Sam muttered. Was Thornton insane? If his guesses were right, the man had murdered two women that they knew of. What would such a man do with the women of a man he considered his enemy?

"Extortion," Vale said. "Perhaps he hopes to keep you from speaking, Hartley, by holding Rebecca and Emeline hostage."

Sam closed his eyes at the thought, trying to keep down the voices inside that urged him to move rather than think. "Thornton is smarter than that."

Vale shrugged. "Even the smartest man can panic."

A man like Thornton would kill if he panicked.

"How far is it?" Sam asked.

Jasper was staring out the window, too, now. "Wapping? Past the Tower of London."

Sam sucked in a breath. They were still on the fashionable west side of London. The Tower was a mile or more away, and the carriage wasn't moving fast.

"I just remembered something," Jasper muttered.

Sam looked at him.

The other man's face had drained of color. "When we saw Thornton in your garden, after we went into your house for tea, he boasted to me about a large shipment he was preparing for the British army."

"Where was it bound?"

Jasper swallowed, then replied, "India."

Sam felt his heart stop in his chest. If Thornton got Emeline and Rebecca on a ship bound for India…

The carriage slowed and then came to a complete stop. Sam looked out the window. A brewer's cart was stopped in the middle of the road, one of its great wheels broken from the axle. He didn't even wait for the inevitable shouting to begin. He opened the carriage door.

"Where are you going?" Vale cried.

"I'm faster on foot," Sam replied. "You continue in the carriage. Perhaps you'll beat me there."

And he swung down and began running.

Chapter Nineteen

At the sight of Iron Heart's white-hot heart, Princess
Solace gave a cry of despair. His agony was too
terrible for her to bear. She ran forward and with
her own hands threw a bucket of water upon him,
intending to ease his pain. But, alas, although the
flames were doused, it is well known what happens
when metal suddenly cools.
Iron Heart's heart cracked with a loud SNAP....
—from Iron Heart

The gun was pressed firmly into Rebecca's rib cage and
didn't move a whit even when the carriage bumped and
swung around corners. Emeline bit her lip. To either side
of her, two great brutes, Mr. Thornton's creatures, sat, effectively boxing her in. She and Rebecca had never even
seen the men until they were inside the carriage. Not that
it would've mattered. Mr. Thornton had shoved his nasty
gun into Rebecca and ordered them both outside and into
his carriage, and Emeline hadn't liked to call his bluff at

the time. The peril of having Rebecca die before her eyes had seemed all too imminent.

Now, after riding with Mr. Thornton and his foul-smelling henchmen, she wasn't sure she'd made the right decision. He still might kill them both once they reached the wharf. She'd been contemplating making an attempt at leaping from the carriage for the last several minutes. Unfortunately, she'd have to make it past the brutes first, and that was without considering the gun pressed against Rebecca's side. Emeline had not a smidgen of doubt that Mr. Thornton would pull the trigger out of spite if nothing else. The man was quite, quite mad. How he had hidden his affliction up until this point was a mystery, because he was a bundle of ticcing nerves now. Mr. Thornton grinned and winked every few minutes, the expression becoming more like a grimace each time.

"Almost there, ladies," he said now, again winking in that horrible way. "Ever been to the East? No? Well, most haven't, I suppose. What a grand adventure we'll have!"

The man to Emeline's right grunted and shifted, the movement releasing a terrible odor from his scarlet coat. The carriage was rattling into the east end of London, the way lined with warehouses. Overhead, the sky outside was becoming progressively darker.

Emeline clutched her hands together in her lap and tried to make her voice even. "You may let us out here, Mr. Thornton. There really is no need to take us any farther."

"Oh, but I enjoy your company so much," the nasty little man cackled.

Emeline inhaled slowly, then spoke quietly. "Our presence only serves as a reason for Jasper and Samuel to continue pursuing you. Let us go and you may escape."

"How kind of you to consider my welfare, my lady," he replied. "But I think that your fiancé and Samuel Hartley will pursue me whether or not I let you go. Mr. Hartley in particular seems quite obsessed. I've had my eye on him"—he nodded to the scarlet-coated thug beside her—"from the moment I heard that he was questioning all of the survivors from our regiment. So, all things being equal, I think I'll keep your sweet company."

Emeline met Rebecca's gaze. The girl hadn't said a word since they'd been forced into the carriage, but in her eyes, Emeline saw the same despair that threatened to overset her own sensibilities. It made no sense at all for Mr. Thornton to have kidnapped them, and the very senselessness squeezed her chest, making her breath come short.

Outside, the rain started, as sudden as a curtain falling at the end of a play. She needed to think, and the time they had might be short.

She very much feared that Mr. Thornton meant to kill them.

THE SKY OPENED up and rain poured down in a drenching torrent. Sam flinched as the first wave hit him like a slap in the face, but he kept running. The rain actually made things a little easier. Those who could immediately sought shelter, fleeing from the streets as fast as they were able. Unfortunately, that still left quite a few vehicles. The brewer's cart, for instance, probably still blocked Vale's carriage. Sam leapt a row of broken cobblestones, turned by the rain into a miniature urban brook, and focused his mind on running. He couldn't do anything about what lay in back of him or what lay ahead. For now, running was his entire being.

The carriage had been somewhere on Fleet Street when it had stopped, but Sam had cut off the busy thoroughfare. He ran parallel to the Thames now, the river out of sight somewhere to his right.

He felt the stretch in the muscles of his legs as he fought for even more speed. He hadn't run like this—full out, in desperation and hope—since Spinner's Falls. Then, no matter how he'd strained, he'd still arrived too late. Reynaud had died.

He swerved to avoid a young girl carrying a baby and crashed into a bulky man in a leather apron. The man swore and tried to strike him, but Sam was already past him. His feet hurt, sharp shards of pain working their way up his shins. He wondered if he'd reopened the wounds on his soles.

And then the smell hit him.

Whether it was from the leather-aproned man or someone he passed now, or maybe it was just a product of his fevered imagination, he didn't know, but he smelled sweat. Male sweat. Oh, God, not now. He kept his eyes open and his legs pumping, though he wanted to cover his face and slump to the ground. The dead of Spinner's Falls seemed to follow him. Invisible bodies that reeked of sweat and blood. Ghostly hands that caught at his sleeves and implored him to wait. He'd felt these wraiths in the forest after Spinner's Falls. They'd followed him all the way to Fort Edward. Sometimes he'd even seen them, a boy's eyes hollowed by fear, the old soldier with his scalp cut away. He'd never known if he'd been dreaming— running while only half awake—or if the dead of Spinner's

Falls had leaked into his living body. Perhaps he carried them everywhere and only knew it when he was in distress. Perhaps he'd always carry them, the way some men carried shrapnel beneath their skin, a silent ache, an invisible reminder of what he'd survived.

He ran through a wash of water, the splashes hitting him in the thighs. Not that it mattered; his clothes had long since soaked through. He was running closer to the wharves now, and he could smell the decay of the river. Tall warehouses rose up on either side of the lane he ran down. His breath came in gasps, and there was a scorching pain in his side. He'd lost track of time, couldn't tell how long or how far he'd been running. What if they were already at the ship? What if Thornton had already killed them?

His mind suddenly flashed a horrific image: Emeline sprawled, naked and bloody, her face white and still. No! He squeezed his eyes shut against the sight and stumbled, slamming to his hands and knees on the cobblestones.

"Watch it!" a gruff male voice shouted.

Sam opened his eyes to see horse hooves inches from his face. He scrambled clumsily away, still on his knees, as the cart driver cursed his ancestry. His knees ached, especially his right one, which must've taken the brunt of the fall, but Sam stood.

Ignoring the driver, ignoring the breath rasping in his lungs, ignoring his pain, he started running again.

Emeline.

THE CARRIAGE MADE a wide turn, and Emeline could see the docks outside the window. The rain was still sheeting down, veiling tall ships out in the middle of the Thames. Smaller vessels crowded between the ships, ferrying goods and sometimes people between ship and shore. Normally, the docks would be full of laborers, prostitutes, and the gangs of thieves that made their livings off filching from the ships' cargos. But because of the rain, the wharf was sparsely populated.

The carriage shuddered to a stop.

Mr. Thornton dug his pistol into Rebecca's side. "Time to get out, Miss Hartley."

Rebecca didn't move. She turned a heartbreakingly brave face to their kidnapper. "What are you going to do with us?"

Mr. Thornton cocked his head and gave his gruesome grin and wink. "Nothing terrible, I assure you. Why, I have a mind to show you the world. Come and see."

Oddly, his mundane pleasantry confirmed all of Emeline's worst fears. She looked out the carriage door at the rain-grayed waters of the Thames. If they got onto a ship with Thornton, they weren't likely to survive the journey. But at the moment they had no choice. Thornton nodded to the men on either side of her.

"Move on," the scarlet-coated henchman to Emeline's right grunted. He wrapped sausagelike fingers about her upper arm, no doubt leaving grease marks. He was slightly the shorter of the two and sported a frayed tricorne. Mr. Thornton must not pay him well, because his boots were nearly all holes and a grimy big toe poked through the leather on one.

Emeline smiled tightly at Rebecca, trying to give her a bit of courage, before gathering her skirts. She stepped out of the carriage and into the rain, the thug's hand still on her. The second thug followed. He was a tall, stringy man with enormously long arms and thinning gray hair.

He hunched his shoulders and stood mute as Mr. Thornton descended with Rebecca.

"Now," Thornton said, smiling. He smiled at *everything.* "Let's hurry. There should be a boat waiting to take us to *The Sea Tiger.* I'm sure you ladies will want to get out of the rain. If we—"

But he didn't finish the sentence. Rebecca pulled abruptly from his grasp, ducking to the side and behind the tall, balding henchman. For a fraction of a second, Mr. Thornton didn't know where to point the gun, and it wavered. Then he grinned that horrible grin and brought the barrel around, pointing it at Emeline's belly.

She froze. There was a long moment in time as she watched him wink and steady his aim, knowing that she was about to be killed.

And then she wasn't.

Samuel ran out of nowhere and threw himself against Thornton's gun arm, deflecting his aim. The gun exploded, sending chips of cobblestone into the air. The tall, balding henchman leaped at Samuel, grabbing him from behind, and all three men went down in a writhing heap of desperate arms and legs. Rebecca screamed and pulled at the balding henchman's coat. The scarlet-coated thug let go of Emeline's arm, but before he could move, she brought her heel down on the toe that poked through his boot. The man howled and lashed out. Emeline saw a burst of white stars as his hand connected with the side of her head, and then she found herself on the ground, lying in a cold puddle of water.

"Are you all right?" Rebecca gasped beside her.

"Samuel," Emeline whispered. He was under all three men now, almost hidden by the legs kicking him, the arms hitting him. They would beat him to death before her very eyes if she didn't do something.

There were no pieces of wood, no stones to pry up. All she had was herself, so Emeline used that. She scrambled to her feet and ran at the awful little man and his henchmen. She clutched a head of hair and yanked. The man she was holding—one of the henchmen—shouldered her aside. Emeline staggered, almost falling, but got up again. She threw herself, kicking, shrieking, clawing, at the bodies attacking Samuel. Out of the corner of her eye, she saw Rebecca pummeling the back of one of the men, her fists small and puny. The rain mixed with hot salty tears on Emeline's face, and she was half-blinded, but she wasn't going to give up. If they killed Samuel, they would have to kill her, too.

Her slipper connected with Mr. Thornton's rump, and he twisted to look at her with a comically astonished expression. Samuel took advantage of the other man's distraction and punched him in the face. Mr. Thornton's head snapped back, and he rolled to the cobblestones, a hand outstretched to break his fall. He made to get up, and Emeline stomped on his outstretched hand, feeling quite pleased when something snapped beneath her heel.

Thornton screamed.

Behind Emeline, a gunshot exploded.

"Good God, Emmie, I had no idea you were so bloodthirsty," a male voice said.

Emeline looked up and saw Jasper descending a carriage with a footman behind him. The footman had a gun in each hand, the right one smoking.

Fear and exasperation overflowed all of her good manners. "Jasper, don't be an idiot. Come help Samuel at once!"

Jasper, not surprisingly, looked startled. "Right you are, Emmie. You two, get off Mr. Hartley. Slowly, now."

The thugs glanced at each other glumly and got to their feet, backing away from Samuel. He lay so still, the rain beating on his pale face.

Emeline rushed to him, terribly afraid. "Samuel." She'd seen him punch Mr. Thornton, but now he didn't move. "Samuel!" She knelt on the filthy, wet cobblestones and tenderly touched her fingertips to his cheek.

He opened his eyes. "Emeline."

"Yes." It was insane, but she couldn't keep from smiling at him in the rain, with hot tears trickling down her cheeks. "Yes." God only knew what she was saying, but Samuel seemed to understand.

He turned his head and kissed her palm with bruised lips, and her heart rejoiced.

Then his gaze sharpened and he looked behind her. "Have they got Thornton?"

He started to sit up, and she put her shoulder under his to help him. "Yes, Jasper has it all under control."

In fact, the footman was tying the two henchmen's hands to Mr. Thornton's carriage while Rebecca held the guns. Jasper had hold of Mr. Thornton.

"What shall we do with him now?" Jasper asked. He looked like he was holding a piece of offal.

"Toss him in the river," the footman growled over his shoulder, and Rebecca smiled at him.

"It's not a bad idea," Samuel said softly, and Emeline had never heard his voice so cold.

Mr. Thornton laughed. "What for?"

Jasper shook him like a dog does a rat. "For trying to hurt Miss Hartley and Lady Emeline, you bounder."

"But I didn't, did I?" Thornton said. "They're not hurt at all."

"You held a gun on them—"

"Pish posh! Do you think any magistrate will care?" Mr. Thornton smiled happily, almost normally. He didn't seem to have any idea the trouble he was in.

Emeline shivered in Samuel's embrace. Thornton's manic confidence that he could win out against Jasper—a *viscount*—was the final evidence that the man had lost his senses.

"You killed a woman in America," Samuel said quietly. "They'll hang you for that."

Mr. Thornton cocked his head, completely unperturbed. "I don't know who you mean."

Jasper expelled an impatient breath. "Cut line. We know you're MacDonald, know you killed that woman, know you betrayed us to the French and their Indian allies at Spinner's Falls."

"And how will you prove all that?"

"Maybe we don't have to," Samuel said low. "Maybe we'll just drown you in the Thames and be done. I doubt anyone will miss you."

"Samuel," Rebecca whispered.

Samuel looked at her, and although his expression didn't change, his voice softened slightly. "But I don't think we'll have real trouble convicting you in court. There're a few survivors who must remember both Mac-Donald and Thornton, and if nothing else, we can ask your father-in-law."

Emeline sucked in her breath.

Samuel nodded. "Yes, that's one of the things I found out today. Thornton has an elderly father-in-law whom he hasn't seen since he married the man's daughter. The father-in-law lives in Cornwall, you see. The man is in poor health, but he's been suspicious ever since his daughter supposedly fell down the stairs. He's been pestering various solicitors to investigate the death, and I met one who finally took on the old man's case on my search today. I have no doubt that if we provide a carriage, he will come to London and testify that this is not the man who originally married his daughter."

Mr. Thornton went into a veritable spasm of winking and grinning. "Try it! The old man's on his last legs. He'll never survive a trip to London."

"Let us worry about that," Jasper said, shaking Thornton again. "You, I think, should be more worried about the gallows." Jasper turned to Samuel. "Do you mind if I borrow your man to escort these three to Newgate?"

Samuel nodded. "Go ahead. I'll take the ladies home in your carriage." He turned with Emeline to walk to Jasper's carriage, but a shout from Thornton stopped him.

"Hartley!" the nasty little man cried. "You might get me for the woman in America, but you won't for Spinner's Falls. I didn't betray the regiment at Spinner's Falls. I'm not the traitor."

Samuel glanced at the man, his face disinterested.

His lack of reaction seemed to inflame Thornton. "You're a coward, Hartley. You ran at Spinner's Falls; everyone knows it. You're a coward."

Vale flushed scarlet and Emeline heard Rebecca's horrified gasp.

But amazingly, Samuel smiled.

"No," he said softly. "I'm not."

Chapter Twenty

Princess Solace cradled her dying husband in her arms, her salty tears bathing his face. And as she wept over him, the dawn broke, the golden rays of the sun flooding the earth. Iron Heart opened his eyes and, looking into the face of his wife, uttered the first words he'd spoken in seven long years....
— from *Iron Heart*

"He needs a doctor," Rebecca said as she helped Emeline push Samuel into the carriage.

Emeline didn't voice the thought out loud, but she had to concur with Rebecca. Samuel looked white under his naturally swarthy skin, and a cut over his eye was bleeding, painting the side of his face with blood.

"No doctor," Samuel mumbled, which didn't exactly help his case.

Emeline met his sister's eyes over his head and saw she was in agreement. Definitely, a doctor.

The slow pace of the carriage made the drive back

through the streets of London nightmarish. By the time they arrived home, Samuel had been silent for half an hour, his eyes closed.

"Has he fainted?" Emeline whispered anxiously to Rebecca.

"I think only fallen asleep," the girl replied.

It required two sturdy footmen to get Samuel up the steps of the town house and into his own bed. Then Emeline sent for the doctor.

An hour later, Rebecca entered the library to give the doctor's report.

"He says it's merely exhaustion," Rebecca said on finding Emeline sitting by the fire half-asleep.

"Thank goodness." Emeline let her head slump against the back of her chair.

"You look exhausted yourself," Rebecca said critically.

Emeline started to shake her head. She didn't want to leave Samuel. But then she found herself dizzy, so she stilled the movement.

Rebecca must've seen. "Go home and rest. Samuel's asleep, anyway."

Emeline humphed. "You're a dear child, but a trifle bossy."

The younger woman smiled. "I've learned from the best." Rebecca held out a hand to help her up, but then a commotion started in the hall.

Emeline looked to the library door in time to see Jasper blow in.

"Emmie! Are you all right?" he asked. "I went to your house, but you weren't there."

Emeline frowned. She was constantly amazed at how

little Jasper knew her. "Shhh! I'm fine, but you'll wake up Samuel with that bellowing."

Jasper glanced at the ceiling as if he could see through plaster and wood. "I suppose he's had a bit of a day, too, what?"

"Jasper—" Emeline began, about to give him a set down, but Rebecca interrupted.

"Do you mind if I leave you? I need to...to"—she knitted her brow, obviously trying to think of an excuse—"make sure O'Hare is all right."

Emeline stared. "Who is O'Hare?"

"My footman," Rebecca said, and sailed from the room.

Emeline was still frowning after the girl when Jasper interrupted her thoughts.

"Emmie."

She turned because his voice sounded grave, and really looked at him. She'd never seen the expression that was now on his face—a kind of weary acceptance.

"We're not going to be married, are we?"

She shook her head. "No, dear. I don't think so."

He slumped into a chair. "Just as well, I suppose. You never would've been able to put up with my foibles. Probably isn't a woman alive who would."

"That's not true."

He gave her a comically old-fashioned look.

"It might not be easy," she amended, "but I'm sure there's a very nice lady out there for you somewhere."

One corner of his mouth curved. "I'm three and thirty, Emmie. If there was a woman who would love me, and more importantly, could *stand* me, don't you think I'd've found her by now?"

"It might help if you stopped looking for her in brothels and gaming hells and tried a more respectable place." Her words were tart, but her delivery was somewhat marred by the huge yawn that split her face.

Jasper jumped up. "Let me see you home so that you can get some proper rest and continue raking me over the coals tomorrow."

Sadly, Emeline wasn't even up to making a token protest. She let Jasper pull her from the chair and escort her outside the few steps to her own door. There he bussed her on the cheek in the same manner he'd used since she was four and turned away.

"Jasper," she called softly.

He stopped and glanced at her over his shoulder with his beautiful turquoise eyes. His body was tall and lanky in the moonlight, his long, comical face full of tragedy.

Her heartstrings pulled. He'd been Reynaud's best friend. She'd known him all her life. "I do love you."

"I know, Emmie, I know. That's the terrible part." His face was wry.

She wasn't sure what to say to that.

He gave a one-fingered wave and then the night swallowed him up.

Emeline climbed the stairs to her own house, wishing she knew what to do about Jasper. She'd barely made it inside when she was descended upon by Tante Cristelle and Melisande.

"Whatever are you doing here?" Emeline asked in tired astonishment at the sight of her friend.

"I came to return your book of fairy tales," Melisande said prosaically. "But when I got here, Mr. Hartley's butler was informing your aunt that something was amiss. I decided to stay and keep her company until we had word. But we were never told exactly what had happened."

So Emeline had to recount the adventure over tea and buns while Tante Cristelle made many interruptions. At the end, she was even more exhausted than she'd been before.

Which Melisande, with her knowing eyes, must've seen. "I think you need your bed as soon as you've finished that tea."

Emeline looked into her cooling teacup and only nodded.

She sensed more than saw Melisande and Tante Cristelle exchange worried glances over her head.

"In a moment," Emeline said, just to stay in control.

Melisande sighed and gestured to the table at Emeline's elbow. "I put your book of fairy tales there."

Emeline looked and saw the dusty little book. It still held fond memories of Reynaud, but it no longer seemed so important. "Whatever did you bring it back for?"

"I thought you didn't want me to translate it?" her friend asked.

Emeline set aside her tea. "I think the fairy-tale book was a link to Reynaud for me. Something to make me sure I wouldn't forget him. But now it's not quite so important to have a tangible reminder of him." She met her oldest friend's eyes. "It's not as if I'll ever forget him, is it?"

Melisande was silent, looking at her with sad eyes.

Emeline reached for the book. She smoothed the tattered cover and then looked up. "Keep it for me, will you?"

"What?"

Emeline smiled and held the book out to her best

friend. "Translate it. Maybe you'll find in it the thing I couldn't."

Melisande knitted her brows, but she took the book, holding it on her lap between both hands. "If you think it best."

"I do." Emeline yawned hugely and not at all politely. "Goodness. And now it's to bed for me."

Melisande accompanied her into the hallway, murmuring a good night before turning to the door.

Emeline started up the stairs and then had a sudden thought, perhaps brought on by the delirium of exhaustion. "Melisande."

Her friend glanced up from donning her shawl by the door. "Yes?"

"Do you think you can watch after Jasper for me?"

Melisande, that sturdy, unflappable lady, actually gaped in astonishment. "What?"

"I know it's a strange request, and I'm half out of my mind with weariness right now, but I worry about Jasper." Emeline smiled at her best friend. "Will you look after him?"

By this time, Melisande had recovered. "Of course, dear."

"Oh, good." Emeline nodded and started back up the stairs, a weight off her mind.

Behind her, she heard Melisande call a farewell, and she must've murmured something in response, but she could only think of one thing.

She needed to sleep.

"DO YOU THINK Mr. Thornton really was the traitor?" Rebecca asked later that night.

She was sleepy, almost dozing in front of the fire. Samuel had risen from his bed to have a belated cold supper with her, and then they'd retired here. She should be asleep; she was so exhausted after the adventures of the day, but somehow something seemed to be missing.

Across from her, Samuel held up a goblet of brandy and looked through the glass into the fire. "I think so." His face was battered, new bruises atop old ones that had barely begun to heal, but it was dear to her nonetheless.

She blinked fuzzily. "But you're not absolutely sure."

He shook his head decisively and drained the glass. "Thornton is a born liar. It's impossible to tell whether he really had nothing to do with the massacre or not. He may not know himself—liars have a way of coming to believe their own lies. I doubt we'll ever be absolutely certain."

"But"—Rebecca stifled a yawn—"you came halfway around the world to find the truth, to put the massacre to rest. Doesn't it bother you that Thornton might not be the traitor?"

"No. Not anymore."

"I don't understand."

A smile flickered across his face. "I've come to the conclusion that I never erase Spinner's Falls entirely from my mind. It's not possible for me."

"But that's awful! How—"

He held up a hand to halt her worried protest. "But what I've learned is that I can live with the memory. That the memory is part of me."

She stared at him worriedly. "That sounds terrible, Samuel. To live with that all your life."

"It's not so bad," he said softly. "I've already lived six years fighting with my memories. I think if anything, it'll be better now that I know the memories are part of who I am."

She sighed. "I don't understand, but if you're at peace, I'm glad."

"I am."

They sat in companionable silence for a few minutes. Rebecca began to half doze. A log popped in the fire, and she remembered that there was something else to discuss with her brother before she fell asleep.

"She loves you, you know."

He didn't say anything, so Rebecca opened her eyes to see if he'd fallen asleep. He was gazing into the fire, his hands clasped loosely in his lap.

"I said, she loves you."

"I heard."

"Well?" She sighed gustily and a little grumpily. "Aren't you going to do something about it? Our ship sails tomorrow."

"I know." He got up finally and stretched, wincing as something pulled in his side. "You're about to fall asleep in that chair, and then I'll have to carry you to bed like a little girl." He held out his hand.

She placed her hand in his. "I'm not a little girl."

"I know that," he said softly. He drew her up to stand before him. "You're my sister grown into a lovely and interesting lady."

"Humph." She wrinkled her nose at him.

He hesitated, then took her other hand and rubbed the backs of her fingers with his thumbs. "I'll bring you back to England again soon, if you like, so that you can see Mr. Green or any other gentleman you might be interested in. I have no intention of crushing your hopes there."

"I don't really have hopes."

He frowned. "If you're worried about our lack of pedigree, I think—"

"No, it's not that." She looked down to watch his large hands holding hers. His hands were tanned even though they'd been in England for weeks now.

"Then what?"

"I like Mr. Green," she said carefully, "and if you want me to continue seeing him..."

He tugged at her hands until she looked up. "Why should it matter to me if you see Mr. Green or not?"

"I thought..." Oh, this was embarrassing! "I thought that you wanted me to encourage him or a man like him. I thought you might like the fact that he's an English-society gentleman, even though he has a silly laugh. It's just so hard to tell what you want."

"What I want is for you to be happy," he said as if it were the most obvious thing in the world. "I might object if you take a liking to a rat-catcher or an eighty-year-old grandfather, but other than that, I don't much care who you marry."

Rebecca bit her lip. Men were so obtuse! "But I want your approval."

He leaned close to her. "You already have my approval. Now you need to start thinking about what *you* approve of."

"That makes it very much harder," she sighed, but she smiled as she said it.

He tucked her hand into the crook of his arm. "That's good. Then you won't be making any hasty decisions." They started up the dim stairs.

"Mmm." Rebecca muffled a yawn. "I do have a favor to ask."

"What's that?"

"Can you offer O'Hare a job?"

He looked down at her quizzically.

"I mean in America." She held her breath.

"I suppose I can," he said musingly. "But there's no guarantee that he'll accept it."

"Oh, he will," she said with certainty. "Thank you, Samuel."

"You're welcome," he replied. They were at her bedroom door now. "Good night."

"Good night." She watched as he turned toward his own rooms. "You will speak to Lady Emeline, won't you?" she called anxiously after him.

But he didn't seem to hear.

THE SUN WAS shining through her window when Emeline woke the next morning. She stared at it dreamily for a moment before its full import hit her.

"Oh, dear Lord!" She jumped from the bed and rang frantically for a maid. Then, afraid the summons would take too long, opened her door and bellowed down the hallway like a common fishwife.

She turned back to her room, found a soft bag to pack, and began flinging things into it willy-nilly.

"Emeline!" Tante Cristelle stood in the doorway, hair still in braids, looking horrified. "What has possessed you?"

"Samuel." Emeline stared at the open bag, clothing spilling out, and realized there wasn't any time for packing. "His ship leaves this morning. It may have already left. I have to stop him."

"Whatever for?"

"I have to tell him that I love him." She abandoned the bag and instead ran to the wardrobe to draw out her plainest frock. By this time, Harris had arrived in the room. "Quickly! Help me dress!"

Tante Cristelle sank onto the bed. "Why there is such a hurry, I do not know. If that man doesn't know already that you have a *tendre* for him, he is an imbecile most severe."

Emeline struggled up from folds of dimity. "Yes, but I told him I didn't want to marry him."

"And so?"

"I do want to marry him!"

"*Tiens!* Then it was very silly of you to become engaged to Lord Vale."

"I know that!" Good Lord, she was wasting time arguing in circles with Tante Cristelle when Samuel's ship might be sailing down the Thames right now. "Oh, where are my shoes?"

"Right here, my lady," Harris said unperturbedly. "But you haven't any stockings on."

"I don't care!"

Tante Cristelle threw her hands up in the air, imploring God in French to come to the aid of her so-deranged niece. Emeline thrust her bare feet into her shoes and hurried to the door, nearly running down Daniel.

"Where are you going, M'man?" her only offspring asked innocently. His eyes dropped to her bare ankles. "I say, do you know you haven't any stockings on?"

"Yes, dear." Emeline pressed an absentminded kiss to Daniel's forehead. "We're going to America, and they don't wear any stockings there."

Emeline left Daniel yelling huzzahs while Tante Cristelle and Harris tried to quiet him. She ran down the stairs, calling for Crabs as she went.

That imperturbable gentleman ran into the hallway looking startled. "My lady?"

"Bring the carriage 'round. Hurry!"

"But—"

"And my cloak. I'll need a cloak." She looked frantically about the hall for a clock. "What time is it?"

"Just past nine o'clock, my lady."

"Oh, no!" Emeline covered her face. The ship would've left by now. Samuel would be out at sea. What was she to do? There was no way to catch him, no way to—

"Emeline." The voice was deep and sure and oh so familiar.

For a moment, she didn't dare hope. Then she dropped her hands.

He stood in the entrance to her sitting room, his coffee-brown eyes smiling just for her.

"Samuel."

She rushed at him, and he folded his arms about her. Still she made sure to get a good grip on his coat.

"I thought you'd left. I thought I was too late."

"Hush," he said, and kissed her, soft brushes of his lips over her mouth and cheeks and eyelids. "Hush. I'm here." He drew her into the sitting room.

"I thought I'd lost you," she whispered.

He kissed her with determination, as if to prove his existence real. His lips gently parted hers, and he tilted her head back. She grasped his shoulders, reveling in this freedom to kiss him.

"I love you," she gasped.

"I know." His lips wandered over her brow. "I was going to stay here in your sitting room until you admitted it."

"Were you?" she asked distractedly.

"Mmm."

"How very intelligent of you."

"Not so intelligent." He pulled back his head, and she saw that his eyes had grown dark and serious. "It was a matter of survival. I'm cold without you, Emeline. You're the light that keeps me warm on the inside. If I left you, I think I'd freeze into a solid block of ice."

She pulled his head back to hers. "Then you'd better not leave me."

But he resisted her urging. "Will you marry me?"

Her breath caught in her throat, and she had to swallow before she replied huskily, "Oh, yes, please."

His eyes were still grave. "Will you come with me to America? I can live here in England, but it would be easier for my business if we lived in America."

"And Daniel?"

"I'd like him to come, too."

She nodded and closed her eyes because it was almost too much. "I'm sorry. I never cry."

"Of course not."

She smiled at that. "It's not the usual thing, to keep a boy by his mother's side, but I'd very much like to have him with me."

He touched the corner of her mouth with his thumb. "Good. Then Daniel comes with us. Your aunt is welcome to come as well—"

"I will remain here," Tante Cristelle said from behind them.

Emeline swung around.

The older woman was standing just inside the doorway. "You will need someone to handle the estates, the money, these things, yes?"

"Well, yes, but—"

"Then it is decided. And, of course, you will make the journey across the ocean every few years so that I might see my great-nephew." Tante Cristelle nodded with satisfaction at having ordered everything and left the room, closing the door softly behind her.

Emeline turned back to Samuel to find him watching her.

"Will it be all right?" he asked. "Leaving all this behind? Meeting new people? Living in a new country, one not quite as sophisticated as this?"

"It doesn't really matter where we live as long as I'm with you." Emeline smiled slowly. "Although, I plan to set a new standard for sophistication and wit in Boston. After all, no one there has been to one of *my* balls."

He grinned at her then, a wide happy smile that with all his bruises made him look like a pirate. "They won't know what hit them, will they?"

Emeline mock frowned, but then she drew Samuel's head back down to hers so that she could kiss him. Sweetly, happily. And as she did, she murmured one more time against his lips.

"I love you."

Epilogue

"*I love you.*"

As Iron Heart's words left his lips, there came a scream from the wicked wizard.

"*No! No! No! It cannot be!*" The terrible little man's face reddened until steam began to shoot from his nose. "*I've waited seven long years to steal your iron heart and make its strength mine! Had you ever spoken in those seven years, I would've won it, and you and your wife would be damned to hell. It isn't fair!*"

And the wicked wizard spun in a circle, enraged that his spell was forfeited. He spun, faster and faster, until sparks flew from his whirling body, until black smoke billowed from his ears, until the very ground quaked beneath him, and then, BANG! he was suddenly swallowed by the earth! But the white dove upon his wrist flew up as he vanished, the golden chain broken, and when the bird alit, it turned instantly into a squalling baby—Iron Heart's son.

And then what rejoicing there was in the Shining City! The people cheered and danced in the streets with happiness at the restoration of their prince.

But what of Iron Heart and his cracked heart? Princess Solace looked down at her husband, held still in her arms, afraid that he was already dead, only to find him whole and smiling back at her. So she did the only thing a princess can do in such a case: she kissed him.

And though many in the Shining City are of the opinion to this day that Iron Heart's heart healed when the wicked wizard's spell was broken, I myself am not so sure. It seems to me that it must have been Princess Solace's love that revived him.

For what else can mend a broken heart but true love?

About the Author

Elizabeth Hoyt was born in New Orleans, where her mother's family has lived for generations, but she was raised in the frigid winters of St. Paul, Minnesota. Growing up, her family traveled extensively in Britain, spending a summer in St. Andrews, Scotland, and a year in Oxford. She earned a bachelor of arts degree in anthropology at the University of Wisconsin, Madison. Wisconsin was also where she met her archaeologist husband—on a dig in a cornfield. Continuing the cornfield theme, Elizabeth and her husband live in central Illinois with their two children and three dogs. She is an avid gardener with over twenty-six varieties of daylilies in her multiple gardens and more hostas than any one person can count. The Hoyt family enjoys taking family vacations that invariably end up at an archaeological site.

Elizabeth loves to hear from her readers. You may e-mail her at: elizabeth@elizabethhoyt.com or mail her at: PO Box 17134, Urbana, Illinois 61803. Please visit her Web site at elizabethhoyt.com for contests, book excerpts, and author updates.

THE DISH

Where authors give you the inside scoop!

From the desk of Elizabeth Hoyt

Gentle Reader,

Lady Emeline Gordon, the heroine of my book, TO TASTE TEMPTATION (on sale now), is an acknowledged expert at guiding young ladies safely through the labyrinth of London high society. So when the notorious and notoriously *wealthy* American merchant Mr. Samuel Hartley needs a chaperone for his younger sister, naturally he arranges for an introduction to the lovely, widowed Lady Emeline. Well . . . at least her social expertise is the reason Sam *gives* for asking for an introduction to Lady Emeline. In any case, whilst researching the book, I examined closely Lady Emeline's own handwritten papers. Amongst them I found the following artifact, which I hope will be of interest to you, my Gentle Reader.

Some Rules for a Young Lady Wishing to Sail the Turbulent Waters of High Society without Wrecking Her Vessel against the Rocks of Misfortune.

1. A young lady's costume is of the utmost importance. Her gown, hat, gloves, fichu, and shoes—

especially her shoes—should show Good Taste but not Excessive Taste.

2. A lady should *never* talk to a gentleman not introduced to her. Some men—I will *not* call them gentlemen—will attempt to circumvent this rule. A young lady must not let them.

3. The kind of Male Rogue mentioned above is, in fact, best handled by a Lady of Mature Years and Quick Wit.

4. A young lady may never let a gentleman who is not a relative embrace her. *Note:* Naturally this rule does not apply to a Lady of a Certain Age.

5. If a lady of any age lets a gentleman embrace her, the lady should be certain that he is a Very Good Kisser indeed. She may require several sessions to be entirely certain.

6. Beware of country house parties.

7. When at a country house party it is imperative that a young lady *not* become cloistered with a gentleman. People with too much imagination may think she is engaging in an Affaire de Coeur.

8. Affairs should *only* be conducted by a Lady of a Mature and Not Easily Heated Disposition.

9. However, it is desirable that the *gentleman* in the above mentioned Affair become Very Heated indeed.

10. Whatever she does, a lady engaging in an affair must never, *never* fall in love with her paramour. That way lies disaster.

Yours Most Sincerely,

Elizabeth Hoyt

www.elizabethhoyt.com

♥ ♥ ♥ ♥ ♥ ♥ ♥ ♥ ♥ ♥ ♥ ♥ ♥

From the desk of Sarah McKerrigan

Dear Reader,

If you're as much of a fan of medieval romance as I am, you know the plots often involve Lady So-and-So being forced to wed Lord What's-His-Name for political gain. But what about the rest of the folk—the butcher, the baker, the candlestick-maker—the commoners, who were free to marry for love?

Sometimes, instead of Brad and Angelina, I'd like to hear about the courtship of John the trucker and Mary the kindergarten teacher. That's what inspired me to write DANGER'S KISS (on sale now). I wanted to weave a tale I could relate to, where the hero and heroine don't live in an ivory tower, don't dine on sweetmeats, and don't always play nice.

DANGER'S KISS is sort of a Sheriff of Nottingham meets The Artful Dodger adventure in which Nicholas Grimshaw, upstanding officer of the law, living happily alone in his thatched cottage, makes the mistake of taking mercy upon a beautiful scam artist by the name of Desiree. And, instead of hanging her for her thievery, indentures her as his servant.

Sleight of hand and sleight of heart ensue as the two clash over what's *right* versus what's *just*, and moral lines become blurred as lawman and outlaw fall recklessly in love. Yet in the end, these two simple folk prove more honorable than their superiors as they work together to foil a nefarious noblewoman's treacherous scheme.

To research DANGER'S KISS, I mingled with a great bunch of peasants—medieval reenactors with fascinating "lives," who were delighted to share their stories. In fact, a marvelous magician named Silvermane showed me the clever sleight of hand tricks that Desiree uses in the book!

I hope readers will find DANGER'S KISS an earthy, refreshing glimpse into medieval times, and I'm wagering the romance and adventure will keep you up all night! Let me know if it did at www.sarahmckerrigan.com

Enjoy!

Sarah McKerrigan

Want to know more about romances at Grand Central Publishing and Forever? Get the scoop online!

GRAND CENTRAL PUBLISHING'S ROMANCE HOMEPAGE

Visit us at www.hachettebookgroupusa.com/romance for all the latest news, reviews, and chapter excerpts!

NEW AND UPCOMING TITLES

Each month we feature our new titles and reader favorites.

CONTESTS AND GIVEAWAYS

We give away galleys, autographed copies, and all kinds of fun stuff.

AUTHOR INFO

You'll find bios, articles, and links to personal websites for all your favorite authors—and so much more!

THE BUZZ

Sign up for our monthly romance newsletter, and be the first to read all about it!